I'm so happy that I met someone who love of jewelry ma... writing and karaoke!

Vengeful Tendencies

Bethany Vale

Bethany Vale

PUBLISH AMERICA

PublishAmerica

Baltimore

First printing

ISBN: 1-4137-3792-7
PUBLISHED BY PUBLISHAMERICA, LLLP
www.publishamerica.com
Baltimore

Printed in the United States of America

Dedication Page: This book is dedicated to the memory of my father, Peter Edward Vale, Jr.

Acknowledgments

I would like to thank the following people for making my world a place worth living:

My husband, Tom, who thinks I'm most beautiful when I'm at my worst.

My mother, Lynette, who taught me right from wrong in a neighborhood where few knew the difference.

My father, Pete Jr., who loved me even when he couldn't love himself.

My grandmother, Margaret, who financed the graduate courses that helped me become a more disciplined writer.

My grandfather, Pete Sr., a talented artist and chef who passed along his enthusiasm for creative endeavors.

My best friend, Donna, the guardian angel who dried my tears during the darkest hour of my existence.

My dear friend, Lenore, who stayed up all night to become my first test reader and raised my confidence with her enthusiasm for my work.

My cousin, Patricia, who let me read to her for hours on end to test the novel's voice.

My agent, K.J. Vigue II, who approaches every endeavor with "aggressive tenacity."

Foreword

Although this book is intended primarily as a "good read," the struggles of certain characters are not just scenarios pulled from dark corners of my imagination. Over the past decade, the state of Michigan has cut millions of dollars for mental health care. In 2002, a $500-million budget shortfall forced a $100-million cut in community health programs, including programs that support the mentally ill. For me, the widely publicized shutdown of state mental institutions meant one thing: I would be responsible for taking care of my dad, who'd suffered from schizophrenia since I was a child.

Determined to pick up where the state had left off, I purchased a single wide trailer and struggled to keep my father's cabinets stocked with basic essentials. For a few precious months, I watched him live as an independent adult and make routine decisions that most of us take for granted. On a special shopping trip for household supplies, he rejected the burgundy towels I'd chosen and threw blue towels into the cart. For the first time in many years, he cared about something tangible.

My role as a caretaker ended with one horrifying phone call. On June 7, 2002, I learned that my father had doused his clothing with gasoline and set himself on fire. A number of witnesses, including children, had spotted him stumbling through a neighbor's yard engulfed in flames.

None of the fictional accounts in this book are as deeply disturbing as the sight I encountered when I entered my father's hospital room. Plump red flesh hung from his face, neck and eyelids. Loose flecks of charred skin clung to his whiskers. Scattered patches of hair dotted his swollen scalp. Despite his ghastly appearance, he still looked like himself. Behind his swollen eyelids, I saw glimpses of the loveable loon who was more like a mischievous playmate than a parent. My head spun with memories of us sneaking outside after Mom went to sleep, going for midnight joy rides up and down Telegraph Road, and sharing Big Boy's famous hot fudge cakes at 3 a.m. on a school night.

The day after my father died, the police officer who'd witnessed his last few moments of consciousness informed me that he blamed the voices in his head for directing him to start the fire. I was hardly shocked by this new piece of information. For the past twenty years, these mysterious voices had haunted his waking moments more effectively than a recurring nightmare.

The decision to share my father's story with readers was not easy, but I feel a strong responsibility to raise public awareness in the most graphic way possible. Unlike chemotherapy or organ transplants, psychiatric care is not a lucrative undertaking for hospitals. A surgeon can cure a patient in minutes or hours, but a psychiatrist requires months or years of intensive therapy. State legislators are planning sweeping changes, but it's our job to monitor their progress and support potential tax increases that could open more hospital beds to the desperately ill.

Prologue

It was the best place to go for a man-sized hamburger or a nice, strong drink. Scotty slipped a little more rum in his Cokes than most bartenders, and he had a way of making folks feel as if it was a special courtesy he extended to friends. Donovan endorsed Scotty's tactics and provided plenty of free popcorn to keep customers thirsty.

Despite the impoverished neighborhood, Donovan's Pub was richly furnished with a solid cherry bar flanked by elegant Roman pillars. Painstakingly crafted in an age when trees were plentiful and labor was cheap, the grand wooden structure that enclosed the bartender's work station was widely regarded as a piece of living history.

There were ample places to relax for introverts and extroverts alike. Quiet souls slipped into isolated booths warmed by candlelight. Socializers liked seats closer to the bar, where an endless parade of women traded glimpses of cleavage for free drinks and idle conversation. Just in case there was any question as to what type of establishment it was, racy photos from pornography's infant age were scattered about the place. Customers particularly enjoyed gawking at a faded grey portrait of a man's bare legs poking out from beneath a buxom blond's flowing gown. The antique photographs were the stuff of local legends, and it wasn't uncommon for curious youngsters to slip inside and sneak a peak. Donovan got a kick out of such mischief until the day Darren Price strutted through his elegant stained glass door.

Darren was the cockiest little twerp he'd ever seen—the kind of kid who would've been remembered, even if he hadn't caused such a ruckus. His sharp, angular face was dripping with metal trinkets, from the hoop surrounding his right nostril to the spikes driven through his left eyebrow. His long dark hair had cherry red streaks running through it. He might've looked hip at a crack house or rock concert, but he stood out like a sore thumb among 50 middle-aged men in flannel shirts and hiking boots. If you managed not to chuckle long enough to get a good look at his face, eyes of pure fire starred back at you.

He was 15, maybe 16 at the most, and no one saw him as much of a threat. His man-sized attitude could not conceal his baby face. Donovan didn't know whether to kick him to the curb or serve him a nice glass of chocolate milk, so he let Scotty do most of the talking.

"I'll have a margarita," the kid said as casually as a businessman orders a drink after work.

Scotty raised one eyebrow in Donovan's direction. "Shaken or stirred?"

"Shaken, if you don't mind."

"Not at all. How about a fancy umbrella to impress the chicks?"

"That would be cool, thanks."

"No problem. Come back in about five or six years, and I'll have it ready for you."

Darren slapped a driver's license on the counter. Scotty studied it closely, running his fingers across the surface as if it were made of silk. "This is incredible," he said. "Absolutely flawless. Wait till I show my boss what kids are doing with their computers these days."

"Perhaps your boss will be smart enough to recognize a real license when he sees one. May I speak to him, please?"

Scotty shook his right index finger in Darren's face. "My boss is a very busy man. You've got ten seconds to get your scrawny ass…"

With that incomplete command still hanging in the air, Darren grabbed hold of Scotty's index finger and snapped it at the second joint. Eyes blazing with fear, Scotty ducked behind the counter to escape further injury. Donovan watched the whole thing from his usual seat at the end of the counter. He was far too disgusted with Scotty to feel any anger toward the kid. The last thing he needed was a sissy representing his establishment.

It was Ron the bouncer who arrived first to assist Scotty. He was a fat, hulking man in a sleeveless denim shirt. It took only one of his beefy hands to lift Darren from the stool by the back of his collar and carry him to the front door. Suspended in mid air, Darren swiped a long-necked bottle from a customer's hand and smashed it over the juke box. Using the jagged edge of the bottle, he quickly tore open the skin on Ron's upper arm. Ron screamed like a schoolgirl, turning every head in the bar with his high-pitched wail.

Donovan took a deep, cleansing breath to expel the anger welling up inside him. As an ex-marine, he was well aware that blind rage had a tendency to manifest itself as terror. Showing no fear and conveying no sense of urgency, he stepped out of the shadows to provide a helping hand. He was not a tall man, but he felt larger than life in his trademark double-breasted suit. With quiet elegance, he twisted Darren's wrist, forcing him to release the bottle.

From that point on, the boy was like putty in Ron's hands. It didn't take much to drag him up the rickety old staircase leading to Donovan's second floor office. He couldn't have weighed more than 130 pounds.

It was nearly closing time when Ron led Donovan to the stuffy little office above the kitchen. Splinters of wood from his battered desk littered the ground. Darren was sprawled out on the floor with his hands tied behind his back and a filthy rag stuffed between his lips. Much to Donovan's surprise, Ron hadn't taken the opportunity to beat the kid senseless. Instead, he'd chosen to remove the jewelry from his face and apply a generous amount of lipstick, eyeliner and rouge. Looking down upon Darren's angry eyes, Donovan got the feeling that the kid would've rather been beaten to death. "Where did you get all the powder and paint?" he asked.

"It was in the lost-and-found bin. Kind of suits him, huh, boss?"

Darren tried to sit up and began to choke violently. The stifled coughs brought fresh tears to his heavily lined eyes. "Take that fucking rag out of his mouth!" Donovan demanded. "The kid can't breath." Ron removed the rag from Darren's mouth and watched him swallow big gulps of fresh air. His small, bony rib cage trembled with each new breath. He tried to speak, but words failed him.

"What's wrong, little girl? Cat got your tongue?"

Donovan took two steps in Ron's direction and stood with his nose pressed to his chin. The fat man's putrid breath gave him something else to be angry about. "Shut the fuck up. You're fired."

"But boss…"

"Get the hell out of my office! If you can't control a child, how can I trust you to have my back?"

Hanging his head in shame, Ron dragged his enormous feet across the dirty tile and shut the door behind him. Donovan quickly knelt to the floor to loosen the rope surrounding Darren's wrists. Upon regaining his freedom, Darren took a furious swing at Donovan's face. He blocked the punch with one arm and grabbed the kid's throat with the other. "Nice job. Your reflexes are impeccable, but your timing could use a little work."

"Let go of me, you son of a bitch!"

"All in good time, my boy. All in good time. Why don't you have a seat?"

Donovan released his grip on the kid's throat and let him fall to the floor. Trembling slightly, Darren rose to his feet and took a short walk around the office. Five large bookshelves covered the walls, displaying assorted concession supplies and huge boxes of soap and toilet paper. A musty old couch sat below a small picture window on the eastern wall. Darren arrived at the couch on his own terms, taking time to study the contents of each shelf and run his fingers along a dusty set of ring binders. Donovan took a seat at his desk and waited for the boy to finish exploring. "You know, I could easily call the cops, but it just so happens that I'm not that kind of guy. Call me crazy, but I've got a soft spot for kids, especially those with certain undeniable talents. If you give me one good reason to let you go, I just might listen."

Darren pulled a stray box over to the couch and used it to prop his feet. "I didn't mean to hurt anyone. I just wanted a drink, and your bartender pissed me off."

"He has that effect on people from time to time. I'm sorry you were mistreated. Now, let's see about getting that drink."

"Don't bother. I'll be leaving soon."

"Not so fast. You owe me for the disruption, and I have a favor to ask."

"What's that?"

"If you ever need anything—I don't give a fuck what it is—I want you to come to me. Always come to me first, Capisce?"

For the first time since he'd entered the bar, Darren cracked a smile. "Quit playing Godfather. For Christ's sake, you're not even Italian. You're wasting your time."

"Am I?"

"You're trying to be my friend. I don't have friends."

"A wise choice. Friends are highly overrated. I much prefer business associates."

"I don't have those, either."

Donovan slammed his fist down on the desk. "What's your game, kid?"

"What's yours!" Darren hissed.

"You really want to know? You think you can handle it?"

"Try me."

Donovan leaned forward in his seat to strengthen the impact of his words. He rarely felt the need to impress people, but tonight was somehow different. "I kill people for money."

Darren rolled his eyes in disgust. "Pussy."

"And why do you say that?"

"I say that because I kill for pleasure."

Chapter One: Five Years Later

Dr. Thomas Rushing was not one to gawk at every short skirt that strutted through his office, but today he could not be held responsible for his wandering eyes. His pretty blond receptionist showed up in a tight little spandex tank that squeezed her breasts right up to his pupils. Her look was unprofessional, to say the least, but he didn't have the heart to tell her so. An office painter was scheduled to arrive any minute, and little miss Brooke had her eye on his young apprentice. At 32, Dr. Rushing was young enough to understand that a crush was very serious business to a college freshman who collected stuffed gorillas and sipped cherry Kool-Aid from a pink thermos.

He was overjoyed when his 10 o'clock client didn't arrive on the hour. Abbreviated time with Darren Price was always a good thing. Plus, it gave him the opportunity to test the comfort level of his new leather couch. Keeping his office door open just a crack, he settled down to eavesdrop on the conversation in progress. He overheard Brooke discussing the merits of semi-gloss enamel with a man old enough to be her grandfather. Despite her intimidating looks, she adored people of all ages and thought nothing of shooting the breeze with a paint-splattered fellow who whistled old Hank Williams ballads and wore tee shirts that declared his love of fishing. The man's apprentice, Curt, was a strapping young lad of few words. His moderately enthusiastic grunt was the last thing Dr. Rushing heard before nodding off to sleep.

He awoke to find Darren standing over him. He was a dark, handsome young man who didn't deserve the good looks God gave him. His angular features were a shade too strong, too irregular for classic good looks, but riveting just the same. In the right clothes, he could've passed for a ruthless businessman. In fact, the way he looked down upon Dr. Rushing was quite businesslike. He could've been a manager chastising an employee for sleeping on the job.

"Save your sarcasm," Dr. Rushing said. "I'm not the least bit embarrassed about being caught with my eyes closed and my shoes tossed in the corner."

Darren chuckled under his breath. "I was merely going to suggest that you wipe the drool from the corner of your mouth. I'm used to you paring your favorite jeans with a rumpled shirt and tie, but slobber I can't overlook."

Dr. Rushing was careful not to let Darren see him dab the corner of his mouth as he crossed to his desk. "Make yourself comfortable. I have something special planned for today." Darren snatched a magazine from Dr. Rushing's desk and flopped down on the couch. The sight of his muddy sneakers on the armrest made Dr. Rushing cringe. It had taken him almost five years to acquire such a fine piece of furniture for his office. If the boy's father wasn't such a dear and loyal friend, he would've referred him to another psychiatrist years ago.

"Reposition your feet, or I'll bill you for the damage."

Darren adjusted his legs so that his sneakers hung over the edge of the armrest. "Is that better? Can we get to this special exercise already?"

"We certainly can. I've created a list of scenarios, and I'd like you to tell me how you'd react in each case. Try not to brood over your answers or weigh your options too heavily. Say the first thing that pops into your head. Is that clear?"

Darren yawned. "Sounds simple enough."

"Okay. You're in the express lane at the grocery store, and you notice that the woman in front of you has a whole cart full of items. What do you do?"

"I try not to let it bother me. Life is much too short."

"Are you just telling me what I want to hear?"

"No, I'm telling you how I'd react to a woman."

"Say it was a man."

"I'd ask if he knew how to read, then I'd spell out the word "express," just to be sure. If he came back with a smart ass reply, I'd make him the sorriest bastard that ever lived."

Dr. Rushing leaned forward to study Darren's face. "It's interesting that you'd react differently to a man. Would you say that you have more respect for women?"

"I have respect only for myself. I wouldn't terrorize the woman because there's no fun in that. It's like setting your sights on a hill when you could be climbing a mountain."

"How is intimidating a man like climbing a mountain?"

"How the fuck should I know? I've never climbed a mountain."

Dr. Rushing sighed. "Okay, Darren, let's move on. You're driving down the road, and someone cuts in front of you. You don't know if it's a man or a woman because it happens so fast. What do you do?"

"I suppose it depends upon my mood. I might just raise my middle finger and move on."

"And what happens if you're in a bad mood?"

"Not a whole hell of a lot. I drive a motorcycle. Do you expect me to get myself killed?"

"I have no expectations. I'm simply asking what you'd do."

"I'd whip out a gun and blow out the guy's windows. Is that what you want to hear?"

"This isn't about what I want. It's about your gut response. Let's move on, shall we? You're walking your dog down the street, and some guy with a rottweiler laughs at your little Cocker Spaniel and says you need to find yourself a real pet. What would you do?"

"I'd fall into step beside him and ask questions about his dog. Are rottweilers smart? Do they train easily? Are they loyal and faithful companions? Can I pet the dog? Can I walk with it? Can I jerk the leash hard enough to cut off the mutt's supply of oxygen and sick my Cocker Spaniel at its throat?"

Dr. Rushing tried not to laugh, but a little chuckle escaped him. "That's interesting."

"What's interesting? Why the hell are you laughing?"

"I have serious doubts that you could subdue an angry rottweiler with your bare hands. Why can't you just admit there would be nothing you could do?"

Darren walked over to Dr. Rushing's desk and slammed his fist down on a pile of dusty books. "Have you been listening to anything I've said in the last ten minutes? I've already admitted I wouldn't go after a car on my motorcycle. I know my limitations, and who are you to imply that I don't?"

"Sit down, Darren. If your goal is to intimidate me, you haven't succeeded."

"On the contrary, I don't get off on intimidating wimps. You wouldn't represent a challenge to me. You probably haven't been in a decent fight since elementary school. Look at your hands, for God's sake. They're positively delicate."

"That's it, Darren. Go after my ego. Assume that I'm self-conscious about some remote physical characteristic. You know better than that, don't you? A strong man's self-esteem is based upon more important traits."

Darren was quiet for a moment. "God, you're good. You really turned that one around on me, didn't you?"

"Well, I try not to be offended too easily. It's an occupational skill."

"Then you won't be offended by my next observation."

"Your *next* observation?"

Darren picked up one of Dr. Rushing's shoes and placed the sole of it against the bottom of his foot. "You're a tall man, but your hands and feet are relatively small. You know what they say about men with small hands and feet?"

"Jesus, Darren. You're not here to speculate about the size of my penis, and I'm not here to dispel your delusional faith in folk tales. Let's try to be productive, shall we? Remember that you have a wonderful father who is paying dearly for this time, week after week, month after month, year after year."

"Don't worry about my dad. It's not like he can't afford this."

"I worry about his emotional well-being. Surely you must be aware of the strain you're putting on him. I know it's not so easy to control your rage, but you should at least try to make the most of our appointments. It wouldn't hurt you to do a little soul searching."

Darren glanced at his watch. "Your time is up. Send me out with a bang."

"I have no closing arguments for you today. Sometimes I think your greatest joy in life is to shock me. I'm glad I can be a source of amusement. If that's all you have, so be it."

"Wanna hear about what I'd do if some guy came running at me with a tire iron?"

"Go home, Darren. And try not to kill anyone on the way."

"Can I fantasize about it?"

"No."

"Can I watch a movie about it?"

"Whatever raises your shorts."

"Can I go on the Internet and look at pictures?"

"Sure. Can I bill your father for another hour?"

Darren rose to his feet. "I'm going, I'm going."

✶✶✶✶✶

Claire Clinton had rare moments of confidence, and today she was experiencing one of them. The floppy, wide-brimmed hat she'd ordered from an exquisite career woman's catalogue matched her sleek, formfitting dress perfectly. Best of all, it cast a shadow of mystery over her face, making her feel like an untouchable femme fatale. Her coordinating blue pumps were a bit uncomfortable, but she was more than willing to put up with the binding pressure on her toes. She hadn't felt this good in a long time. Perhaps she'd never felt this good at all.

Passing by the bagel shop on the corner, she entertained the possibility of ordering a nice vanilla cappuccino. Did she dare go in there with all of those people? Aside from a brief stroll through a deserted art museum, she hadn't entered a public place in more than three years, but today she felt she could handle it. The hat was her secret weapon. It lessened the possibility of making accidental eye contact with strangers and rendered her almost anonymous. Studying her dim reflection in the coffee shop window, she decided that she was indeed fit for public display. She liked what the dress did for her long, fluid silhouette. It made her shoulders appear broader and her waist slimmer by comparison. She was normally obsessed with the idea of losing five pounds, but today she felt positively slim. She decided to forgo her coffee and head straight over to Dr. Rushing's office. After all, the whole ensemble was purchased with him in mind. Why waste it on a room full of strangers?

She arrived to find Dr. Rushing's office in complete disarray. Tarps covered every piece of furniture, and a little old man stood upon a ladder with a paintbrush. Brooke sat at her desk leafing through a mail order catalog. A second painter stood over her shoulder, pointing to various items and sneaking peeks down her low-cut top. He didn't appear to be very happy when she pulled her breasts from his line of vision and rushed to the door. "Claire!" she squealed in that excited little way she addressed people. "I have something to show you!"

Claire glanced at the glossy page Brooke held before her eyes. It displayed several throw pillows in various colors, shapes and fabrics. She didn't see the need for decorative pillows in a business office, but the vast selection was impressive nonetheless. "Very nice. Is that the catalog you were going to let me borrow?"

"You can keep it. I've already placed an order for the navy blue tweed."

Dr. Rushing poked his head out of the office and spotted Claire standing over Brooke's desk. "What's the holdup? Is Brooke showing you everything in the catalog?"

"I'm almost done with her," Brooke said. "I just want to show her the wallpaper border I put up in the bathroom."

"All right. Make it quick."

The first thing Claire saw when she entered the restroom was her own reflection. The damned mirror was right in her line of vision when she entered the door, and a row of decorative vanity bulbs lit up her face like a string of flood lights. All at once, she was reminded of the gaping imperfections she was able to forget for a few glorious moments. One of her eyes was situated half an inch higher than the other, and her nose slanted hopelessly to the right. As if that wasn't bad enough, her jaw line was more pronounced than Jay Leno's. All the beautiful clothing in the world could not disguise the fact that she looked more like a circus freak than a stylish young businesswoman.

"What do you think?" Brooke asked, making a sweeping gesture with her right arm. In that skimpy little outfit, she looked like one of the models on *The Price is Right*. Claire was overcome by a sudden urge to rip the little top to shreds, but deep inside she knew that Brooke's big blue eyes and cute button nose didn't make her the happiest person on Earth. She craved approval like anyone else, and this decorating project was extremely important to her.

"It's just beautiful," Claire said, gazing up at the wallpaper border. "You have a definite flair for this sort of thing." It really was an excellent pattern for the tiny room. Multicolored pastel swirls gave the space a light, airy feel. The rest of the room was just as impressive. Brooke had managed to create a sense of depth and dimension by adding a rectangular mirror with little wooden slats glued to the front. The end result was a cosmetic window that looked every bit as inviting as a real glass pane.

The phone rang in the outer office, forcing Brooke to tear herself away from the conversation. Claire was tempted to linger in the bathroom and hide from the world, but she knew Dr. Rushing would find a way to lift her spirits. He was one of the few people in her life who looked right past her disfigurement and saw the beauty within her soul.

Not that Dr. Rushing was a saint. Every so often, Claire noticed his eyes lingering in Brooke's direction, and she wondered if his commitment to her well-being was as brotherly as he made it out to be. There was no getting around it. Dr. Rushing had an eye for beautiful women, and that was that. No fancy hat was going to make him stand up and take notice of her physical charms, and she couldn't really hold that against him. After all, didn't most men admire pretty women? And didn't most women adore handsome men? Wasn't there some unwritten law which stated that people were supposed to go out and find the most attractive mate that their own looks would allow them to snare?

Claire smoothed her dress and turned to leave the bathroom. She could only feel grateful that she'd had the opportunity to confront her reflection in a more realistic light. At least she wouldn't walk into Dr. Rushing's office with any false hopes.

*****

Darren felt like a fat worm stuffed into a drinking straw as he inched along the air duct running above Dr. Rushing's office. The points of his elbows ached under the pressure of his own weight. His forearms rubbed painfully across the corrugated steel shaft.

A small handgun burned a hole in his pocket, but he resisted the urge to load it. He wanted to savor the adrenaline rush that came from skulking in dark corners, studying a building's architecture and identifying all possible exits. Bullets were quick and efficient. Plans were dangerous, messy and fraught with complications.

He didn't intend to hear Dr. Rushing's appointment with the disfigured girl who'd passed him coming into the office with her eyes glued hopelessly to the ground. He couldn't see anything, but he could hear her soft, timid voice rising up through an air vent. "You look fabulous, Claire," Dr. Rushing said. "Love the hat." Darren suppressed the urge to laugh. The dude was such an ass kisser.

"I feel a little silly," Claire said.

"Nonsense. It looks great on you! I trust you wore it to the concert."

Claire's voice fell to a whisper. "I didn't make it to the symphony. I gave the tickets to my aunt."

"That's the last thing I wanted to hear. I was so sure you'd make an exception this time. You've been wanting to go for months."

"I'm so sorry, Dr. Rushing. I can't live the kind of life you want me to live. It's just not me."

A subsequent lull in the conversation was punctuated by the sound of rustling papers and creaking cabinet doors. "A friend of mine passed along a poem written by a woman who attends his literary group. I'd like to share it with you."

Darren cringed. His dad passed along poems like joints or sticks of chewing gum. He was quite possibly the corniest son-of-a-bitch alive.

"Lord help me to see through the eyes of a child," Dr. Rushing began. "Instill me with the desire to play more games and engage in more unproductive activities. Don't let me feel silly when I spend time fantasizing about what I might become. Let me walk along your beautiful beaches without worrying that I look fat in my swim suit."

Darren stroked his gun. The man obviously deserved to be shot.

"Help me to find endless joy in a package of cherry flavored Pez. Allow me to watch an entire evening of television without worrying that the dishes are piled to the ceiling. Let me look forward to birthdays instead of dreading them."

It suddenly occurred to Darren that this poor woman was shelling out $50 an hour to hear a poem about cherry flavored Pez. He only hoped she had good insurance.

"Help me not to care what coworkers think of my haggard face when I wake up too late to apply makeup. Let me fantasize that I'm a princess and believe it's true. Don't let me get angry when I discover a new stain on the couch. Help me to understand that the world is made to be lived in."

Claire's soft voice rose up through the vent. "That's beautiful, Dr. Rushing."

"I have something else for you. A magazine clipping. Did you know that the average woman uses about 20 personal hygiene products each day—everything from hair spray and mouse to lipstick and mascara?"

"That's insane."

"And do you know how many products the average man uses?"

"Six or seven?"

"More like five. What does that tell you about women, Claire?"

"We're obsessed with our appearance."

"Exactly. Imagine how much simpler life would be if you could stop worrying about the way you look and concentrate on the beauty that surrounds you. A man enjoys a walk along the beach without worrying that he doesn't look sexy in his swim trunks. He doesn't care if his eyes are framed by dark circles and his hairstyle isn't in vogue. He's going to go out and have fun anyway, and he's going to project an air of confidence that attracts others."

Claire chuckled a bit. "So a man is like a child in many respects."

"Very funny. You know what I'm driving at. Inner peace projects outward."

Darren wanted to be sick. Was Dr. Rushing actually trying to convince her that a new attitude would suddenly make her the most desirable fuck in town? The guy was out of his mind. Darren knew the value of a good white lie, but Dr. Rushing's lies seemed a few shades darker. "You make it sound so simple," Claire said.

"It *is* simple. Don't you see? Happiness is not found—it's created. You're responsible for constructing your own joy by making the effort to do more of the things you love. Do you honestly believe the average person walks around feeling happy all the time?"

"No, but I do believe the average person is happier than me."

Dr. Rushing sighed. "Tell me something, Claire. What do you think the average person does after work?"

"I'd say most people eat dinner and watch television."

"And what do you do after work?"

"I pop a chicken patty into the microwave and flip through the cable guide."

"I rest my case. You're already having just as much fun as the average person most of the time. Your looks certainly don't prevent you from doing what the average person does after work, and there's no reason why they should prevent you from joining that aerobics class you've been talking about or enjoying an evening at the symphony. You have some challenges, that much is true, but you're not crippled. Look at me, Claire. You're not broken."

Darren hoped Claire wasn't buying all this crap. Of course she wasn't as happy as most girls her age. Most chicks were getting laid, and that was certainly more interesting than eating microwave chicken parts in front of the television.

"I suppose you're right," Claire said.

"It is written that Helen of Troy had a face that could launch a thousand ships. Her greatest gift was her beauty, and she used it to command great respect. I believe we all have a special gift that commands respect. Your gift is the ability to make others happy. I've been in practice for almost five years now, and I'm sad to say that I don't usually enjoy myself. I don't particularly like getting out of bed on Mondays, but when I walk over to my appointment calendar and see your name, I have something to look forward to. You seem to have that effect upon a lot of people. It's no accident that Brooke brought her decorating books to the office today. She was looking forward to your visit, and she couldn't wait to show you what she'd done to the bathroom. Your mom tells me that the children at your nursery school light up like Christmas trees when you walk into the room. If you don't believe me, you should at least believe the children. You're beautiful just the way you are."

Darren pictured a radiant smile on Claire's face. No, he felt a radiant smile. He sensed that she liked hearing the lies almost as much as Dr. Rushing enjoyed telling them. The two of them were as co-dependent as a hooker and a pimp. She needed a knight in shining armor, and he needed to be one.

"One more thing," Claire said as the hour drew to a close. "If appearances are so irrelevant, why do you spend so much time looking at Brooke?"

Darren reveled in the long silence that followed. He could hardly believe Claire had called Dr. Rushing to the couch. He didn't think she had it in her.

"Do you remember that painting I showed you at the art museum?" Dr. Rushing asked. "The one with the flaming orange sunset over the canyon?"

"*View From a Cliff Top* by Andre LeBlanc."

"Wow. I can't believe you remember the title and artist of a painting I showed you four months ago. That officially makes you the coolest person on the planet."

Darren rolled his eyes in disgust. Why didn't they just get a room and be done with it?

Claire laughed a bit. "If I recall, that painting covered half the wall."

"Exactly. Don't you see? The painting is a bit like Brooke. I certainly enjoy looking at it, but it would be a bit cumbersome to take home."

Darren was glad to hear Dr. Rushing sounding more like a real man for a change. The woman he cared for so deeply was not the woman he wanted to fuck. He was not the paragon of virtue Darren's father believed him to be, and that thought brought a massive smile to Darren's face.

Chapter Two

Benny Simpson walked slowly along the curb in search of stray cigarette butts. He wished he could step into his favorite coffee shop and bum a smoke from one of the regulars, but he had only thirty cents in his pocket. The manager, who was easily young enough to be Benny's son, wouldn't allow him to sit around without ordering anything.

He didn't understand what was wrong with teenagers these days. They were so brutally cold and apathetic. They laughed at his dirty clothing and rode their bikes through mud puddles just to splash him on the street. How was he supposed to stay clean if they kept doing that? They would end up killing him one day, he just knew it.

It wasn't his fault he couldn't shower. Water had a tendency to block the intricate network of radio waves surrounding his body. Twenty years ago, key nerves running along his spine had been replaced with threadlike fiber optic wires. It was all part of a CIA experiment to enhance human ability to transmit messages over time and distance. Government surgeons had performed the operation during his very first stay in a mental hospital. They did whatever they wanted to do in those places. If you dared to speak of the horrors you had endured, they could always claim you were crazy. That was their game, and they played it well.

He was just about to give up when he spotted a nice, juicy Marlboro with five or six drags left on it. Who in their right mind would discard a bone with so much meat? "An angel, that's who," a feminine voice whispered in his ear. It was the voice of a cousin who'd died of Leukemia at age 16. His favorite cousin.

"Jenny?"

He listened very hard for a reply, but his seventh-grade teacher kept disrupting the frequency. "You're disgusting!" she shouted in her sharp, abrasive voice. "Take that filthy cigarette out of your mouth. You could get a disease."

"I'll have a mint when I get home."

"A mint will only cover the smell of your breath. You must wash your lips with soap and gargle with Listerine."

"I will, I will. I'll do it as soon as I get home."

"You're lying!" said his first wife. She interrupted whenever she felt like it. The bitch had no manners whatsoever.

"I'm not lying! I'll do it as soon as I get home."

"Sure you will. You don't even own a bottle of mouthwash."

"I'll pick some up on the way home."

"How? You can't afford it. You haven't worked in 20 years."

"Leave me alone! I told you I'll get a job as soon as the recession is over."

As he argued with his ex-wife, a woman in a big blue Easter hat came strolling up the sidewalk. She looked quite wealthy in her sleek, tailored dress and fancy blue pumps. It was just the opportunity he'd been waiting for. "Excuse me, Miss! Could you spare a dollar?"

Keeping her eyes set firmly on the ground, the woman scurried past.

"Please!" he shouted at her back. "I haven't eaten today."

Slowly, as if turning against an ocean current, the woman shifted her body in his direction. About six feet separated them, but she still felt the need to clutch her purse with both hands. "Stay right there. I may have a roll of quarters." As she fumbled through her purse, Benny noticed that her face was all distorted and out of whack. He wondered if the CIA had gotten hold of her, too. He desperately wanted to ask, but the timing didn't feel right.

"Here you go," the woman said, rolling the loot across the sidewalk at his feet. "Promise you won't buy alcohol with it."

"I've been seven Saturdays without wine."

"That's wonderful. Keep up the good work."

Benny deposited the roll of quarters in his pocket. "Would you like a cup of coffee? I'll buy."

"That's very sweet of you, but I'm nearing the end of my lunch hour. I have to get back to work."

"I'm not hitting on you. Is that what you think?"

"Not really."

"I'm not a rapist, either. You don't have to be afraid. I can hardly get an erection these days."

At long last, the woman cracked a smile. "Who says I'm afraid?"

"I don't know. People think all kinds of things about me, but they're usually wrong. I'm hard-wired to send out negative signals, but the signals are false. They get me in all sorts of trouble. You know all about it, don't you? I sense that you've dealt with the CIA. We could talk about it, if you like."

"I'd love to, but I really have to get back to work. Take care of yourself, okay?"

"I will."

"Promise?"

"Yes, I promise."

*****

It was not the best place to eat in town, but it was certainly the fanciest. A grand piano took up too much space at the center of the room, forcing waiters to maneuver in circles with huge platters of lamb, duck and porterhouse steak. A gaudy crystal chandelier showered light in every direction, casting vivid reflections on the cherry wood tables and adding a sharp twinkle to the wine glasses. Darren wondered how the staff managed to keep the glossy wood so free of streaks and scratches. Perhaps he'd ask his father, who was already fifteen minutes late for their weekly lunch appointment.

Darren passed the time picking little white flowers from the fragrant centerpiece. How like his dad to ruin a perfectly good lunch with the sickening sweet scent of water lilies. He didn't understand the need for such adornments or the desire to produce them. He pictured five little old ladies in the back room sticking stems into cones and trading ancient remedies for colon troubles and vaginal dryness.

Dr. Roland Price arrived at half past noon. He didn't seem to care that his son had been waiting for almost 30 minutes. He strode past the piano in a crisp navy suit and planted a light kiss on Darren's cheek. "Jesus, Dad. I told you to stop doing that."

"Nonsense, my boy," Roland said in his unique half-British accent. "There's nothing wrong with public displays of affection."

Darren hated everything about his father's foppish manner and flawless diction. The guy moved to the States shortly after his 20th birthday, but he still insisted upon sounding more important than everyone else. He went around slapping backs and kissing cheeks like a raging fag in heat. Even his relatives back home didn't act like that. Darren suspected that his father's exuberant displays of emotion were an attempt to help mold his deviant child into a more compassionate young adult. Conventional wisdom held that disturbed youngsters needed all the love they could get, but Darren had no desire to be coddled.

When the waiter noticed that Roland had finally arrived, he smoothed his jacket and came running over with a bottle of wine. "I'm so sorry," he said, dusting the table with a soft, velvety rag that reeked of furniture polish. "Have you been waiting long?"

"Not at all. I was just settling in. Bring us the usual, please."

Darren rolled his eyes in disgust. He couldn't understand why everyone fawned over his father. The guy earned a pathetic salary as a professor of literature at a small private university. The gleaming red Porsche in the parking lot was a gift from his mother, and the sprawling estate he called home was inherited from a great aunt. He had no business calling himself "doctor" and rubbing elbows with mayors and corporate executives. He didn't know the first thing about running a business, and politics bored the living hell out of him. His influential friends were only kept around to serve as a buffer against mediocrity. Most of them were former students, like Dr. Rushing. Roland fixated on the brightest, most talented kids in his class and coaxed them into his inner circle as they grew into successful young adults. People loved to hear him speak and didn't mind spending endless hours at his fireplace discussing the outdated philosophies of assorted dead poets.

"How was your appointment?" Roland asked, sniffing his glass of wine like a real connoisseur.

Darren yawned. "Ask me about anything but that."

"Fine. Have you given any thought to the possibility of finding a job?"

"My appointment with Dr. Rushing was just grand."

"Do you feel that you're making any progress?"

"It's been four years, Dad. I think it's safe to assume that I've made all the progress I'm going to make. If you want the truth, the guy doesn't know his ass from a hole in the ground. If I locked myself in a room with three good psychology texts, I could gather more knowledge than he's absorbed in eight years of schooling."

"Dr. Rushing is a good man, Darren. A stellar human being. You'd do well to listen to him once in awhile."

"If you love him so much, why don't you just fuck him and get it over with?"

Roland cleared his throat. He was a slender man with pale blue eyes and a neat white beard. He looked smashing in a suit, and he knew it. "Why must you say things like that? It's quite unsettling."

"I say things like that to get a rise out of you. If you haven't figured that out yet, you don't deserve that silly piece of paper hanging on the wall in your office."

"I worked very hard for that piece of paper."

"I know, I know. You walked five miles to school in the snow, and when your boots fell apart at the seams, you made your own moccasins from the hide of a Wolverine, which you killed with your own bare hands."

Roland threw a napkin across the table at his son. "All right, all right. You've made your point. My wealth is inherited, and I've never toiled a day in my life. I love what I do, and it certainly doesn't feel like work to me. I'm a lucky bastard, but at least I'm grateful for what I have. What's your excuse?"

"I don't make excuses for myself. I am what I am."

"Good Lord. Where have I failed you?"

Darren leaned forward in his seat and met his father's gaze with an impudent smile. "It all started when you decided we should eat lunch here until the end of time. If you really wanted to be my friend, you'd learn to accept me for who I am. You can start today, if you like. Just down the street, there's an Irish pub with a projection television so large you'd swear you were looking into a whole other dimension. Let's cancel our order and go watch the fight."

"I despise boxing."

"Fine. So go home and wait by the fire. I'll call Dr. Rushing, and you can regale him with a spirited discussion of Nathaniel Hawthorne's provocative use of imagery and symbolism. Does that sound like good fun to you? Are you getting a stiffy just thinking about it?"

Roland dropped his wine glass on the table, splashing deep red liquid over the exquisite centerpiece. A smile of pure radiance came over his lips. "My God, Darren. You're… jealous. Just look at you! You're positively green with envy. It's a beautiful color on you, my boy. You really do love me, don't you?"

Darren opened his mouth to speak, but Roland wouldn't allow it. Raising one finger to his lips, he stood up from the table and stepped backward toward the door. "If you say one thing to ruin this moment, I'll reclaim the title on your motorcycle."

Darren threw a napkin over the spreading puddle of wine. "I love you, Dad," he shouted across the room. "I love you to pieces."

✱✱✱✱✱

Roland despised traffic jams as much as any busy traveler, but today he was grateful for the opportunity to hunt for his cell phone. If his calculations were correct, Dr. Rushing would just be settling down to a fat pastrami sandwich.

Before his young friend could manage a quick 'hello,' Roland shouted into the receiver, "He loves me!"

Dr. Rushing cleared his throat. "Thanks for the unbridled enthusiasm. My hearing wasn't quite dull enough. Who loves you?"

"Darren, of course. He loves me, loves me, loves me."

"Stop. You're scaring me. Did he make this declaration at lunch?"

"There was no declaration, but I got the message loud and clear. You could say we had a moment."

29

"That's wonderful, Roland. But I'm not sure why you're so surprised. Darren is a fan of yours from way back."

"Please. He thinks I'm a twit. And perhaps I am."

"I don't know about that. I seem to remember a story about a boy who dragged his mattress down two flights of stairs just to be your new roommate."

Roland adjusted his grip on the wheel to keep from drifting into the next lane. The mere memory of his sappy six-year-old child made his heart lurch. Darren couldn't sleep alone after the divorce, but he thrived in every other way possible. On his first trip to Paris, he became so infatuated with a young tour guide that he sketched her face onto the back of a rumpled bus schedule. The resulting caricature looked as if it had been produced by a child twice his age.

Impressed by his son's natural talent, Roland hired an art tutor who led Darren on fantastic excursions through the woods surrounding their fifty acre estate. Under the direction of Jill Peters, a talented art major enrolled in one of Roland's literature courses, Darren learned how to draw animals and landscapes with astonishing accuracy. When a good, hard rain prevented him from sketching his surroundings, he drew fantasy worlds of lavender skies and pure white deer with angel wings.

"Do you think we've lost him for good?" Roland asked.

Dr. Rushing spoke slowly, as if reaching for words. "No life stage is permanent. We change and grow every single day." Roland sensed his dear friend was just being nice. Darren's extreme aggression was more than just a stage. It was a part of him, like the tiny mole on his earlobe or the sharp contours of his brow.

His face had changed overnight. Around age 11, the pointed elven features of his youth morphed into the hardy features of a pint-sized man. A strong Cro-Magnon forehead sprouted from his skull. Rugged cheekbones popped out beneath squarely chiseled eye sockets. And then there were the mothers, arriving in pairs to describe senseless acts of arson and vandalism: windshields smashed to bits with a baseball bat, obscenities spray painted across the front of million dollar homes, burning bags of feces on front doorsteps.

As in most civilized communities, they kept it to themselves. Roland covered the cost of all damages and wrote additional checks to a string of overpaid youth counselors. They characterized Darren as a spoiled rich kid flipping society the bird, but Roland wasn't so sure. Even then, he sensed a dark rustling within Darren's soul.

One afternoon, Jill arrived early to find Darren torturing six tiny blue jays fresh from the nest. Through hysterical tears, she explained that he'd been squashing the poor creatures with his bare hands and using their blood to create abstract smears upon a blank canvas. A subsequent investigation of Darren's tree house turned up five more canvases and a whole bag full of blood-encrusted knives. Each canvas had its own label: squirrel, frog, racoon, rabbit and cat.

Faced with the extraordinary challenge of identifying a suitable punishment for murder, Roland brought his dilemma before a panel of students in the form of a fictional story. After reading the account of Damian Pierce and his slaughtered gerbils, each young scholar was to write a short composition on how Damian's father could address the problem. Much to Roland's surprise, a young psychology major by the name of Tommy Rushing presented a plan more feasible than any suggestion put forth by Darren's prestigious youth counselor. With a heavy heart, Roland peeled dozens of sketches from the kitchen wall and put Darren's cherished art supplies into a safe. That very evening, he brought home the most adorable puppy he could find, an energetic Cocker Spaniel with weepy brown eyes.

This was the deal: Each time Darren did something to improve the dog's quality of life, one of his artworks would be returned to the wall. He could also reclaim one item from the safe—within reason. A whole pad of paper would not be counted as one item, nor would an unopened box of colored pencils. Roland's love was unconditional, but his respect was a privilege earned slowly, piece by piece, one day at a time.

In an effort to acquire more supplies, Darren struggled to think of new and exciting ways to help the dog lead a more comfortable existence. During winter months, he fashioned crude moccasins of burlap to keep its paws warm on long, snowy walks through the woods. In the summer, he shaved the dog bald and applied cool lotion to its skin. In one particularly outlandish bid to increase his daily supply of paper, he began to brush the dog's teeth each morning.

Eventually, Roland awarded points for displaying kindness toward all living creatures. Darren could earn a blank canvas by feeding squirrels or helping to install concrete birdbaths around the property. One fine afternoon, he climbed a tree to return a fallen baby bird to its nest. Moments later, he watched the mother swoop down and attack the child. Enormous round tears poured from his eyes as he asked his father why a parent would do such a thing. Roland explained that the baby now carried a human scent, which the mother probably interpreted as a threat. Sniffing his own arm, Darren tried to determine if he carried the scent of a bird. Is that why his mom fled the country with his sister?

Despite a newfound appreciation for animals, Darren had considerably less respect for humans, including himself. In the 7th grade, he developed a bizarre fascination with body piercing and drove a safety pin through his own nostril. When the school bully dared to make fun of his new look, Darren cornered him in the bathroom and sealed his nostrils shut with a stapler.

Darren's middle school antics were nothing compared to the dirty deeds he pulled off in high school. With the help of a shiny new motorcycle, he ventured into the roughest neighborhoods he could find and spray painted rival gang signs in selected territories, causing vicious rumbles that often made the evening news. Roland learned of his son's secret hobby when he discovered a series of newspaper articles in a scrapbook hidden under Darren's mattress. He didn't have to ask if the anonymous prankster described in the articles was his son. He felt it with his very soul.

When Darren asked for permission to turn the guest house into his very own bachelor pad, Roland saw no reason to withhold the privilege. He was secretly proud of his son's prowess with women and hoped this new hobby would make a life of crime seem dull by comparison. His instincts proved accurate. For more than a year, Darren kept himself busy indoors.

The peace ended as abruptly as it began. The chain of events seemed to happen all at once, like a series of cannons exploding in the night. Darren stumbled home one morning with a painted face and assorted scrapes and bruises. His beloved jewelry was gone, and he refused to talk about where he'd been. The following day, he cut class and took the longest ride of his life, passing through several states and running out of money before calling home from Clearwater, Florida. As Roland headed to the airport on a mission to save his only son, Darren was arrested for chasing two young men through the street on his motorcycle. According to the police report, the men were forced to climb a guardrail and roll down a steep embankment to safety. When asked why he'd do such a thing, Darren swore he never intended to hurt anyone physically. He was merely curious about the nature of fear and the amount of psychological torture necessary to drive a grown man to tears.

After a court-ordered stay in juvenile hall, Darren was required to take anger management courses that did little to curb his violent temper. Out of sheer hopelessness and frustration, Roland paid a visit to the imaginative young man who'd helped him reform Darren's attitudes toward animals.

Friends argued that Roland should've chosen a more experienced therapist, but he simply wouldn't hear of it. Darren had never taken authority figures seriously. He needed a brotherly kind of mentor, and Dr. Rushing seemed like the perfect candidate. He was young enough to appreciate a good single's bar but wise enough to understand that there was more to life than partying and skirt chasing. He liked motorcycles and dreamed of owning one, but he was far too practical to invest in a vehicle that couldn't carry him to work through sleet and snow. He was the kind of guy a teenager could relate to and an older man could respect. Or so Roland thought.

"Do you ever regret taking Darren under your wing?" Roland asked.

Once again, his dear friend was heartbreakingly polite. "Of course not. What is life without a good challenge?"

*****

Dr. Rushing had just finished eating lunch when Benny wandered into his office with a cigarette dangling from his lips. He looked worse than ever in a mud-splattered raincoat with buttons missing down the front. Tattered bits of shoestring were laced through the button holes to hold the jacket closed. His long dark hair looked like it hadn't been combed in days. "There are no ashtrays in here," Dr. Rushing said. "You'll have to take that outside."

Benny spit into his palm and placed the tip of his cigarette into the saliva. Wiping his hands down the front of his coat, he wandered about the office in search of a waste basket. The poor man was so intent on finding a place to toss his cigarette that he didn't notice the glorious spread of food waiting for him on the coffee table. A fat pastrami sandwich sat upon a clean napkin with a side of potato chips and two chocolate-covered doughnuts. The new couch was covered with an old quilt to catch any drips or stains.

"Have a seat," Dr. Rushing said. "I brought a little something for you."

Benny took a doughnut and left the sandwich untouched. "I've already eaten, but thanks anyway. I like your sandwiches."

"Would you like me to wrap it for later?"

"Yes, please."

As Dr. Rushing slipped the sandwich back into its tin foil shell, he listened to Benny carry on a short conversation with an imaginary friend. "Captain Janeway doesn't have time to consult everyone on board," he mumbled under his breath. "She does the best she can to represent the minorities, and the homosexuals, too."

On days like this, Dr. Rushing wasn't sure if he should feel sorry for Benny or envy him. The man was so lost in his own world that he didn't have the capacity to worry about everyday concerns. He had plenty of friends, if only in his head. It wasn't the best existence, but Benny found it preferable to downing Clausoril on a daily basis. He complained that the stuff made a hole in his mind. Perhaps it was better to have bizarre thoughts in full clarity than weak impressions through a dull and unrelenting fog.

"Did you bring your medication?" Dr. Rushing asked.

Benny handed him a little brown bottle. "It doesn't matter," he shouted at the ceiling. "He can have it. What do you care?"

"There are too many pills in this bottle. Why haven't you been taking your medicine?"

Benny shook his head. "I'm not going to tell him. YOU tell him."

"Listen to me, Benny. I'm supposed to make out a report if you don't take your medication. If I do that, they could put you in the hospital again, and your SSI checks will stop coming. Remember how hard it was for us to find you a place? I assume you like your freedom and independence."

Benny dropped his half-eaten doughnut onto the napkin. "Please, don't tell on me. I'll start taking my pills, I swear."

Dr. Rushing looked down at Benny's mismatched tennis shoes. Unfortunately, he didn't really have the power to send him back to the hospital. Statewide budget cuts had stripped him of that power more than a year ago. "Do you remember what we discussed last week?" he asked.

Benny's eyes wandered up to the ceiling. "I'm not going to the Marina. I don't like it there."

"Benny, do you remember what we talked about last week?"

"You said the voices aren't real. I'm only imagining them because I'm sick. I'm not like other people. I hear things that other people can't."

"Well, it certainly appears as if you've been listening to me. The real question is, do you believe that?"

"How can I believe that when there's so much evidence against it?"

"What evidence?"

"There's a man at the bus stop who sells incense. I see him talking to them all the time."

"Has it ever occurred to you that the man at the bus stop could have the same type of illness you do?"

"I have a cousin in New York who hears voices, and he's an engineer. He graduated at the top of his class."

"Plenty of brilliant people are affected by schizophrenia. In fact, there's a strong correlation."

"So how come I haven't reinvented the wheel?"

"I didn't mean to imply that every schizophrenic person is a genius. The point is that there's a biological explanation for the voices you hear. Did you know that pictures of your brain look different from pictures of the average brain?"

"They do?"

Dr. Rushing opened a textbook and pointed to a picture of a schizophrenic person's brain displayed beside a picture of a healthy person's brain. "Take a look at this. See how the ventricles are enlarged?"

"Does my brain really look like that?"

"Cross my heart. In fact, your chemical makeup is different as well. There's enough dopamine in the left hemisphere of your brain to give me a contact buzz."

"Maybe that's what's helping me tune into stations you can't pick up. Maybe you're the one who can't see things as they really are."

Dr. Rushing sighed. "Let's try this another way. Can you remember a time when the voices didn't exist?"

"Yes. I was just a kid. Not even twenty."

"If you had passed that man at the bus station as a teenager, what would you have thought?"

"I would've thought he was nuts."

"I rest my case. The signs of schizophrenia usually become apparent in late adolescence or early adulthood. As a healthy young man full of joy and natural optimism, you had the tools to separate fantasy from reality. Can you even remember how good that felt? If you're willing to show a little faith, I can try to get that feeling back for you."

Benny's bottom lip quivered. "You can?"

"Yes, but only if you believe in me. You have to take your medication religiously. That means every single day. Do you understand?"

Benny stood up from his seat and brushed the doughnut crumbs from his lap. "I understand. The CIA isn't going to like this one bit."

✱✱✱✱✱

Brooke gasped in horror at the sight of Benny dipping his fingertips into a bucket of blue paint. "Watch out!" she shrieked. "Don't get that on your coat."

"What's the idea!" Curt shouted from the top of his ladder. "We're trying to do a job here."

Benny backed into a corner. "I... I only wanted to check it for you. They said it could be toxic."

"*Who* said it could be toxic? There's no one here but us." Benny took a few steps forward and brushed past the coat rack. "Hey!" Curt shouted. "Don't you dare get that shit on my jacket."

Brooke nudged Benny toward the bathroom. "Don't pay attention to him.

Let's get you cleaned up."

Curt stepped down from his ladder. "You can't go in there with him alone!"

"Don't worry," Benny assured him. "I can't get an erection."

Curt shook his head. "You can't say that to a lady!"

"Why not?" Brooke asked. "I know what an erection is. And anyway, I only planned on washing his hands."

Dr. Rushing appeared in the doorway. "Is something wrong out here?"

"You bet your ass something is wrong," Curt said. "Isn't there a place for guys like him?"

Brooke felt blood rising to her cheeks. "Curt, may I see you outside for a moment?"

A brisk October wind swept over Brooke's shoulders as she stepped into the small courtyard connecting her office building to the coffee shop next door. Curt offered his jacket, but she refused with a polite nod. She could hardly believe she'd worn such a skimpy top to impress him.

Curt pulled a pack of Newports from his shirt pocket. "Thanks for getting us a break. I could really use a smoke."

Brooke snatched the cigarette from his mouth and broke it in half. "I didn't bring you out here for a break. I thought you could use a lesson in diplomacy."

"Oh yeah?"

"This is a psychiatrist's office. If you plan to finish your work here, you'll have to accept the fact that some of our clients have difficulties."

"Difficulties I can handle. That guy has major malfunctions. Shouldn't he be in a group home or something?"

"It's not that simple. He's wandered away from five of them."

"So send him to the hospital."

"If Benny were a factory worker with medical insurance, he could get a room at a private institution, but the government isn't going to foot the bill to keep an impoverished man under lock and key."

"That's insane. There must be some way to get him off the streets."

"In order to secure a placement in a public institution, he would have to commit a violent crime of some sort, thus proving himself to be a public danger. He could also get there by way of a suicide attempt. His last placement resulted when he jumped off a bridge and landed in a sewage canal. They held him for a few days and released him back to the streets."

Curt looked puzzled. "So there's no place at all for folks like that?"

"St. Mary's Catholic Church operates a shelter on Chesterton Boulevard, but it's not the most therapeutic place. Benny would have the opportunity to spend the night sitting against a brick wall or to compete for one of 50 beds in a dingy grey basement that shelters close to 400 people, many of them homicidal or suicidal."

Curt's expression softened a bit. "I guess it's nice of Dr. Rushing not to let Benny rot away in that hole."

"Well, he normally tries to distance himself from the shelter types, but Benny is special. He appeared out of nowhere one dark, snowy night when Dr. Rushing slammed his car into a guardrail. Before leaving the scene of the accident to flag down a police car, he tossed his tattered raincoat over Dr. Rushing's shoulders. If a man with so little in life has the decency to offer his only protective garment to a stranger, he deserves a little kindness in return, don't you think?"

Curt draped his jacket over her shoulders. "Look, I didn't mean to be insensitive. My mom is on Valium for her nerves. It's not like I don't understand what it means to be around someone who's a little unbalanced. I suppose we all have a few demons residing in dark corners of the mind. What will happen to Benny? Will he be sleeping at the shelter tonight?"

"Thankfully, he has a place of his own now. Dr. Rushing and I have spent a good deal of time helping him secure what little government money is available to him. That amounts to $370 per month, plus food stamps. To make ends meet, Benny goes shopping with an impoverished mother in his apartment building and trades the groceries for any amount of cash she can offer. With any luck, he'll never have to set foot in that shelter again."

*****

Darren shifted positions in his worm hole and slammed his face against the corrugated steel wall. A sharp clang reverberated through his head as flecks of color danced behind his eyelids. Breathlessly, he listened for an acknowledgment of the careless noise he'd made, but Dr. Rushing didn't seem to notice. He was busy trying to convince some wacko that the paint on the walls wasn't going to make everyone sick.

Darren should've gone home after lunch, but the temptation to go back and listen to another one of Dr. Rushing's sessions was much too great. He'd gotten such a kick out of Claire's appointment that he wanted to see if Dr. Rushing was filling anyone else's head with lies. He was now convinced that lying was a well-practiced ritual around Dr. Rushing's office. He could hardly believe Dr. Rushing had told Benny the medication would magically turn his life around and make him feel like a young man again. No amount of dope would quiet the demons in that freak's head.

Even after Benny left the office, Dr. Rushing continued lying to clients. When Brooke asked if he could visit a client who'd recently broken her leg, he instructed his bubbly young receptionist to tell the woman he didn't make house calls. Less than five minutes later, he left the office to visit a fellow by the name of Rivard. On his way out, he joked that he probably wouldn't want to return after spending the afternoon in a luxurious mansion with an indoor tennis court and swimming pool. From that comment, Darren concluded that Dr. Rushing had no problem paying professional visits to rich folks.

Darren tried to remember his early conversations with Dr. Rushing in the days before they started killing time with silly exercises. Had Dr. Rushing used lies on him? The man certainly knew how to kiss ass, that much he could remember. He asked questions about Darren's motorcycle and made believe he was interested in motorcycles himself. He even took Darren to a wrestling match to prove that he understood where bad boys were coming from. When that didn't work, he encouraged Darren to take up boxing as a social outlet for the red-hot rage that boiled deep within him.

Darren saw through Dr. Rushing's act right away. The guy was obviously more screwed up than half his patients. He felt a burning need to turn clients into friends, and that was just plain sick. Where would it all end? Was he going to start complimenting every ugly face in town and feeding every poor person within a 30 mile radius? His obsessive need to play savior was highly unprofessional. In Darren's book, Dr. Rushing was no better than the dentist who got caught squeezing tits or the gynecologist who was arrested for exploring vaginas without gloves. The man refused to recognize his boundaries.

Dr. Rushing had crossed his most fatal boundary when he turned Darren's dad into his own surrogate father. So what if he lost his own dad at a young age. Did that give him the right to steal someone else's? The young psychiatrist was everything Roland wished his own son could be, and he didn't mind flaunting it. He kept a master list of Roland's favorite books so that he could toss literary references into casual conversations. He always showed up with a bottle of Roland's favorite wine, even when he couldn't afford it. He took up smoking cigars by the fire, a practice that once disgusted him. His initial attempts to get close to Darren were obviously designed to impress the old man. If he could fix the boy no one else could help, he would officially become Roland's hero. If only there were some way to prove Dr. Rushing a quack. If only Darren could show his father that he was a more capable and efficient human being than Dr. Rushing could ever hope to be…

Chapter Three

They warned him not to marry Brittany, but he'd refused to listen. He was just foolish enough to think he had an irresistible Woody Allenish sort of charm that appealed to younger women. God forgive him, but he honestly believed his keen intellect and offbeat sense of humor compensated for his funny little looks. Standing naked before the mirror on that cool October afternoon, Mr. Rivard finally saw himself for what he really was: a scrawny, 50-year-old man with big ears, coke bottle glasses and a receding hair line. A man with a fatal weakness for little girls. A man who'd rarely been loved for what he was, just what he could provide.

He could've settled down with Deloris Brown, the plain but efficient secretary who'd served him well for more than 25 years. As far as he knew, she was the only person in the world who saw potential in him before the money started rolling in. Instead of spending the best years of his life with a good woman, he'd chosen to date strippers and finance their drug habits. At the time, he didn't think of it as paying for sex. He saw himself as the life of the party— the lucky little guy always surrounded by beautiful young women.

He'd married Brittany at a time when the prospect of settling down didn't seem half bad. He was almost 45, and she was almost grown up. Though she needed a fake I.D. to order alcohol, she was an enthusiastic travel partner and an excellent listener. No matter where they chose to have cocktails, she made sure to make him feel like the only person in the room. He learned the truth when he began to lose his sex drive. He'd always been prone to depression, but this time was serious. He could no longer satisfy Brittany in the manner she was accustomed, and that worried him deeply. His greatest fear was that she'd grow bored with his lack of vitality, but that trivial concern was replaced by a whole new set of worries when he overheard her talking to a girlfriend on the phone.

"I have good news and bad news," Brittany had said. "The bad news is that Rick is going through another one of his little depressions. The good news is that I probably won't have to sleep with the old bag of bones for quite awhile."

Mr. Rivard might've recovered from that first insult, but Brittany proceeded to discuss all of the reasons why sleeping with him was the most difficult job she'd ever held. She hated the loose white flesh hanging from his ribs. According to her, the sight of him naked was even more repulsive than the sight of an Ethiopian child dying in the corner of some filthy little hut. She was even more disgusted by his putrid breath, which smelled of hard boiled eggs and raw fish. Finally, there was his lumpy old prick. The thick, twisted veins running through it were the most sickly shade of purple she'd ever seen. "Can you imagine taking that thing into your mouth?" she had asked.

Mr. Rivard never recovered from that day. He'd battled depression since childhood, but low self-esteem was a new adversary. Had he been a joke to all of them? Had he spent his entire life among women who found him repulsive? What a tragic, tragic waste of time.

His vast advertising empire was no consolation prize. The striking accomplishments of his youth mattered nothing to him at this moment. The fine oriental rug beneath his feet was just a place to stand while he drew a hot bath. The rich green velvet drapes covering his windows were just another barrier between him and the sun. The luxurious hot tub at the center of his master bedroom suite was a cesspool where morbid temptations flooded his mind.

He filled the tub with bubbles and sank into deep, warm oblivion. As the Jacuzzi jets spread thick white foam over the surface of the water, he was suddenly reminded of his greatest pleasure in life: sleep. Would it be so wrong to sink under the water for ten seconds? How about twenty, or even fifty? If he could just lose consciousness, it might happen naturally. With any luck, it would be called an accident.

"Is everything okay?" a familiar voice asked. Mr. Rivard opened his eyes to find Dr. Rushing standing over him. Was it Monday already? Had he been taking naps and baths all weekend long? "Fine. Everything is fine."

"Have you disconnected the intercom again? Your maid is worried sick. She's afraid to walk into your bedroom unannounced."

"I'm fine," Mr. Rivard said. "Would you like to feel my pulse?"

"That won't be necessary. Are you feeling any better this week?"

"About the same, I guess. Food doesn't taste good. Golf is no fun anymore. Masturbation has lost its charm. Even my dog is bored with me."

Dr. Rushing crossed to the window and opened the think velvet drapes. "It would help if you let a little light in here. How's business?"

"Excellent. Ever since I fired those mid-level managers at the Houston office, overhead is down ten percent. I've got Deloris running everything."

"And your mom?"

"She's fine, too. She's out shopping for me again. Would you like to see what she bought me last week?" Mr. Rivard reached for a remote control device on the ledge of the hot tub. Lush velvet curtains retracted to reveal a gigantic televison screen.

Dr. Rushing's eyes widened in amazement. "Wow! That's one hell of a setup you've got there. I'd kill for something like that."

"Too bad I don't watch television."

"Your mom obviously thinks you should start."

Mr. Rivard sighed. "I've always envied television watchers. I don't understand the ability to become lost in someone else's fantasy. What a gift. What a remarkable gift."

"Maybe you should create your own fantasies."

"Too late. They've all come true."

"Have you ever considered writing your own screenplay? It might do you some good to imagine a world more exciting than your own. At the very least, a new project would give you a reason to get out of bed in the morning."

"I suppose I could try."

"Do you mean it? Are you really willing to set a plan in motion?"

"No, I'm trying to make you feel better."

"This isn't about my feelings. Are you taking your medication?"

"Yes."

"Religiously?"

"Of course. I eat it right from my priest's hand."

Dr. Rushing laughed. "You're pretty funny for a guy who fantasizes about death."

"What's so strange about that? Even the grim reaper has a sense of humor."

"And how would you know that?"

"I've seen him. He wears pink boxers under his robe. He's a harmless sort, really. Very misunderstood."

"So, you identify with the grim reaper?"

"It was a joke, for heaven's sake. Don't analyze it."

"You started this. Let's see if you can finish it. Why is the grim reaper misunderstood?"

Mr. Rivard looked up at the grand cathedral ceiling. "I think he's very merciful. He knows there's a way out, and he shows up at your darkest hour to lead you through the door."

"Not everyone is looking for a way out. On the contrary, most folks want to stay in the game as long as they can."

"Only because they've been brainwashed. We're taught that we should struggle and fight to the very end. Hardship is supposed to mold us into better human beings and help us appreciate the good times when they finally arrive. I'm living proof that there's not always a light at the end of the tunnel."

Dr. Rushing paced circles around the hot tub. "And what was at the end of your tunnel, Mr. Rivard?"

"Boredom. Disillusionment. The realization that there are no goals left to accomplish."

"So invent new goals."

"It's not that simple. A person who has everything can't always think of new goals."

"Let me ask you this: when you were just a child, what did you dream you'd become?"

Mr. Rivard flexed his tiny arm. "The heavyweight champion of the world."

"Good! Let's go with this. What else did you dream about?"

"Being an airline pilot."

"There you go! Have you ever considered getting a license to fly your own plane?"

"It wasn't the flying part I dreamed about. It was the stewardesses."

Dr. Rushing slapped his palm against his forehead. "I can see you're not going to make this easy for me. Just write the damned screenplay. If you can't think of a goal, I'm more than happy to assign one."

* * * * *

The newspaper described Aunt Millie's Farm as a quaint wildlife park with an abundance of natural charm, but Roland wasn't easily impressed. The property surrounding his estate was home to a gaggle of Canadian geese and dozens of white-tailed deer. He could hardly become excited over a duck pond surrounded by small children clutching bits of stale bread in their chubby little fists.

"Is it just me, or do these ducks look a little fat to you?" he asked.

Dr. Rushing laughed. "I suppose they do, now that you mention it. I was actually thinking the kids around here could use a little exercise."

They shared a little chuckle at the sight of a super-sized toddler tossing Reeces Pieces into the water. It was one of those extra lazy afternoons where adults congregated on benches with newspapers in their laps. Even the children looked a bit lethargic with their walkie talkies and hand-held video games.

The pond was surrounded by eight wooden cottages with colorful hand-painted signs. There was a time when the place was considered to be a decent

42

fishing hole, but Aunt Millie had long since put a stamp of commercialism on the property. People came from miles around to sample overpriced hunks of fudge from her little pink sweet shop with the white picket fence. The cries of children begging for money were ever-present outside the waterfront toy store famous for popularizing the duckling key chain and flashlight set.

"I have a surprise for you," Dr. Rushing said, retrieving a tiny plastic duck from his pocket. "I'm told this little guy can swim, waddle and quack in three different languages."

Roland held the tiny duck in his hand like a little lump of gold. Years ago, when Dr. Rushing complained that it was impossible to find suitable birthday gifts for a wealthy bastard who had everything, Roland had assured him that simple tokens of the heart pleased him most. Ever since then, Dr. Rushing had made a game of supplying him with useless trinkets. It was a gesture that Roland appreciated deeply. His own son hadn't presented him with a gift in more than 15 years.

"Did Darren treat you well today?" Roland asked.

"Well, he didn't stab me with his pencil. I suppose that's a good sign."

"I should never have dumped him in your lap. It wasn't a very nice thing to do to a young man beginning his career."

Dr. Rushing snatched the duck from Roland's hand and set it upon the ground. Instead of waddling along the shoreline, it took three steps and dove head first into the sand. "You don't have to apologize for your son's behavior. I'm not his high school principal. I'm here to help him in any stupid way I can. Sometimes, that includes listening to him shoot off at the mouth."

"You shouldn't have to take that kind of abuse. I'd understand if you decided to call it quits."

Dr. Rushing kicked the duck into the pond. "Are you suggesting I can't handle him?"

"Not at all. I'm just saying it wouldn't hurt you to be careful. You're not exactly one of his favorite people. That's why I called you here—to tell you that his emotions have become more intense."

"His emotions have always been intense."

"You don't understand. He's extremely jealous of you. He just about told me so at lunch."

"I don't believe you. He'd never admit to such a thing."

"He didn't exactly say it outright, but believe me, I caught the drift. I think he may be reaching out to me. I have the feeling he wants you out of the picture so we can work on our relationship."

Dr. Rushing looked at the ground. "I see."

"This doesn't mean we can't go to the symphony or show up at the same book club meeting. It just means we could be a little more careful about flaunting our friendship."

"That makes sense. Instead of me dropping by next week, you could pay me a visit for a change. There's a case of German beer in my garage with our names on it."

"Splendid! I don't believe I've ever tried German beer."

"There's a first for everything. I only ask that you don't take Darren out of therapy until you've found another psychiatrist who's willing to take him on. He needs a place to vent. It's the one thing in the world he can't go without. I'm certain of that."

Roland laid a gentle hand upon his young friend's shoulder. "You really care about him, don't you?"

Dr. Rushing raised a finger to his lips. "Shh. Don't let it get around."

* * * * *

Claire sat in the middle of her living room floor gluing slats of wood onto the face of an old mirror. She'd liked Brooke's makeshift window so much that she wanted to create a similar piece for her own bathroom. She didn't have many things to be proud of in life, but her modern studio apartment provided great comfort and joy. She treated it like a castle, and for all practical purposes, it was. There was nothing small or stuffy about the expansive room that greeted visitors when they walked through the front door. It had a surprisingly high ceiling and beautiful French doors that opened onto a modest balcony overlooking a neatly manicured courtyard. Best of all, the place was dirt cheap because the tiny kitchenette was hardly a comfortable place to prepare a meal, and the bathroom contained a shower cubicle instead of a full bathtub.

Claire didn't mind sacrificing hot baths and extravagant meals. She was quite satisfied to fill the main room with every comfort imaginable. Her large, overstuffed sofa cradled the spine in the most gentle way possible, and its distinctive cream color gave the room a light, airy feel. A splash of multicolored throw pillows added a hint of character and pizzazz. A painting of abstract color swirls completed the look, tying all contrasting shades in the room together.

Her collection of electronic luxuries was even more impressive than the decor. Unlike many of her young coworkers at the daycare center, she didn't spend her extra cash at single's bars and shopping malls. She threw all of her money into this special place of refuge, and it showed. A dream computer system will all the bells and whistles sat upon a beautifully finished oak desk in the far corner. She'd made payments on the system for more than a year, and now it was finally hers, free and clear. The most impressive piece in the room was a large, free-standing plasma television. Less than one month after she'd paid off the computer, she stumbled upon a web site offering outrageous deals on the monster sets. She wasn't crazy about the idea of going into debt again, but she couldn't resist the urge to turn the one-room apartment into her own personal movie theater. She was a girl who took her entertainment seriously. After all, she spent a lot of time indoors.

The computer and television set were an amicable pair of friends who kept her company and conspired to keep her sane. Her father joked that she had enough recorded movies and downloaded music to entertain a third world nation. She didn't have many visitors to share in the experience of her little castle, but she often dreamed of inviting Dr. Rushing to dinner. Perhaps if he ever grew tired of staring at beautiful women, he might consider gracing her couch with his presence.

In the meantime, she would have to settle for the company of her Internet boyfriend, Walt, otherwise known as Johnny Cool. She had no illusions about the fact that it was a pretend relationship, but she enjoyed chatting with him just the same. She suspected the picture he provided when they first met in a chat room was scanned from a magazine, but she could hardly fault him for that. The photo she had sent in return was a snap shot of Brooke.

It all started as a lighthearted flirt fest, but as the months wore on, the two of them developed a deep friendship, and Claire became more and more curious about Walt's life. Was he really a veterinarian at some animal shelter in Arizona? Did he honestly own a home in one of Scottsdale's most prestigious neighborhoods? Was he truly a single man with no children and no real commitments? If so, why hadn't some beautiful young woman snatched him up? Claire decided that tonight was a good time to find out the answers to these questions. A few days ago, Walt had provided her with a phone number and specified that she should only call on Sundays. She was just devious enough to bother him on a Monday night. Her hands shook as she dialed the number, but her voice remained steady and calm. "May I speak to Walt McKenzie, please?"

A froggy female voice shouted in her ear. "Walter! It's for you."

As Claire waited for her young veterinarian to pick up the extension, she wondered if the abrasive voice belonged to his wife. She could forgive just about any lie, but she had no patience for married men who used the Internet to live out their adulterous fantasies. Her fears were laid to rest when a deep but pleasant voice came over the receiver. "You can hang it up now, Mom."

Without hesitation, Claire dove into a sales pitch she'd repeated a hundred times while working as a telemarketer the previous summer. "Hello, my name is Beth Werner, and I'm calling on behalf of Regency National Bank and Trust. I'm pleased to inform you that you've been pre-approved for our prestigious Gold Traveler's Card."

"Sorry. I don't travel much."

"That's quite all right, Mr. McKenzie. Our card is accepted at many major hotels, restaurants and tourist attractions in your area. And best of all, you'll receive a ten percent discount each time you use it."

"What's the catch? Is there a high interest rate on purchases?"

"Not at all. We offer zero percent financing for the first year. After that, a reasonable APR of 13.9 percent will apply."

"That's not bad. Can you send me an application?"

Claire did a private little dance on her living room carpet. This was going more smoothly than expected. "I can take your application over the phone, if you like. But first, you must be aware that this call may be monitored for quality control purposes."

"That's fine."

"All right, Mr. McKenzie, I have your address listed as 4123 Wellington Lane in Scottsdale, Arizona. Is that correct?"

"No, I live at 4359 Aztec Circle in Phoenix."

"I'm sorry. My mistake. I was reading the address directly above yours on my list. It's been a long day."

In addition to a correct address, Claire was able to secure more personal information about Walt than a seasoned private investigator. She learned that he was a single 40-year-old man with no children and no outstanding debts. He earned minimum wage as a cage cleaner at a local animal shelter, and he didn't have a car payment. He had no criminal record, and he didn't find it the least bit peculiar that she'd asked such a question. He didn't have a mortgage because he lived at home with his parents. All in all, he was an excellent candidate for a credit card. His low-paying job was not a strike against him because he had very few financial obligations. In fact, he probably had more disposable income than the average 40-year-old man with three kids and a mortgage.

Not that Claire cared about Walt's money. She simply wanted an accurate picture of who he really was. She was pleased to discover that he really did work with animals. That meant most of the amusing anecdotes he shared were heartfelt stories about real, honest-to-goodness events in his life. The previous week, he'd spent a good deal of time talking about a three-legged mutt that was scheduled to be put to sleep. He found it amazing that the dog had survived a brutal accident and healed very nicely without the help of antibiotics. Though he saw several stray dogs put to sleep each month, he wasn't going to let this particular mutt slip into oblivion. The creature had made it this far, and perhaps there was some good reason.

Encouraged by her success on the phone, Claire decided to try for an accurate picture. She was bound and determined to find out why an intelligent, kind-hearted man like Walt had never found a wife and moved out of his parent's home. Was he disfigured, like her? Was he handicapped in some way? Was he a closet psychopath who used a handsome photo to lure young ladies to his parent's basement? She desperately wanted to know.

On a hunch, she scanned a photo of her mom's most haggard girlfriend and paid a visit to Walt's favorite chat room. When he appeared on line, she used the nickname "Wildflower" to strike up a conversation with him. It didn't take long to establish a rapport. They were both articulate people who possessed the gift of gab. After downloading the unflattering picture Claire had sent, Walt sent a real picture of himself. Much to Claire's surprise, there were no horns sprouting from his forehead and no vampire teeth protruding from his upper lip. He had a sweet, boyish face with a baby moustache and dark round eyes. His big secret was that he was morbidly obese. She wasn't good at judging height and weight, but she estimated he must've weighed more than 400 pounds.

Claire was not attracted to the man in the photo, but she wasn't turned off by him, either. She desperately wanted to send a real picture of herself to set the record straight, but she couldn't find the courage. She suspected that even a fat mamma's boy wouldn't be attracted to a circus freak with a raised eye socket and exaggerated jaw line.

Just before bed, Claire visited Walt's favorite chat room with her usual nickname, November Rain. She was happy to learn he'd adopted the three-legged pooch and named it "Gimpy." She had always loved his twisted sense of humor. Before signing off, Claire told Walt about the strange man she'd encountered on the street earlier that day. Was she wrong to turn her back on a lonely soul in need? Would it have killed her to buy him a cup of coffee and listen to him babble for just a little while? Could 15 minutes of her time have changed his day? His week? His life?

Walt assured her that it was not a good idea to befriend the deranged. The very fact that she felt guilty for blowing the man off indicated she was more kind and sensitive than most people. She couldn't save the human world anymore than he could save the animal kingdom. He died a small death each time an animal was eradicated, but he couldn't very well adopt every one of them. Despair was a sad fact of life, and it was best to just accept that and move on.

That night, as Claire drifted off to sleep, a vivid picture of the deranged man's face appeared behind her eyelids. She knew exactly what he meant about negative signals. She gave them off herself. People took one look at her face and ran the other way.

*****

Dr. Rushing had never called a client after midnight, but he was a man who believed that certain circumstances warranted the breaking of rules. Breathlessly, he dialed Claire's number and let the phone ring for several minutes.

"Hello?" she answered wearily.

"Go turn on your computer."

"Dr. Rushing? What time is it?"

"Just do what I say. I've mailed you a link to a web site. Do you have a dedicated line? I mean, can you stay on the phone and go on the Internet at the same time?"

"Does a crack head have a pipe? Of course I have a dedicated line."

Dr. Rushing waited for Claire to open his e-mail message and click on the link it contained. When he heard her gasping for breath, he knew that she was staring at the very same image that lit up his own computer screen. Halfway across the world at a concert hall in Germany, a real symphony was in progress. A white-haired conductor stood before the orchestra working his wrists in swift, jerking motions. "Turn up your speakers!" Dr. Rushing commanded.

Together, they cranked the volume and let the energizing medley of trumpets, flutes and violins flood the phone line.

Chapter Four

Five Days Later: Saturday Night

Darren liked to prepare a wide variety of foods, but he particularly enjoyed handling raw chicken flesh. It was the same color as Caucasian skin, and it had a curious rubbery quality that felt good in his hands. Firm yet flexible, it made a faint ripping noise when torn with a serrated knife.

Chad Whitaker's high-pitched scream overpowered such noises when Darren tore his abdomen with a dagger. As the young college student writhed in agony on his bed, Darren couldn't resist the urge to run his fingers along the fresh slit that ran down the length of the guy's torso. *Chicken skin.*

"Please!" Chad whined through runny nostrils. "My safe is downstairs in the pantry. The combination is written in my phone book under "X." Take anything you want. I mean it, anything!"

Darren smiled. "How much is there?"

"Three, maybe four thousand dollars."

"Which is it? Three or four?"

"Three and a half, maybe. I don't know! I beg you for mercy. I'm dying here."

Darren couldn't help but laugh. "It's just a superficial wound. If I'd wanted to kill you, your guts would be spilling over the edge of the bed."

Chad tried to sit up, but his wrists were tied to the headboard. The blood-soaked sheets entangled his legs. "The keys to my car are in my coat pocket. It's yours for the taking."

Darren took a peek out the bedroom window. A brand new Mustang stood in the driveway. "You call that transportation? I had a better vehicle when I was sixteen."

Chad began to cry for the umpteenth time. "What do you want from me?"

"I want to know how an accounting student can afford to pay cash for a brand new car. Should I assume that internships are more lucrative these days?"

"I don't know what you're talking about."

Darren ran the tip of his knife under Chad's toenail. "Stop lying to me."

Chad's short, choppy breaths interrupted the flow of his speech. "I'm…

sorry. I can... still... take it back."

"Now we're talking. Where's the rest of the money?"

"I... don't... have anymore money."

Darren ran the very tip of his knife along Chad's penis, creating a superficial razor scratch. He waited for the pain to register on the guy's face, but it was too late. An eerie calm had overtaken him. His placid eyes moved slowly around the room, as if absorbing every minute detail. Darren recognized the all-encompassing stare of a man who'd suddenly accepted his own impending death.

Furious with himself for taking the mission too far too soon, Darren wrapped a blanket around Chad's abdomen and applied direct pressure to his wound. If he wasn't careful, the dude would start to lose consciousness. "You're going to be okay. I'm not going to kill you, I promise."

Chad's voice came out as a whisper. "You're lying. I can feel it."

At the last possible moment, Darren spotted a snapshot of a young brunette tacked to Chad's bulletin board. Her dark, round eyes were framed by the thickest lashes he'd ever seen. "Does she love you?" he asked.

"No."

A smile came over Darren's lips. He'd lost his edge, and it was time to regain it. "I'd be willing to bet that she does love you. She'd probably freak if you didn't call her tomorrow. She might even drive by your house to investigate."

"Please, no!"

"I'm a very patient man, Chad. I'll wait for her."

"The money is buried behind my neighbor's garage. She doesn't even know it's there."

"Is the body there, too?"

"What body?"

Darren brushed his lips against Chad's ear. "Has your girlfriend ever been raped?"

"The body isn't intact. I hacked the remains and set them on fire."

Darren didn't hesitate to drive the dirty steel blade through Chad's heart.

*****

Samantha Becker was known for her infectious smile, but tonight she wondered if customers could sense the deep black anger brewing in the pit of her stomach. After enduring scores of snide comments laced with sexual innuendo, she had only twelve dollars in her pocket. Didn't she deserve better tips for putting up with such nonsense? She hated to obsess about money, but there were things she desperately needed to get done after work. The first item on her agenda was a trip to the pharmacy to renew her son's prescription. Just when his ear infection was starting to clear up, he'd dumped half a bottle of the precious antibiotics into the toilet.

Mercy came in the form of a $50 tip from Darren Price, her all-time favorite customer. He'd always been a big tipper, even before she started sleeping with him. The way he looked tonight in his faded jeans and crisp red windbreaker, she was half tempted to toss *him* a wad of cash.

"You look great tonight," Darren said as he took command of an isolated corner booth. "Did you lighten your hair?"

Samantha's heart fluttered a bit. "It's just a lemon rinse. The citric acid brings out the highlights."

She wanted to ask him about the black garbage bag stuffed under his arm, but his mile-wide grin threw her off guard. Where was the dark, brooding kid who sipped endless margaritas alone in the corner?

Lots of younger waitresses had made a play for Darren's attention in the past year, but she had something they didn't. She was permanently bound to a marriage she couldn't leave, and there was no chance of her choking off his freedom or making unreasonable demands of his time. As much as she hated the sight of her unemployed husband, he was a convenient babysitter. Darren couldn't help her in that department. Sure, his family was rich, but that didn't amount to anything. He wasn't the fatherly type. Not that Darren didn't have feelings for her. He could be surprisingly gentle when he wanted to be. She had watched him grow up over a period of five years. Long before the relationship turned sexual, he'd been a brotherly type. He'd asked for her opinions on a variety of issues from his strained relationship with his father to his sudden desire to cut his long hair. He didn't ask to meet at the hotel later, and that didn't necessarily bother her. If anything, she was a bit worried about him. He was getting a little old to play criminal. It was time for him to get serious about finding a respectable job, enrolling in college and taking up with a girl who had a little more to offer him.

A few minutes after Darren headed for Donovan's office, Samantha came face to face with a person she thought she'd never see again. Ron the bouncer was settling into one of the tables in her section. She desperately wanted to buy him a beer and ask what he'd been doing with himself all these years, but instead she panicked. Did Donovan still have some kind of grudge against him? What would Darren do if he emerged from the office to find Ron casually sipping a drink? Should she ask him to leave or simply ignore him until she had the opportunity to speak with Donovan? In the end, she decided that some things were better left alone.

*****

Donovan was pleased to see Darren arrive with a black garbage bag under his arm. He poured the kid a drink and motioned for him to have a seat on the musty old couch opposite his desk. "How much did you recover?" he asked.

"Almost all of it. The Mustang is in the parking lot."

"And the body?"

"Burned beyond recognition."

"Very good. My client will be pleased."

"Do you mind if I ask who the kid rubbed out?"

"Not at all. It was a secretary who monitored the ledgers."

Darren tasted his drink. "What a dumb ass. He couldn't have been more sloppy. He didn't even bother to create a password on his computer. Copies of his boss's financial records were stored on his hard drive. I saved them for you. The disk is in the glove box."

Donovan tapped his fingers on the desk. "Speaking of sloppy, my cleaner tells me you left quite a mess. Was that necessary, Darren?"

"The kid was a murderer and a thief. Should I have made dinner?"

"You're a murderer yourself. Have you no mercy?"

Darren fidgeted in his seat. "Don't look at me like that. I got the job done, right?"

Of course he got the job done, Donovan thought. He always got the job done. Who could complain about a hit man who killed with a smile and asked for no pay? In exchange for his valuable services, Darren only required the use of a goon or two once in awhile. He was a vengeful kid, no doubt about it. If practical reasons prevented him from wasting one of his enemies, he'd find another guy to do it, simple as that. There was only one problem: Donovan's conscience. He didn't know he had one until Darren stumbled into his bar.

He'd always been able to separate his career from his personal life, but the kid was something different. Sitting before him was a boy not much older than his own son—a kid who attended the same private school, learned from the same teachers and ate in the same cafeteria. How did two teenagers growing up in the same neighborhood and enjoying the same financial advantages turn out so differently? His own son was a college track star with a string of beautiful young ladies at his heels. Darren was certainly handsome and intelligent enough to live such a life, but somewhere along the line, he'd made different choices. He seemed to be haunted by personal demons too sinister and grotesque to imagine. Donovan had exploited that vulnerability on the night he invited Darren into his inner circle, and he would regret that move for the rest of his life.

"This psychiatrist you want me to waste—is he *your* doctor?"

"Good guess."

"Is he aware of your dealings with me? Does he know how much blood is on your hands?"

"He knows only what my father has told him about me. His knowledge of my extracurricular pursuits doesn't extend beyond my senior year of high school."

"So why kill him?"

The color suddenly left Darren's face. "Are you backing out of the deal?"

"Of course not. I'm just curious as to why you hate him so much."

"He's poisoned my father's mind against me. He's mismanaged my personal care and the care of others who depend on him. Rest assured, Donovan, my reasons are sound."

Donovan leaned back in his chair and lit a cigarette. "All right, Darren. Just say when."

*****

Ron Warner sat in a quiet corner of Donovan's Pub waiting for a familiar face to acknowledge his presence. Samantha had passed by his table three times without blinking, and Scotty had quietly refused to serve him a drink. Was there no mercy and forgiveness in the world? What would it take to get a beer in this fucking hole?

Ron hated being ignored worse than anything in the world. Back in high school, kids were so afraid to tease him about his size that they refused to look him in the eye. On graduation day, an auditorium full of ecstatic teens clapped and cheered each time a new student approached the podium. Only two people clapped when Ron accepted his diploma: Mom and Dad.

The day he was able to turn his hulking physique into his greatest asset was the happiest day of his life. It all started simply enough. He was having a drink at Donovan's Pub when four drunks plunged head first into an old-fashioned brawl. It was a messy kind of fight that endangered other people and left broken chairs and overturned tables in its wake. Ron knew he had to do something. When he sprang into action, a collective hush fell over the room. He went after the largest drunk first, snapping his arm behind his back and shoving him head first into the juke box. The remaining three drunks tried to gang up on him, but he absorbed their sloppy jabs like a punching bag. When he noticed people staring in awe and admiration, he was overtaken by an irresistible urge to put on a show. He lifted one drunk over his head and tossed him over the edge of the bar. The pain in his back was incredible after that, but he forged ahead nonetheless. He beat the two remaining drunks to a pulp and carried them out the door like rag dolls.

From that moment on, Ron was king of his own little corner of the universe. Donovan made him head bouncer and offered him double the salary he earned at the local steel factory. Ron enjoyed driving a brand new truck and having extra beer money in his pocket, but the financial perks paled in comparison to the social benefits. For the first time in his life, girls looked directly into his eyes when they spoke, and guys slapped him on the back in passing. People stopped their conversations when he walked into the room and went back to the beginning of their stories just to include him. He got laid more often than some of the thin guys who trolled the depths of the bar in search of a piece of ass.

His whole life fell apart that fateful night when a young Darren Price sunk a broken bottle into his arm. Even before he dragged the kid into Donovan's office, he sensed that his boss would never look at him the same way again. It was the scream that did it. If he could've gone back and relived that moment, he would gladly have swallowed his own tongue to stifle that high-pitched wail of terror.

God help him, but he was afraid of the kid. Spooked to the very core. Even after he'd managed to tie Darren's hands behind his back, an inexplicable feeling of doom rose and fell within his chest. The boy's vicious tongue cut to his very soul.

"You scream like a girl," the kid had said between clenched teeth. "Like a fucking little girl."

Ron eyed Darren's piercings with disgust. "Look who's talking. You wear more costume jewelry than my grandmother."

"You're just jealous because I can take the pain. You'd scream like a baby if someone took a needle to your face."

"How would you know?"

"I can tell by looking at you. You're a mamma's boy, aren't you? Someone's been feeding you much too well. When's the last time you were laid? The Reagan administration?"

Ron took a deep breath to suppress the violent rage that boiled within him. His first impulse was to blacken the kid's eye, but he suspected Donovan would want first crack at him. He had no desire to alienate his boss twice in one night. For lack of a better outlet to vent his frustration, Ron took a makeup case from the lost-and-found bin and painted Darren's face. He didn't want to stuff the rag down his throat, but the kid kept biting him. Streams of blood trickled down his wrist as he tried to finish the sloppy job he'd started. When the make over was complete, Darren looked more feminine than a supermodel in pink. His smooth, young face made a perfect foundation for the makeup, and his extra long hair framed the whole look to perfection. It was a proud moment when Ron held a compact mirror before Darren's eyes. "Who's the little girl, now?" he asked. "I don't know many guys who would look so pretty in drag. In fact, I don't know any at all."

Trembling with rage, Darren rammed his heels into the side of Donovan's desk. It was a fit like nothing Ron had ever seen. His first kick knocked a bottle of wine to the floor. His second, third and fourth kicks weakened the entire frame. His fifth kick sent chunks of wood flying through the office. Ron should've been happy that he'd finally broken Darren's spirit, but he felt genuinely sorry for the kid. He was just a baby. What could've happened to mess him up so badly?

When Darren began to bang his head on the hard tile floor, Ron was utterly terrified. He was forced to grab a cushion from the couch and slip it under the kid's neck to prevent serious injury. For more than 10 minutes, he watched Darren's head strike the pillow and felt his own heart sink further and further into his chest with each blow. He was dangerously close to reciting a prayer when Darren finally passed out.

Remembering it now, Ron had the feeling Donovan would've been a little more sympathetic if he'd known how impossible the kid was to control. In fact, he was betting on that feeling. If his feeling turned out to be wrong, he could always keep working at the steel mill. If it turned out to be right, he could reclaim the beautiful life he'd lost five long years ago.

The walk from his favorite corner booth to Donovan's second floor office was excruciating. He half expected the rickety old staircase to collapse under his enormous weight. He'd always understood that the bar he loved was a place fraught with hidden dangers, but he never imagined he'd come face to face with Darren again. Watching the young man step out of Donovan's office was like looking at a continuous video tape of the night his whole life ended and his descent into isolation began. The kid was older and more powerfully built, but that didn't mean much. His short hair provided a clear view of the sharp, angular features that haunted Ron's dreams. Two tiny bald spots on his left eyebrow served as further proof that he was just a more grown-up version of the little freak who walked into the bar with a face full of metal on that dismal

September night.

The encounter couldn't have lasted more than five seconds, but in that fleeting moment when Ron held Darren's gaze in the doorway of Donovan's office, an eternity slipped by. He didn't know why Darren smiled, or why he stepped aside and let him pass so gallantly, but he assumed the kid's reasons were as dark as the night sky.

Donovan spoke only after Darren had vanished from sight. "Ronald Warner! Do my eyes deceive me?"

"Don't shoot," Ron said, holding his arms in the air as a joke. Inside, his heart pounded a hole through his chest.

"Don't look so nervous. It doesn't become you. Have a seat, my friend."

The word "friend" was like music to Ron's ears. His heart slowed a bit as he sank into the old familiar couch. "How's business?"

"Not very good, I'm afraid. Drinks are getting stronger and less expensive by the minute. It's the only thing that keeps 'em coming to my side of town."

"I'm sorry to hear that," Ron said. "I truly am."

Donovan flashed him a rare smile. "I know you are, Ron. You just might be the only person in the world who loves this hole as much as I do."

"I suppose this isn't a good time to ask if you could use a little weekend help."

"There's never a good time to ask, but I'm glad to see you just the same. My temper gets away from me. You could've come back the next day."

Donovan's words cut right to Ron's soul. It was about as close to an apology as the man ever came. "Thanks, boss. I appreciate that."

"Aren't you going to ask me about the kid?"

"I'd rather not."

"He's pure evil. Kills for kicks and doesn't expect to be paid."

"Who could compete with that?"

"You could, Ron."

"Me? I've never killed anyone in my life."

"Exactly. You wouldn't have the stomach to do what Darren does."

"What do you mean?"

"He leaves messes for me. Insists upon torturing his victims."

"So why use him?"

"I told you, Ron. His rates are reasonable."

"My rates aren't bad, either."

Donovan picked up a stray pencil and rolled it between his thumb and forefinger. "Oh yeah?"

"I'd be willing to hang out on weekends, free of charge. I could bust a few chops now and then, and you could tip me for my trouble. Otherwise, you wouldn't have to pay me to sit around and drink with the guys."

Donovan snapped his pencil in half. "I'm ashamed of you, Ron. Why aim so low? A real man would stand up for himself."

Ron swiped Donovan's beer from the desk. "It was wrong of you to fire me. I want my job back, and I'm not leaving until I get it."

Donovan laughed so hard he nearly fell out of his chair. "Now that's more like it!"

* * * * *

Mind racing with images of Chad Whitaker's bloody torso, Darren flew down the highway on his cherished Harley Davidson. He usually didn't risk drawing the attention of local squad cars, but tonight was a night made for speeding. The road was free and clear for miles ahead. The street lamps stretched out before him like a thousand tiny moons arranged to light his way. It felt strangely good to be young on this cool October night. The world was an ever-changing place, and he was up for the challenge. He liked the idea that he could change and grow with each passing year, learning more and more as he went along. Ron had helped to remind him of that.

Just 30 minutes ago, he felt lost. The fat man's bulging eyes sent him back to a time when he had no control over his own destiny. Laying on that dirty floor with a face full of makeup was more than just humiliating: It was torture in its purest and most extreme form. He'd tried to kill himself, but Ron was merciless. The fucker wouldn't rest until he'd brought Darren to the darkest and most vulnerable hour of his existence. Perhaps murder wasn't the best way to avenge oneself. Real power was all about finding a man's trigger and nailing it. Physical torture had its limitations. Chad proved that. Once he'd given up on the idea of living another day, no amount of pain could affect him. He could only be touched by visions of the girl he loved. No weapon in the world was a match for that picture on his bulletin board, and Darren was lucky to have spotted it.

Darren wondered if Dr. Rushing had any special triggers. What did he value most in life? What weaknesses could be tapped? Were there any cherished pictures on his bulletin board? A bullet was too quick for him, and a knife wasn't much better. Why not send him out with a bang?

Chapter Five

Sometimes they believed Kelly, and sometimes they didn't. If she said she was having trouble sleeping, they slipped her a little white pill. If she asked for a razor to shave her legs, they told her it wouldn't be possible. If she claimed to be dying for a cigarette, they issued her a pass to the courtyard without question. If she announced that Satan visited her in dreams, they nodded their heads condescendingly.

Betty was her favorite nurse because she didn't mince words. "It doesn't matter what you believe," she would say. "Just remember that people don't always want to hear about it. If you ever want to find a job, make some friends and lead a normal life, you'll learn when to keep your mouth shut."

It was Betty who slipped her the cosmetics. Nothing fancy, just a small bottle of foundation to get rid of the dark circles and a little mascara to darken the eyelashes. She always knew she could be pretty when she tried, or even when she didn't. It was a confusing gift, but one that had served her well since childhood.

She thought she might have a shot with the sweet young security guard with the nice ass. If she played her cards right, he might provide her with a place to stay upon her release. Perhaps he would even support her while she looked for a job and tended to some unfinished business. Anything was better than going home. She could learn to love him, if that's what he needed. Most people weren't so hard to love, aside from her parents.

She found him in the television lounge around midnight. He hated to miss his late night talk shows. He didn't mind it here, and that's what she liked about him. Any guy who could find joy in a hell hole was a guy who could be happy anywhere. He generally made the most of his shift, even when he looked tired. He ate endless mints and whistled ever so softly as he roamed the corridors on hourly patrols. Sometimes, he stopped to flirt with the old nurses and look at pictures of their daughters. He didn't need a reason to make people feel good. He did it instinctively.

He didn't look away from the television when she sat down beside him. "Does Betty know you're out of bed?" he asked.

"She doesn't care as long as I don't wake anyone else."

"She could give you something to sleep, if you like."

"No thanks. I'm weaning myself off the pills. If I'm going to lead a productive life, I'll have to learn to get by without them."

Finally, he looked at her. "Are you sure that's a good idea?"

"I'm positive. As long as I have my happy pills, I shouldn't need anything else."

"You didn't seem very happy last week."

"That was just a nightmare. By the way, thanks for your discretion."

"You can thank Betty. She got you calmed down pretty quick."

"I'm feeling better now—honest. I don't have nightmares anymore."

"I'm glad to hear that. You don't really believe all that Satan crap, do you?"

Kelly looked away. She had hoped he'd be too polite to bring that up. "It seems real only in dreams. I had to learn how to separate fantasy from reality. Once I did that, the dreams weren't so frightening. In fact, I learned how to control them."

"You learned to control your dreams?"

"Sure. It's a simple technique. Would you like to hear about it?"

"Okay."

"There's a certain point in many nightmares when you half realize you're dreaming, but you just can't wake up. Have you ever been there?"

"Many times. I've read that the body releases natural chemicals that paralyze you so you won't act out your dreams."

"That's exactly what I'm talking about. If you can imagine a different outcome in the grip of that paralysis, you'll incorporate that outcome into your dream."

"You know, I think I've actually done that before."

"Really?" Kelly asked, scooting just a little closer. "Tell me about it."

As Vince dove into the story of his most frightening childhood dream, Kelly realized he wasn't so different from other men she'd tried to seduce: He didn't miss an opportunity to talk about himself. She made sure to hang on his every word and widen her eyes at selected points in the story. She dared not comment on the part where he found himself barreling toward the edge of a cliff on a skateboard. She suspected he'd never believe how close he came to Satan each time he confronted his own mortality.

They talked for nearly an hour, stopping only to grab a couple Cokes from the vending machine down the hall. She was surprised to learn that he was a full-time college student. Did the man ever sleep? His ultimate goal was to become a hard-nosed private investigator like the ones he read about in detective novels. His ambition was impressive, but she couldn't understand why some men felt the need to confront danger. Perhaps he was a bit too much like Darren.

She was on her way out of the lounge when she summoned the courage to make her final move. "So, if I ever want to run a background check on my neighbor's second cousin, I can find your number in the phone book?"

"Sure. Why not?"

"In that case," she said with a wink, "I'll steal a copy of the Yellow Pages."

She knew it was a decent closing line. She could feel his eyes upon her as she slipped out of the lounge and made her way around the corner. She was deliciously aware that her long black hair had a tendency to flow behind her as she walked. She half expected him to follow her, but she knew the risk was much too great.

Half an hour later, a sliver of light from the hallway cut through her darkened room. It was Vince creeping past the door and closing it behind him. He paused for a moment to remove his pants before slipping into bed beside her. Her heart hammered against her rib cage as he inserted a cold hand beneath her flimsy institutional gown. She opened her mouth to him in the moonlight, savoring the taste of his soft, probing tongue. He tried to enter her, but she squirmed beneath him in protest. It had been far too long since she'd relished the heat of man's touch. She wasn't about to settle for a few quick thrusts from a half-dressed security guard.

Slowly, as if removing a bandage from a wound, she unbuttoned his starchy uniform shirt and peeled the formal black socks from his swollen feet. Rectangular impressions from his belt were still etched along his waistline. It appeared he was no stranger to the twelve-hour work day. What he really needed was a little TLC.

She worked her hands over every inch of his skin, paying special attention to a tight bundle of nerves along the side of his torso. His deeply satisfied groans sent shivers through her very core. The opportunity to please a man was the only reward she sought, but she was nicely surprised when he ran his tongue down her abdomen and came to rest at the warm juncture of her thighs. His intense hunger for her flesh told her that he needed this almost as much as she did. Perhaps people on the outside weren't as fulfilled as they liked to believe.

*****

It was usually too loud for Dr. Rushing to notice what a lonely place his house had become. His basement office was equipped with a television set and two computers so that he could play video games, download music and watch rented movies at the same time. Upstairs, a radio played constantly to drown out the terrible silence that hung in the air like a great fog.

He never felt there was something missing in his life until those cases of German beer arrived on his doorstep. They were a gift from an old college friend who used to drink the stuff like Kool-Aid and pass it along to anyone who seemed to need an excellent buzz. The beer brought back fond memories of bon fires at the beach, and Dr. Rushing felt the sudden urge to call every name in his phone book.

As much as Roland wanted to spend a night away from home, he was busy correcting an endless stack of essays. None of Dr. Rushing's old classmates could make it, either. They were all tuckered out from dance recitals, little league games, amusement parks and bickering wives.

Perhaps it was time to find a wife and fill the house with screaming children, battery-operated machine guns, talking dolls and hand-held video games. Though he hadn't been involved with anyone in the past few years, his dating history wasn't exactly limited. Much to his mother's dismay, he'd gone through a Don Juan phase in his early twenties. She once said his interest in a girl began and ended the moment she spread her legs. He argued that it was a young man's God-given right to explore the female anatomy, and she promptly smacked him upside the head for bringing her hero into a discussion of casual sex.

Despite a hot temper and a quick right hand, Mrs. Rushing wasn't such a bad mom. She made sure to deliver her whacks near the top of the head, avoiding painful contact with the cheek and outer ear. She drew blood two– or maybe three–times max.

He couldn't really fault her for losing her temper. He liked to pester her while she washed dishes and never missed an opportunity to tie her apron strings in knots or make fart noises by pressing the small of his back into the freshly mopped linoleum. She'd failed to provide him with a little brother or sister to torment, and he wasn't about to let her forget it. Her tight curly perm and bulldog face didn't scare him. She was a stout, cartoonish figure whose pointy toes stuck straight out from beneath the hem of her floor-length housecoat.

The truth be told, he much preferred to hang out with his dad. A man of many talents, Gregory Rushing could balance a basketball on the very tip of his index finger and coach scores of undisciplined brats to local and state championships. He skipped stones farther across the lake than any well-practiced third grader and ate frosted flakes straight from the box like potato chips.

As far back as he could remember, Tommy's greatest wish was to win a spot on the school basketball team in order to become more like the kind of fellow his dad slapped on the back after a good game. He tried very hard to conquer a long-standing depth perception problem, but he always wound up sinking his baskets into an imaginary hoop three feet away from the real net.

Since he had little hope of impressing his father on the basketball court, Tommy set out to prove his manhood in the classroom. On the eve of his eighth birthday, he made a serious dinner table announcement that he planned to become a doctor.

"What kind of doctor?" his mom asked between bites of overcooked tuna casserole.

"The regular kind," Tommy said proudly.

"A family practitioner?"

Tommy had to think about that question for a moment. Was a family practitioner the smartest kind of doctor, or were there even smarter kinds? His grandmother kept regular appointments with a foot doctor for bunions, and his mom saw a stomach doctor for ulcers. He didn't know which kind of doctor was smartest, but he was reasonably certain he didn't want to touch bunions or ulcers with his bare hands. "I want to be a head doctor," he said.

From that moment on, things were different in the Rushing household. Instead of sports magazines and comic books, Gregory brought home real texts for his son to read. The first was a children's science manual called, *My Brain, Your Brain.* The star of the book was a disfigured boy with a transparent forehead that showed every lump and bump across the surface of his frontal lobe. Tommy immediately felt sorry for the kid. His head was way too big for his body, and he had an annoying habit of explaining every aspect of his daily routine: "When I want to ride my bike, my brain tells my feet to step on the pedals. When I feel hungry, it's really just my stomach telling my brain to tell my arm to reach for an apple. Are you feeling hungry? What is your brain telling you?"

Tommy's brain told him to put the silly book away and look for more useful information in the family's well-worn set of encyclopedias. With a little help from his dad, he spent a whole summer sketching rough diagrams of the human brain and nervous system. He even took time to label his drawings, copying super-sized words he could not yet understand. He particularly liked the term "medulla oblongata." He and his father repeated that phrase several times each night before bed, just to hear themselves pronouncing it.

He lost his father to stomach cancer at age 13. It was a chapter of his life he preferred not to think about. He called it "voluntary repression," as opposed to the kind of repression that happened on a subconscious level. He didn't like the word "denial" and rarely used it, even with clients.

What was he going to do now that Roland sensed the need to find Darren another psychiatrist? He'd already lost one father. Would fate be cruel enough to take another? Somewhere in the back of his mind, he realized his patients' parents weren't supposed to be up for grabs, but professionalism was never one of his strong points. He wouldn't let Roland slip quietly out of his life like an old college buddy with new responsibilities. He would keep sending him wine and filling his mailbox with useless trinkets until the old man told him to take a flying leap.

With nothing else to do but sit alone, Dr. Rushing made himself the guest of honor at his very own party. He defrosted a steak in the microwave and threw it over a low flame on the gas grill. As it slow cooked to perfection, he took a seat in his favorite lawn chair and downed five cans of the bitter German brew.

It was a little chilly for comfort in his backyard, but the more he drank, the less it bothered him. He no longer cared that the dead leaves littering his yard had reached ankle height, and he was not particularly worried about the pile of lumber in his garage that was slated for the construction of a new deck. He concentrated on the stars above his head and the way they seemed to grow dimmer with each passing moment. By midnight, they were like faded flecks of light with no shape or definition.

He was finishing yet another beer when his cordless phone rang. He didn't want to answer it, but when he saw Brooke's name flash across the caller ID window, curiosity got the best of him. "I'm not really home," he whispered into the receiver. "It's a figment of your imagination."

"Dr. Rushing? Are you… drunk?"

"Yes, but it's not my fault. An old friend sent me two free cases of beer. I couldn't very well pour them down the sink."

"Am I disturbing your party?"

"Yes, but I'm glad you called. I've been meaning to talk to you about your office attire. It's not very pra-fesh-null."

Brooked laughed. "It's interesting that you've chosen to point that out with slurred speech. Aren't you going to ask why I'm calling you at such an ungodly hour?"

"No."

"Dr. Rushing!"

"Okay. Why are you calling me, damn it!"

"I'm worried about Claire. I just got off the phone with her."

Dr. Rushing stood up and fell back into his seat. "Claire calls you at home?"

"What do you expect? I'm her only friend."

"And what am I? Chopped liver?"

"You're an authority figure. It's not the same."

"I'm her best friend, and you know it."

"Are you going to let me finish, or not?"

"I'm sorry. Tell me about Claire."

"She's all excited about this guy she met on the Internet. She wants to fly halfway across the country to meet him in person."

Dr. Rushing felt as if he'd been slapped in the face. "Jeezus. I'll have to take a walk with her. I mean, have a talk with her."

"You can't! She trusted me with a very personal secret. Besides, it's not that serious just yet. She hasn't even shown him a real picture of herself, but she's starting to suspect he won't care what she looks like."

"Brooke, *all* men care what a girl looks like."

"Not in this case. He's kind of on the heavy side."

"How heavy are we talking?"

"About 400 pounds."

"Jeezus! He's a fucking whale."

"Maybe so, but his weight isn't what concerns me."

"You mean there's more?"

"Yep. Are you ready for this?"

"Hit me."

"He's a 40-year-old recluse."

Dr. Rushing crushed his empty beer can in his fist. "That settles it. I'm going to call her right now. She's not flying halfway across the country to meet some fat old man in his fat old town. She's better than that."

"I can't believe you're being such a jerk about this. I wish I'd never told you."

"I'm sorry. It just frightens me to imagine her spending her life with some other person who's afraid to set foot in public. Claire is special. She needs someone who can help her to develop all of the wonderful qualities she keeps hidden."

Brooke's tone was suddenly sarcastic. "Someone like you, maybe?"

"That's absurd."

"Come on. I know you like her. You totally want to send her flowers and write her name in your notebook ten thousand times. It's disgusting. You're old enough to be her father."

Dr. Rushing slammed his fist down on the patio table. "I am NOT old enough to be her father!"

"Sure you are. Lots of 13-year-olds are having kids these days. It was the movie of the week on channel eleven."

"Fuck off, Blondie. My father was almost twelve years older than my mother."

"That's different! Women needed older men to support them in those days."

"It is NOT different!"

"It is so!"

"What makes you think I'm the kind of loser who'd blow a nut over some girl who's just barely old enough to share a case of beer with me?"

"Well, for starters, you used to have a crush on me."

Dr. Rushing spit into the phone. "Bullshit!"

"I had to quit wearing miniskirts because of you."

"There's a difference between ogling a woman's body and having a crush on her."

"So, you admit you were ogling my body?"

"I'm not going to discuss this with you. I absolutely refuse."

Dr. Rushing hung up the phone. Two minutes later, it rang again. "I'm not home!" he shouted into the receiver.

"Don't hang up! I don't think you have a crush on me. Men just like to stare. It's no big deal, honest. I know you're not in the habit of dating little girls, but I do think there's something unprofessional about your feelings for Claire. You can't talk about proper attire one minute and get all jealous over a client the next. It's insane! Either you're a professional, or you're not a professional."

Dr. Rushing stood up to stretch his legs and fell flat on his ass. Gasping for breath, he stretched out on the cool grass and looked up at the night sky. "You're right. I should be acting in Claire's best interests, even if that means letting her make a few mistakes. She's old enough to make adult decisions."

"Bingo."

"So, why burden me with all this top secret info if I'm not allowed to do anything about it?"

"I never said you couldn't do anything. Do you still keep in touch with that Bob guy? You know, the private investigator?"

"Are you kidding? He's the one who sent the beer."

"Perfect. Why not have him check this guy out? His name is Walt Simpson, and he works at some animal shelter in Phoenix. It wouldn't hurt to find out if he's as sweet and harmless as Claire makes him out to be. We can't stop her from chasing hunches, but we can damned well make sure she's headed to a safe destination."

Dr. Rushing smiled. "Excellent idea, Einstein. Your brain's almost as big as your heart."

* * * * *

It seemed like a typical Sunday morning. Slats of sunlight filtered through the window bars, casting pinstriped shadows over Kelly's blanket. A pair of sneakers squeaked across the linoleum outside her door. That meant the janitors were still at work, and it would be at least another hour before breakfast. The smell of ammonia drifted up to her nostrils. It was so strong she could taste it in the back of her throat.

Throwing back the covers, she went straight for the window, her bare feet slapping the cold tile along the way. Brilliant orange and yellow leaves clung to the branches of oak trees lining the outer edges of the courtyard. A quaint cobblestone path cut through the center of the property, leading to nowhere in particular. The landscape reminded her of a scene straight out of one of Darren's paintings. If nothing else, he was a talented bastard.

She tried not to think of the way Darren's moist breath caressed her cheek when he bent to kiss her. The very taste of his skin was a pleasure more profound than any sensation she'd ever known. He could be astonishingly gentle when he wanted to be, but that was a lifetime ago. His hidden charms were irrelevant now.

Shivering to the core, she snatched the blanket from her bed and wrapped it around her shoulders. That's when she noticed the brilliant red rose on her pillow. Her heart jumped to her throat as she ran her fingertips along the soft velvet petals. Did Vince really see something in her? Had she affected him so deeply in just one night?

She'd expected him to leave right after their secret tryst, but he'd remained by her side for more than an hour. With nothing much to do in the dark room, they passed the time gossiping about other patients and covering their mouths to stifle the laughter. Now, there was a beautiful red rose to serve as evidence that he'd enjoyed himself in more ways than one. It didn't matter that he'd probably plucked the rose from the beautiful bouquet adorning the reception desk. A stolen rose was better than no rose at all.

She wondered if Vince kept a gun at home. He wanted to be a private investigator, but that didn't necessarily mean he liked the idea of having a lethal weapon stuffed in the drawer of his night stand between a paperback novel and a bottle of aspirin. Most people didn't think the way Kelly's parents had taught her to think. They didn't worry about strangers crouching in bushes and live each day as if it could be their last.

She wondered if Darren still lived in the quaint little guest house behind his father's estate. If so, it would be relatively easy to sneak up on him. He wasn't the kind of person who locked his doors and barricaded his windows. He was the kind of person who necessitated the invention of locks and barricades. His very presence on Earth was like a festering boil on the backside of mankind.

If she could eradicate that boil, she would be doing the whole fucking world a favor. In one fail swoop, she could right all the wrongs of her past and extricate the demons from her very soul.

*****

The piercing cry of an ambulance pulled Dr. Rushing from the depths of slumber. Breathlessly, he rushed to the window and peered out into the cold night. Time stood still on the street below. The moon was full and strange. A twinkling star glided past his window on a gentle breeze. Was this for real? Since when did stars swing so close to home?

A dull, aching sensation pounded the back of his skull. The piercing cry grew louder and louder until he reached over and slapped the anti-panic button on his alarm clock. "Damn," he said to no one in particular. "Damn it all to hell."

Was it morning already? Didn't he just lay his head down on the pillow a few moments ago? He remembered talking to Brooke, the little blonde genius. She knew, even when he couldn't see it himself. She didn't need eight years of college to look right down to the bottom of his soul. She fucking knew. Was it that obvious? Did Claire know as well? Had he ever shown a little too much enthusiasm in her presence? When did it all start, anyway? When did he stop looking at her as a disadvantaged child and start seeing her as an equal? Was it that day at the art museum? How come she remembered the complete title of his favorite painting, anyway? Wasn't that a bit much to remember after four months? Did she feel it, too? Was he more than just an authority figure in her life?

His headache was accompanied by a powerful thirst. Of course. A hangover. He hadn't had one since college. He'd almost forgotten how horrible they could be. If he could just gather the strength to open his eyes, he could stumble–or crawl—into the bathroom and get a drink from the faucet.

Had he remembered to replenish his supply of Dixie cups? The last thing Dr. Rushing expected to see when he opened his eyes was a knife glinting in the morning sunlight. The blade was less than an inch from his nose.

"Let's play a game, shall we?" a sinister voice whispered. "I'll pull a list of scenarios from my ass, and you can smell it."

"Darren!"

"Spare me the shock. You knew you were dealing with a psychopath. In fact, it was you who delivered the diagnosis. What a horrible label to slap on a 16-year-old child. What were those phrases you wrote in your book? Extreme lack of emotion? Inability to feel remorse? I took a peek one day. You should never get up to pee with a psychopath in the office."

Dr. Rushing took a deep breath to clear his head. A gun was strapped to Darren's belt. It was pointless to put up a fight. He would have to try and talk his way out of this mess. "I was only trying to help you. Whatever you're feeling right now, you must understand that my primary goal was always to help you."

Darren dropped to his knees beside the bed. "Liar! If you cared so much about me, why didn't you have me committed?"

"On what grounds? You were a punk kid who got off on intimidating other people. Every school has bullies. Should we send them all to the funny farm?"

"You knew I fantasized about killing people."

"I fantasize about fucking my secretary, but it doesn't mean anything. A thought is just a thought. It's there one minute and gone the next. You trusted me with your darkest desires, and I respected that. Should I have committed you for honesty?"

Darren's hot breath warmed the side of Dr. Rushing's cheek. "You're good with words. You have a way of twisting things around to suit your purpose. I used to admire that quality, but I've grown bored with it. I'm going to ask you again, Dr. Rushing. Why didn't you have me committed?"

"A psychiatric hospital is no place for a teenager. I thought you'd be better off with your father."

Darren sliced through the skin on Dr. Rushing's throat. The pain was minimal, but he felt a stream of blood flowing down his neck. "That was for lying to me. The next cut will be deeper."

Dr. Rushing shivered with fear. The incision had hurt just a little more than a typical razor scratch, but that didn't mean it wasn't a serious wound. As a doctor, he was well aware that adrenaline was his best friend right now. It could've been keeping him from feeling the full force of the pain. "What do you want me to say? What is it you'd like to hear?"

Darren rose to his feet. "Just once, I'd like to hear the truth from you. Why didn't you have me committed?"

"I thought I could help you. I was just arrogant enough to believe I could change your life."

Darren clapped his hands together in an exaggerated display of applause. "Very good, Dr. Rushing. Anything else you'd like to add?"

"I didn't know what I was doing. You were one of my first clients, for God's sake. Deep down, I knew your case was more than I was qualified to handle, but your father was so insistent. He believed in me at a time when I couldn't believe in myself."

"How touching. You toyed with my mind for five years to impress my father. What a joke."

"It wasn't like that, Darren. You've got it all wrong."

"Don't contradict a man with a knife. I wonder what my father would say if he knew you were such a God damned quack."

"I'm truly sorry you think of me as a quack. I may not have been able to help you in a profound way, but you have to believe that I gave it my best effort for a very long time."

"Okay. I'll buy that. But what about the others? Have you given them your best effort?"

"I'm not sure what you're talking about."

Darren made a deeper incision across Dr. Rushing's throat. "You're lying again! You know how I feel about liars! You told Claire there's no reason why she can't be just as happy as anyone else. You told Benny the voices aren't real, when you know damned well they're very real to him. You said the medication would change his life, but we both know it'll take more than a steady supply of pills to quiet the demons in that freak's head."

Blood trickled down Dr. Rushing's chest and soaked his pale blue sheets. "How... how do you know about Claire and Benny?"

"You're missing the point! How do you expect to cure people if you can't acknowledge what they believe to be true?"

Dr. Rushing reached deep within his heart to find the most honest answer he could provide. The truth was startling, even to him. "I don't expect to cure them. I try to give them a little something to hold onto. I try to help them leave the office feeling a little better than they felt when they arrived."

Darren hopped onto the bed and did a quick little dance atop the covers. "The truth shall set you free!"

"I'm sorry, Darren. I'm so sorry."

"Don't apologize. Words mean nothing to me. Actions speak volumes."

"I'll do anything you need me to do."

"First of all, I want you to acknowledge that the pain your clients feel, no matter how irrational, is very real."

"I'll acknowledge that."

"And I want you to stop visiting that rich guy. Why should he enjoy house calls just because he can afford to pay you more than anyone else? Is he any more fucked up than the rest of them?"

"I'll never visit him again. I promise."

"That's not good enough! I want you to fix him and everyone else."

"You're asking for the impossible! Certain aspects of mood and behavior can be altered with medication, but some of my clients cannot be cured. You know that, Darren. You know that as well as I do."

Darren jumped down from the bed and stood once again at Dr. Rushing's side. "You have too little faith in the people who put their lives in your hands. How do you expect to help clients if you can't imagine them in a better place? I could do a better job of curing people with one hand tied behind my back. You don't deserve the authority you've been given, and it's high time someone took it from you."

Tears streamed down Dr. Rushing's face. "Please, Darren. I'm too young to die."

Darren tossed Dr. Rushing a roll of duct tape. "Relax. I'm much too disgusted to take pleasure in ending your pain. Wind the tape around your ankles, please."

Dr. Rushing's hands shook as he fumbled with the thick silver tape. In his mind's eye, he saw himself rolling across the floor with bloody eye sockets and severed limbs. Darren obviously didn't plan to make this quick and clean. He was the kind of freak who would go for the maximum punishment he could devise.

When more than five minutes passed without incident, Dr. Rushing found the courage to ask the very question he least wanted answered. "If you aren't going to end my life, what are you going to do?"

Darren flashed him a wide-toothed grin. "Isn't it obvious? I'm going to steal it."

$$\ast\ast\ast\ast\ast$$

Mr. Rivard raised his coffee cup to divert the waitress's attention from a heated debate at the counter. Apparently, the Sunday morning regulars at

Ted's Diner were hell bent on proving they could use a cigarette lighter to cook a raw egg without breaking the shell. The middle-aged blond adjusted her hair net and wandered over to Mr. Rivard's table with a fresh pot of coffee.

"If I were a bartender, I'd have to cut you off. What's that you're working on?"

Mr. Rivard suddenly noticed that several wads of paper had spilled over the edge of his table. "I'm attempting to write a screenplay about my life."

"That's enough!" the waitress shouted across the room. "You're going to break it."

Mr. Rivard wondered why the abrasive blond had taken the time to ask a question if she wasn't interested in hearing the answer. Perhaps she'd change her tune if she knew how many hurdles he'd jumped in the past 30 years. His first bout with depression came at age sixteen when his father brought home a used Mustang for his birthday. At the time, a gently used vehicle was a luxury for a grown man, let alone a child whose driver's license had not yet arrived in the mail. With great pride, his father explained that the car was in excellent condition and would last for years to come. A young Rick Rivard went to bed that night with a terrible phrase stuck in his head: "years to come." He couldn't imagine himself living long enough to see his first car deteriorate with age. Even as a teenager, a profound and irrational sense of doom resided deep within his soul.

Driven by the unshakable fear that he wouldn't live to see age 30, young Rick became obsessed with the challenge of leaving a legacy behind. Refusing a management position at his family's shoe factory, he launched Rivard Enterprises, an advertising agency staffed by English majors and art students. By the end of his senior year in college, he had 200 solid clients throughout the metropolitan area. At age 29, he merged his company with an established corporation and became a nationally recognized force in the advertising industry. He not only lived to see his 30th birthday: He rented a stadium to celebrate.

When laid out in black and white, his history covered less than 70 pages. Initially, the writing project had been a therapeutic undertaking because it led him to recall pivotal experiences in his life and learn from them all over again. He wrote constantly for days on end, stopping only to take naps, make coffee or pay visits to various diners where no one knew him or cared to know him.

Something peculiar happened as he approached the middle of his first draft. All of a sudden, there seemed to be nothing left to write about. By age 35, he had an aggressive marketing team to secure new accounts and a first-rate management team to maintain them. Various scouts traveled the country in search of smaller agencies to buy out, and lawyers worked out the details. On paper, his business grew faster than the cockroach population in Florida, but he wasn't exactly sure how or why.

His creativity stopped flowing when he realized that the middle section of his screenplay depicted an endless procession of lawyers bringing papers for him to sign. It was quite possibly the dullest story ever written. Once his main focus shifted to acquiring more and more agencies to merge with his own, he'd become little more than a pencil pusher with detached control of an empire that operated like a well-oiled machine.

Perhaps he should've listened to Dr. Rushing in the first place. He was supposed to invent an imaginary world more exciting than his own. He could've created a place to get lost in, but instead he chose to stumble around in a reality that had never quite been what he wanted it to be. He would know better next time. He would avoid autobiographical sketches at all costs and concentrate on designing the most fascinating fictional world ever conceived.

Chapter Six

Sunday night, Vince's footsteps made rhythmic tapping sounds on the linoleum as he made his way down the corridor. The mint in his mouth tasted just a little sweeter than the same brand had tasted just a few days ago. The dim hallway seemed just a little brighter, and the cold, institutional smell of ammonia didn't bother him half as much. He no longer whistled softly to pass the time. He poured out his heart in song.

He once read that it was nearly impossible to feel unhappy during the beginning stages of a good courtship. Natural endorphins flooded the brain, turning ordinary moments into profoundly rich experiences. Even the clinically depressed showed remarkable—if temporary—progress when caught in the grip of a budding romance.

Maybe "romance" wasn't the right word. He wasn't exactly taking Kelly to dances and pinning corsages on her chest, but the fleeting moments he spent by her side were precious just the same. She had this crazy way of making him feel like he was the only person in the whole world who really mattered. She didn't just open her mouth to receive his tongue: She kissed his eyelids and moved slowly down his face before setting her sights on his lips. He'd never been the center of someone's universe, and it felt strangely incredible.

His own girlfriend had never made him feel that way, even in the beginning. She was a chatty prom queen type who still got a kick out of displaying old cheerleading trophies on the mantle. He sometimes had to remind her that high school was only a four-year period in life, and past accomplishments weren't the only thing that defined her as a person.

When he thought of how he pursued her in his senior year, it made him sick to his stomach. He was easily one of the best looking guys in school, but that wasn't good enough for her. Only a quarterback or a debate team captain would do. She wouldn't touch a man who couldn't raise her social status, and Vince didn't stand a chance in those days. He was a quiet kid who sat in the back of the classroom reading magazine articles on every subject under the sun from health and fitness to psychology and international affairs. Ironically, his hunger for knowledge didn't extend to academic pursuits. His teachers often pointed out that it wouldn't have killed him to approach textbook assignments with the same raw enthusiasm.

His prom queen didn't warm up to him until he dated a couple of her friends after graduation. Once she realized other girls on her level perceived him to be a good catch, she couldn't get down his pants fast enough. It felt like a big victory back then, but now Vince realized how much of a failure it was. He'd spent the last four years of his life with a girl who corrected his grammar in public and monitored his clothing purchases to make sure he didn't wear anything slightly out of style. He was never successful enough for her and never as talented as the overachievers she bragged about dating in high school.

Not that Kelly was a perfect replacement. Vince knew it took more than a couple of earth-shattering kisses to define real love. A funny farm wasn't the best place to shop around for a new girlfriend, and he wondered if he was half crazy for attempting it. A thousand questions ran through his mind each time he slipped into bed beside her. Was she truly nuts, or was she just a person who'd slipped along the pathway of life? The statistics weren't encouraging. A depressing number of crazy folks slipped in and out of reality their entire lives. The point was that he knew very little about Kelly, and it was time to start asking questions.

He knew something was wrong the moment he stepped behind her door. The acrid smell of her sweat filled the room. Her lifeless limbs were tangled in the sheets. Her cherished blanket lay on the floor in a big white heap. Carefully, he slipped into bed beside her and studied her face in the pale moonlight. Her eyes danced in circles beneath their lids. A nervous twitch lifted one corner of her mouth into a smile and dropped it back down. She thrashed from side to side for a moment then collapsed like a rag doll mixed up in the sheets. Another nightmare was in progress.

As much as he wanted to evaluate any stray words that might escape from her lips, he thought it best to wake her before the screaming started. A profound sense of disappointment flooded his heart as he grasped both of her shoulders and shook her back to reality. Maybe she really was crazy. Perhaps the nightmares would continue for the rest of her life.

The moment she opened her eyes, a look of sheer terror came over her face. She stared at him as if he were a complete stranger. His mind understood her confusion, but his heart felt the sting of rejection. He was suddenly reminded of the way his girlfriend pretended not to recognize him when she passed him in the hallway back in high school.

"It's me, Kelly. It's just me."

"Vince?"

"Yes. I'm here."

"Thank God," she said, burying her face into the crook of his neck. "Thank God."

He held her until she began to drift off to sleep. "Talk to me!" he demanded. "Was it the Satan dream again?"

"I don't know."

"What happens in the dream?"

"A madman is chasing me and my friends through the woods with a chainsaw. We should've left the campsite after the first beheading, but we felt an inexplicable urge to hang around and sing songs by the fire."

"Stop it, Kelly. This isn't the movie of the week. Tell me what happens in your dream."

She pushed him away. "Don't do this to me. I can't tell you anything because I'm afraid of what you'll think. I fear I've already lost you."

Vince stroked her long black hair. "I'm not going anywhere. I only want to help you make sense of things."

She scooted back into his arms. "I'm afraid there's no sense to be made. I'm sitting in a dark corner of this cave-like dwelling. Hundreds of souls are pressed against my naked body. I can't see them, but I can smell their foul breath and feel their bare skin as they brush past. Some one—or some *thing*—leads me through the crowd to a separate chamber within the cave. A small, helpless man is writhing in pain on the ground. His skin is covered with hundreds of tiny round depressions, as if someone took a piercing gun to his abdomen. He hates me with every fibre of his being. I can smell the animosity dripping from his pores and taste his bitter blood in the back of my throat. My first instinct is to run, but my arms and legs won't obey. I can only watch in horror as he picks up a jagged stone and slices through both of my breasts. The pain is more severe than anything I've ever felt, and it only gets worse. He uses his bare fist to crack my breastbone and holds my beating heart in his tiny hand."

He pulled her closer. "Is this man Satan?"

"No. Satan is an invisible force that pulls me from the man's grasp and delivers me to a separate chamber within the cave. I open my eyes to find that I'm laying on the ground with my hands and feet bound to four stakes. Satan is standing over me with lust in his eyes, and he wants me as much as I want him. My senses are on fire, but I'm frightened by my own desire. I know that if we bond, I'll belong to him. That's when I wake up screaming."

Vince was utterly speechless. He almost wished he hadn't forced her to describe the terrible images that haunted her in the dead of the night. Perhaps a little levity would lighten the moment and put her at ease. "So, tell me. Does Satan have big horn-like extensions protruding from his scalp? Does he carry a pitchfork or any of that crap?"

"Of course not. Satan is beautiful. He was God's highest angel, remember?"

"What does he look like?"

"This is where it gets good. He looks like a person I once knew. An old boyfriend, to be exact."

"Your ex-boyfriend is Satan?"

Kelly laughed. "Crazy, isn't it?"

"Not really. I've dated Satan for the past four years. What do you think it means? Are you still recovering from a particularly painful breakup?"

"If only it were that simple."

"So what's the Satan angle all about?"

"Well, if you can believe my psychiatrist, I'm suffering from a profound sense of guilt. I did many things in my youth that I'm not very proud of as an adult. I've cleaned up my act since then, but deep down, I fear that I'm headed straight to hell for my sins. The dream is a subconscious manifestation of that fear."

"I see. And your idea of hell is having sex with your ex-boyfriend."

"That's one way of putting it, but my psychiatrist says sex is more of a metaphor in this case. It symbolizes the unification of two souls. Bonding with my ex would be the equivalent of becoming exactly like him. And that's my worst nightmare."

Vince stroked the side of her face. "What was this guy like?"

"Violent yet fragile. Beautiful in the most ugly way possible."

"Are you going to tell me about the things you feel so guilty about?"

"Yes, but not now. You've been here much too long. If you're not careful, you'll be stepping out as the day crew arrives."

"What are they going to do? Fire me? This isn't exactly the job of my dreams. I'll find another."

Kelly was quiet for a moment. Vince didn't know anything was wrong until a small drop of liquid hit the side of his neck. "Are you crying?"

Kelly's voice was much too calm. "No."

"I felt the tear. Why are you crying?"

"I have a tendency to drool after a bad nightmare."

"That was almost funny. Please, talk to me."

Kelly shifted positions so that her face was no longer inches from his neck.

"If you don't mind losing this job, it means you wouldn't mind leaving me behind."

"No! That's not what I meant. It's just a boring job, that's all. If I found a better job, I'd come back and..."

"It's okay. You don't have to sugarcoat the situation. I know that I'm an exciting diversion from your nightly routine, and I'm happy to be that for you, if only for awhile. This isn't exactly torture for me. Did I ever tell you what a nice ass you have? It was the first thing I noticed about you."

Vince sprang to his feet. "Well, I'm taking this ass out the door. Maybe then you'll believe I don't want to get myself fired just to get away from you."

"Will I see you tomorrow?"

"Yes. If you had a clock, you could set it by my arrival."

*****

Dr. Rushing had never been more grateful that he'd gone into debt for a wide screen television for his basement recreation room. It wasn't the most pleasant thing to sit in a straight-backed chair with his arms tied securely behind him, but at least he had entertainment at a time when a fellow's own thoughts were likely to drive him insane.

He'd always meant to rip out the dismal walnut paneling, but he'd never gotten around to it. Even with all the lights on, the room was just one or two shades brighter than a cave. An old avocado green refrigerator stood in the far corner, holding juice boxes and snacks that were of no use to him in his current predicament.

The only thing he couldn't handle was the gag. His mouth had been crammed with cloth for so long he'd stopped producing saliva. He would've killed for just one sip of the warm Coke sitting across the room at his computer station.

Earlier that day, he'd practiced moaning and groaning as loud as he could. He knew there was little chance of a passing neighbor coming to his rescue, but it only made sense to exercise his vocal chords just in case.

Although his ankles were still bound together with electrical tape, he could scoot around the room at will. He was encouraged by the fact that the legs of his wooden chair made a harsh scraping sound against the old tile. He also liked the idea of having a vase in the middle of the coffee table. If the opportunity arose, he could scoot into the table and knock it to the floor.

Deep within his heart, he realized he couldn't blame his predicament entirely on Darren. By the time he took him on as a client, he'd already developed a highly personal relationship with Roland. It was now painfully obvious that he should never have gotten professionally involved in a friend's affairs. Beyond that, it was ludicrous to force a disturbed youngster to compete for time with his father.

It all began innocently enough. Shortly after Dr. Rushing wrote his freshman composition on Damian Pierce and the slaughtered gerbils, Roland began to invite him to poetry readings at an artsy fartsy tavern off campus. The readings were generally attended by graduate students and English majors, but he embraced them with the enthusiasm of a serious scholar. In just one semester, he managed to find his way into Roland's exclusive circle of friends, which included doctors, lawyers, entrepreneurs and local politicians who'd impressed him with their performance in the classroom. Dr. Rushing was by far the youngest student ever to secure a seat by Roland's fire, and Darren resented him for it.

Since the fireside chats usually ran past midnight, an eight-year-old Darren was often sent to bed when things were just warming up. His attempts to eavesdrop behind the bannister were a constant source of amusement to guests. It all seemed hilarious at the time, but to a disturbed child, the sense of rejection must have been profound.

By the time Dr. Rushing opened his own practice, it seemed only natural for Roland to seek his professional assistance. After all, he'd been the only person to come up with a viable solution to address Darren's cruelty toward animals. With a few haphazard strokes of a purple ink pen, he'd managed to solve a devastating crisis that had stumped practicing psychiatrists twice his age.

Flattered by Roland's undying admiration, Dr. Rushing broke all the rules. He shared privileged information with Roland, summarizing appointments and comparing notes on Darren's behavior. Holed up at restaurants, concert halls, country clubs and basketball stadiums, they made an adventure of sipping wine, sharing secrets and identifying creative strategies for dealing with Darren's problems.

They both suspected Darren had never stopped finding outlets for his aggression, but they could never pin anything on him. When he disappeared for days at a time, they could only assume he wasn't spending his weekends at Disneyland. When he returned home with mysterious scrapes and bruises, they could only guess he hadn't tripped while helping old ladies across the street. Just what did he do with his time, anyway?

As Dr. Rushing stared at the can of warm Coke on his computer desk, it occurred to him that he might not live long enough to learn the answer to that question.

*****

Jeffrey Turner wasn't in the habit of skulking around office buildings at 3 o'clock in the morning, but he would've done just about anything for his dearest friend. Even if Darren hadn't provided such a detailed account of the building's hidden pathways, he would've gladly thrown a rock through the front window and risked going to jail in order to get Darren the information he sought.

He'd sailed into the building long before security guards locked the main entrances. He passed the next several hours napping in a cramped air vent. Luckily, his tiny frame was custom made for the space. He didn't experience so much as a leg cramp or a stiff muscle.

Dr. Thomas Rushing's computer was a pathetically outdated piece of machinery. Darren had worried that his files would be protected by access codes, but nothing could've been further from the truth. The case histories Darren requested were stored in a basic word processing program. File names coincided with each client's last name. Jeffrey decided not to tell Darren how simple it was to gain access to the information. If Darren had known the operation was something he could've performed himself, he might not have contacted Jeffrey in the first place.

As he copied the files onto disk, his mind drifted back to a time when Darren didn't need an excuse to call upon him. The two of them had spent many exciting nights cruising the worst neighborhoods they could find on Darren's motorcycle. Darren made a game of searching for gang symbols and drawing maps of the territories in which they were found. He was in love with danger, and Jeffrey was in love with him.

Ironically, the two of them couldn't have been more different. Back in high school, Darren sat at the back of the classroom because he couldn't stand being around other people. Jeffrey sat at the back of the classroom because other people couldn't stand being around him. Darren wore long hair, leather jackets and eyebrow studs in a place where khaki pants and preppie sweaters were the norm. Jeffrey stocked his closet with carbon copies of the puffy sweaters in a desperate attempt to fit in.

Not that his hip clothing did much to bolster his image. He was the kind of guy whose sexual orientation could be determined at a glance. He always envied neutral gay males who passed themselves off as well-dressed straight men. He would've given his right arm for a stronger jaw line and a deeper voice. His finely chiseled features were perfectly and hopelessly beautiful. His deep blue eyes were framed by the kind of lashes that women used mascara to create. If he'd had the slightest desire to grow his hair long and go shopping for a dress, he could've unseated the homecoming queen.

He first came to Darren's private school in his senior year. A horrific encounter with a group of bullies at his former school had forced his parents to take second jobs to pay his tuition at Parrington. Their hope was that children from upper class families would be more cultured and sophisticated. Jeffrey expected to ride out his final year of high school in relative comfort, but he quickly found that rich kids could be even more brutal than their middle class counterparts.

Less than one week after he came to Parrington, a couple jerks from swim class broke into his locker and stole his clothing, forcing him to roam the hallways in a pair of swim trunks. Wet and shivering from head to toe, he went looking for the punk who picked on him most. This wasn't the first time something like this had happened to him. Despite their fancy cars and bloated SAT scores, the students at Parrington weren't original thinkers, and their pranks were no more inspired than the pranks he'd endured in public school.

He was arguing with the guy he suspected of masterminding the caper when Darren came strolling down the hallway. David Whipple was a tall young man with a naturally muscular build and a naturally dull mind. He should've graduated two years earlier, but he hung around just to make people's lives a little more miserable. Darren eyed him like a spot of bacteria and grabbed a handful of his collar. "Did you steal Jeffrey's clothes?" he asked.

"Of course not."

"Then you won't mind opening your locker."

"I told you, I didn't steal anything from the little fag."

Darren whipped out a switchblade knife. "I said, open your locker."

David fumbled with the combination lock. As suspected, Jeffrey's clothing was wadded into a ball and stuffed into the upper compartment where books should've been. Darren retrieved the extra small sweater and held it before David's eyes. "This doesn't look like your size."

David retreated a few steps. "Come on, man. I was just messing with him."

"Apologize," Darren said.

"No! If he can't learn to take a joke now, he'll never make it in the real world."

Darren slashed David's shirt open with his knife. "Apologize, or you'll be the one walking around with no clothes."

"It's okay!" Jeffrey shouted. "I've got my stuff back. That's all that matters."

Later that day in history class, Jeffrey couldn't take his eyes off Darren.

As usual, he sat in the back of the classroom with a sketch pad while everyone else took notes on the lecture. Something about the way he chose to remain apart from the others was downright sexy. Jeffrey had spent most of his life caring too much about what others thought of him, but Darren didn't appear to give a rat's ass what other people said or did. He wasn't the most warm and compassionate soul on the planet. So why had he gone to such great lengths to defend a classmate? Was he just looking for an excuse to wield his knife, or was there some hidden meaning behind his actions?

Over the next few months, Jeffrey learned the answers to those questions. Deep within his heart, he wanted to believe Darren saw something special in him, but that just wasn't the case. Darren was still in love with some chick who'd dumped him the previous summer, and he wasn't looking to get involved in any kind of romantic relationship. When he needed sex, he found it at a place called Donovan's Pub, where grown women considered motorcycle ownership to be the ultimate aphrodisiac. Most of the gals assumed Darren was an adult who looked young for his age. The fact that he had his very own fuck pad in the woods lent credibility to his case. Only the bartender, the owner and the head waitress knew the truth.

Having a friend was an incredibly new and profoundly satisfying experience for Jeffrey. Guys weren't exactly waiting in line to be his pal. They either wanted to date him or beat the snot out of him, and that was that. Even those who claimed to have feelings for him wouldn't be seen with him in public. Darren was unique in that he didn't value other people's opinions. He offered his friendship as a pure and unconditional gift, never caring who thought it was strange that he chose to hang out with the resident fag.

Besides Jeffrey, Darren had two other friends who often wandered over to his private table in the back of the lunchroom. The first was Jessica Flint, a talented sculptor he'd met in art class. Jessica hated Darren's brutal sketches of human suffering, but she admired his talent nonetheless. The two of them never grew tired of discussing form and technique. She was a bubbly girl with long reddish hair and sparkling green eyes. She might've been a cheerleader or a majorette if she hadn't weighed 250 pounds.

Darren's other friend was the biggest loudmouth ever to walk the halls of Parrington High. Dale Truman seemed to have absolutely no control over his frequent urges to cut people down. Darren first took notice of him when he verbally assaulted the homecoming queen in gym class. She'd gained about ten pounds over the winter semester, and her sloppy sweat pants added additional bulk to her small, delicate frame. Out of nowhere, Dale declared she wasn't fit to grace the inside cover of the yearbook. He added that she was a first class bitch who didn't deserve all of the attention classmates lavished upon her.

Darren jumped to Dale's defense when three jocks descended upon him. He wasn't particularly fond of Dale at the time, but he was never one to pass on the opportunity to join a good brawl. With a little teamwork and a lot of blind anger, Dale and Darren were able to draw an impressive amount of blood before the gym teacher swooped in to break up the fight.

Dale's introduction to Darren's private lunch table didn't go smoothly. In less than a week, he got the idea he could tell his new friends how to live their lives. He had a brutal talk with Jessica about her weight and suggested that pizza and doughnuts were not the best choices for a person her size. Next, he turned his attention to Jeffrey, calling him a pussy and a spineless wimp. He insisted Jeffrey should stop wearing puffy sweaters to impress a shallow group of people who hated his guts. If he couldn't accept himself for who he was, how did he expect anyone else to accept him?

Jeffrey remained silent during the verbal assault, looking to Darren for protection. Much to his surprise, Darren did nothing more than laugh his ass off. "Do me!" he insisted.

"You're easy," Dale said. "You hide behind a mountain of hair because you're afraid someone might notice you're actually not so scary looking. You walk around with sharp objects stuck in your face to give the impression that you're the kind of dude who can take a fair amount of pain. Your dark, mysterious image is largely a product of your own creation. You're no stronger than the average Joe, just a lot more fearless. You hang out with losers like us to give people a few more reasons to hate you. You're happiest when you stare conflict in the face, and we give you the opportunity to do that a lot more often."

Shortly after Dale's vicious tirade, the unthinkable happened. Jessica replaced her beloved pizza and doughnuts with yogurt and tuna fish sandwiches. Jeffrey stopped wearing puffy sweaters and found the courage to say hello to a guy he'd only messed with in private. Darren paid a long overdue visit to a barber and removed every hunk of metal from his face.

As the months wore on, the four of them established a bond that Jeffrey considered to be unbreakable. When Jessica got down to 160 pounds, she made an unexpected play for Darren's affection. They dated for a few months, but the romance fizzled shortly after graduation. In his characteristically perceptive way, Dale commented that the only thing Darren and Jessica ever had in common was their awesome talent.

Jeffrey did everything he could to hold onto his best friend after graduation, but Darren was increasingly preoccupied with private concerns. He dropped by once in a blue moon to take Jeffrey for midnight rides on his motorcycle, but he was a loner by nature, and no amount of wishing or hoping could change that.

Jeffrey wasn't sure why Darren had taken a sudden interest in studying the case histories of three psychiatric patients, and he didn't particularly care. He could've taken a peek inside the envelope Darren instructed him to leave on the receptionist's desk, but he didn't. For the first time in ages, Darren had trusted him with one of the private concerns that kept him so occupied, and that was good enough for him.

*****

Brooke was used to arriving at the office an hour before Dr. Rushing. It made her feel good to dust the bookshelves, organize the files and have coffee waiting. He didn't require such things of her, but she wouldn't have it any other way. Lots of girls her age toiled in fast food restaurants for slave wages. She had a good thing going, and it didn't hurt to show a little appreciation.

She unlocked the office door with her personal key and fired up the coffee pot. She was searching the desk drawer for her bottle of energy supplements when she spotted an envelope sitting near the phone. It contained a type-written letter from Dr. Rushing:

> Brooke,
> I regret to inform you that I'll be leaving town immediately. An old friend has sustained serious injuries in a car accident, and there's no one available to take care of her small children. I feel a strong obligation to help her through this difficult period.
> Please cancel all appointments and send letters of regret to my clients. Do not begin rescheduling appointments until you hear from me.

Brooke sat down at her desk to re-read the note. It was just like the good doctor to go rushing to a sick friend's side, but this was a little weird. She wasn't aware he had any close female chums. Perhaps it was an old girlfriend or college soul mate he'd never mentioned.

The last time he rushed out of town for an uncle's funeral, he left a long list of instructions. Among other things, she had to write checks for rent and utilities, stop by his house to collect mail and cancel reservations on his appointment calendar. Why didn't he leave instructions this time? Perhaps he

83

assumed she knew the drill. But if he was in such a hurry, why did he take the time to fire up the computer and type a note? Last time, his instructions were scribbled on the back of a pizza flyer. It seemed odd that he would choose to scribble long messages and type short ones. Maybe he was making an effort to get more organized.

Brooke decided to play it by ear. She would pay the bills as they arrived and check his mail in a few days. In the meantime, she had phone calls to make and form letters to write.

*****

Monday night, Vince's mind raced forward in time as he completed his hourly patrols. He could hardly wait to meet with Kelly. The fact that she was about to expose all of her sins didn't scare him. If anything, he was strangely excited by the idea that she had a past. He'd never dated a bad girl type, but he'd fantasized about plenty of them.

To pass the time, he tried to imagine what Kelly's life was like before the guilt caught up to her in nightmares. For some reason, he pictured her as a dancer in a strip club. Perhaps she'd dated a few older men in hopes of elevating her financial status. Maybe she'd dated a few women as well. What if she'd failed to report her income to the IRS? She might've spent time in jail with other hot young bad girls. Very exciting stuff!

He wasn't prepared for the truth about Kelly's past. As he listened to her describe her early childhood experiences, he came dangerously close to breaking down in tears. He didn't know much about the things that went on in dark corners of the inner city. He was a suburban kid himself. He hardly knew what to make of Kelly's shocking tale.

*****

Kelly's earliest memories began at age five or six. The big red car was an ugly thing with rust spots on the outside and torn seats that bled stuffing on the inside. She waited there while her mom roamed the neighborhood. It was called working, but Kelly didn't see how wandering around was like carrying plates at the diner, which was what her mom used to do.

Some days, it felt as if the car was getting smaller and smaller. She believed the car would eventually melt under the sun like cassette tapes left on the dashboard. She knew it was possible because the whole car closed in on her one day while she slept. When she woke up, her nose was pressed against the ceiling and her whole leg was caught in one of the big holes in the steering wheel. Her mom said it must've been a dream, but that didn't mean it didn't really happen. Her mom told lies when they were useful.

Sometimes, it was so hot in the car she couldn't breath. On days like that, her mom left a Styrofoam cooler filled with ice. If she dipped her feet for just a few minutes, her whole body would get cold. She'd tried the trick with her hands once, but it didn't work the same way.

She was allowed to open the window, but only just a little. If a grown person's arm could fit into the space, the crack was much too wide. Just in case someone ever tried, Kelly had a little black box on a string. Sometimes, out of sheer boredom, she pulled the string and listened to the alarm for a second or two before replacing the pin lock. It was loud enough to make her jump in her seat, but not louder than the alarms on newer cars around town. That meant she needed the little knife for backup. If you could believe what her mom said, there was a big vein down the center of the wrist that controlled a person's life. You were supposed to be able to kill a grown person by stabbing that spot, but Kelly doubted that would work.

Most of the time, she didn't worry about hands reaching into the window. She'd never seen a single thing go wrong in the back of the big parking lot where she lived. She wasn't afraid of the world outside, and she wasn't about to duck when people walked by. She looked at picture books to pass the time and studied big glossy photos of places she wanted to visit. Her favorite was a picture of five sailboats cruising into the sunset. She imagined that living on the water would be much nicer than living in a car. She figured she could swim half the day and catch a few fish for dinner. In the evening, she could swim to other boats and visit with friends. If she ever had to pee, she wouldn't have to fuss with the jar and worry about leaks and splashes. She could hang her butt right over the edge of the boat.

If her mom popped in to check on her all day long, that meant there wasn't much work to be found. She liked it better when her mom stayed gone because she'd always come back with plenty of money for pizza and movies at the drive-in. Her mom didn't go to regular theaters because she couldn't bring the pipe. Without the pipe, she couldn't feel happy, not even for a minute.

Kelly often wondered why it took more than pizza and movies to make grownups feel good. Her grandmother liked vodka with a squirt of lime. Her grandfather smoked little cigarettes that smelled of skunk and burning leaves. Neither one of them liked the pipe because they were sure it could kill a person, or at least make them wish they were dead. Kelly didn't believe the pipe could be all that dangerous. It was just a little something that went along with pizza and movies and long nights by her mother's side. It contained some kind of magical medicine that held things together, if only for awhile.

Sometimes, but not very often, her mom brought men to the car. Some were light colored, like Barbie's Ken. Others were dark as night with hair as thick as carpet. When the men came, Kelly had to wear earmuffs with radio speakers inside and sleep with a woolen cap pulled over her eyes. She often wondered if one of the men could've been her father, but she never felt brave enough to ask.

It was a crazy night when her mother let her stay up and talk to the man with the bundle of flowers. He was a nice enough guy with friendly eyes and skin the color of coffee with cream. She held her arm next to his and saw that it was the closest match she'd ever seen. "You must be my daddy," she said.

The man laughed so hard his belly shook. "No, but I'm applying for the job."

"Do you have a house?"

"Yes, I do."

"Will I have my own bed?"

"Not at first, but you'll have a sleeping bag in your very own room with plenty of dolls to play with."

Kelly twisted her face. "I hate dolls."

"And why is that?"

"They're mostly too light, and the dark ones are too dark. I want a doll that looks like me."

"That's a tall order," her mom said. "They don't make dolls as pretty as you."

"How come?"

"Because you've got the beauty of the whole world in you. You have the hair of a Geisha girl, the skin of a Nubian princess, and the finely chiseled features of a Victorian queen."

"Quit making it sound so fancy."

"Fine. You're part black, part white and part Japanese. Is that better?"

"What does 'chiseled' mean?"

"Soft and delicate, like the features of a Barbie doll."

"Was Daddy like Ken?"

"Well, he liked to think he was. He certainly had plenty of Barbies."

"Is that why you left?"

"He left, sweetheart. Always remember that. I'm not perfect, but at least I'm here."

The new house wasn't much cleaner than the car. There were cracks in the walls, and the carpet smelled like pee from all the dogs. The two pitt bulls were young and crazy. They played tag all over the house and took turns pooping in the kitchen corner. The rottweiler was a gentle old soul who used the bathroom outside. Molly had arthritis in her hips, and Kelly wasn't allowed to sit on her back or ride her like a horse. Molly was also the bitch of the house. She didn't allow the pit bulls to cross into the front room. They made her nervous, and she didn't like them near Kelly. She was happiest sleeping on the floor beside Kelly at night. If anyone dared to open the door, she growled like a monster and bared her teeth.

People came and went as they pleased at the new house. Lots of money changed hands, and little macadamia nuts were treated like diamonds. No one ever died from hitting the pipe. In fact, Kelly's mom seemed happier than ever. There was plenty of money for pizza, movies and trips to the casino. In just a few months, Kelly had a bed of her own and a whole closet full of brand new clothes.

Her new daddy was a good man with more friends than he could count. His name was Carlos, but people called him "brother." Blacks and whites had the crazy idea they were related to him, but Kelly knew better. His real brothers lived in Mexico, and their skin was somewhere between white and black.

Kelly loved her new daddy with every piece of her heart. He put a fancy lock on her door and told all his brothers to stay away from her room. He said special girls deserved a special place for all their beautiful things, and he really meant it. He used the computer to order handmade dolls from Indian reservations in Arizona. The Indian dolls looked more like Kelly than dolls from the department store, and they had the most beautiful handmade outfits she'd ever seen. One day, Carlos brought home a big glossy catalog with dolls from all over the world. Kelly was happy to learn that most people on Earth were neither white nor black. By age seven, she had so many dolls that Carlos had to build special shelves to hold them.

The beautiful dolls led Kelly to believe she was some kind of rich girl. Her friend Clarissa had only three dolls, and they had dirty hair. Clarissa's dad sold rocks, too, but everyone said he liked to smoke his profits. Carlos did much better because he had a secret Kelly wasn't supposed to tell. He was something called "big time." He made friends at golf courses in faraway places and shared the pipe with them for free. They liked him so well they never quit calling. Golf course people didn't know of any other place to find rocks, so Carlos made up any price he wanted. That's why he needed a fireproof safe for all his cash.

One day, the dolls stopped coming. So did the pizza and the movies and the shiny little rocks that kept Mom and Carlos happy. There was talk of a big bust somewhere far, far away. Carlos said the well was dry. The brothers stopped coming around with their dollars. Her parents were suddenly different people. They spent half the day fighting and the other half pacing the floor. They took long drives around the city at night, stopping at different houses and coming out with just a little of the stuff they needed to get by. They said Kelly would have to go to work if she wanted to keep eating pizza and collecting dolls.

Her job was mostly easy. Carlos explained that the dirty neighborhood where she lived was only a small corner of the world. Just a car trip away, there were clean brick houses with shiny new cars in the driveway. The playgrounds were nicer, too. There wasn't so much broken glass to worry about, and bums weren't allowed to sleep on the benches. It was Kelly's job to make friends in such places and get herself invited to their homes.

Carlos warned her that some of the people she would meet were going to be cold and snotty, especially the pure white ones. It was important to remember that white people from rich neighborhoods were not the same as white brothers living in the ghetto. They had a different way of talking and a different way of dressing. Even their music was not the same.

Although he could barely read or write, Carlos was some kind of expert on folks who could. When he first came to America, he worked as a caddy at five different golf courses. He learned he could get better tips if he tried to sound more white. He promised Kelly she'd go further in life if she completed two simple exercises each day. First, she had to copy three paragraphs straight from the newspaper. Next, she had to read them aloud until she sounded just like the news people on television.

Kelly was amazed by all the things she could learn about the world by eating dinner at different houses. Some kids came home from school and waited all afternoon for their parents to get home from work. Other kids were watched from the moment they set foot in the house to the moment they went to sleep at night. Most kids had more freedom than she did. They were allowed to take walks down the sidewalk in front of their own homes, and they didn't need a horse dog for protection.

Of all the things she learned, Kelly was most surprised to find that rich folks didn't stay in one place day after day, month after month, year after year. They needed to get away from their pretty homes almost as much as Carlos and Mom needed the pipe. Some folks had cabins in faraway places, and their children spent long summers fishing in real lakes and riding four wheelers down rugged trails in the woods. Other folks took yearly vacations to places like Disney World and stayed gone for weeks at a time. Carlos kept a big list of families and their work schedules. He also kept track of who was going on vacation. Kelly wasn't sure why he wanted to know exactly when each family was leaving, but she always tried to find out anyway. She asked so many questions that some parents wanted to know why she cared so very much. Her answer was always the same. She'd never been anywhere special, and she just wanted to know what it was like.

At first, Kelly wasn't sure why Carlos kept bringing home so many stereos and television sets. She didn't think twice about it until the day she woke up and spotted a friend's CD player sitting in the kitchen corner beside a big pile of dog poop. The CD player was special because the outer shell was made of pink plastic, and it came with its very own unbreakable disks. There was no mistaking it. It was the Pretty Princess Music Maker, her friend Gina's favorite toy. Kelly was so angry that she went into her parents' bedroom and glued little flowered barrettes in Carlos' hair. When that didn't wake him up, she spread grape jelly over his face and called Molly to lick it off. "What's the idea!" he shouted.

"That's what you get for stealing my friend's CD player!" she screamed.

Carlos pushed the dog aside. "Let's get one thing straight, little girl. The kids you meet at the playground are not your friends. They're pawns in our little game of chess. Understand?"

"I don't like chess."

Carlos grabbed a handful of Kelly's hair. "You'll learn to like it!" Kelly left Carlos with tears in her eyes and stayed hidden in her bedroom all day. The more she looked around at her beautiful doll collection, the more ashamed she felt. Her room was like a miniature palace sitting smack dab in the middle of a junkyard. Carlos didn't mind stepping over dog poop in his own kitchen, but he made sure her walls had a fresh coat of paint and her floors were covered with clean rugs. Her four poster bed was the nicest piece of furniture in the house, and the outfits in her closet were even prettier than the outfits rich girls wore. For some reason, Carlos wanted her to have the best of everything. Maybe he looked at her light brown skin and saw shades of himself.

From that day on, Kelly did her best to be a good worker. She quickly learned that the stuff Carlos brought home was more valuable than it looked. Designer clothing and tennis shoes could be traded with neighbors for food stamps. A gently used television set was worth fifty bucks at the pawn shop and even more on the street. Necklaces and rings were as good as cash. They could be traded at the dope house on the spot.

Over a two-year period, six of her friend's parents were killed in robberies.

Every once in awhile, people stayed home when they were supposed to go out, and Carlos got caught. He didn't like to shoot people, but sometimes he ran into heroes who tried to surprise him with a hand gun or baseball bat. He said there was no place for heroes in his game of chess.

Kelly pushed the murders to the back of her mind until the day those religious people came knocking at her front door. She didn't usually open the door for strangers, but this guy had a little boy with him. She immediately wondered if she could get herself invited to his house. "May I speak to your parents?" the father asked. He was a white guy with acne scars sprinkled over his cheeks. She felt kind of sorry for him. The boy already had a few pimples on his forehead.

"My dad isn't home, and my mom is asleep."

"That's okay. We'll come back later."

Before Kelly could agree to the plan, the son stepped forward. "Would you like to know how to get into heaven?" he asked.

Kelly was fascinated. She liked the images of angels she'd seen on televison and knew that heaven was a place where people walked around with smiles 24 hours a day. "Tell me."

"There are lots of ways, but you can start by doing good things for people. I go to the grocery store for old folks who can't do it themselves. My dad brings boxes of pizza to the homeless people at the bus station."

Kelly looked down at her feet. "What happens if you don't do good things for people? What if the things you do make people want to cry?"

The father stepped forward. "We'll discuss this when your mom wakes up," he said.

Kelly told the man to come back for dinner, but he never made it through the door. Her mom called the pit bulls to the front room and warned him that he shouldn't go around bothering people at suppertime. Kelly was confused by her mother's behavior. Why scare people who only want to show you how to get into heaven?

The next day, Kelly asked one of her rich friends what happened to people who couldn't get into heaven. Shelly Whipple was a chubby little girl with very clear opinions on the subject. Between bites of chocolate-covered raisins, she described a place called hell and explained what happened to people who were sent there. "First, they throw you into a dark cave and make you confess every bad thing you've ever done in your life. Then, they set you on fire and let you burn for eternity."

"Eternity?"

"Forever and ever."

"That's impossible. Wouldn't you eventually go up in smoke?"

"The devil won't let you die. He wants you to suffer until the end of time."

A shiver crawled up Kelly's spine. "That's the scariest thing I've ever heard."

Later that night, Kelly held her fingertip over the flame of a lighter to find out what fire felt like. She was shocked by how much the pain increased with each passing moment. Six seconds were just about all she could stand. She couldn't imagine spending an eternity on fire. The pain was ten times worse than any bruise or belly ache she'd ever had. For almost two weeks, Kelly nursed her blistered fingertip and avoided touching things with it. Her mom gave her aspirin to ease the pain, but the pills didn't take away the images that haunted her dreams. Night after night, she saw herself trapped in a fiery cave blistered from head to toe, screaming and screaming until the end of time.

It didn't take long for Kelly to figure out that Mom and Carlos were headed straight for hell themselves. Maybe that's why they liked the pipe, because it helped them forget. Kelly started on the pipe when she was 11 years old. It helped her reach a level of bliss she'd never experienced, not even when swimming in a rich friend's pool or opening a brand new doll on Christmas morning. It kept her awake for days at a time and helped her to collapse into a dreamless state. Not dreaming was the best part about it.

By age 13, she was a master at raising the cash to support her habit. She no longer needed to steal rocks from her parent's bedroom because she had more than three suppliers in the neighborhood. She shared the pipe with friends at school and got them hooked in just a few days. When they couldn't come up with the cash to buy more, she accepted compact disks and computer software as payment.

By age 14, she figured out that she needed to go where the money was. She rode the bus to rich areas and seduced any well-dressed boy she could find at the mall. She shared the pipe with her new friends and accepted cash for ever-increasing quantities of the stuff. Her cell phone rang day and night. Eventually, she didn't have to take the bus anymore. A steady stream of clueless suburbanites were willing to drive all the way to the city just to meet her on the corner for a few minutes. Like Carlos, she set her own prices and demanded full payment on the spot.

The bottom fell out when she was 16 years old. An in-house school security officer caught her hitting the pipe under the bleachers. She was able to shake her addiction while serving a six-month sentence in juvenile hall, but the nightmares never went away. On a conscious level, she knew she wasn't entirely to blame for the murders Carlos committed, but her subconscious mind never let go of the notion that hell was an unavoidable destiny.

Chapter Seven

Mr. Rivard dumped a small container of cream into his coffee and watched the deep brown liquid fade to tan. All was quiet at Ted's Diner this time of the evening, but he couldn't appreciate the opportunity to relax. A killer migraine rocked his skull. A blank pad of paper sat mockingly on the table before him. He desperately wanted to create a fantasy world to get lost in, but he was fresh out of ideas. He was sure he'd find inspiration at the very place where his first screenplay took shape, but he'd turned out to be wrong. His previous attempt at writing was nothing more than a walk down memory lane. This journey was a little different. He had to pull scenarios from thin air, and the possibilities were excruciatingly endless. He was just about to call it a night when a young man in a red windbreaker took a seat beside him at the counter. His sharp, chiseled features were immediately stunning and somewhat overbearing. "Could I get some paper from you?" he asked.

Mr. Rivard tore a few sheets from his notebook. "Is that enough?"

"That should be plenty. I'm supposed to have a poem ready by tomorrow morning, but I'm not doing so well."

Mr. Rivard tried not to laugh. What were the chances of running into another person with writer's block at this time of night? Just how many artistic insomniacs were walking around the city with uncompleted projects eating away at their hearts?

"So, you're a writer?"

"Not exactly. I'm a lazy student who thought it would be easy to rack up some English credits with a creative writing class."

"In that case, you should've taken a course in lit appreciation. Writing is only fun when you care very deeply about the subject of your piece."

"Maybe that's my problem," the kid said. "I don't care enough about anything."

Mr. Rivard looked out the window. "I can certainly relate to that. Does that Harley outside belong to you?"

"Yeah."

"Most guys your age would kill for a bike like that."

"I guess so."

Mr. Rivard sighed. What could he say to a boy with too much time on his hands and not enough enthusiasm to enjoy it? "Someone has given you a little too much money to play with."

The kid looked surprised. "Is it that obvious?"

"If you want the truth, yes. I know a Devon Croft windbreaker when I see one. And your bike is truly spectacular. It's an interesting combination, to say the least."

"The jacket was a Christmas gift from my dad. I never really looked at the label. I don't pay much attention to that kind of stuff."

"Good for you. It's a silly way to choose a coat, don't you think?"

"I suppose so."

"Maybe it's time to start choosing your own coats."

The kid was silent for a moment. "Why do I get the feeling you're not just talking about my apparel?"

"I'm sorry. I don't mean to be judgmental. I just feel like I know you in more ways than you'd guess. Can I ask you something?"

Darren rolled his eyes at the ceiling. "You might as well."

"Have you ever had a job?"

"Not really."

"Well, I think you should get one. And don't go looking at your father's place of business. Do something you like, and do it just for you."

"Sounds simple enough. Maybe I'll ask the waitress if they need an extra cook around here. I've always wanted to walk around with grease stains down the front of my shirt."

"This isn't a joke. When I was your age, I felt like my whole life had been mapped out from the cradle to the grave. It didn't matter if I worked my ass off or stayed home in front of the television. The outcome was the same either way. I was just a spoiled rich kid, and people viewed me that way no matter how hard I worked or didn't work. There was no room to grow or change. I was just a stagnant mass of flesh and bone, dead in the water before my 21st birthday."

The kid motioned for the waitress to fill his empty cup. "All right, Mister. You have my attention."

They talked for what seemed like hours, drinking countless cups of coffee and building curious contraptions with whatever materials they could find. The kid was an artistic soul who could fashion an impressive go-cart from toothpicks and make it roll across the table on a track of ordinary drinking straws. Mr. Rivard had the distinct impression there was nothing his young friend couldn't do under the right circumstances. "If you like to build things, you'll understand why the time is ripe to begin shaping your destiny," he said. "You claim there's nothing left to care about in this world, but it's only because you have nothing to call your own. When I was your age, I found a dirty little apartment downtown and paid the rent with tips I earned as a bartender. I sank the rest of my money into a three-person ad agency that everyone said would fail. When I discovered it was possible to make the first one work, I bought a couple smaller agencies and merged them. To make a long story short, I merged my way to a disgusting new level of wealth. Believe it or not, I just wrote a screenplay about it. You can have a look, if you like."

The kid's face lit up. "I'd be honored to read it. It sounds like you've really managed to take control of your life."

Mr. Rivard looked away. "If only that were true. I'm afraid the best years are behind me now. I've found that life is a journey, not a destination. The real joy lies in the struggle."

"So start struggling. Get yourself a studio apartment and share your last crumb of food with the cockroaches."

"That's absurd. A billionaire doesn't live in a one-room apartment."

"Why not? Who says you have to keep spending all the money you've piled up? Go somewhere and start a brand new company that has nothing to do with advertising, and do it without any help from existing bank accounts."

Mr. Rivard laughed. "That's damned near impossible. I'll need office space, computer equipment, a secretary or two…"

"I didn't say it would be easy. I thought you said life was a journey! Or were you just bullshitting me?"

"Come on, kid. Don't do this to an old man with a migraine."

"What if I told you that I have a truly original product you could market? That's more than half the battle, isn't it?"

"Not necessarily. It's much more difficult to promote a new business in this day and age."

"That's not true. You can put up a web site for next to nothing."

"Don't believe everything you read. The market is saturated. I don't care if you need a lug wrench or a bottle of herbal supplements, there's an Internet guru standing in line to sell it to you."

"You're pretty negative for a guy who makes his living helping companies to compete in a global marketplace."

"You're forgetting that I deal with money people. My clients have the capital to invest in the production of television commercials that direct traffic to their web sites and store fronts."

The kid wheeled his go-cart across the table. "So, you're telling me that it's impossible to advertise a web site without promoting it on television? What about search engines?"

"Search engines are a joke. If you don't believe me, try entering the keyword 'vitamin.' I guarantee that the largest vitamin producers in the country will appear at the top of your list every time. The little guys will be buried so far down the list that they might as well not be there at all. I'm telling you, kid. Money makes the world go round."

"So how do folks with no startup capital succeed in the business world?"

"If you want the truth, I have no clue. If you need a grandiose ad campaign that dazzles potential customers with compelling words and images, I'm your man. If you want to sell chocolate chip cookies from your basement office, I don't know what to tell you."

"I refuse to believe that. You started your first ad agency in a studio apartment."

"It was a different era. Competition was scarce."

"And courage was plentiful."

Mr. Rivard smashed the little toothpick go-cart with his fist. "Are you calling me a coward?"

"Yes, sir. And a pessimist, too."

"Okay, kid. If I take a look at this miracle product, will you ease up on the name calling?"

✲ ✲ ✲ ✲ ✲

Vince had a little score to settle with Kelly. She was supposed to wait up for him tonight, but he'd entered the dark room to find her fast asleep. She definitely deserved to be punished.

Carefully, he grasped a small section of her beautiful hair between his fingers and used it to tickle the inside of her nose. She woke with a start, slapping her face as if swatting a fly. "You're such a brat!"

"Shh. You'll wake the neighbors."

Kelly tried to whack him over the head with her pillow, but he snatched it from her hands. "Your reflexes are pathetic."

"Give me back my pillow!"

"Nope. You don't deserve it."

"Damn it, Vince. Give it to me!"

"No. I think you're way too attached to this pathetic hunk of foam. I've decided that I'm only going to let you use it for two more weeks."

"You can't do that."

"Oh, yes I can. If you're still clinging to this particular pillow 14 days from now, I have complete authority to throw you out on the street."

"What are you talking about?"

"I'm talking about budget cuts. Massive statewide budget cuts."

"I don't understand."

"It's really quite simple. They can't afford to keep you."

"But why me? Am I not as crazy as some of the others?"

Vince threw the pillow at his new love. "Don't flatter yourself, honey. Close to half the people on this floor are looking at an early release."

"Even Jack Singleton? He still thinks he's Spiderman's long lost son."

"Jack is good as gone."

"And Linda the liar?"

"Hasta la vista."

"You can't be serious. Where will they go?"

Vince pulled Kelly into his arms. "I don't know what will happen to them. I can only speak for one person, and you're coming with me."

*****

Mr. Rivard couldn't have been more impressed with the charming wooded estate Darren called home. He'd expected a luxury dwelling with more space than a single family could use, but he never imagined a lush tract of land with more buildings than several families could occupy.

The main house was a church-like dwelling with a pointed steeple nestled among the treetops. Quaint cobblestone pillars kept the place from feeling too grand or self-important. A neat brick sidewalk circled around the back of the house, where four wooden cottages dotted the landscape. Each structure was stained with a rich almond glaze and trimmed with contrasting pastel colors. The doors and shutters of the pool house were done in a light buttery yellow. The gardener's home was trimmed in a pale, earthy shade of green. The guest house—as Darren called his humble bachelor pad—was accented in a light dusty rose.

Mr. Rivard took a deep breath and savored the strong aroma of Alberta spruce and pine. "I'm at a loss for words. This is truly breathtaking."

"I think it's disgusting. It's a blatant display of wealth."

Mr. Rivard felt a slight twinge of embarrassment. If anything, his own home was a blatant display of prosperity. His ex-wife had convinced him to buy an ultra modern palace with angular planes and oversized tinted glass windows. He'd always felt the sparkling glass structure reeked of opulence and industrialism.

"If you think this is bad, you should see my place. It has all the warmth and character of a steel rod."

As they shuffled into the guest house, Mr. Rivard was horrified to discover that Darren had turned the interior of the quaint cottage into his own private dungeon. He was obviously striving for a gothic feel, but the look wasn't put together well. Grotesque oil paintings covered every inch of wall space from ceiling to floor. A pair of Victorian arm chairs were upholstered in rich red velvet to compliment the black Queen Anne sofa. A dingy plaid recliner stood in the corner as a reminder of a time when the place was probably decorated like a country cottage. The charming cobblestone fireplace didn't fit into the picture. An eerie portrait of a dead fish graced the mantle. "Please tell me you didn't drag me all the way out here to look at these paintings."

Darren's mouth dropped to a frown. "You don't mince words, do you?"

"I didn't get to the top by keeping my opinions to myself. I could sell tampons to menopausal women, but I couldn't convince a blind man to pay good money for these paintings."

"That's a shame. I took you for a man who likes a challenge."

"And I took you for a visionary. I suppose we were both wrong."

Mr. Rivard was on his way out the door when Darren stepped in front of him with a gun. "I brought you here to do a job, and you're not going anywhere until you've finished."

Mr. Rivard couldn't help but laugh. He'd longed to die since he could remember. It seemed absurd that his wish would finally be granted in this charming little corner of the woods. It was almost too good to be true. "I hope you have the balls to pull that trigger. I've dreamed of this moment for more years than you've been alive."

Darren reached into the pocket of his Devon Croft windbreaker and pulled out a switchblade knife. "You've dreamed of death, but have you imagined the possibility of slow and unrelenting torture? It's not a desirable fate, I assure you."

Mr. Rivard was struck by a vision of himself sprawled out on the floor with deep slashes over his naked chest. The thought of enduring so much pain sent his heart on a roller coaster ride. "What do you want from me?"

"I want you to sit down and come up with a decent plan of action that requires little money and absolutely no help from an overpaid team of executives."

Mr. Rivard sat down on Darren's black velvet sofa and took a closer look at the paintings he'd judged so harshly upon entering. The vast majority were brutally honest depictions of pain, suffering and death. It seemed his young friend never missed an opportunity to document the little tragedies he saw in everyday life. In one particularly disturbing piece, an elderly woman with raw boils on her neck clutched a crumbling bouquet of dead flowers. Her tattered white dress clung to the contours of a frail body and outlined her sagging breasts. In another gross representation of everyday life, dozens of hairy black flies feasted upon the carcasses of three small birds. The image was so large you could see their bulging eyes and detect a faint whisper of motion in their tiny wings. A shiver crawled up Mr. Rivard's spine. He could almost feel their little legs crawling across the back of his neck.

It seemed that no creature on Earth was too small or insignificant for Darren to paint. In a portrait called "Rainy Day," a handful of plump, juicy worms were scattered over a slab of wet pavement. A large tennis shoe loomed above them, casting an ominous shadow upon the ground. "The worm painting is meant to capture that fleeting moment between life and death," Darren explained. Mr. Rivard could've done without the commentary. To him, it was just an ordinary scene from an ordinary day that wasn't worth documenting on canvas.

The portrait above the mantle was a bit more remarkable. Although it was just a picture of a dead fish floating in pond scum, something about it was quite moving. The creature's pale, yellowish eyes had an unmistakable human quality about them. It was almost as if the damned thing had a soul.

Not all of Darren's paintings depicted average, run-of-the-mill deaths. In a series called "Circus of the Dead," he used five separate canvases to depict freak accidents that might happen in an environment where death-defying feats are performed on a regular basis. In the first painting, the mutilated head of a lion tamer sat upon the ground beside a vicious white tiger. In the second, two trapeze artists were shown falling to their deaths. The third and fourth paintings depicted tightrope and high dive catastrophes. The fifth was a particularly brutal representation of a knife-throwing accident. The victim in this scenario had a dagger protruding from her eye socket. Streams of blood trickled down her neck, staining her sequined costume and producing a fine puddle on the ground near her feet.

Just when Mr. Rivard thought he'd seen it all, Darren led him down a narrow flight of stairs at the back of the house. "And now," he said with the smile of a proud parent, "I'd like to show you a very special group of paintings hidden away in the cellar. I don't keep them in the living room because I believe their impact is diminished when displayed among so many others."

"The Hunted" was Darren's most cherished collection because it depicted game animals tearing humans limb from limb. Timid creatures such as deer and rabbit were the most vicious of all predators in his fantasy world. Mr. Rivard was sure he would never forget the image of a dainty fawn feasting on the abdomen of a terrified hunter. The fawn had vampire-like teeth, which it used to tear organs from a gaping hole in the hunter's belly.

Despite Darren's exaggerated tendency to paint the world as a horrifying place, there were a few gems hidden in his cellar. A portrait titled "In the Clouds" presented an aerial view of the magnificent estate he called home. "The Optimist" was a loving portrayal of his father tending to the rose garden on the western end of the property. "The Cold War" was a light-hearted depiction of his Cocker Spaniel chasing a squirrel. The background in this painting was especially breathtaking. A bright pinkish sunset hovered over a small pond in the woods. The trees were alive with color and motion. Their vibrant leaves glowed like drops of flourescent green gold.

The most stunning of Darren's paintings was a portrait of a young woman in a simple white gown. Her strong, exotic features were both odd and beautiful at once. It was almost as if Darren had pulled an exaggerated vision of perfection from his own mind. Just as he made his sunsets a little pinker and his trees a little greener than normal, he'd given her more warmth and color than the average woman. Her wide, cat-like eyes were more blue than the sky on a clear August afternoon. Her long black hair was so glossy it produced a faint halo of light above her head. Her smooth, flawless complexion was the color of caramel.

"She can't be real," Mr. Rivard said. "Who has that coloring? She's just too beautiful."

"Beauty is an inner quality," Darren replied. "In her case, it radiates outward."

"If you could show me more paintings like this, I'd have a much easier time marketing them."

"I appreciate the compliment, but she's not for sale."

"How about the old man in the garden? I could sell that one, if you like."

"That one is off limits. You can start with the circus series."

* * * * *

Jenna Lamarr hopped onto her treadmill and set the timer for 45 minutes. She'd been lazy about sticking to her exercise regime lately, but that was about to change. Her boyfriend of four years hadn't touched her in weeks. She usually had to fight off his advances when he came home from work and slipped into bed beside her, but lately he'd been falling asleep on the couch. That could only mean he was getting it somewhere else.

She wondered how a busy guy like Vince could find the time to carry on an affair. He worked midnights as a security guard on the mental health wing of St. Benedict's Memorial Hospital. He arrived home around 7 a.m. and took a three-hour nap before heading off to class at the local community college. He returned home from school without delay and took another nap before going back to work.

She concluded that he must've been seeing a nurse. The ancient box of condoms in his top drawer had been replaced with a newer, more expensive brand. She started counting them a week ago. She noted that three lambskin condoms had disappeared from the box in the last four days. The least he could've done was keep the new box in his glove compartment. He cared so little about her feelings that he hadn't even bothered to hide them.

She supposed she couldn't really blame him. She'd spent the last few years criticizing his lack of ambition and comparing him to more successful men she'd dated in high school. About a year ago, something within him snapped. He began taking college courses, lifting weights at the gym and reading endless detective novels. If she wasn't careful, some other woman would end up sharing a life with the new, improved man she'd worked so hard to create. She wondered if he would put a down payment on a house and let the bitch decorate it any old way she pleased. It wasn't fair. Strong women who encouraged their men to take chances were always made out to be the villains. The cute, demure types swooped in to collect the prize after most of the work was done.

She was sprawled out on the couch wearing nothing but a smile when he walked through the front door. He took one look at her and dropped his keys on the floor. "Who are you, and what have you done with my girlfriend?"

Jenna forced a laugh. "She's out for the evening. Would you care to have a little fun before she gets back?"

"Actually, I'm exhausted. I could really use a hot bath."

She followed him to the bathroom and closed her arms around him from behind. He smelled of cheap sex and institutional hand soap. "Please," he said. "I've had a long night."

"All of your nights are long. That never stopped you from waking me at the crack of dawn."

"Maybe I got tired of begging. Maybe it's too late."

She slid her hand down to his crotch. "It's never too late."

"Jenna... "

"Who is she, Vince? Who is she, and what does she mean to you?"

"I don't know what you're talking about."

"I've been counting your condoms, honey. We can work through this if you're honest with me."

Vince looked at her as if she were hardly worth fighting for. "What if I don't want to work through it?"

Tears stung Jenna's eyes. She didn't know the answer to that question.

*****

Mr. Rivard began his quest to market Darren's paintings by familiarizing himself with the world of modern art. While Darren leafed through magazines on the living room sofa, he sat quietly at the computer and visited dozens of web sites offering genuine oil paintings at various prices. The overwhelming majority of works he encountered were inspired by the world's natural beauty. Land and seascapes were popular, as were cottage scenes and floral bouquets of every texture and color. Certain animals found their way into many of the outdoor scenes. Deer and mountain lion seemed to be in vogue. Dogs, cats, and horses were often plastered into scenes where they didn't belong.

Mr. Rivard's journey through cyberspace only confirmed his early suspicions. Most people had no desire to decorate their homes with brutal depictions of pain, suffering and death. Throughout the ages, there may have been a few artists who became famous for their use of blood and gore, but that didn't mean they enjoyed commercial success while they were still alive. Darren would be lucky to find one or two eccentric souls with a taste for the grotesque and a pocketbook deep enough to indulge it.

Mr. Rivard closed his eyes to block out the blinding glare of the computer screen. Obviously, he wasn't the marketing wizard so many people believed him to be. For too many years, he'd thrown money at every obstacle blocking his path, producing high budget television commercials for clients who could've gotten away with modest print campaigns. Worse yet, he'd relied upon a high-powered creative team to do all the writing and brainstorming. Now, at the ripe old age of 55, his mind was like the ancient Mustang hidden away in his garage: rusty and useless from decades of neglect.

He dreamed of restoring the jalopy because it reminded him of a time when he didn't believe he'd live long enough to see his first car deteriorate. To him, the old hunk of junk served as verifiable proof that miracles could happen. If a 45-year-old car could be restored to working order, why couldn't his mind? Weren't both things worth saving?

Perhaps all he needed to do was exercise the long neglected mass of tissue between his ears. He began by typing a list of some of the creative marketing strategies he'd developed back when most of his clients were small businessmen with limited resources. Three pages later, he was astounded by the number of clients who'd depended on him to keep their struggling businesses afloat. His walk down memory lane led him to recall his dealings with Roger North, the owner of a small guitar shop on East Maple Avenue. Roger was facing bankruptcy when Mr. Rivard convinced him to organize a concert featuring three amateur rock bands and create a contest whereby ten local teens could win cheap acoustic guitars.

Almost overnight, Roger's humble establishment became the after-school hot spot for young music lovers. Any kid who could play with decent accuracy was encouraged to perform a song or two from a makeshift stage near the back of the shop. Guitar sales skyrocketed, but that was only half the story. Roger brought in a hot dog cart and made a small fortune selling sodas and snacks. The following year, he moved his business to a larger building and expanded his product line to include a wide range of musical instruments.

Mr. Rivard leaned back in Darren's swivel chair to analyze the core reasons why Roger's concert had turned out to be such an effective marketing tool. In essence, the event had provided an opportunity for like-minded individuals to come together and celebrate their passion for music. For many teens, buying a guitar was the perfect way to capture the spirit of the event and bring it home in a box.

Mr. Rivard wondered if it would be possible to assemble a large group of people who shared Darren's love for grotesque images. It was a great theory, but how would he find a bunch of creepy folks preoccupied with pain, suffering and death?

The answer came to him in a sudden flash of inspiration. Each year, millions of movie goers paid good money to watch celebrated madmen such as Freddy Krueger mutilate human bodies in every way imaginable. A certain percentage of horror fans took their films so seriously that they were willing to travel long distances to attend premiers and conventions. Obviously, a startling number of Americans enjoyed gawking at images that made Mr. Rivard sick to his stomach. Perhaps Darren's art wasn't so outlandish after all.

His heart fluttered wildly as the details began to take shape in his mind. He envisioned a major outdoor Halloween bash with special incentives to attract hard core horror fans. Guests would be encouraged to dress up as their favorite movie characters, and spectacular prizes would be awarded to those with the most realistic costumes. Darren's art would be on display in a custom tent decorated to look like a haunted house. Even if his paintings didn't sell, the price of admission would more than cover the cost of organizing the event.

There was only one problem. What kind of "spectacular" prizes could be awarded to winners? It took the promise of ten free guitars to attract teenagers to Roger's concert. What would it take to entice folks to come have a look at Darren's macabre portraits? He couldn't exactly hire celebrities to sign autographs or hand out extravagant prizes. Darren had made it abundantly clear that the overall marketing plan should be inexpensive to carry out.

Without fully realizing it, Mr. Rivard began to think aloud. "If I were a horror movie nut, what could Darren do to get my attention?"

Darren mumbled a few words from behind his magazine. "I could paint a picture of Freddy Krueger removing your flesh with a potato peeler."

Mr. Rivard would've laughed at the joke, except it was much too brilliant to be funny. What if Darren could paint a realistic portrait of a celebrated madman killing the winner in some horrible fashion? What a grand—and inexpensive—prize that would be! The villain in the portrait would be the winner's favorite pop culture icon. The winner would also decide exactly how he wanted to be mutilated on canvas, even if it involved a potato peeler. It was a sick way to draw a crowd, but then again, it was a sick world, wasn't it?

Mr. Rivard was pondering that very thought when a loud, guttural snort jolted him back to the moment at hand. Spinning around on his swivel chair, he saw Darren fast asleep on the sofa. His gun was on the coffee table beside an empty Coke bottle and two sandwich crusts. The knife was on the end table about a yard from his reach.

God save the little twerp! Was there any point in continuing with this charade? If Darren really needed a seasoned professional to help market his paintings, he could've easily hired one with his father's money. If he cared one bit about Mr. Rivard's progress, he never would've fallen asleep with his weapons out of reach. All of a sudden, it seemed obvious that Darren had only wanted to get him excited about facing a new challenge. No wonder he slept so soundly. He'd already gotten exactly what he wanted.

Mr. Rivard snatched the gun from the coffee table and pointed it at Darren's head. "Rise and shine!" he shouted in a disgustingly enthusiastic tone of voice. "We've got a big day ahead of us!"

Darren sprang to attention. "What the hell?"

"You fell asleep, stupid. I've been racking my brains to come up with the best marketing strategy ever written, and you fucking fell asleep."

Darren grinned. "Since when have you started to toss such colorful words into your sentences?"

"I don't know."

"Try it again without the proper participle ending."

"Okay. I've been racking my brains to come up with the best marketing strategy ever written, and you fuckin' fell asleep!"

"Excellent! I'm going up to bed now, but feel free to finish what you've started. There's plenty of food if you're hungry, but stay away from my Pop Tarts, capisce?"

Mr. Rivard watched Darren disappear up the stairs. Was the kid afraid of anything? What would it take to get his attention?

It didn't take long for Mr. Rivard to find the largest, most impressive butcher knife available in Darren's kitchen. Minutes later, he hopped into bed beside his young friend and pressed the shiny silver blade against his throat. "I've been rackin' my fuckin' brains to come up with the best god damned marketing strategy ever written, and you fuckin' fell asleep, dick head!"

Darren trembled with laughter. "Stop! You're killing me."

"Come on, asshole! Don't you even want to hear about my plan? What the fuck! I can't be excited about this alone. Would it hurt you to give a shit about something for a change? I don't want you to do this because you think a little project would breathe new life into my jaded old heart. I want you to do it because you believe in yourself and your ability to reach people."

Darren retrieved a notebook and pen from his bedside table. "Okay," he said. "Let's hear about this fuckin' plan."

✱✱✱✱✱

On his day off, Vince woke to find some big changes around the apartment. All of Jenna's fancy perfume bottles had disappeared from the bedroom dresser. The closet that sheltered her gigantic shoe collection was almost empty. The floral print pictures she'd begged to hang were tucked away in a big box.

Best of all, her vast collection of scented candles was nowhere to be seen. He'd always hated those glorified hunks of wax in dainty glass containers. They burned so strongly that he could often taste them in the back of his throat. Perhaps now he could sit down to a decent meal without choking on the essence of jasmine, freesia and water lily.

He was preparing a giant bacon-and-tomato sub when he noticed the most startling change of all: Jenna's old cheerleading and homecoming pictures were stuffed into the garbage bin under the sink. He'd shattered one of the glass frames with his empty mayonnaise jar. It didn't make sense. Jenna's favorite pastime was going through old pictures with her friends. New visitors to the apartment were treated to an explanation of every cheerleading trophy on the fake brick mantle. Why did she suddenly want to dispose of those memories? Was it because he liked to criticize her for living in the past? Did he really have that much power to hurt her with his words?

He found her soaking in the bathtub with a ton of green goop slathered over her face. She quickly rinsed it away when he appeared in the doorway, as if he'd suddenly become someone worth impressing.

"I rescued your pictures," he said, dropping them on the rubber bath mat near the tub. "Something tells me you'll wish you had them one day."

Jenna wouldn't look at him. "You can burn them for all I care."

"Don't even say that! It took a lot of work to win three state championships. Not everyone can do a triple somersault from the top of a pyramid and land on both feet."

"It was a double somersault, and I thought you hated those pictures."

"I only hate them because they remind me of a time when you wouldn't give me a second look."

"How do you know I wasn't looking? I could've been glancing sideways."

"Do you expect me to believe you returned my admiration on some level?"

"Of course I did. You weren't exactly chopped liver. All my friends thought you were hot."

"But you didn't notice me until I started screwing them. I suppose it would've been different if I'd been class president or captain of the football team."

Jenna looked at him as if he were crazy. "No one ever said you had to be class president. I would've been happy to see you complete a homework assignment or two. That's the thing about you, Vince. You can't admit that you're somewhat lazy and unmotivated. I'd give my right arm for just one ounce of the natural intelligence you possess. You were easily one of the smartest kids in school, but you insisted on reading magazines in class. You could've graduated with honors, but you barely squeaked by. Was it so wrong to want a man with an ounce of ambition?"

Vince sat down on the edge of the tub. "I guess I never really looked at it that way."

"Don't get me wrong. I'm not trying to imply that I've been an angel. I shouldn't have made a habit of comparing you to all the men I could've ended up with. I suppose I thought I could get what I wanted by hurting your feelings. I knew it would take drastic measures to get you interested in setting a career goal, but I didn't have to go about it in such a mean and awful way. Please say you'll forgive me. Even if we wind up living at opposite ends of the globe, I have to know that you don't hate me."

The pain in her eyes was so intense that Vince had to look away. Glancing down at his feet, he spotted her cheerleading pictures on the ground, and he suddenly realized why he hated them so much. Jenna was a girl who went after what she wanted, no matter how impossible the goal. Just four years out of high school, she was less than a semester away from a master's degree in chemistry. Three local school districts were interested in hiring her as a teacher, but she was holding out for a more prestigious position at a research lab. Vince was just beginning to learn how difficult it was to hold a job and take classes, but she'd been doing it for years. She obviously had something he didn't—a natural spark that propelled her forward with no prompting from friends, family or authority figures.

Could it be that he was drawn to Kelly because he needed to be able to impress someone? Someone who was happy that he had a job and peed standing up? Could he really base a relationship on the fact that she was easy to please? Wasn't he better off with a woman who would keep pushing him to realize his full potential?

Better off, perhaps, but not happier. In Kelly's arms, he never felt more alive. It wasn't just her exotic beauty or her dirty little ways. There was a certain innocence about her—a strong belief that each day was a gift and the world was made to be lived in.

Vince helped Jenna from the bathtub and wrapped her shivering body in a towel. He couldn't go on like this forever, but for just this moment, it was nice to have two beautiful women in love with him. Decisions like these were never easy, and he was running out of time.

*****

"Remember," Darren said, propping the phone between Dr. Rushing's ear and shoulder, "if you say one word about where you are and what I'm doing, I'll yank the chord from the wall. Test my reflexes, and you'll end up staring at the business end of a gun."

Dr. Rushing nodded. He had no desire to argue with Darren this morning. He'd been listening to him brag about Mr. Rivard's progress for the past few days. He was curious to find out how much of his outlandish tale was true. Beyond that, he was happy to participate in any exercise that didn't involve extended use of a gag. The taste of his own saliva was as refreshing as a quart of lemonade.

Darren had acquired the cordless phone from the bedroom so he could listen to the conversation every step of the way. The cord attached to Dr. Rushing's phone was laced through Darren's fingertips so he could yank it from the wall on demand. The handle of a small gun peeked out from the waistband of his jeans. There was no disputing he meant business.

Mr. Rivard's tone was casual and upbeat. "Dr. Rushing! I thought you were out of town."

"I am. I just wanted to check on my favorite client."

"Stop. You're flattering me."

"Of course I am. I was hoping you'd write me into your will."

The two men shared a good laugh. "So, how's your friend?" Mr. Rivard asked.

"Two broken legs and a fractured rib. She'll be okay, but she's in no shape to chase a toddler around the house. That's where I come in. But enough about me. How are things with you?"

Mr. Rivard dove into an animated discussion of his recent brush with death. Apparently, it had taken the threat of physical torture to pull him from the depths of self-pity and get him interested in identifying new goals. "It's not just this particular project or this particular young man," he gushed. "It's the idea that I have the power to make a difference in someone's life. Darren came to me as a spoiled brat with no real desire to work and no idea what he wanted to get out of life. Now, he's running around town shopping for Halloween decorations and sending four-page e-mails packed with marketing ideas and preliminary outlines for taking his business to the next logical level. If nothing else, I've helped him to develop a clear vision of his future, and I know I can do the same for other young people. This morning, I contacted my attorney about setting up a charitable organization to provide expert counseling and generous grants to would-be entrepreneurs. I won't be able to help everyone who applies, but there's no reason I can't hire a few people to read business plans and forward me the very best of the best."

Darren hopped onto the coffee table and shook his ass in Dr. Rushing's face. His snide little victory dance made Dr. Rushing's blood boil. It was obvious he considered this to be some sort of competition. To him, Mr. Rivard's happiness was nothing more than a victory to dangle in front of his opponent's eyes.

As the conversation wore on, Dr. Rushing became increasingly distracted. It was a bit hard to concentrate with Darren jumping on furniture, patting his own back and playing an imaginary trumpet to illustrate the concept of tooting one's own horn. When it all got to be too much, Dr. Rushing decided to toss a little cloud over the parade.

"I hate to play the pessimist, but isn't this going to get a little expensive? You can deplete an entire fortune financing other people's dreams."

Mr. Rivard laughed. "I don't intend to foot the bill myself. That's the beauty of my line of work. I've spent a lifetime helping successful entrepreneurs climb to new heights. I know a boatload of people who don't mind shelling out big bucks to attend charity luncheons. The more expensive the meal, the more important they feel. I was thinking of charging $2,000 a plate to start."

"Two thousand dollars! Are the plates encrusted with jewels?"

"Of course not. But the opportunity to network with other business leaders is worth its weight in gold. Put it this way—I don't expect many last-minute cancellations."

Dr. Rushing was finally beginning to see the whole picture. This was a clear victory in every sense of the word. In the most unorthodox way possible, Darren had helped Mr. Rivard to help himself. This new charity would serve three important purposes. First, it would provide him with a steady stream of new challenges. Next, it would validate his existence by allowing him the opportunity to help young people realize their dreams. Finally, it would strengthen his ties with industry leaders around the country. Why didn't he just run for president while he was at it?

Dr. Rushing continued to feel bitter long after Darren replaced the gag and left him alone with his thoughts. As hard as he tried to focus on past victories in his life, he couldn't shake the image of Darren and Mr. Rivard wedged into a small booth at the local diner, laughing and talking well into the night. As he drifted off to sleep, he saw a clear vision of an elderly Mr. Rivard on his death bed thanking Darren for making his twilight years the very best years of his life.

He awoke with a start. Since when was he such a jealous creature? If he truly cared about Mr. Rivard, he should've been happy to hear that someone had finally broken through to him. Perhaps jealousy wasn't just an irrational emotion experienced by siblings and possessive spouses. It was an intense fervor that had the power to eat away at one's very soul. Maybe Darren wasn't so crazy after all. At a very young age, the only person who'd never left him developed a strong attachment to an outsider. No wonder he felt the need to prove himself. Like Mr. Rivard, he was struggling to validate his existence.

A deep black fear moved through Dr. Rushing's spirit. Who would Darren try to fix next, and what would he do when he was satisfied that he'd proven himself?

Chapter Eight

Friday afternoon, Claire found herself behind the wheel of a rented van large enough to swallow her old Volkswagen Beetle. According to the slip of paper on the dashboard, she was looking for a church-like mansion nestled in the woods of Cloverlawn Estates, an exclusive gated community on the rich side of town.

Earlier that day, she'd received the most incredible message on her voice mail at work. A fellow by the name of Darren Price wished to donate an extravagant collection of toys from his youth. He was even willing to load the truck and reimburse rental fees.

As she bobbed along the rough gravel road connecting Cloverlawn to the outside world, she felt like a 16-year-old enjoying her first unsupervised road trip. If only Dr. Rushing could've seen her march into that rental office and request an application form. His long-standing suspicions were right on target. She was more than capable of dealing with strangers if given the right incentive.

Her confidence faded when a handsome young man with precisely sculpted features greeted her on the cobblestone path. Despite his warm smile, he reminded her of the kind of guy who used to point and stare in junior high.

He earned his first brownie point when he looked directly into her eyes. If he was shocked by her appearance, it didn't register on his face. Perhaps she was the bad guy in this scenario. It was never acceptable to form opinions about a person based on exterior qualities.

"Glad you could make it," Darren said, as if her schedule was loaded with more exciting things to do.

She could barely look at him. "The pleasure is all mine. I wouldn't miss this opportunity for the world."

She was surprised to discover that the impressive mansion in the foreground was just one of the exquisite structures dotting the landscape. On the northern end of the estate, four wooden cottages encircled a plot of lush green land adorned with polished boulders and miniature pines.

She soon learned that those quaint little cabins housed untold treasures. Nothing could've prepared her for the sight of a miniature house crammed with child-sized furniture, appliances and cookware. She couldn't resist the urge to peek into cabinets, flip switches and open drawers. Even the little blue refrigerator had its own ice maker!

Eyes glued to a ceiling adorned with sparkling purple stars, she wandered into the family room and stumbled over a miniature red corvette with real leather seats. A little green army figure hung from its rear view mirror. "Don't tell me," she said, lifting the plastic hood. "There's a real motor in here."

Darren looked at his feet. "I know what you're thinking. What kind of spoiled brat has his own car with a real motor!"

"Actually, I was just wondering how you managed to keep this stuff looking so brand new. I play with children eight hours a day, and I know how destructive they can be."

Darren squeezed his rear end into a tiny recliner upholstered in rich brown suede. "If you want the truth, none of this stuff impressed me as a child. My father bought it to keep me from spending every waking moment in the woods. As you can see by the condition of the car, his plan backfired."

Claire crossed to a large picture window overlooking a brilliant cluster of pines. "I can see how you'd be tempted to explore your life away." She wanted to add that she'd never spent much time outdoors as a child, but she doubted he wanted to hear about her sad and lonely existence.

"I could take you on a tour, if you'd like. It's really quite breathtaking."

"That's very nice of you, but shouldn't we start loading the truck?"

Darren shot her a wicked grin. "One of the advantages of being a spoiled rich kid is that you don't always have to do things for yourself. I'll have the groundskeeper put things in order." Claire couldn't believe the generosity of the young man sitting before her. He obviously had some hidden motivation. His spoiled rich kid comments were a clear sign that he felt guilty for having it so good. If he took the poor ugly girl for a walk in the woods, he could feel a little better about his many blessings in life.

Claire was shocked by the evil and petty thoughts that sometimes popped into her head. Darren had offered a very generous donation before he'd ever laid eyes on her. Was it so difficult to believe he was just a nice guy who felt like taking a walk on a crisp autumn afternoon? His other alternative was loading the truck, and that was certainly less interesting. Why was she suspicious of anyone who wanted to spend time with her? Why not take this rare opportunity to explore a pristine area of town she'd only seen from her car window?

Darren's tour began at the northern end of the estate, where clusters of oak, hickory and walnut formed a barrier between wooded and residential areas.

Farther into the woods, a large pond nourished a precisely planted circle of maple and beech with brilliant red and yellow leaves. A cool autumn breeze rippled the water and produced rustling sounds in the air. The place was alive with color and motion.

Darren raised a finger to his lips and instructed her to remain completely still. Fifty feet in the distance, a graceful fawn strutted to the water's edge for a drink. Upon spotting them across the pond, it quickly turned and darted back into the woods. Darren explained that several species of animals visited the pond on a regular basis. From his old tree house along the water's edge, he'd spotted white-tailed deer, muskrat, woodchuck, racoon, beaver, rabbit and skunk. Fifty years ago, hikers passing through the area might've encountered black bear, porcupine, red fox, elk or wolverine.

"As a kid, I used to imagine that my awesome skills as an explorer led me to discover species long considered to be extinct from the area. I fantasied about encountering a big black bear, wrestling it to the ground and bringing its hide to school for show and tell."

Claire laughed. "It's funny how a girl's fantasies differ from a boy's fantasies."

Darren stopped to inspect a tiny trail of paw prints. "What did you fantasize about as a child?"

"Barbie dolls coming to life, leprechauns in the basement, Tom Thumb prancing about the cupboards."

He slipped his arm around her shoulder. "Sounds like you needed a friend."

Though his gesture was purely platonic, Claire couldn't stop her hands from shaking. Deep within her heart, she still suspected his actions were motivated by pity, but that no longer mattered. She concentrated on the warmth of his body, the pressure of his touch, and the smell of his light musky aftershave.

* * * * *

Kelly reached under her mattress for the little red pen she'd managed to steal from the nurse's station. The rules at the institution were ridiculous. If they were so afraid she'd stab herself or put out an eye, why were they releasing her more than a month early?

She decided not to waste time worrying about that. She felt happy for the first time in years. She'd almost forgotten how powerful love could be. It penetrated the spirit like a double shot of Nyquil, soothing those persistent aches and providing more than enough comfort to get through the night.

She wondered if Darren had ever managed to find love again. There was a time when he considered her to be the love of his life, but his problems had turned out to be more than she could handle. It took a special person to assume the role of savior, and she wasn't strong enough to be that for him or anyone else. She was damned lucky Vince had agreed to be a guardian of sorts. Did she deserve a love so pure and unconditional? Perhaps some people were put on Earth to be strong for others.

She didn't waste time obsessing over Darren these days. Her spirit was so full of love there seemed to be no room for hatred. Instead of stewing over all the things that had gone wrong with her life, she tried to remember all the things that were right. That's what the pen was for. She liked to make lists of all the exciting things she planned to do upon her release.

Finding a job was her top priority. There was an entry level position available at the office in Vince's apartment complex. He'd brought her an application to fill out, along with several brochures from businesses close to home.

The second item on her list was dance lessons. She had no lofty goals in that department, but she thought it would be nice to develop grace and learn an artistic skill. Just once in her life, she wanted to be a person with hobbies and interests. It didn't hurt to have something to look forward to on a Saturday evening.

The next item on her list brought a gigantic smile to her face. She was determined to find a pure bred rottweiler pup, no matter what the cost. Her childhood dog had died while she was locked away in juvenile hall. She'd never forgotten how safe she felt laying beside Molly on the bedroom floor. Perhaps Molly was another guardian of sorts—a creature put on Earth to serve and protect.

Last but not least, she wanted to buy a truckload of scented candles. Candles were strictly forbidden at the institution, and she missed them dearly. She'd discovered the joys of aroma therapy while sharing an apartment with her friend Clarissa after her stint at the juvenile home. When the killer cravings began to resurface, she found great comfort in lighting every candle in the house.

After finishing her list, she passed the time doodling on the back page of her notebook. She began with basic hearts then moved on to stick figures and caricatures. Without fully realizing it, she started to scribble the image of an anorexic woman with ratty hair and wild eyes. Her extra large pupils were fixed at opposite corners.

No! It wasn't possible. That woman was gone forever, wasn't she?

★★★★★

Surrounded by gruesome oil paintings and outlandish sculptures, Claire stuffed her hands into her pockets to keep them from shaking. She couldn't take her eyes off a frighteningly realistic portrait of a young circus performer with a knife protruding from her eye socket. "I like the way you've decorated for Halloween," she said, for lack of anything better to talk about. "Where in the world did you manage to find all these gruesome portraits?"

"Actually, I painted them myself, and I keep them in place all year."

A shiver crawled up Claire's spine. "You do?"

"Relax. I'm mostly harmless. My publicist describes me as an up-and-coming artist with an uncanny flair for capturing the true essence of death. In just a few weeks, we're holding a grand outdoor exhibition with special incentives to attract horror movie fans."

Claire fixed her eyes upon the door. Although Darren had a perfectly reasonable explanation for his freakish hobby, she was downright nervous. Handsome or not, he was still a relative stranger. She must've been crazy to follow him home based on the smell of his musky aftershave.

"Stop that," Darren said.

"Stop what?"

"You're calculating the number of steps to the door."

"Is it that obvious?"

"Yes. Would you please relax for a moment? If I were a celebrated author of ghost stories or an award-winning director of horror films, you'd feel perfectly safe to sit and have coffee with me. Why is it so dreadful to paint the kind of images Americans pay good money to see in theaters?"

Claire suddenly felt like a fool. For the first time in her life, a handsome man had expressed genuine interest, and all she could do was throw questioning stares around his living room. How dare she discredit something as deeply personal as a man's art? "I'm so sorry, Darren. I didn't mean to sound as if I were disappointed in…"

"It's okay. I've disappointed everyone, especially my father."

"You don't understand. I would never judge anyone. I dropped out of high school, for God's sake. I change diapers and wipe snotty noses for a living. Your line of work is certainly more impressive than that."

Darren draped a comforting arm around her shoulder. "I'll tell you what. Let's just start over. Let's throw away every dull and awkward word we've spoken and pretend we're on a date in a movie. Let's tell everyone we spent the evening talking about music, art, religion and politics."

Claire looked directly into his eyes for the first time. Had he really used the word 'date'? It was almost too good to be true. "It's a deal."

It wasn't so difficult to sit and talk with Darren once she made an effort to understand what made him tick. For most of the evening, she listened to him brag about the new publicist who'd recently come into his life. He didn't have many friends, and it was quite liberating for him to spend time with a person who supported his dreams and visions for the future. The two of them had some very original ideas for turning Darren's grand estate into an expansive Halloween wonderland.

She was shocked by how comfortable she felt sitting close to a young man. She didn't mind looking him in the eye when she spoke or brushing her shoulder against his body when she laughed. It felt good to be taken seriously for a change. The only person who came close to making her feel this way was Dr. Rushing, and that didn't count because she paid him.

She didn't start feeling insecure until she spotted that portrait of the dark, mysterious woman dressed in white. She didn't notice the painting at first because it was propped against the wall in a dark corner of the living room. For some reason, Darren had taken it down from the wall. An ex-girlfriend, perhaps?

"A penny for your thoughts," Darren said.

Claire turned away from the painting. She'd been staring at it so long there was no pretending she hadn't noticed. "I was just wondering about that portrait in the corner."

"A long lost love," Darren explained. "Way lost."

Claire hesitated. "She's very beautiful."

"Beauty is an inner quality," he said.

Claire wanted to be sick. As a child, her mother had always told her that true beauty was found within the heart. It was an automatic response designed to make her feel better about the way she looked. She wondered if Darren was using a variation of that same line to make her feel better right now. The thought wasn't worth dwelling on. She'd been having a lot of fun until the moment she spotted that painting, and she wasn't about to let long-standing insecurities ruin her special evening. She decided it would be best to change the subject.

"That's an interesting piece above your mantle. I don't think I've ever seen a portrait of a dead fish."

"Would you prefer a garden bursting with flowers or a sailboat drifting on the ocean? How about a mountain range at dusk or an eagle soaring over the horizon?"

"It's not that I would prefer another image. I just think that one is sort of peculiar."

Darren looked directly into her eyes. "Why must it be peculiar? Why can't a dead fish be beautiful? That's the thing about me, Claire—the thing that disappoints so many people. I see beauty where others can't."

Darren placed his hand under Claire's chin and guided her face to his. As he brushed his mouth against her quivering lips, a single tear blazed a trail down her face.

* * * * *

"You must be crazy!" Jerry shouted between bites of fried mozzarella sticks. "Are you that desperate for a new piece of ass?"

Vince clenched his fists under the table. His brother could be a real idiot when he wanted to be. "She's not just a piece of ass. God, I knew I shouldn't have told you about this."

A tiny blond waitress wandered over to a nearby booth with a wet rag in her hands. Jerry watched her bend over the edge of the table as if he'd never seen a girl scrubbing coffee rings quite so gracefully. "Hey, Susie!" he shouted. "Come over here for a second."

Vince watched Susie's long pony tail bob up and down as she bounced over to the table. He wasn't sure why Jerry was so interested in bringing a stranger into the conversation, but he didn't expect much from a guy who once started a bon fire with a collection of women's undergarments left at his apartment.

"Take a look at my brother here," Jerry said. "Would you say he's fuckable?"

Little miss Susie had a surprisingly tough voice. "Get over yourself, Jerry. Don't ask me shit like that."

"I'm serious. Junior here is having some self-esteem problems. I'll double your tip for an honest answer."

Susie placed her hands upon her hips and shot Vince a coy smile. "Yeah, I'd say he's definitely fuckable."

"Good girl. Bring us another beer, will ya?"

Vince threw a dirty spoon across the table at his brother. "Was that necessary?"

"I was only trying to prove a point. New ass isn't so hard to find, especially for a guy like you. For God's sake, quit dipping your prick in the funny farm."

"You're not listening to me, Jerry. I think I'm in love with her."

"Don't talk to me about love. You only feel that way because it's new. Trust me on this one. Inside every woman, there's a repressed bitch waiting to be

116

set free. Some chicks have more control over their inner bitch than others, but believe me, it always comes out eventually. Why waste time breaking in a new bitch when you can work on the one you've got?"

"You're so eloquent, Jerry."

"Thank you. If you want the truth, I can't understand why you're looking to trade up. Jenna has a damned good head on her shoulders. That girl is going to bring some serious money to your table one day."

"You're awful."

"Don't judge a man until you've walked a mile in his shoes. Do you really want to end up like me, supporting some bitch with no skills, praying she won't divorce you and go after everything you've got? Wake up, little brother. Don't look a gift horse in the mouth. If Jenna doesn't want to choke the chicken, find someone on the side who will. I can hook you up in that department. That's what brothers are for."

"Thanks but no thanks. Do I look like I need to be hooked up? Open your ears for just two seconds, will ya? I'm in love with the girl!"

Vince stuffed another mozzarella stick into his mouth. "All right, all right. I believe you. I've been in love before—I think. I know what it can do to a guy's head. But consider this: Kelly is locked up for a reason. They don't just put you in a mental institution when you've had a bad week. Her whole life has been one big setback after another. I know you want to save her, but what if it can't be done? You've got a heart of gold, but you're no psychiatrist. You could be setting yourself up for a lifetime of grief."

Vince laid his head down on the cold table. "Now, you're speaking my language."

✶✶✶✶✶

Claire had always worried that her first kiss would be an awkward moment that showcased her insecurity and lack of experience. Much to her surprise, kissing was a bit like learning to drive a car. The longer she did it, the less awkward it felt.

She was also relieved to discover that there was no right or wrong way to do it, as people claimed in high school. It was all about establishing a mutual rhythm. The tongue was a highly flexible instrument of pleasure. It could be used like a feather to tease and caress or wielded like a weapon when passions ran high. A perfect balance could be achieved by alternating between the two extremes.

Just when she began to feel comfortable with Darren's natural rhythms, he introduced a new variable into the equation—his hand. He began by slipping it up the back of her blouse and moving it gently over her shoulder blades. Slowly but surely, he was able to unfasten her bra and work his fingers around to her bare breasts.

A sudden bolt of fear shot through her heart. Wasn't this the part where decent girls were supposed to stop? She'd always thought of herself as a good person, and she certainly didn't want her handsome new companion to perceive her as an easy kill. Did she dare to seize his hand and move it away from her breasts? Would she come off as a prude if she refused to engage in a little harmless foreplay?

She was just about to close her fingers around his wrist when a wicked little voice inside her head warned her not to ruin the moment. Who was she fooling, anyway? She wasn't your typical wide-eyed 20-year-old with countless phone numbers stored in her Palm Pilot. She'd never had the luxury to pick and choose. In all likelihood, this would be the opportunity of a lifetime. Whatever the consequences, she was determined to experience the full range of Darren's talents.

Leaning her head against the back of the couch, she watched him fumble with the buttons on her blouse. The sight of him taking her left breast into his mouth sent strange currents up and down her thighs. She continued to watch as he slid down to her navel, savoring every flick of his soft, pink tongue.

As he took down her zipper, he paused for a moment to look deeply into her eyes. She could tell he was searching her face for signs of approval. Looking down upon him with a smile, she granted him permission to slide her jeans down over her thighs.

The way he looked at her naked body made her feel like a hunk of Godiva chocolate on a silver platter. She'd never had the opportunity to gauge a man's reaction to her slim, curvy figure. His wicked little grin was by far the most moving compliment she'd ever received. He spent the next few minutes running his lips along her inner thighs. She thought she'd never felt such a miracle as the way his hot breath caressed the surface of her skin. Was this the reason why the girls at work were always going out to find new dates? Could this explain why hair salons, clothing boutiques and cosmetic companies stayed in business?

She expected him to whip out a condom at any moment, but instead he did the craziest thing: He parted her lips with his fingertips and flicked his tongue into her moist center. Sharp currents of ecstacy danced along her inner walls. When he stopped to tease the little nubble that throbbed with an almost painful pleasure, she found herself gasping thick handfuls of his hair, pushing him deeper and deeper into the abyss.

Before she could fully grasp what was happening, an involuntary shudder moved through the pit of her stomach. All at once, her vision grew dark and her whole body began to tremble. She clenched her teeth to stifle her own whimpering.

She collapsed on top of a generous heap of throw pillows. She couldn't remember the last time she'd felt so relaxed and content. She wallowed in that feeling of inner peace until it occurred to her that Darren deserved a little reward for his outstanding work. She reached for his zipper, but he caught her hand and pushed it away. She didn't know whether to feel disappointed or relieved. "But don't you want to…"

"Not if it'll hurt you."

"I can take a little pain. It's… gotta… happen sometime."

"Yes, but that doesn't mean it has to happen tonight. Trust me on this. You'll be much more relaxed if we put it off a little and get to know each other first."

Claire couldn't believe her ears. Weren't men supposed to be pigs? According to the girls at work, didn't they always put their own pleasure first?

"If you didn't plan on finishing, why did you do all of that?"

Darren threw her a seductive wink. "Just think of it as a gift."

✱✱✱✱✱

Dr. Rushing leaned back in his wooden chair and made a mental list of all the action and suspense movies he'd seen in the last year. If you could believe what you saw on television, it was possible to rub your wrists together behind your back and create enough friction to eat through the fibers of a good rope, or even a good layer of duct tape. He'd seen scores of leading men and half a dozen supermodels perform the trick, but it wasn't so simple in reality. The longer he did it, the more he felt like breaking down into a fit of tears.

He should've known better than to attempt such a stunt. Now, in addition to feeling caged and restless, his wrists were on fire. He wondered how many layers of skin he'd torn in the process of trying to escape. He longed for a tube of antibiotic ointment and a nice clean bandage.

It was well past midnight when Darren stumbled down the stairs and removed the gag from Dr. Rushing's mouth. He'd been kind enough to bring a large pizza and a case of Mountain Dew. The light, clean essence of rose blossoms overpowered the aroma of the food. "Did you manage to get any sleep?" he asked.

"What kind of question is that? If you'd wanted me to rest, you'd have provided me with better accommodations."

"Sorry about that. I could transfer you to the couch for a while, if you promise to be good."

"How about loosening this tape? I think I've lost all sensation in my fingertips."

Darren used his pocket knife to cut through the layer of duct tape encircling Dr. Rushing's wrists. Searing pain radiated through his biceps. His arms had been secured behind the chair for so long that they no longer felt like extensions of his body. His ankles were still bound together, but he could stand at will. "Rub your hands together," Darren said. "It'll help get the blood flowing."

"Thanks, Doc. How about an aspirin? Look at my wrists, for God's sake. Have you no mercy?"

Darren studied the deep friction burns that marred Dr. Rushing's flesh. "Very impressive. You've got more fight in you than I would've guessed."

"Is that what you're doing? Testing my fight?"

"I've already told you what I'm doing."

"Oh, yes. I must've forgotten. You're fixing my patients."

Darren smiled. "And you haven't even thanked me."

"What should I thank you for? Destroying bonds of trust I've formed with blood, sweat and tears?"

"Don't be so dramatic. Your bonds with patients aren't as strong as you'd like to believe."

"How would you know? Have you looked inside their minds?"

"No, but I've been further inside Claire's head than you'll ever get."

The realization hit Dr. Rushing all at once. The rosy fragrance that followed Darren inside the door was the scent of Claire's perfume. "You son of a bitch!" he screamed, springing up from his chair and diving into Darren's torso like a linebacker. They crashed to the floor with a dull thud that knocked an empty glass from the computer table. It shattered to a thousand pieces on the cold tile. Taking advantage of his position on top, Dr. Rushing closed his fingertips around Darren's throat and watched the blood drain slowly from his face. "What did you do to her!" he demanded. "What the hell did you do!"

"Something you should've done a long time ago," Darren gasped.

Dr. Rushing was sure he held Darren's life in his hands. His only mistake was hesitating to choke off the kid's last breath of air. The moment he loosened his grip on Darren's throat, he could feel the strength returning to his opponent's limbs. A pair of trembling arms overturned him.

Locked in a violent embrace, they rolled across the floor and came to rest upon a thick bed of glass. Dr. Rushing cried out in agony as the razor sharp chunks sliced through his tee shirt and leapt into his flesh. Searing pinpoints of pain quickly melted into a dull, throbbing sensation that spread over his entire back. He was all too aware that the sudden liquid warmth surrounding his body was a pool of his own blood. Darren smiled down upon him, his thick red windbreaker glistening with fine crystal slivers. Dr. Rushing tried to speak, but his last bit of strength left him in a rush of air. His last thought was that he should've killed the son of a bitch when he had the chance.

He awoke to the smell of rubbing alcohol. A slab of hard tile froze the side of his face. Was he sprawled out on the bathroom floor? Was that Darren's bare foot just inches from his cheek? A small rope secured his arm to the sink's pedestal. The sound of dripping water grated on his nerves.

The pain of rolling over broken glass paled in comparison to the agony of having it removed, bit by bit, with a pair of old tweezers. It took every ounce of his strength to remain calm and collected as Darren performed the intricate operation. "This was so unnecessary," Darren said. "Physical torture wasn't on my agenda."

Dr. Rushing took a deep breath. "Was it on the agenda with Claire?"

"Of course not. I think it's safe to say she'll go to bed feeling much happier than she felt when she opened her eyes this morning."

"You can't go on like this, Darren. You can't inject yourself into people's lives and perform experiments with their mental health."

Darren tossed a hunk of glass into the waste basket. "Why not? Isn't that what your line of work is all about? You're just jealous because it was me who finally gave Claire the very thing she needed most."

"That's not true. A mercy fuck is the last thing Claire needs at this juncture of her life."

"Who says it was all about mercy? Believe it or not, she's got a hot little body under those baggy drawers."

Dr. Rushing banged his head on the hard tile. "I'd prefer not to discuss that."

"How come? Is it a little too painful? Why don't you just admit you screwed up? You've had plenty of opportunities to sweep Claire off her feet, but you didn't take a single one of them. And why is that?"

"I'm a professional, Darren. My work is governed by certain standards that…"

Darren twisted Dr. Rushing's arm behind his back. "What did I tell you about lying to me?"

"All right, all right! I didn't go after Claire because I wasn't sure if I could

see myself in a relationship with someone who is... is..."
Darren tightened his grip on Dr. Rushing's arm. "Say it!"
"Disfigured. Broken. Physically unattractive. Are you happy now?"
Darren let go of Dr. Rushing's arm. "On the contrary, I couldn't be more depressed. You call me a psychopath, but I'd never consider hurting someone I love the way you've hurt Claire. How could you enjoy her company, consume her energy, win her trust and then hold back the one thing that could make her whole? You disgust me."

Dr. Rushing was silent for a moment. "You're right, Darren. I'm shallow and weak-minded. I should've gone after what I wanted, but that gives you no right to take it from me. Claire deserves to be in a relationship with someone who truly cares about her."

"Who says I don't care about her? You know absolutely nothing about the way I feel."

"I don't doubt that you feel some kind of spark, but you can't enter a relationship based on the goal of fixing someone. What happens when she becomes that happy and confident person you want her to be? She'll be like every other girl in town, and you'll lose interest in the project."

"Maybe so, but that doesn't mean I can't show her a little happiness right now. Every girl deserves to know what it feels like to be loved by a man at least once in her life. It doesn't matter if it lasts 30 days or 30 years, the experience of it will transform her permanently."

Chapter Nine

Benny stretched out on a thick bed of leaves and took a good look up at the sky. On days like this, when the atmosphere was blue as the ocean and still as a lake of glass, he could see reflections of the world around him. The sun was like a great ball of fire leaking across the sky. He couldn't tell where the treetops ended and their reflected images began. He closed his eyes to escape the harsh light. Hazy orange impressions shimmered behind his lids, filling his head with an almost liquid warmth. He might've fallen asleep if it weren't for all the humming. Some junkie in a ski cap was determined to get noticed. That was the problem with public parks. There was always someone stepping into your personal space.

The kid couldn't have been much older than 20. His patchy brown beard couldn't hide the flawless condition of his porcelain skin. He obviously hadn't been on the streets for long. A fellow's face could turn to leather overnight.

"You need something?" Benny asked.

The boy smiled down at him as if he were looking upon an old friend. "I was just wondering if you were going to smoke the rest of that cigarette."

Benny glanced down at the extra long ash clinging to the tip of his Marlboro. He didn't remember lighting it, and now there were only a few drags left. "Take it," he said.

"I appreciate it, man. I got a whole package of beef jerky here, if you want some."

"Save your food. You'll wish you had it later. In the meantime, you need to find yourself a coat. Have you tried the Salvation Army?"

"Thanks, but no thanks. I ain't dealing with no government organization."

"The Salvation Army isn't the government, is it?"

"Sure it is. It's got the word "army" in it, doesn't it?"

"Yeah, I guess you're right."

"I know I'm right! They're everywhere, but I've learned how to outsmart them."

Benny eyed the kid skeptically. "Sure you have. How old are you, anyway?"

The guy said he was 20, but he acted like a teenager. His name was Darren, and he carried a fancy red lunch bag with matching plastic thermos. The set was the exact shade as his red windbreaker, and it bore the same logo. There was a mother in his life somewhere, even if he didn't go home to her every night.

For the next hour, they combed the park in search of lost treasures. The kid found five empty cans and a decent Timex watch hidden beneath a crisp bed of leaves. Benny found some loose change embedded in the dirt near the swing set, but it was mostly pennies and nickels. They were just about to call it a night when Benny stumbled upon a woman's handbag under a remote picnic table at the far end of the park. "Well, I'll be damned!" he shouted. "You feel like pizza tonight?"

To avoid the scrutiny of passing joggers, Benny urged his new friend to follow him to the tiny studio apartment he called home. He wasn't used to visitors, so he felt the need to explain the graffiti on the walls. "I like to draw sometimes," he said, pointing to a childlike portrait of a clown with balloons.

The kid wasn't listening. He was too busy studying a detailed sketch of an eyeball that covered the old window shade. "You feel watched," he said.

Without much effort or concentration, Darren took a piece of chalk from the window ledge and softened the outer edges of the pupil. Next, he added eyelashes and tiny lifelike creases in the skin. The effect was that of an eye half-closed and half-interested.

With that small detail out of the way, Darren joined Benny in the corner of the room, where a mountain of old coats served as a bed. They dumped the contents of the purse on the floor and looked at one another in bewilderment. There seemed to be no end to the amount of junk a gal needed to get by. In addition to a real leather wallet stuffed with cash, they found countless utensils for the application of makeup, a full bottle of hair spray, a whole package of fresh wipes, two lamb skin condoms, a tiny tube of toothpaste, two granola bars and a clean pair of cotton panties stuffed into a zip-lock bag. "I have first dibs on the condoms," the kid said.

"Take 'em. I won't be needing them anytime soon."

"Good. You can have the fresh wipes."

Benny studied the trial-sized package of feminine deodorant cloths. "But these are for a woman's privates!"

"That doesn't mean anything. You can use 'em like fresh wipes for your hands. It's all the same ingredients. They just print flowers on the package and sell 'em for a higher price."

Benny stuffed the package of feminine wipes into his pocket. "Good thinking."

Around 7 o'clock, the kid left to order pizza from the pay phone down the street. Benny used the time to go through the big black wallet. He found several credit cards in the name of Andrea Moyer and a little purple checkbook with white butterflies printed across each page. He wished he hadn't spotted the driver's license with the young redhead's picture. She was one of those femme fatale types with an ultra sleek haircut and brazenly seductive eyes.

"Put that picture away!" demanded his seventh grade teacher. "It's turning you on, isn't it?"

"It is not!"

"You ought to be ashamed of yourself. She's young enough to be your daughter."

"I was just looking at her picture, for God's sake. I mean her no harm."

"So why do you have an erection?"

Benny cupped his hand over his crotch. "It's just the thought of some young redhead who likes sex so much that she carries her own condoms and a clean change of panties. They didn't make girls like that in my day."

"Sure they didn't. What about that Kimberly bitch? She sure took you for a ride, didn't she?"

Kimmy Watkins was the last person Benny wanted to think about. He quickly found a pair of scissors and snipped every card in Andrea's wallet, including the license. His old teacher fell silent. She almost never stuck around to watch him do the right thing. "Where did you go!" he shouted. Get back here!"

The kid returned just in time to catch Benny shouting at the wall. "Who are you talking to?" he asked.

For the first time in years, Benny felt embarrassed about his little quirk. "I hear voices sometimes. It's no big deal—honest. I'll ignore them if you want."

The kid shot him a look of pure horror. "Please tell me you don't answer them every time they speak."

"Why shouldn't I?"

"Because it makes it easier for them to keep tabs on you!"

"What are you talking about?"

Darren tossed his ski cap into Benny's lap. "Put this on. I don't expect you to understand. You'll just have to trust me, okay?"

Benny slipped the cap over his head. "I trust you."

"Good. Can you still hear them?"

"Yes. They want to know who you are."

"Don't answer! It's a trap. They've lost the signal, and they want to get a fix on you. Understand?"

Benny nodded in agreement. "How did you know about the signal?"

"You wouldn't believe me if I told you. We have to get out of here, at least for awhile."

✶✶✶✶✶

Darren guided Benny down the winding cobblestone path that led to the swimming pool on the eastern end of his estate. He'd managed to convince his new friend that he was just a groundskeeper with full access to the spectacular property. Benny didn't question why a fellow with such an important job would be napping on park benches and searching for lost coins in the park. That was the most charming thing about the guy. He didn't always take the time to connect dots.

Benny eyed the pool with an uneasy grin. "You don't really want to go swimming in the cold, do you?"

"Don't worry about it. The dude who owns this place is so damned rich he can afford to keep the temperature like bath water."

Benny took a step backward. "I still can't go in there. It just might... kill me."

"What are you talking about?"

"There are electrical currents running up and down my spine. That's how I'm able to communicate with people from a distance."

Darren suppressed the urge to laugh. "You're confusing electrical currents with radio waves. You'll be just fine. You aren't plugged into anything."

"You don't understand! My whole nervous system is woven together with..."

Darren tuned the man out. One way or another, he was going to get the dude to take a bath. He had no intention of spending endless hours with a bum who reeked of armpits and ass.

Turning away from the pool, Darren dropped his pants just below the base of his spine to reveal a nasty scar from an old skirmish he cared not to remember. The thug had left him with a jagged knife wound that circled his lower back and barely missed the crack of his ass. "You see this!" he shouted. "I know all about what the government does to innocent people. And you have the nerve to bitch about a few little wires. How would you like to have a computer chip stuck in your ass?"

Benny traced his fingers along the hideous scar. "My God," he said through chattering teeth. "You're just a baby..."

Darren spun around to face his new friend. He couldn't understand why the sight of tears pouring down Benny's face made him feel like crying himself. Since when was he such a little girl? "Don't worry about me. I removed the chip with a razor blade. I'm free and clear now. My greatest concern is for you."

Benny's lips began to quiver. "I… can't remember the last time I was anyone's greatest concern."

"Then you'll let me help you?"

"I don't know. Will you have to cut me?"

"Not at all. In your day, they didn't use computer chips."

"What did they use?"

"Threadlike cables, like the ones bundled together inside telephone wires."

"So how do you get them out?"

"You can't get them out, but there's a way to damage the receptors and render them useless. You'll need an organism with the ability to extract fluids from beneath the skin."

"Like a leech?"

"Yes, like a leech. It may take a few applications. You'll have to be strong. This process isn't for the faint of heart."

Benny dropped his pants to his ankles. "I don't care. Let's do it!"

"Not so fast. First, we have to make sure no one has a fix on you. You can jam the signal by soaking in warm water. It will temporarily…"

Before Darren could complete his thought, Benny dove into the swimming pool.

$$*\ *\ *\ *\ *$$

Claire would never have called Darren if she had known there were concert tickets burning a hole in his pocket. "I told you," she said for the fifth time. "I can't deal with public places. It's just something you'll have to accept."

"So how did you get the moving van for the toys? Surely you must've paid a visit to the rental office."

"That was different. It was a rare opportunity for the children."

"So think of me as a four-year-old with a big Kool-Aid moustache. I'm begging you, Claire. Come to the concert with me."

"No."

"Fine. Stay home and stare at the television. I'm going out to live my life."

Claire slammed the phone into its cradle. Was this what it meant to have a boyfriend? If so, she wasn't sure if she could handle it. She liked the safety and comfort of her overstuffed sofa. It was certainly more inviting than a dark stadium packed with screaming teenagers. There was only one problem: The sofa didn't hug back.

It didn't take long for her to start feeling guilty. She'd criticized Darren's art on their first date. Shouldn't she make an effort to understand his music? She quickly logged onto the Internet and found pictures of the heavy metal band known as Sick Puppy. She was intrigued to discover that the group's physical appearance was somewhat similar to the legendary rock band KISS. Members of Sick Puppy didn't appear in public without their costumes, and fans often imitated their animalistic makeup designs.

Claire raced to the phone to call her only friend. She was happy to learn that Brooke didn't have a date for the evening. She had plenty of time to visit the Halloween specialty shop at the mall. Less than an hour later, Brooke showed up at Claire's front door with a Sick Puppy makeup kit under her arm. They experimented with different looks all afternoon and settled on the lion-like facade of Damon Lamont, the band's charismatic drummer.

Posing in front of the bathroom mirror, Claire was amazed to discover that she radiated pure feline sex appeal. The makeup lent itself well to her natural features. The super-thick black eyeliner did an amazing job of balancing her uneven eyes. The dark tan coat of powder softened the contours of her nose and cheek bones. The prosthetic chin piece wasn't necessary because Claire's jaw line needed no augmentation. With a little help from a blow dryer and a tube of styling gel, Brooke was able to turn Claire's limp blonde hair into an expertly tousled mane. "You look absolutely stunning!" she gushed. "You were totally meant to go to this concert."

"You really think so?"

"I wouldn't say it if I didn't mean it. You're a real video vamp—except for one thing."

"What's that?"

Brooke hiked up her skirt and stepped out of her sexy black lace tights. "Put these on!"

"What's the point? My skirt is too long to show off the lace pattern."

Brooke reached for a pair of scissors on the vanity table. "I can fix that."

"No! My mom gave me this skirt for Christmas."

Brooke shot her a wicked grin. "Do you want to be sexy or not?"

$$*****$$

With a stiff self-conscious walk, Claire made her way up the cobblestone path leading to Darren's house. She wasn't used to the feeling of wind blowing through extra wide slashes in her clothing. Her newly altered skirt was just barely long enough to cover her panties. Brooke had made damned sure she looked the perfect picture of a slutty lioness.

She paused at the door. She hadn't told Darren she was coming because she'd wanted it to be a surprise. What if he'd invited a friend to use the extra ticket, or even worse, a girl? He wasn't exactly her boyfriend yet. He was free to invite anyone he pleased, and there weren't many girls who'd be opposed to stepping out with a handsome young man from an upper class family.

She was considering that possibility when the door swung open. Darren looked more handsome than ever in faded jeans and a black leather jacket. She instantly recognized the seductive look in his eye. For the second time in her life, she felt like a hunk of Godiva chocolate. "Still have that extra ticket?" she asked.

"It just so happens that I do."

"I was afraid you might've given it to some lucky young lady."

Darren pulled her into his arms. "The only lady I'd dream of taking is you."

It was no small accomplishment to straddle the back of Darren's motorcycle in a tattered mini skirt. To keep it from riding up her legs, she was forced to adjust the fabric every few minutes. As they approached the open highway, she felt as if her upper thighs were on display to the entire world.

Barreling down the road at 75 miles per hour was the most frightening experience of her life. She desperately wanted to adjust her skirt again, but she didn't dare let go of Darren's shoulders. Billboards and neon signs flashed by her eyes in a dizzying rush of color. She felt as if she might be sick at any moment.

She managed to make it to the Metro Dome without throwing up on her date. Her fake whiskers had perished in the ride, but Darren assured her that it didn't detract from her overall look. He added that her wind-blown hair was sexier than ever.

He put a firm grip on her hand to direct her through the crowded lobby. A legion of bodies pressed against their backs, propelling them farther and farther down the great hallway until she felt as if she were floating on a sea of people. The presence of a thousand beating hearts didn't frighten her. She took strength from each one of them. Her elaborate makeup was the warmest security blanket she'd ever known. For the first time in her life, she made eye contact with strangers and acknowledged their smiles with a confident nod. The bodies propelled her into an enormous circular room where echos danced on thin air. Theater style seats climbed up the walls in every direction. Her head swam with flashes of color and light. A complete stranger passed her a joint.

"No thank you!" she shouted.

"What?"

"I said no thank you!"

Darren's arm felt good around her shoulder. The warmth of his body compensated for the cold ride to the stadium. She had the distinct feeling that this would be a night to remember.

Until the music started.

An electric guitar cried out in agony, blowing her ear drums apart at the seams. The crowd nearly pissed itself with excitement. She felt like the only person in the room who couldn't identify the song from the first few riffs. Some crunching sounds were accompanied by speed drumming and intense feedback from the amplifiers. The effect was like standing inside a trash compactor without ear plugs. This wasn't your typical hard rock or heavy metal music. It was totally void of heart and soul, logic and reason. Sick Puppy only *wished* they sounded like Kiss.

Most of the lyrics were indecipherable, but the main chorus barreled through her head like a freight train:

Poke me, prod me, put me to shame.

Suck all the blood from my last good vein.

Screw me, do me: Don't call me tomorrow.

Make me wait a week: Let me wallow in my sorrow.

Darren pulled Claire a little closer and buried his face in her tousled hair. To him, this was the language of love.

Later that night, he brought her to a special midnight screening of his favorite horror movie. He insisted there was no reason to be nervous about sitting in a dark room with a bunch of people who only cared about what was happening on the giant screen in front of them. She no longer had the desire to argue. She wanted to get as much mileage out of her costume as possible.

Far Beyond Twisted was the story of a young doctor who enjoyed skinning people alive and monitoring how long it took for their hearts to stop. The movie disturbed Claire to the core, but she was able to make the evening bearable by burying her face in the crook of Darren's neck. God how she loved the smell of his hair, the taste of his skin and the feel of his soft cotton tee shirt against her cheek. She basked in the warmth of his body heat until the credits came rolling across the screen.

By the end of the night, she found herself wishing she could skip past the dating rituals and stay home wrapped in Darren's arms. She could just barely tolerate the activities that pleased him most. Their conversations were fairly pleasant but uninspired. It took too much energy to discuss the finer points of a movie she'd watched through clenched eyelids.

None of that seemed to matter when he stepped behind her bedroom door. She was awestruck by the joy and wonder of human closeness. Every nook and cranny of his body was dear to her heart. She liked the gentle slope of his neck and the strong outline of his collar bone. The skin on his upper thighs was as soft as the bottom of a baby's foot. She enjoyed running her hands along his spine, stopping briefly to brush her fingertips across the jagged scar that circled his lower back.

They explored one another's bodies with their hands and mouths, perfecting the art of climax without penetration. Her first encounter with him had been all about receiving, but she quickly learned it was just as intoxicating to give. She savored the sense of authority and control, drunk on her own power to manipulate a man's body, mind and spirit.

*****

Benny clenched his fists so tightly that he could feel the tips of his fingernails ripping into his palms. "Is this going to hurt?" he asked.

"Not really," Darren said. "Trust me, the psychological horror of it is much more frightening than the physical pain."

Benny's eyes wandered over to the jar of slimy black leeches on Darren's coffee table. "How long do they have to stay on me?"

"Just long enough to damage the fragile network of wires beneath the surface of your skin. Five minutes should do it."

"Five minutes!"

"Okay, three minutes."

"Are you sure that's long enough?"

"I'm positive. Are you going to remove your shirt or not?"

Benny did as he was told. "Sorry. I've always hated going to the doctor's office."

"This isn't an office, and I'm not a doctor. Lay down, please."

Benny did a belly flop onto the couch. Just when he was starting to feel a little more relaxed, his seventh grade teacher zeroed in on his frequency. "What in the world do you think you're doing!" she snapped. "This *can't* be sanitary."

The tiny creatures felt cold and slimy on his skin. There was a slight stinging sensation followed by the most beautiful music he'd ever heard. "What's that noise?" he asked.

"What noise?"

"The piano. Who's playing the piano?"

"That's my radio. It's been on since we walked in the door."

"That's strange," Benny said. "I really hadn't noticed."

✶ ✶ ✶ ✶ ✶

Martha Patterson removed the basket of sunflowers from her kitchen table to make room for the giant poster-sized crossword puzzle Benny held in his hands. "My goodness!" she said with a wink. "I'll be six feet under by the time we solve this one."

"It's not as tough as it looks," Benny assured her. "Darren made it himself."

Martha used the front of her housecoat to dust a pair of reading glasses that hung from a rusted chain around her neck. "Is this for real? Does he really want us to come up with a synonym for 'meadow muffin'? I must admit I have no clue."

Benny counted the number of blanks available to enter the answer. "Cow pie!" he shouted. "The answer is cow pie."

Martha laughed and laughed until her old bladder nearly sprung a leak. Sunlight filtered through her threadbare yellow curtains, infusing the room with a cheery amber glow. The aroma of fresh raisin bread and homemade chicken pot pie wafted through her tidy kitchen. She wasn't used to eating so well, but it was something she could learn to live with.

Life had a funny way of working itself out. The crazy neighbor who kept her awake at night with his constant jabbering would now become a much needed source of income. Her whole life had changed the day his nephew stopped by with a checkbook to buy a little slice of her time. The food stamps they shared were another bonus. Up until Darren stepped in, Benny had been trading them for small amounts of cash barely adequate to pay his utilities. The young mother who'd worked out the deal used her own welfare checks for drugs. Just what was the world coming to?

Taking care of Benny wasn't as difficult as Martha thought it would be. She brought him along on trips to the pharmacy and reminded him to refill his prescriptions. She kept track of his Medicaid card because he had a tendency to misplace it. When he didn't feel like taking his pills, she could usually find a way to sneak them into his food. He particularly liked chocolate milkshakes with mounds of whipped cream. She made them extra sweet to disguise the taste of the medication.

The one thing she didn't have to remind him about was rent. The landlord's wife made a habit of checking his mail near the end of the month to make sure his SSI checks didn't get lost among all the million dollar offers. Benny took such offers seriously and waited patiently for a surprise visit from Publisher's Clearinghouse. He was so obsessed with his junk mail that he overlooked his monthly bills. When prompted, Benny took his check straight to the convenience store down the street and cashed it on the spot. He gladly handed over every cent of his income for the opportunity to remain in the building. Dismal as it was, he loved his tiny apartment. Years of sleeping on park benches had taught him the value of a nice warm hovel. Before his nephew brought the bed, he'd slept on a pile of old coats from the Salvation Army. Martha often wondered how Benny had survived before his nephew stepped in. His monthly check from the government was barely enough to cover rent. He begged for change and hunted for bottles when he could, infuriating neighbors with constant requests to look through their garbage. A slice of pizza from the convenience store was a treat he had to earn. He filled zip-lock bags with stray cigarette butts to quiet his other nagging hunger.

Strange as he was, Benny made good company in the morning when his mind was relatively clear. They liked to work crossword puzzles and help one another solve difficult questions. Benny's nephew was particularly concerned about exercising his mind. He provided plenty of magazines, tabloids and puzzle books to keep Benny occupied. He even delivered a cell phone so that Benny wouldn't be stuck without a line of communication in the event of an emergency. Most of the time, he only used it to call Publisher's Clearinghouse.

After Benny left for the evening, Martha settled down to watch her programs with a nice bowl of fruit salad. Directly overhead, the hard soles of Benny's new winter boots pounded the floor like horse hooves. There was a time when the sound of him pacing back and forth drove her to the medicine cabinet for a special little pill, but now the constant noise was a strange comfort. As long as she could hear him moving around, she didn't have to worry about him peeking into garbage cans or begging tenants for spare change. He no longer needed to panhandle, but he kept right on fighting for survival just the same. She supposed some things about him would never change, no matter how much money flowed into his life.

✶✶✶✶✶

Darren drove slowly along Chesterton Boulevard in search of an unkept man in a tattered yellow raincoat. He was supposed to have dinner at Claire's house this evening, but Mrs. Patterson had called to inform him that Benny had flown the coup. The only clue to his whereabouts was a small notepad with a Chesterton address scrawled across the front.

Darren switched on his father's favorite classical music station to calm his racing heart. This was more responsibility than he needed right now. Would he ever be able to make solid plans with his new girl? Just when life was beginning to take a turn for the better, he'd been saddled with a 50-year-old child who couldn't remember to take a bath or tie his shoelaces without prompting.

He spotted Benny just south of the Chesterton Shopping Plaza. A big stuffed giraffe filled his trembling arms. A mixture of rain and sleet plastered his long hair to his forehead. What the hell was he thinking? Was he determined to end up with pneumonia? With anger brewing in the pit of his stomach, he eased his father's Porsche to the side of the road and opened the passenger side window. Freezing rain infiltrated the car and disappeared into the plush velour seat. "What are you doing out in this weather!" he shouted.

"Hitchhiking," Benny replied, as if such a pastime was as natural as breathing.

"Hitchhiking? Good Lord! You were instructed to contact me when you needed transportation."

Benny chuckled. "You sound like an Englishman when you're angry."

"Just get in the car, damn it!"

Benny wedged his big wet giraffe into the space between the driver and passenger seats. The creature's silly buck-toothed grin fueled Darren's fire. "Shut the door. We're going home this instant."

"No!" Benny whined. "I have important things to do. That's why I didn't bother you. I knew you wouldn't take me."

"Take you where?"

"To visit Chrissy."

"Chrissy?"

"One of my friends at the shelter. I promised to come see her as soon as I got my life together. Now that you've helped me do that, I can't just forget about her."

Grumbling to himself, Darren shifted into drive and got his elbow caught between the giraffe's front legs. He couldn't go on like this. Even with Mrs. Patterson's help, Benny was a handful. He got a notion to do something and followed it through without thinking.

The shelter was a dismal place with dark cinder block walls. The moment they entered the lobby, a gangly man in hospital scrubs grabbed Darren's elbow. "How nice of you to come," he said, pulling Darren through a long corridor lined with men sitting on the floor. "I trust you have an appointment."

Darren stopped. "I didn't know we needed one."

"Don't pay attention to him," Benny said. "He's no doctor."

"Nurse!" the man shouted. "We have trespassers."

A stout woman in a floral smock rushed to their side. "Benny! Where the heck did you come from? I haven't seen you in ages."

Benny wrapped his arms around the woman's neck. "I'm back, and I brought my friend, Darren."

The woman extended her hand. "It's nice to meet you, Darren. My name is Marge. I'm a volunteer from St. Mary's. I'd offer you a bed, but the inclement weather has brought a small army to our door. Shall I put you on the waiting list?"

Benny chuckled under his breath. "You'll be waiting till June."

"Actually, we don't plan on staying long," Darren said. "Benny just came to visit a friend."

"Aw," the woman said, as if she'd just spotted a puppy. "You came to see Chrissy, didn't you?"

Since men and women slept in different areas of the shelter, Darren and Benny had to wait for Marge to bring Chrissy up from the basement. As they crouched along the great hallway lined with stragglers, Darren spotted a man chewing on a cigarette butt. Steams of tobacco-stained saliva clung to his chin. Darren nudged Benny with his elbow. "Toss that dude a cigarette, will ya?"

"I can't. There's no smoking inside the shelter. Besides, he would only eat it."

Darren closed his eyes to block out the sight of a young man changing his underwear. "Does he have to do that here?" he asked.

"Where would you like him to do it? In the rain?"

Darren spent the next several minutes with his eyes glued to the floor. If anyone else took a notion to exposing genitals, he didn't want to see it. The sounds and smells that floated about his head were enough to contend with. He was amazed by the number of people who spent time conversing with imaginary voices. With so many warm bodies stuffed into the corridor, wouldn't it be easier to chat with a real person?

The moment he stood to stretch his legs, he was sorry he'd allowed himself to take a good look around. At the end of the great hallway, three men were slumped over in wheelchairs with bandages wrapped around big round stumps where their feet used to be. "My God," Darren said. "The next time I feel sorry for myself, I'm going to remember those gentlemen."

"Are you kidding?" Benny said. "The diabetics are the lucky ones. They never have to wait around for seats."

"But I thought this was a facility for the deranged, not a medical clinic."

The gangly man who believed he was a doctor stepped in to clarify the situation. "We take the folks everyone else turns away, from the ranting schizophrenics to the homicidal crack heads. The men in wheelchairs came from the hospital. It's my job to massage their legs and help stimulate circulation."

Darren whispered in Benny's ear. "I thought you said that guy wasn't a real doctor."

"It doesn't matter what he believes as long as he's willing to help."

Marge stepped into the hallway with a young blonde in fleece pajamas. Benny jumped to his feet and threw his arms around the girl's neck. "Chrissy!" The stuffed giraffe fell to the floor between them.

"What's that?" she asked, grabbing the curious creature with dry, cracked hands covered in fresh blisters.

"A present for you," Benny said.

Looking almost frightened, Chrissy inserted three fingers into her mouth. "Don't worry," Marge said. "I'll keep it in the office so no one steals it. You can come look at it anytime you like."

Benny emptied the contents of his sagging pockets. Tubes, bottles and brightly colored packages struck the floor like items spilling over the edge of a grocery cart. Darren stepped to the center of the hallway to prevent the genital flasher from intercepting the goods. "I'll go get a bag," Marge said.

Darren finally understood what Benny had been doing with the extra pocket money flowing into his life. There were bottles of aspirin and freesia perfume oil, fresh bandages and tubes of pricey antibiotic ointment. Paperback novels adorned by air-brushed pictures of young heroines in flowered hats indicated that Benny had put a good deal of thought into his purchases. Fifteen packages of bubble gum rounded out the clutter.

Chrissy regarded the stock pile with a smile that lacked one tooth. The blush of late adolescence burned brightly in her cheeks. Darren guessed she couldn't have been much older than eighteen. "She doesn't have a dad," Benny whispered, as if that were some sort of shameful secret in this day and age.

"Offer her some gum," Darren said.

"I don't like gum," Chrissy replied, chewing frantically on her fingertips.

"Would you learn to like it for me?" Benny asked.

Her radiant smile returned. "I'll try anything for you."

Chapter Ten

Darren sat alone on his couch gazing up at his beautiful paintings. As much as he liked the idea of holding a grand Halloween exhibition, he wasn't sure if he wanted to part with them. Each piece held special meaning only he could understand. Would potential buyers love and cherish them as he did, or would his most precious works end up collecting dust in leaky basements and musty attics? He especially hoped the circus series wouldn't end up in a garage sale twenty years from now. The images expressed on those canvases began as a collection of sketches scribbled in the back of his fourth grade math book. His first field trip to the circus had been a terrifying experience. Each time a daring young performer began a new stunt, he expected a freak accident to occur. His classmates had laughed when he hid his face in his hands, but to him, it was no joke. For nearly two months after the event, he dreamed of mutilated lion tamers and beautiful women with daggers protruding from their eye sockets.

The nightmares had stopped after he got them down on paper. Once he took a good look at the images haunting his dreams, he was able to see how ludicrous they were. When did you ever hear about a tightrope or knife throwing accident? The answer was never.

The worm painting was another gem he wished he could hold onto. That summer his father encouraged him to feed the animals of the woods, he became obsessed with the idea of protecting all God's creatures, including the slimy ones that served no clear purpose. How was a worm's life any less valuable than a human's? Worms didn't cheat, lie, degrade or humiliate. They caused no problems for anyone, yet they were particularly vulnerable to something as random as a casual misstep.

A knock at the door intruded upon his thoughts. Pulling on a pair of sweat pants, he stumbled through the living room and flung the door wide open. His father was radiant in a pale blue suit with matching pinstriped handkerchief peeking out from the breast pocket. The hem of his tailored slacks fluttered softly in the wind, revealing a pair of pinstriped socks.

"You look lovely," Darren teased. "Where the hell did you find a handkerchief to match those socks?"

"Never mind that. I have a surprise for you."

Darren ignored the picnic basket in his father's arms. "Did you actually go to a fabric store to find a swatch of pinstriped material?"

"If you must know, I have an extensive collection of handkerchiefs and socks. Sometimes, when I walk into my closet, things just fall into place. May we eat breakfast now?"

Darren turned on his best English accent. "Yes, we certainly may."

He continued speaking in his father's tongue as they enjoyed a feast of hot buttered biscuits and homemade jam. "To what do I owe the honor of this visit?"

"Knock it off. I haven't seen you in awhile. I was just wondering if you were still alive."

Darren pinched himself hard enough to leave fingernail impressions on his wrist. "I can still feel pain. I suppose that's a good sign."

Roland cleared his throat. "There's been a steady stream of traffic around here lately. May I inquire about your sudden interest in making friends?"

"No, you may not."

"Come on, Darren. You never include me in your life. You could at least tell me a little something about the girl."

"Her name is Claire, and she works at a daycare center."

"Is it serious?"

"I'm not entirely sure. Would you like it to be?"

"This isn't about what I'd like. Just tell me how you feel."

"If you must know, I can see myself with her for quite awhile. I kind of like her innocence. The world seems a little different when I look at it through her eyes."

Roland grabbed his son's buttery hand. "That's beautiful, Darren."

"She also gives one hell of a blow job."

"Good Lord! Is it so difficult for you to express genuine sentiment without putting a macho spin on it?"

They finished their breakfast in silence, passing condiments across the table like two polite strangers. Roland ate with a napkin in his lap, while Darren preferred to catch drops of butter and jam with his pants. He made sure to chew with his mouth open, just to make his father's skin crawl.

He waited patiently for the old man to leave for work, but Roland remained firmly planted in his seat. When the terrible silence threatened to drive Darren mad, he tossed his butter knife across the room to savor the sound of it striking the stainless steel sink.

"Don't you have someplace to be?"

"I haven't been late in fifteen years. I think they'll forgive me this once."
Darren ran from the kitchen and did a nose dive into the couch. "All right!"
he shouted. "I give up! Ask all the questions you came to ask."

Roland raced into the living room on white patent leather shoes. His
expression reminded Darren of a dog begging for a bone. "Who was the man
in the swimming pool?"

"Some crazy dude I met in the park. I'm sort of helping him out. Actually,
you're helping him out, if you want to get technical."

"Me?"

"Yes. I'm using your checks to help support him. I was hoping you wouldn't
mind."

"Just how much is this costing me?"

"About a thousand dollars so far. I bought him a nice bed and a good pair
of boots for the winter."

"That's not so evil, I suppose."

"I'm glad you're not angry. I was thinking of giving him my televison set."

"The big one?"

"Yes. He has nothing in life. A little entertainment might do him some
good."

A smile came over Roland's face. "What can I say? Give him anything you
wish. I must admit I'm quite proud of you. This is an amazing development,
indeed."

Darren yawned. "Are we done now?"

"Not quite. I want to know about the little man with the glasses."

"We're business partners. He wants to help me host a grand Halloween
exhibition to sell my art."

"Am I financing that, too?"

"Not at all."

"Please be careful, Darren. The business world is full of vultures who prey
upon rich young investors with big dreams."

"This isn't about money. The guy is a self-made billionaire. That's
billionaire with a "b," as opposed to millionaire with an "m," which is all you'll
ever be. Trust me, he's got enough stock to make you look like a charity case."

His father looked puzzled. "If this isn't about money, what's it about?"

"Shared visions and dreams."

"Since when do you have dreams?"

"Since I met Mr. Rivard."

Roland's voice was suddenly laced with contempt. "So, that's his name,

Rivard?"

"Yes. We've decided we need more challenges in life."

"And how did you arrive at this conclusion?"

"It's a long story. We met in a coffee shop. There was an instant rapport."

Roland began to pace the floor. "Where do you plan on holding this exhibition?"

"Here, of course."

"Here? That's not possible."

"Why not?"

"I'm not insured for this kind of thing. What if someone falls and breaks a hip or has a seizure in the pool?"

"No one is going to have a seizure in the pool."

Roland crossed to the front door. "If this Rivard fellow is so filthy rich, let him use his own property to carry out his dreams!"

*****

Darren was barreling down the highway on his motorcycle when his cell phone rang. He normally wouldn't have taken the time to pull over, but he had people who depended on him these days. He hated to admit it, even to himself, but that made him feel important.

He couldn't have been more annoyed to hear his father's voice come over the receiver. "What the hell do you want? I'm on the shoulder of the freeway, for God's sake."

"You'll be fine," Roland said. "A Mack truck couldn't bowl you over."

"Could we get on with this, please? Cars are splashing me."

"I just wanted to apologize for my behavior this morning. I've been under a good deal of stress and..."

"Give me a break. Stress had nothing to do with it. You were glowing bright green with envy."

Roland was silent for a moment. "Yes, I suppose I was."

A tear escaped the corner of Darren's eye. "It's a beautiful color on you, Dad."

"You really think so? It doesn't clash with my blue pinstripes?"

"Not at all."

"I was thinking. This Halloween exhibit doesn't sound like such a bad idea. You could set up on the eastern end of the property near the pool house."

"I appreciate the sentiment, but everything is fine. I informed Mr. Rivard of the change in plans after you left this morning. He's got people preparing his property as we speak."

"He certainly moves fast. I'm so sorry, Darren."

"Don't worry about it. I'll tell you what. When this is all over, we can tell Mr. Rivard and Dr. Rushing to take a flying leap."

"I'm not sure that's the most healthy way to deal with this. If we're going to behave as adults and maintain some semblance of respect, we must allow one another to choose our own friends. I like what Mr. Rivard has done for your outlook. If this is what having a mentor is all about, I'm all for it."

Darren clenched his fist. "That's not what I wanted to hear, and you know it. Fuck the exhibit! If you'll agree not to see Dr. Rushing, I'll break all ties with Rivard."

"You're asking a great deal of me. Thomas has played an important role in my life for the last ten years. You've only just met Mr. Rivard. I'm more than willing to find you another psychiatrist, but my personal friendships are sacred."

"And your relationship with your son isn't?"

Roland sighed. "I didn't say that. Stop putting words into my mouth. What if I asked you to end your relationship with Claire because I felt threatened by her? Would you do it?"

Darren didn't have to think about his answer. "No, I wouldn't."

"There you have it. We'll live as adults and let one another forge our own relationships. Now, if you'll excuse me, I've promised to join Thomas in the destruction of a case of beer tonight. I couldn't make it last time, so it's important for me to be there this evening."

Darren's heart skipped a beat. How could he have forgotten to send his father a copy of the letter announcing Dr. Rushing's departure? "You're on your way there *right now*!"

"Yes, Darren. You don't have to shout. I can hear you just fine."

"Have you cleared the parking lot?"

"No, I just got into my car."

"Stay right where you are. Don't leave yet, okay? I'll be back in a second."

Darren took to the open road with a vengeance, flying through red lights and weaving in and out of traffic like a man on a suicide mission. He wasn't sure how long his father would stay on hold, but he assumed he could get at least five minutes out of the old man.

It took approximately 20 minutes to get to Dr. Rushing's house. He hid his motorcycle in the shed, just in case his father was already in the vicinity.

Dr. Rushing was fully prepared for a visitor. The moment Darren slammed the front door, a hideous scraping sound drifted up the basement stairs.

Proceeding in the direction of the noise, Darren found Dr. Rushing scooting frantically across the tile on his wooden chair. Darren's whole body shook with fear. His father was going to arrive any moment, and there was no way to get Dr. Rushing out of the house without a struggle. He wasn't going to walk quietly up the stairs with a gun in his back. He was going to make a scene or die trying.

A sharp knock at the door brought Darren's racing heart to a dead stop. The blood curdling howl of a neighbor's dog filled the air with an unmistakable sense of doom. Dr. Rushing tipped his chair into the coffee table and knocked a glass vase to the floor. It seemed to shatter in stereo, sending little slivers of glass into Darren's eardrums. He could only hope his father hadn't heard the horrible crash.

Left with no further options, Darren snatched a medical encyclopedia from the desk and whacked Dr. Rushing over the head. Much to his horror, the blow didn't render him unconscious. He twitched violently in his seat, eyes wide as two saucers.

The knocking continued and continued. The neighbor's dog fell silent. Tears of madness streamed down Dr. Rushing's cheeks. Darren was suddenly reminded of the two men he'd chased through the streets with his motorcycle as a teenager. It had all been a game to him then, but now he saw that a man's breaking point was no laughing matter.

Darren buried his face in his hands to block out the sight of it all. Was hurting his father's dearest friend the same as hurting his father directly? He couldn't think about that... wouldn't let himself think about that. In his head, he recited a childhood rhyme about an old woman who swallowed a fly. The knocking grew faint and disappeared altogether.

That night, when the property was swallowed by a blanket of darkness, Darren found Dr. Rushing's keys and quietly escorted him out to the car. He fell into the back seat like a rag doll, never bothering to grunt in protest or use his legs as weapons. Darren considered untying his arms and removing the gag. There seemed to be no fight left in him.

After transporting his hostage to the cellar of the guest house, Darren drove Dr. Rushing's car back to his house. It was then that he noticed the little note taped to the front door.

> Tommy,
> I'll have you know that I showed up after work to help destroy that case of German beer you've been bragging about. Since your car is still in the driveway, I must assume

you left with someone else. If it was a hot date, I forgive you. Otherwise, you receive a failing grade for the day. Either way, you owe me a bottle of Grauman's finest for my trouble.
–Roland

Darren wanted to be sick. Since when did Dr. Roland Price, connoisseur of fine wine, jump at the chance to kill a case of beer? Darren had practically begged him to go out for a beer on his 21st birthday, but he'd insisted upon making reservations at a fancy restaurant known for its exquisite private label wine. The implications were clear. Roland's blood coursed through Darren's veins, but his heart belonged to the adopted bastard in the cellar.

* * * * *

For three days, Dr. Rushing watched Darren go about his business without comment. Each evening, he came to the cellar with a new Halloween mannequin that bore no resemblance to the cheerful scare crows found on front porches around town. Using foam rubber masks and clothing stuffed with straw, he was able to create a virtual army of monsters, zombies and demons. He chose only the most frightening and realistic masks that money could buy, avoiding cartoonish representations at all costs. Sometimes, when the cool moonlight filtered through the small window at just the right angle, Dr. Rushing felt as if the freakish dummies would come to life and swallow him whole.

In the dead of the night, when Roland was fast asleep, Darren removed the gag from Dr. Rushing's mouth and brought him upstairs to relax in the recliner with his hands tied loosely in front of him. If he was feeling generous, he played movies until the sun came up. Dr. Rushing secretly prayed for the opportunity to get lost in a good screenplay, but he never dared to ask for it. He was certain Darren would withhold the privilege if he knew how important it was to him. He was particularly puzzled by Darren's fascination with a low budget film called *Into the Grave*. It was a poorly acted and marginally frightening story about three witches who struggled to maintain control over a town of Satan worshipers. At one point in the movie, the elder witch's mask came unglued from her neck. The sun shone through cracks in her cave when it was supposed to be night, and her fingernail polish often changed from red to black within the same scene. Despite such inconsistencies, Darren popped the movie into his VCR for a few minutes each night, usually just before bed. Dr. Rushing said on his fourth night in front of the television, "I don't know how you can stand to watch this. It's just too damned realistic."

"If you must know, this was the very first movie that ever scared the living hell out of me as a child. I watched it over and over again until it lost its power to frighten me."

Dr. Rushing couldn't help but analyze that comment. "So, the movie is a comfort to you?"

"I guess you could say that. Isn't laughter a comfort to everyone?"

That night, Darren treated Dr. Rushing to a no-holds-barred horror fest. Popping movie after movie into the VCR, he pointed out dozens of classic "B" movie moments guaranteed to arouse a chuckle or two. Dr. Rushing shook with laughter when he saw ten zombies dragging their feet across a field that was supposed to resemble an ancient burial ground. Fresh clumps of cow manure clung to their feet, causing several actors to slip across the grass and struggle to recover their balance.

For one fleeting moment, Dr. Rushing felt he could become friends with Darren under the right circumstances. If they could enjoy a night of watching movies, perhaps they could find common ground elsewhere. Those feelings of warmth and kinship vanished with the waning moon. Just before dawn, Darren inserted the gag and escorted Dr. Rushing back to the cellar. The mannequins that occupied his corner of the room weren't so frightening anymore. Their twisted faces were suddenly the most hilarious thing he'd ever seen.

The following night, Dr. Rushing came up from the cellar to find the television missing. It was easily one of the saddest moments of his life. He immediately wondered how he'd cope with the constant silence. As Darren helped him settle into the old plaid recliner, he feared sleep would become his only comfort and joy.

He awoke to find the phone in his lap. It was time for another one of Darren's victory calls, and there was nothing he could do about it. Or perhaps there was nothing he *wanted* to do about it. He looked forward to any exercise that would connect him to the outside world.

Benny's tone was comfortingly optimistic. He didn't ask how Dr. Rushing had found his new number, and he didn't seem to care. "You'll never guess what I'm doing!" he shouted into the receiver.

"What's that?"

"Watching the news on my brand new wide-screen television! There's a water main break down on Central Avenue. If you hurry, you can catch it."

"I thought you didn't care for television."

"That's because I could never concentrate on it. The voices have left me now. I found a way to outsmart them."

Benny told Dr. Rushing about his young friend with the leech collection. He seemed to have an incredible amount of faith in Darren's ability to diagnose and treat symptoms that had plagued him since early adulthood. He was absolutely certain the voices would never return, and Dr. Rushing couldn't tell him otherwise. Darren had the telephone chord laced through his fingertips. If he dared to utter one word of skepticism, the connection would be lost.

"Are you taking your medication?" Dr. Rushing asked.

"I think so. I caught Mrs. Patterson dissolving it into my milkshake."

"Mrs. Patterson?"

"My upstairs neighbor. She cooks me dinner every night."

Dr. Rushing looked at Darren. "That's awfully generous of her."

"Well, she's lonely. You know how old people are."

Dr. Rushing felt a sudden wave of relief. Darren's methods were unconventional, but at least he wasn't endangering his most fragile patient. It didn't matter if Benny's peace of mind came from a bottle or from a strong belief in the healing power of an outlandish medical procedure. The point was that he hadn't felt so good in years.

Benny went on to discuss a few of the hobbies he'd recently discovered. He'd just borrowed a stack of tabloids from Mrs. Patterson so he could keep up with the personal lives of folks he saw on television. He found great joy in working crossword puzzles, especially in the morning when his head felt clear. Sometimes, when Mrs. Patterson wasn't around, he stood before his window and studied the neighborhood with a pair of binoculars he'd found in the park. "I can't get over the things I've never noticed!" Benny said. "Like the way small children jump over cracks in the sidewalk instead of stepping on them. And I love how fashions have changed since I was a boy! Tailored slacks are a thing of the past. Darren is going to buy me a pair of sloppy, wide-legged jeans with droopy pockets, like the rappers wear. Think of all the things I can carry around with me! Not to mention, they make a great place to store the little treasures we find in the park."

Dr. Rushing pictured Benny and Darren crawling through the grass in search of lost jewelry and coins. A friendship like that was the very thing Benny needed most in life. He seemed to feel a certain connection to the world after a long and terrifying separation. Dr. Rushing had promised himself he would no longer allow jealousy to eat away at his heart, but it was getting more and more difficult by the minute. In a ridiculously short period of time, Darren had pulled Benny from his hallucinogenic world and delivered him back to reality. It was an admirable feat that Dr. Rushing hadn't been able to accomplish in more than eight months of therapy. Perhaps he wasn't as competent as he once believed himself to be. If he ever broke free from Darren's control, he wasn't sure if he would return to his practice at all.

Did he dare mention these insecurities to Darren? An admission of failure was exactly what the kid wanted, but what would happen when he got it? Would he gloat for awhile and lose interest in the project, or would he slit Dr. Rushing's throat the moment it became clear that his whole life's work was a joke?

He decided that a diplomatic approach would be best. He would have to find a way to rejoice in Darren's victory without admitting his own defeat.

"I'm so proud of you," he said after hanging up with Benny. "I wish your father could see how you've changed that man's life."

Darren looked at Dr. Rushing as if *he* were the one who needed intensive therapy. "*You're* proud of *me*?"

"Of course. There was a time when I believed you were incapable of such warmth and compassion. It's nice to know that I was wrong."

"This isn't about compassion. It's about proving you to be a quack."

"I don't consider myself a quack. I do the best I can with the time and resources available to me. Don't forget that I deal with more than 50 clients each week. I don't have time to take them for treasure hunts in the park, and I certainly can't afford to hire babysitters. Nonetheless, you are to be commended for your efforts. All of my clients should be so lucky to have a friend like you."

"He's NOT my friend."

"I don't believe that. You could've stopped with the food and medication, but you chose to furnish his apartment and provide him with all the little luxuries he's gone without for so many years. Where's your television, by the way? Was Benny watching it when I called?"

Darren folded his arms in front of him like a child refusing to go to bed. "I never used it anyway."

"Sure you didn't. Your collection of horror movies could fill a warehouse."

"Just shut up, okay?"

"Very well. But first, let's have a drink to celebrate Benny's triumphant return to the real world!"

Chapter Eleven

Kelly was disappointed to discover that St. Joseph's Women's Shelter looked more like an old warehouse than a place of refuge. Donated hospital beds covered every inch of floor space in the enormous grey room, forcing residents to navigate around bodies on their way to the bathroom. Women of all ages milled about the place, stopping at different beds to visit with friends or antagonize foes. When a skirmish broke out, Sister Mary Louise Parker reminded instigators that they could easily be reassigned to a cold bench outside. Her threats didn't scare anyone because the warehouse itself was only a few degrees warmer than the parking lot.

As luck would have it, Kelly was assigned to the bed next to Deb McFadden, a rude and confrontational bitch who'd accompanied her on the bus from the institution. She passed the time humming softly to avoid being drawn into a conversation with the haggard old woman. "You're pretty damned cheerful for someone whose new home is a 30-year-old hospital bed," Deb said. "Whose been blowing sunshine up your ass?"

Kelly buried her face in the pillow. "This is NOT my home. I don't plan on staying another night."

"Oh yeah? Is your guardian angel swooping down to find you an apartment?"

"Not exactly."

"Well, tell her to get you a job while she's at it."

"Actually, I have a job waiting for me across town."

"Really? And who is going to provide cab fare?"

"I have a ride, thank you very much."

"From who? Your guardian angel again?"

"If you must know, he's more like a knight in shining armor."

Deb was overcome by a fit of laughter. "If Lancelot cares so much about you, why didn't he come and get you when you were released?"

Kelly pulled the covers over her head. She didn't owe Deb McFadden an explanation of any kind. She couldn't be released to Vince's custody because Vince was an employee of the hospital. He didn't want her to write his name on the release form because it would raise suspicion that something was going on between them. She wound up on the bus to the shelter because she had to state a destination in order to receive clearance. It was an age-old policy designed to keep lunatics from roaming the streets upon their release.

It would all be over soon enough. Vince's shift ended at 6 a.m., and he was coming straight downtown to pick her up. The only thing left to do was catch a decent night's sleep.

She woke to the smell of powdered eggs wafting through the old warehouse. She'd choked down so many spoonfuls of them at the institution that she could smell a reconstituted breakfast a mile away. She could hardly wait to raid Vince's refrigerator.

Sinking a little farther down into the covers, she imagined what it would be like to have breakfast with her new man each morning. Would they flip through the paper and discuss the day's events like two people who belonged to the world at large? Would they marvel at the power of their high-speed juicer like a couple of newlyweds caught in an infomercial? Would he sneak up behind her as she stood over the stove and slip his arms around her waist, just to show he cared? She was so lost in her commercial that she kept her eyes closed a little too long. It slowly dawned on her that the smell of powdered eggs wasn't a good sign. If breakfast was already cooking, wasn't Vince a little late?

She threw back the covers and sprang to her feet. Could Vince have gotten lost on his way downtown? He was a child of the suburbs, after all. The city was a big, scary place filled with one-way streets and extra tall buildings. If you made a wrong turn, you couldn't just swing around and go back to the street where you'd made the mistake. You had to go around the block and catch the next street headed in your direction.

Spotting Sister Mary Louise, Kelly raised her arm, as if to ask a question in class. The old woman hobbled over to her bed and laid a gentle hand upon her shoulder. "Yes, dear?"

"Did anyone leave a message for me this morning?"

"I'm not sure. What's your name?"

"Kelly Donovan. You checked me in last night."

"Of course, dear. I don't recall anyone leaving a message for you. There was something for a Lynette Peters and a Valerie Margaret."

"Could you double check for me, please?"

"Certainly. I'll be just a moment."

A "moment" became twelve hours. Kelly passed the time smoking borrowed cigarettes with a group of women who congregated on the front steps to trade gossip and watch the cars go by. She didn't dare go inside because she wanted to be the first person Vince saw when he came strolling up the sidewalk. It somehow fit better into the commercial.

Despite the horrendous wait, she remained in good spirits. It had been months since she'd enjoyed the privilege of smoking more than one cigarette at a time. She felt supremely light-headed, as if she'd spent the afternoon smoking marijuana instead of tobacco. Or maybe she'd been watching the cars pass for so long that her head was beginning to swim.

Perhaps Vince had car trouble and couldn't find help. He drove an old Buick that guzzled gas like a motorboat and broke down every few weeks. He was always complaining about the money involved in keeping it on the road. If he'd broken down near the shelter, he might be searching for her on foot. The moment that possibility entered her head, she was struck by a vision of him roaming the city streets, calling her name at the top of his lungs. The image was so clear that she could see his breath in the wind and perceive his frustration and fear.

She decided it would be best to go looking. The streets were her first home, and she felt a certain connection to them. Others had perished in their battle against the city, but she'd survived against incredible odds. If she could rise above all that, she could certainly find a man lost in the fog.

She realized too late that she should've borrowed a coat. The crisp October wind stung her eyes and drove a chill to the very core of her frail body. She sought comfort in a cloud of steam rising from a manhole cover on the street. As she walked along the faded yellow line that ran down the center of the road, she had the distinct feeling that she'd found her magical path, like Dorothy and her yellow brick road.

It didn't matter that Vince could've been stranded on any one of several roads. She had a feeling about East Maple. It was the kind of street that could make you forget about the soot-stained warehouses and abandoned office buildings found in most areas. For more than 50 years, local politicians had fought to keep it clean and unadulterated, diverting endless tax dollars to the upkeep of its beautiful parks and historical residences. Yes, East Maple was a place where good things happened. Perhaps the only place in the city where good things happened.

She was startled by the squeal of oversized tires on the wet pavement. An old man left his pickup and rushed to her side. His deeply lined face was kind and brutal at once. "What's wrong with you!" he screamed. "You can't just wander down the middle of the street in the fog! You could've gotten yourself killed."

Her hands began to shake. "I'm sorry. I didn't realize..."

"Where's your coat? It's freezing out here!"

"I don't... have one."

The man removed his faded brown parka and threw it over her shoulders. "Take mine. Would you like me to call someone for you? I have a cell phone in my truck."

A tear came to Kelly's eye. "There's no one to call."

"There's a women's shelter a couple miles from here. I could take you there, if you'd like."

"No, thank you. Someone is coming for me."

The man's face suddenly softened. "Are you sure about that, sweetie?"

"I'm sure."

"Would you at least go sit in my truck and wait? It's nice and warm in there. If it'll make you feel better, I'll call my wife and let you speak to her. You can't be too careful these days."

They circled the block until deep furrows appeared above the man's brow. Kelly declined the opportunity to use his cell phone and chose to fiddle with the heater vents instead. He flipped through countless stations on the radio, stopping only to catch the end of an old Sinatra ballad. Finally, he pulled into a stranger's driveway and fixed her with a penetrating gaze. "Where are your parents?" he asked. "Surely you must have a home."

"I hate my mother," she replied.

"Don't ever say that. Life is a long and winding road. Over time, the very people we hate most can become our greatest allies."

Kelly laughed a little. "You obviously don't know my mother."

"That doesn't matter. I only have to know the nature of things. I'm going to let you in on a little secret. I married the same woman two different times because I didn't know how to treat her when I was young. I screwed around until I found someone desperate enough to fall in love with a liar and a cheat. And do you know what I discovered? If you cancel one relationship, you'll end up replacing it with a brand new set of complications. It's best to work on fixing what you've got. Don't ever turn your back on love."

Kelly didn't have the strength to argue with a man who claimed to have seen and done it all. A thousand little noises were mixed up in her head, from the distant wail of a siren to the steady hum of the radio and the shrill bark of a neighborhood dog. The old man's craggy voice was just another sound to contend with. She recited her mother's address to shut him up.

This was all Darren's fault. He'd driven her over the edge and turned her into something no man could want. Vince might've stuck around if it hadn't been for the nightmares. In the end, he'd probably decided that her mental quirks were more than he could handle. He had the best of intentions, but when it came right down to it, who could blame him for not wanting to shack up with a lunatic?

Would it always be this way? Would she spend the rest of her life drifting from one public institution to another? How many shelters and funny farms would she have to endure before finding a place to call home?

It was all Darren's fault. All his fault! He'd turned her into a murderer— a person destined to live through hell on Earth and beyond.

She didn't bother to wake her parents. Experience had taught her that neither one of them had much to offer. She loved Carlos with all her heart, but in reality, he was just another link in the chain of events that had led her down the road to insanity. She didn't wish to wake him, didn't want to find comfort in his arms, didn't need to feel sorry for the very person who'd delivered her to Darren's front door.

All she needed from him could be obtained from a trip to the hall closet— a warm coat, a bit of cash, and a small hand gun, fully loaded.

✳ ✳ ✳ ✳ ✳

Benny might've stayed asleep if it weren't for all the shadows. Sometime during the night, flourescent moonbeams had burned holes through his flimsy window shade. Streams of light bounced off every flat surface in his apartment, turning ordinary walls into vast projection screens like the ones found in theaters. Reflected images of the past moved over his room in a frightening rush of color and sound.

A pair of ballroom dancers glided across his closet door. He liked the way the woman's ruffled petticoat swirled about her shapely legs. Would he ever dance like that with a woman again? He saw Kimmy Watkins in her silky lavender prom dress. A brush of that fabric against his neck was enough to set storms brewing in the pit of his stomach. Her moist, warm kisses lingered on his lips for years to come. He had a life once, damn it. He really had a life.

"Kimmy was not your life!" his ex-wife shouted. "You only dated her for a month."

Benny sat straight up in bed. "Yes, but it was a damned good month."

"I gave you ten years of my life! Shouldn't that count for something?"

"It was seven years, and they were miserable."

Benny's wife began to cry. "It might've been different if you hadn't talked to the voices more than you talked to me."

Benny slapped his hands over his ears. He didn't know much about keeping

152

a marriage together, but he was certain a woman had no right to punish a man for matters beyond his control. Maybe it was best that Kimmy had decided to move away for college. He would've only made her life miserable too.

He couldn't help but think of his young friend Darren. How many girls would he disappoint on his voyage through life? He seemed convinced that the jagged scar on his back would put an end to the voices for good. He was far too young to realize that life had a way of spinning out of control. Would he cut himself again, or would he come to accept that some things couldn't be fixed?

"Darren can't help you now," whispered Benny's seventh-grade teacher. "If you want to know the truth, he never really helped you at all."

Benny reached for the stocking cap on his bedside table. "That's not true! He brought the television and introduced me to Mrs. Patterson. You're just jealous because I have friends now. You liked me best when I had nothing better to do than argue with you."

"Nonsense! I only want to help you see things as they really are. Go ahead and cover your head with that ridiculous cap. It won't block me. I'll keep coming back."

Benny rushed to the bathroom and turned on the shower. The distant sound of a piano grated on his nerves. His teacher's shrill voice sent spikes through his ear canal. "Oh my darling, oh my darling, oh my darling Clementine..."

"No! Not that song! Sing any song but that."

"Rosy lips above the water blowing bubbles mighty fine. But alas I was no swimmer, so I lost my Clementine."

Dense clouds of steam rose from the bathtub and expanded to fill the air. His teacher's voice grew faint and disappeared. "I can't hear you!" Benny shouted at the ceiling. "Who's crazy now, Clementine?"

* * * * *

Mrs. Patterson's frantic voice crackled over the receiver. "He's doing it again!" she screamed. "Pacing the floor, talking to himself, yelling at people who aren't even there! I woke to find water dripping through the ceiling onto my antique doll collection. It turns out he flooded his apartment on purpose. Do you hear me, Darren? On purpose! He seems to think he can block radio waves in the air with steam."

Darren's heart turned over in his chest. "He's using HOT water?"

"Yes! It eventually ran cold, but only after he scalded his hands and feet."

"Put him on the phone."

"I can't! The police are up there with him now. I'm so sorry, Darren. I didn't know who else to call! You live so far away, and he doesn't have anyone else who can..."

"It's okay, Mrs. Patterson. How badly is he hurt?"

"Badly enough for them to call an ambulance!"

"Have you spoken to him?"

"Yes. He wants me to call a man named Rushing. He says he's the only person who can help him now."

Darren slammed the phone into its cradle. What had he done to the poor man? He'd encouraged Benny to take frequent baths in hopes that it would have a placebo effect, like the leech procedure. As long as Benny believed the voices couldn't reach him, he wouldn't hear them anymore, right?

"Wrong," Darren mumbled. Benny was on his way to the hospital, and it was all his fault. There was nothing he could do about his physical wounds, but he desperately wanted to know how he could right some of the other wrongs. He looked over at Dr. Rushing, who was fast asleep in the recliner with his hands tied loosely in front of him. Did he dare to ask for his advice? Would it be like admitting defeat? Would this failure serve to cancel out his other two victories?

Darren pulled two glasses from his liquor cabinet. He used the first to pour himself a double shot of Jack Daniels and smashed the second on the hardwood floor.

Dr. Rushing sat straight up in the recliner. "What's the matter?"

"Nothing. I just dropped a glass."

"How long have I been asleep?"

"A few hours, I guess. Would you like to watch some televison? I could bring the small set down from my bedroom."

It looked as if a candle had been lit behind Dr. Rushing's eyes. "Yes, that would be great!"

Darren cleaned up the broken glass while Dr. Rushing watched a rerun of the evening news. He'd never seen a man so absorbed in an account of a neighborhood recycling project. Perhaps the isolation was beginning to crush his spirit. Any news from beyond the guest house was good news to him.

Darren was careful to wait for a commercial break before hitting Dr. Rushing with the questions that burned deep within his heart. "Tell me something. Why do you suppose Benny thinks government surgeons implanted wires into his spine?"

"I don't know. Why did our ancestors believe thunder and lightening were clear signs that the gods were furious? When something frightening happens, there's a natural tendency to invent explanations for it. I once had a schizophrenic client who believed he'd been struck by lightening as an infant. I went to college with a fellow who was convinced the voices he heard came from inside the television."

"If Benny started hearing voices again, what could I do to stop it?"

Dr. Rushing looked deeply concerned. "Is he hearing voices, Darren?"

"Of course not. But it occurred to me that it could happen eventually. A placebo can't last forever, can it?"

"I would suggest a little hand holding. Talk to him, be his friend, and make damned sure he's taking his medication. How long has he been hearing voices?"

Darren was struck by the sudden urge to grab Dr. Rushing by the throat. "He's *not* hearing voices."

"Damn it, Darren! Do you want my help or not?"

Darren downed the rest of his drink and smashed the glass against the wall. "You think you know everything, don't you?"

"What are you drinking, Darren?"

"Mr. Harvard man—the apple of everyone's eye. Even the janitors in your office building buy you Christmas presents."

"Stop it. I didn't go to Harvard, and you know it."

"Well, you might as well have."

"Please tell me what happened with Benny. I have no intention of gloating. I don't care if it's you or me who is finally able to break through to him."

"Sure you don't! You're loving every minute of this, aren't you? You think I'm pathetic. I can see it in your eyes. As much as you'd like to rip the heart from my chest, underneath it all, you have only pity for me."

"That's not true, Darren."

"Need I remind you that I've already fixed two people you couldn't reach? I've helped Mr. Rivard to see that life is worth living, and I've shown Claire what it means to be loved by a man."

"Of course you have. In fact, I'm very proud of you."

"Don't placate me, asshole! I've fixed them, and you know it."

"That remains to be seen. I wish you all the luck in the world, but you have to understand that real therapy takes time. You can't keep equating humans with cars. They don't go into the shop one day and come out fixed the next."

Darren dropped the phone into Dr. Rushing's lap. "I've fixed Claire, and I can prove it."

"Don't do this, Darren. You're only hurting yourself."

"Call her!"

"But it's 3 o'clock in the morning."

"So what! Are you scared she'll tell you how much her life has changed now that someone gives a damn about her?"

"If I call her, will you put a cap on that Jack Daniels?"

"Sounds fair enough. Shall I dial her number?"

* * * * *

The phone ripped Claire from the depths of a peaceful slumber. "Hello?"

"Claire? It's me. Sorry to call so late, but..."

"Dr. Rushing! I thought you were out of town!"

"I'm on my way home. I was just calling to see how you're doing."

"I'm great. Did you think I'd fall apart in two weeks?"

"Of course not. I knew it would take at least three or four."

Claire laughed. "You seem to be in good spirits. How's your friend?"

"She's recovering quite nicely. What's new with you?"

"So many things! I'm not sure where to start. Do you have about three hours?"

"I don't know. It'll cost ya."

"Just put it on my tab."

Claire's head swam with silent thoughts as she described her first trip to the Price Estate. She couldn't believe Dr. Rushing had taken the time to call her from clear across the country. Even with so much turmoil going on in his life, her welfare was among his immediate concerns.

It was sort of like that other time he rang her up in the middle of the night. He'd crossed a very serious line just to share a little music and laughter. For some reason, it was very important for him to share in the joy of that Internet broadcast. Did other doctors do that sort of thing with their patients?

Of course they didn't. His concern for her went far beyond professional boundaries. The real question was, how far? Was she kind of like the little sister he never had, or was she something much more than that?

There was no better time to find out than the present. If he was the least bit attracted to her, he surely wouldn't want to hear all the juicy details about her new relationship. If there was a jealous bone in his body, she was about to find it.

She relived the details of her first encounter with Darren, carefully sugar-coating the X-rated parts. Using terms such as "messing around," "making out," and "down there," she provided a fairly accurate picture of what happened that night.

"Wow," Dr. Rushing said. "Sounds like you've been busy in my absence."

"I shouldn't be telling you all of this, but you're the only person I can talk to about deeply personal matters. I was tempted to call Brooke, but when it comes right down to it, our relationship is based on small talk and a shared interest in decorating."

"Don't worry about it. An amazing thing has happened in your life. Of course you're bursting to talk about it."

"I'm afraid to get too excited about this. What if the whole thing is sick?"

"Sick? Why would you say that?"

"Just before we kissed for the first time, Darren made a point to tell me that he sees beauty where others can't. What if I turn him on because I'm just as grotesque as his art? What if I'm sort of like his Bride of Frankenstein?"

"Claire, I don't ever want to hear you speak that way about yourself again."

"It's true, and you know it."

"It is most certainly *not* true! Your perception of what others think is totally distorted. I once heard a guy say you had a hot little body, and he was quite serious."

"Please. You're making that up."

"I am not."

"Who said it?"

Dr. Rushing hesitated. "One of the men who came to paint the office."

"Are you serious?"

"Dead serious."

Claire was silent for a moment. "What do *you* think of my body?"

"I'd prefer not to discuss that."

"Fine. I'm hanging up now."

"Wait! Your body is… very proportional. Not too thin and not too fat."

"Spoken like a true diplomat."

"Tell me more about this Darren fellow."

"He's quite talented. He can paint almost anything with astonishing accuracy. I saw a portrait of his ex-girlfriend. She makes Miss America look like chopped liver."

"That just proves he's interested in all types of women. Your assumption that he's searching for a Bride of Frankenstein is totally false."

"I never thought of it that way. Thanks, Dr. Rushing."

"You're welcome. Are you going to be okay with this now?"

"I guess so. A handsome rich guy wants to take me places and buy me stuff. What more could I ask for? A movie star?"

"Aren't you a little young to be so jaded?"

"I'm *not* jaded. I'm just not sure if Darren and I are right for each other."
"What makes you say that?"
"His motorcycle scares me. I guess I'll get used to it, but I'll never learn to like his music or his art. We saw a band called Sick Puppy at the Metro Dome. What a waste of a perfectly good evening! I can't help but wonder if I'd be dating him if he weren't the only guy in town who's willing to be seen with me."
Claire heard the distinct sound of glass shattering in the background. "Dr. Rushing? Are you okay?"
His voice quivered. "I'm… I'm fine. I just dropped my beer. It sounds as if you're thinking of cutting this Darren fellow loose."
"No way! Are you kidding? I haven't even experienced the full range of his talents yet. I want to go all the way—several times if I can help it."
Claire waited for Dr. Rushing to express concern about her sudden desire to lose her virginity. Much to her surprise, he didn't warn her to slow down or encourage her to wait around for the right person to come into her life. Only his choppy breaths gave away a hint of emotion. There almost seemed to be two sets of lungs blowing into the receiver. After much hesitation, Dr. Rushing spoke. "I trust you'll make sure this Darren fellow wears a condom."
"Is that all you have to say?"
"What would you like me to say, Claire?"
"Tell me not to do it. Tell me there are other options available to me."
Dr. Rushing mumbled something about professional standards just before the line went dead. The persistent hum of the dial tone was by far the most infuriating sound Claire had ever heard. The one time she'd found the courage to push the subject of their not-quite-professional relationship, he'd dropped out of the conversation. Perhaps he wasn't half the man she'd always believed him to be.

✶✶✶✶✶

Darren toyed with the phone chord he'd just ripped from the wall. He was determined not to look at Dr. Rushing, no matter what it took. He'd never felt more humiliated in his life, not even when Ron the bouncer painted his face and showed him exactly what a real sissy looked like.
"Come on, Darren," Dr. Rushing said. "It's really not so bad. No one has to know about any of this. Cut me loose, and I'll make us the biggest, sloppiest breakfast of our lives."
"How typical of you. I've brutalized you and taken over your life, and now you want to give me a pep talk with extra cheese and bacon. How does it feel

to always be right? What's it like to be so fucking noble and selfless?"

"Darren... "

"Please don't say another word. The more logical you are, the more it makes me want to wrap this chord around your neck."

"You'll do nothing of the kind. If you'd wanted to kill me, I'd be dead already. What do you say we skip past the theatrics and go straight to the part where we laugh about what fools we've been—you for tormenting me, and me for tormenting Claire."

Darren crossed the room slowly. "That'll never happen because I'm not the person you think I am. I've been molded by experiences you'd never imagine, and I've learned the hard way that it's best to destroy a threat before it destroys me. If I let you live, you'll always be the son my father wished he could've had and the man Claire really wanted in the first place."

Before Dr. Rushing could voice another logical argument, Darren tossed the phone cord over his neck and tightened it with ever-increasing force.

*****

Kelly bent over her favorite little pond to splash her face. The ice-cold water stung her cheeks in a curiously refreshing way. She'd been running down jagged trails for so long it was nearly impossible to absorb a chill from the cool October wind. A fierce animal sweat soaked her clothing down to the socks.

In years long past, the woods surrounding the Price Estate had been a place of comfort and refuge. As a child, she'd fantasized about building a cabin from branches that littered the ground after thunder storms. One fine August afternoon, Darren helped her construct a fort larger than her bedroom at home. They were just naive enough to think they could hide from the whole world in there.

Kelly wished she could rebuild that fort, throw Darren inside and secure it with the strength of ten thousand nails. If she had known then what she knew now, would she have found the courage to seal the door?

Of course she wouldn't have. She'd loved him more than life itself. Even then, he was terrifyingly beautiful. And he'd grown into something even more amazing. The simple, quiet love she felt for Vince was but a gentle breeze compared to the hurricane of passion that swept through her heart each time Darren pulled her into his arms.

Perhaps she'd loved him too much. She'd allowed herself to become something else just to please him. And he would do it to someone else if she didn't stop him.

The trail leading to Darren's house was frozen in some places and muddy in others. The soles of her standard-issue tennis shoes were barely adequate to provide traction. If she slipped and broke a leg, no one would hear her scream. The cab driver had warned her not to venture into the woods at night, but she'd told him to mind his own business.

The guest house was illuminated by a full moon. After all these years, it still reminded her of the gingerbread house in Hansel and Gretel storybooks. Now, she understood that the cheery paint job and neat cobblestone path were all part of a grand facade. It was nothing more than a house of horrors.

Peering into the window, she saw Darren hunched over a man in a recliner. His trembling shoulders told her he was locked in battle. The man's legs kicked and quivered as he struggled to break free from Darren's grasp. She briefly wondered what he'd done to arouse Darren's scorn. She decided it didn't matter. Darren shouldn't be allowed to kill again—not ever.

She retrieved the gun from her father's coat pocket and delivered a direct shot through the glass. She didn't expect to hit her target on the first try, but Darren's sudden loss of equilibrium indicated he'd been hit in the back. The blood was overwhelming. It seeped through the back of his white shirt and dripped from the back pockets of his faded jeans. As she watched him stumble forward and collapse, she felt a sudden liquid warmth radiate through her limbs. She recognized the feeling immediately. His blood was coursing through her veins. Its bitter taste clung to the back of her throat.

A light switched on in the main house. The family cocker spaniel bolted from the back door and headed in her direction. She turned to run but was startled by the sudden appearance of a crackled image in the shattered window. The anorexic bitch was back, and her pupils were fixed at opposite corners.

✳ ✳ ✳ ✳ ✳

The old woman's skin was like the tissue paper Benny used to find in Christmas boxes. A bright network of purplish veins shone through the surface of her sagging cheeks. Her long white hair was as soft and dry as shredded cotton balls.

He might not have recognized her if she hadn't wheeled over to his side of the courtyard and asked for a match. Her froggy voice was as harsh and abrasive as the day he last saw her. The detached mole hanging from her chin was still as plump as a California raisin.

"I hope you're happy, Mrs. Benedict."

"How... how do you know my name?"

"Don't give me that crap. I was one of your students. No one forgets Benny Simpson. You've got a nerve to keep tormenting me. I graduated more than 30 years ago."

"I'm a teacher?"

"You used to be, a long time ago."

"Yes, I suppose I was. Could I get a light, Lenny?"

Benny was surprised to see the old woman raise a pencil to her lips. "I can't light that!"

"Sure you can."

"But it's a piece of wood!"

Mrs. Benedict held his gaze with her cloudy blue eyes. "Give me those matches, damn it! I've had tubes up my ass all day. The least you could do is let me enjoy a good smoke."

Benny handed the woman his cigarette. "Take a drag off mine, but don't get your spit on it. It wouldn't be sanitary. I'd have to rinse with Listerine, and God knows I can't afford it."

He thought it was rather rude of her to turn away and smoke the whole thing by herself. Now, he would have to find someone to loan him another. Good thing there were plenty of addicts to choose from. The hospital courtyard was always crowded, even at 4 o'clock in the morning. No matter how sick or tired folks felt, they never seemed to forget how badly they wanted to smoke. Even some of the nurses couldn't resist the urge to step outside, and they were supposed to set an example.

"Don't mind Mrs. Benedict," said a comforting female voice. Benny turned to find a young nurse with perfect white teeth to match her uniform.

"But she stole my only cigarette!"

"She doesn't realize that. Just look at her."

Mrs. Benedict was now fascinated with a trial-sized bottle of vanilla scented lotion. An innocent smile came to her lips as she passed the open bottle under her nose. "Mmm."

"Don't eat that!" the nurse shouted. "It's for your hands."

Benny shook his head in disgust. So many years wasted. So much energy misapplied. A whole lifetime up in smoke.

* * * * *

The sight Roland encountered in his guest house at approximately 4 o'clock in the morning shot painful spikes into his chest. His only son lay face down on the floor in a pool of blood. His dearest friend sat lifeless in the recliner with a telephone chord wrapped around his neck. A portion of the chord entangled

Darren's left wrist, connecting him to Dr. Rushing in a bizarre fellowship of death.

Roland collapsed on the couch to collect his thoughts. What on God's Earth could've happened? After his cocker spaniel dragged him out of bed by the sleeve of his pajamas, he'd rushed outside to discover a woman stumbling among the pines. She was gone now, and so was everything he loved. He wouldn't have the opportunity to watch his wayward son grow into a responsible young adult. He would never again enjoy the comfort of his best friend's company by the fire. Was there a reason to go on living? He wished he could've died right along with them.

A strange, whistling sound jolted him back to the moment at hand. His eyes darted about the room in search of the source. Dr. Rushing's nostrils flared. A nervous twitch tugged at the corner of his eye.

Roland bolted across the room to loosen the chord that held his friend's life in check. Dr. Rushing choked on his first breath of air and fixed him with the questioning glance of a terrified animal. "Darren!" he gasped. "Where... is... Darren?"

Roland fumbled with the rope encircling Dr. Rushing's wrists. "He's dead, Thomas. There's nothing we can do."

Dr. Rushing scrambled out of the recliner and knelt beside Darren's blood-soaked body. "I can't find a pulse!"

Roland grasped his dear friend's wrist. "What's done is done."

"How can you say that! It may just be that my hands are numb from the rope. I can barely feel my fingertips. Send for an ambulance, and bring me a clean bed sheet. Your son is losing blood fast!"

"He'll do it again, Thomas. He's done it before, and we both know it."

"We know nothing!"

"But he tried to strangle you!"

"No! He never would've killed me, as much as he wanted to. The chord was tight around my neck, but not tight enough to close my airway. He looked down into my eyes and asked for help—begged for it, like a child asking not to be abandoned. A shot rang out, and he stumbled forward. The momentum of his fall pulled the chord even tighter."

Roland was struck with a profound sense of guilt. As he rushed to the linen closet for a pair of sheets, he had the ominous feeling that his actions were futile. By hesitating to stop the blood more quickly, he'd doomed his son to certain death.

A police and rescue team arrived on the scene within ten minutes. With all the confusion, Roland could just barely remember calling them. A fierce headache stabbed the back of his eyes. Through ringing ears, he heard Dr. Rushing explain that Darren was a disturbed patient who used scare tactics as a cry for help. He made it sound as if the "skirmish" was partly his own fault. He should never have become professionally involved in a friend's affairs. Roland couldn't help but stare at the young doctor he'd come to love so dearly. In many ways, he felt as if he'd been granted the gift of a second son. And what a brilliant son Thomas was. He seemed to be keenly aware that all casual statements leaving his lips would help seal Darren's fate. He spoke with grace and compassion, painting a picture of a terrified youngster in dire need of a long rest in a caring and professional environment.

The paramedics were loading Darren onto a stretcher when the police called Roland outside. Did he recognize the young woman lying on the ground with a gun just inches from her fingertips?

—Yes. Her name was Kelly Donovan, Darren's closest childhood friend.

Did he know why she'd fired the gun through Darren's window?

—She must've seen the struggle and tried to put an end to it.

It was all speculation at this point. A nasty lump on the girl's forehead explained why she was out cold, but how did it get there? Had she fainted from the shock of it all, or had she slipped on the half-frozen mud? Why was she carrying a gun in the first place? Was she as disturbed as Darren? Did she have some kind of grudge against him?

The answers came in the form of a journal delivered to the hospital by Kelly's stepfather, whose wallet was found in the pocket of her coat. Kneeling before Roland on the cold waiting room floor, Carlos explained that he'd lived with the terrible secrets of his past for long enough.

Chapter Twelve: The Past

The first time Kelly laid eyes on Darren, he was a hyperactive nine-year-old who could swing from one end of the jungle gym to the other like a trapeze artist at the circus. His pencil-thin arms were so astonishingly delicate she feared they would break under the strain of his own weight. He didn't look like a good candidate for one of Carlos' robbery schemes. His parents obviously couldn't afford to feed him well enough.

Taking a peanut butter sandwich from her back pack, Kelly approached Darren and asked if he wanted a bite. Just then, fat ass Shelly Whipple wheeled over on her bicycle. "Don't talk to him!" she demanded. "He has AIDS."

"AIDS?"

"It's a disease faggots get from rubbing their butts together. That's why he's so skinny."

"Get out of here. He's not old enough to rub butts with anybody."

"You don't understand. His dad is a faggot, and he passed the disease on to his son."

Kelly looked up at Darren. "Is your dad a faggot?"

"Nope. He's a college professor."

"That doesn't mean anything," Shelly said. "You can be a faggot and a professor at the same time."

Kelly made a mental note to put Shelly's family at the top of Carlos' list. "How would you like a mouth full of dirt?"

"Go on and try it, bitch face. I'm way bigger than you."

Kelly grabbed a handful of Shelly's long blond hair and pulled her off the bike. She hit the ground with a surprisingly loud thud, splitting her bottom lip on the oily metal chain. The sight of her blood made Kelly's heart smile. "The bigger they are, the harder they fall," she sneered.

Eyes blazing with anger, Shelly jumped to her feet. "But the smaller they are, the farther they fly!"

Before Kelly could step out of the way, Shelly came charging at her like a bull. The impact of her head on Kelly's stomach was excruciating. The blow knocked the wind from her chest and sent her flying through the air. She came to rest on a soft patch of grass five feet away from the spot where she'd been pushed.

Shelly was doing a snide little victory dance when Darren approached. Grasping both of her chubby cheeks in his hands, he cleared his throat and hocked a giant spit ball at her face. "Look who has AIDS now!" he screamed.

Eyes filled with spit, Shelly swung her fits at a target she could no longer see. Darren danced in front of her, ducking her jabs like a proud peacock.

When Shelly's older brother rushed to her defense, Kelly knew there was no more time for games. Grasping Darren's arm, she made a break for the dense row of trees that ran along the northern border of the property. After running nonstop for what seemed like 20 minutes, they passed through the woods and came to rest at a giant clearing with lush green grass. A golden brown house with light pinkish trim stood near the back of the clearing, looking curiously like the gingerbread house in Hansel and Gretel storybooks. Several yards beyond the cottage, a red brick church stretched up to the sky.

Darren panted like a dog trapped in a hot car. "That's my house! Let's get something to drink." Kelly headed straight up the cobblestone path leading to the gingerbread cottage. She was surprised to see Darren running for the church. Didn't he say he was going for a drink?

"Come on!" Darren shouted over his shoulder. "Last one there is a big fat turd!"

He led Kelly through the back of the church first. The room he called a kitchen was more like a small restaurant. Real leather booths like the ones in diners were built into the walls. The oversized appliances were made of stainless steel that glinted under a large skylight. A whole boatload of pots and pans clung to a rack suspended from the ceiling. "How many people live in this house?" she asked.

"Just me, my dad and the maid."

"So how come you need so many pots?"

"I don't know. I never thought to ask."

As Darren mixed an extra-sugary batch of raspberry punch, Kelly studied the unique collection of sketches that covered every inch of space along the dining wall. She recognized the little pond in the woods as the backdrop for many of the outdoor scenes. Though she'd only passed the pond once, she remembered its curious half-moon shape and its position within a circle of trees. "Who drew all this stuff?"

"I did."

Kelly zoomed in on a picture of three rabbits drinking from the water's edge. "Did you trace those rabbits into your picture?"

"I don't trace anything. I see things in a certain way and put them down on

paper."
"That's amazing."
"Not really. My dad says everyone has a gift. Mine just happens to be drawing."
Kelly's mouth dropped to a frown. "I don't have any gifts."
"Sure you do."
"Oh yeah? Like what?"
"Like you're the prettiest girl I've ever seen. That's a gift, isn't it?"
Kelly looked down at her feet. She couldn't understand why her insides suddenly jumped to her throat. The feeling was awful and wonderful at the same time. "Show me the rest of the house!" she demanded.

Kelly had never seen a spectacle so grand as the Price Estate. The dining room had a massive chandelier with hanging crystal teardrops that shimmered above a shiny wooden table long enough to seat 20 people. No matter where you looked, a beautiful painting stared back at you. She became lost in a world of radiant blond angels and half-naked cherubs—a world where gowns fluttered and infinite happiness could be found in the sharing of grapes.

The front parlor was a stuffy place with old fashioned doll house furniture. She was almost afraid to step on the light mauve carpet or brush past the creamy silk sofa in her dirty play clothes. The family room had a pool table, a fireplace and a television screen taller than Darren himself!

There were only three bedrooms in the big house. The largest one had fancy glass doors that opened into a giant bathroom with a hot tub and a skylight. Darren's room had a big bed in the shape of a rocket ship and a real basketball hoop built right into the wall. The third room was where the maid slept. Darren was not allowed to open that door. Kelly was amazed to discover that the whole upstairs was just a bunch of empty rooms. You could run from one end of the long hallway to the other and listen to the echo of your footsteps race behind you. She figured a person could turn at least ten cartwheels before running out of floor space. To prove her theory, she did hand springs across the floor until she came to the window at the end of the hallway.

They spent the afternoon practicing gymnastics until Roland came upstairs to see what all the thumping was about. He urged them to come down for dinner, but Darren wouldn't hear of it. He hated roast duck and wanted the maid to prepare bacon sandwiches instead. Roland commented that he didn't care if the boy ate worms as long as he showed some interest in nutrition.

While the maid prepared a special supper just for him, Darren constructed a tent from old blankets and rusty metal folding chairs. Kelly wondered why he would choose to camp indoors when there was such a fine tree house near

166

the pond and a real, honest-to-goodness swimming pool on the eastern end of the property. Maybe he didn't need all that stuff to be happy. As they shared a supper of bacon and fruit loops inside the tent, she wished Mom and Carlos would learn to find joy in simple pleasures.

It didn't take long for Kelly to figure out that Darren was different from the boys who sent her Valentines at school. As amazing as his life was, he didn't like to go on about himself. He didn't bore her with sports talk or brag about all the kids he could whip in a fight if it came right down to it. Instead, he asked endless questions about her life. He wanted to know her favorite color and her least favorite day of the week. He asked if there was a certain food she liked so much she could eat it every single day for the rest of her life. He wondered how long she could hold her breath under water, how much she could eat without puking and how far she could run without stopping. Most of all, he wanted to know why she didn't hesitate to stand up to a girl twice her size.

Kelly explained that learning to fight was as important as learning to ride a bike in her world. "Where I come from, you're nothing if you can't kick ass. It's like being able to walk or talk. You're not even a whole person unless you know how to scare other people and make them toe the line. You're something less than a person, like an ant crawling along the sidewalk or a worm rolling around in the mud."

"Are you serious? Where do you live, in a boot camp?"

Kelly laughed. "No, I live in an old green house on a dirty little street that runs behind a junkyard. There's a police station right around the corner, and even the cops can't keep people from stealing cars and breaking into houses. Gangs rule the playgrounds, and if you dare to set foot in their territory after dusk, you could get yourself shot or even worse."

Darren looked a bit confused. "What could be worse than getting shot?"

"Getting raped."

"Is that when a guy throws you down on the ground and rips off your shirt to get a look at your boobs?"

"It's worse than that. It's when a guy forces his parts into your parts."

Darren screwed up his face. "Gross! I'm glad I'm a boy. Has that ever happened to you?"

"No, but it happened to my friend Clarissa, and she couldn't come back to school for five whole months. I'm not supposed to talk about it because it makes me have nightmares. When something upsets me, I dream about it over and over again until my head hurts."

"That's awful. I wouldn't go near that playground if I were you. You could get your parts hurt, too."

"Not me! I have two pitt bulls for protection and a rottweiler that weighs more than a full grown man. No one messes with me when I walk down the street. With the right command, my baby will rip a man's eyes out of their sockets."

"Wow! I wish I could take your rottweiler to school with me."

"How come? Do people pick on you all the time?"

Darren looked at the floor. "Yes."

"Why do they think you're gay?"

"Because my father speaks with an English accent and wears pastel suits with matching socks and handkerchiefs."

"I think that's classy."

"You do? It makes me want to puke."

"Your dad should be able to wear what he wants. You can't judge a person by the way they dress."

"It's not just that. They think he's a faggot because there's no mom in my house."

"That's stupid. You know what you need?"

"What?"

"A crash course in kickin' ass."

"It wouldn't matter. I'm so small a girl could lick me."

"That's not true! You just have to know a few tricks. Like did you know you can blind a guy by shoving your palm up his nostrils?"

"Really?"

"Yes, really."

"Do you know any other tricks?"

"Sure. If a bigger guy punches you, it's a waste of time to punch him back. Raise your right arm like you're going to hit him, and slam your foot into his nuts. Don't get too confident when he's doubled over in pain. He can come back and surprise you. Knock him over while he's still recovering his balance and kick the living shit out of him."

Darren's eyes lit up like candles. "Show me!"

For the next hour, they practiced fighting maneuvers. In the beginning, she played the role of the attacker, and he defended himself against her advances. When they tired of that, they reversed their roles. As the evening drew to a close, Darren threw a punch that grazed the side of her chin. It felt more like a play slap than a serious attempt at self-defense. "You hit like a girl," she said. "We'll have to work on that next time."

When Kelly met Carlos at the playground that evening, she had an amazing tale to tell. She bragged about a boy who could draw pictures as clear and accurate as the ones found in books. His name was Darren, and he lived smack dab in the middle of a junkyard on the other side of the woods. His arms were thin like pencils because his family couldn't afford groceries, and his maid served Fruit Loops for dinner.

"Slow down," Carlos said. "If Darren's family can't afford groceries, how do they pay the maid?"

Kelly's heart skipped a beat. "She works for free because she's like a mom to Darren."

Carlos shook his head. "No one works for free, my love."

"Some people do."

"You know what I think?"

"What?"

"I think you're lying to Carlos."

"I'm not lying."

"If memory serves me, there is no junkyard beyond those trees. There's a small gated community nestled in the woods. The area is well known for its mansions."

"Mansions?"

"Big pretty houses like the ones where movie stars live."

Kelly was silent for a moment. "It doesn't matter, anyway. There's a big fancy alarm system—the best money can buy. And then there's all the dogs. Five or six of them at least."

"Shit!" Carlos said.

Kelly breathed a sigh of relief. "I guess we'll have to check out some of those other mansions, right?"

They drove home in silence, never bothering to sing along with the radio or finish the alphabet game they'd started on their way to the suburbs. Just before they reached the outskirts of the city, Carlos pulled the car to the side of the road and looked directly into her eyes. "Why do you lie to me?" he asked. "I would lay down and die for you, and this is how you repay me."

Kelly struggled to think of a good excuse for her deception. "I only lied because I didn't want you to try anything that would get you arrested. I meant what I said about the alarm system. Darren had to punch in codes to get through the back door."

"And the dogs?"

"I lied about that part."

Carlos raised an eyebrow. "What's the place like?"

"It's real pretty, but there's not much to steal. The whole upstairs is nothing but empty rooms—honest. The downstairs has some nice stuff, but the television is way too big to carry alone, and you can't exactly sling the pool table over your shoulder. It's not the kind of place with lots of portable gadgets laying around. Everything is built into walls or special nooks. There was some fancy china in the dining room, but nothing you'd be interested in. Good luck selling flowered plates at the crack house."

"Any jewelry boxes?"

"I didn't see any. Darren's mom lives in England with his sister, and she took all the jewelry with her when she left. I know because I asked the maid if there was anything to play dress up."

Carlos ran his fingers through Kelly's long hair. "That's my girl," he said. "She has the instincts of a cat."

That night, a strange feeling moved through the pit of Kelly's stomach. She wasn't sure what led her to crawl through the dark house and crouch beside her parent's bedroom door. She only knew that her pretty little bedroom was no longer a place of refuge. Her parents could no longer be trusted to rule her life. They were dangerous, dangerous people.

Sure enough, they were talking about the mansions in the woods and the startling fact that Kelly was able to find her way into one of them. They considered using Kelly to steal China and silver, but it seemed like such a waste to go after trinkets when untold riches were sitting in the family's bank account. They thought about kidnaping Darren and asking for a ransom, but the odds weren't in their favor. Even if they succeeded in exchanging the boy for a briefcase full of cash, the bills were sure to be marked. Besides, a man as rich as Roland didn't have to rely upon an overtaxed FBI force to help him track down kidnappers. With a few phone calls, he could have the very finest private investigators in the country working for him. It was risky, risky business. If they landed in prison, what would happen to their little girl?

Finally, at half past midnight, they concluded that some opportunities were simply not worth the risk.

*****

The Present

Lingering just outside the hospital waiting room with a tattered copy of yesterday's newspaper, Dr. Rushing tried to appear as if he wasn't beside himself with curiosity. The stout Hispanic man had Roland's attention, and there was no getting it back. The two of them had wandered over to a desolate corner of the waiting room with a hand-written manuscript. It was abundantly clear they wanted to be left alone.

How did it all come to this? Darren was currently undergoing surgery to remove bullet fragments from his buttocks. All in all, he was the luckiest son of a bitch in town. If just one of the fragments had struck a fraction of an inch higher, he could've been paralyzed for life.

The stout man's daughter was in much greater danger. The lump on her head had swollen to the size of a golf ball. There was no telling when she'd wake up. The longer she remained unconscious, the greater her chances of slipping into a coma.

Dr. Rushing's heart went out to both of them, but he could hardly feel depressed. He was grateful to be alive at all. In spite of a nagging sore throat, he downed three cups of hot chocolate and two bags of barbeque potato chips. He couldn't recall the last time stale food from a vending machine tasted quite so sweet.

To pass the time, he made a mental list of all the things he'd been putting off in life, including the purchase of a motorcycle, a trip to Hawaii and a long overdue visit to his mother in Florida. Above all, he wanted to make things right with Claire. Listening to her describe her dates with Darren had been the most difficult thing he'd ever had to do. The mere thought of them groping each other in the dark made him want to smash windows with a baseball bat.

If only he had acted on his feelings a little sooner, he could've been that special person with whom she shared her first sexual adventures. He could've taken her to her first real concert and introduced her to the simple joy of having someone to hang out with on a Saturday night. How could he have been so shallow and immature? If life was just a never-ending homecoming dance where men were defined by the beauty of the women standing next to them, he had no desire to attend the ball.

What he really wanted was a girl who shined in blue jean moments. He didn't need a prom queen to accompany him on long walks or help him choose movies at the video store. He longed for a loving and attentive person who could breathe new life into all the dull moments that came between work and sleep, and Claire held the power to do that for him. He'd always felt strangely excited in her presence. He couldn't wait for their Monday appointments, and it showed. The night he called to tell her about the web broadcast was a prime example of his need to include her in everyday adventures. He'd been reaching out to her, even then.

He planned to make time alone with Claire as soon as possible. He didn't worry that she already had a boyfriend who was currently laid up in the hospital. She may have been flattered and aroused by Darren's advances, but she'd made it abundantly clear that he was just a fun alternative to what she really wanted in life. It was too late to catch Claire on her way to work, so he decided to pay a visit to her apartment around 5 o'clock. In the meantime, he had eight hours to kill, and he was itching to find out what had happened to Benny.

The ride to Benny's apartment took longer than it should've. Rush hour traffic kept him on the freeway for close to two hours. Normally, he would've grown more and more impatient with each passing moment, but today was a very special day. He thought of the traffic jam as a grand reintroduction to the hustle and bustle of everyday life.

His mood took a sharp turn for the worse when Benny's neighbor told him about the freak accident that had occurred the night before. Gripped by a sudden rush of fear and anxiety, he jumped behind the wheel of his car and headed straight back to the hospital. The nurse who directed him to Benny's room was a tall redhead with expressive green eyes. Ever so tactfully, she explained that Benny's first degree blisters would heal much more quickly than his mind. She was particularly concerned about Benny's tendency to roam the corridors on bandaged feet. He made frequent trips to the courtyard for cigarette breaks, talking to himself along the way. A wheelchair had been provided, but he refused to use it.

"It gets pretty hectic here," the nurse said. "I'd love to accompany your friend to the courtyard, but I'm usually much more busy than I'd like to be. Is there a chance we could redirect him to a "special" wing of the hospital until he's well enough to be released?"

"You don't have to dance around the subject of Benny's mental condition. I'm the man's psychiatrist."

The woman flashed him a set of brilliant white teeth. "I see. Aren't you a little young to be a doctor?"

Dr. Rushing managed a polite nod. He couldn't remember the last time a beautiful woman's smile failed to make his heart flutter. "You may redirect him anywhere you wish."

He found Benny pacing the floor with an unlit cigarette dangling from his lips. The bandage that should've been wrapped around his swollen right hand was tossed carelessly over the radiator.

"Hello, Benny."

"Dr. Rushing! Thank God you're here. We have to find my friend Darren.

He's in great danger."

"Sit down for a moment. I'm sure he'll be okay."

"You don't understand! He thinks the government put a computer chip in his spine. A few years ago, he ripped himself open with a razor blade to remove it! He thinks he's cured now, but he'll do something even more horrible if the voices come back. And believe me, they *always* come back."

"It sounds as if your friend may be sick."

"You don't know the half of it! He lives in a mansion and pretends to be poor."

"Why would he do a thing like that?"

"Because he's lonely. He wants people to think he's a regular guy, but he'll never be regular because of the voices."

"What makes his voices so different from yours? What makes you regular and him crazy?"

Benny looked at Dr. Rushing as if he were three years old. "Do I have to spell it out for you? We're BOTH crazy. He just doesn't know it yet!"

Dr. Rushing slipped his arm around Benny's trembling shoulders. "I have to hand it to you, my friend. You've got more going on in your head than I give you credit for. How long have you known that the voices aren't real?"

"Not nearly long enough. If only she could've stumbled across my path sooner."

"Who are you talking about?"

"My seventh-grade teacher. She has a room right upstairs! Would you believe she doesn't even remember me?"

"Don't let it bother you. Teachers see hundreds of new faces each year."

"That's not the point! She has Alzheimer's disease. She goes around smoking pencils and tasting hand lotion. She's much too preoccupied to be monitoring the life of an old student she never liked in the first place. The voice I hear bitching all the time can't belong to her. It must come from someplace inside my head."

Dr. Rushing felt a smile tugging at the corners of his mouth. "I'm so proud of you, Benny. You have no idea how proud."

"This isn't about me. If I give you Darren's address, would you check on him for me?"

"Of course I will."

"And would you get him to a hospital?"

"I'll get him the help he needs. I promise you that."

Chapter Thirteen: The Past

Carlos allowed Kelly to play with Darren a few times a week, as long as she promised not to forget about establishing relationships with other children in the area. On rainy days, they made a game of sharing gross secrets in their tent, like the fact that Kelly used to pee the bed and the revelation that Darren didn't mind the smell of his own farts. Eventually, the game evolved into a competitive sport, and they took great pride in grossing each other out. They insisted upon chewing with their mouths open to see who could produce the largest slime ball. They kept track of who could spit the farthest and ate cold beans from a can to get an edge in farting contests.

On sunny days, they roamed the woods in search of animals and reproduced everything they saw on paper. Kelly's rough sketches looked like the work of a kindergartner next to Darren's elaborate drawings, but he cherished them just the same. He made room for her art on the kitchen wall and sent her home with vivid sketches of his own.

As spring unfolded before her eyes, Kelly discovered that the woods were a sacred place where tiny miracles happened each day. If you learned to stay completely still, you could catch a whole family of racoons walking single file along the edge of the pond. If you could get used to the feeling of mud seeping between your toes, you could peer down into the water and watch crayfish use their funny little claws to hunt tadpoles. If you laid down on your back and looked straight up at the sky, you could watch the treetops dance in changing currents of wind.

Their competitive spirits followed them wherever they went. Since Darren couldn't lick her in a fight, he took great pride in trapping more critters than she could catch. He filled mason jars with leeches and threw crayfish into sand buckets by the dozen. It took about a month for her to learn his secret. Each evening before dusk, he sank three buckets into the mud along the shoreline. When she wasn't looking, he retrieved the buckets and netted any creature that caught his fancy.

Sometimes, other children visited the pond to trap critters in mason jars and watch them grow over time. Older boys used the pond as a private place to smoke marijuana and trade pictures of half-naked women rolling around on the hoods of fast cars. Shelly Whipple's brother David was almost 13 years old, and he could get the kind of pictures that elementary schoolers would pay good money to look at. The women were completely naked in his photos, and they were much too busy to roll around on top of cars.

The day after school let out, David stopped by the pond to help Darren build a crude raft. He seemed to have forgotten all about Darren's confrontation with his sister, but Kelly knew better. He was desperate to sell a picture of two women munching carpet for $20. Rumor had it that his parents never gave him money because he always came home smelling like marijuana. Other kids at the pond had placed small bids on the picture, but Darren was the only one who carried ten dollar bills.

"Why would I want to buy a picture of two girls making it?" Darren asked. "That's a little weird, isn't it?"

"What are you talking about? This picture is hot."

"What's so hot about two girls?"

"Jesus. If I have to explain why this picture is hot, you must be as queer as everyone says."

"I'm not queer."

"Oh yeah? You play with little girls, don't you?"

"How does that make me queer? You're the one showing off pictures of lesbians."

A group of younger children snickered. David's face grew red on the spot. "Two girls making it is hot. If I had a picture of two guys, that would be queer. I wouldn't expect you to know the difference. You're a little faggot if I ever saw one."

Kelly's blood began to boil. "He's not a faggot, and nobody wants to look at your stupid pictures. Go show them to someone who cares."

David inched toward Kelly with frightening precision, as if calculating the number of steps from his spot in the sand to hers. When she turned to run, he lifted her off the ground and tossed her into the pond. Her butt hit the mud with a big slurp. Each time she tried to stand up, it sucked her back down again.

Darren held out his hand to help Kelly to her feet, but David grabbed hold of his collar to keep him from advancing forward. "Go ahead and save her," he sneered. "She's waiting for her faggot in shining armor."

David's taunting quickly took on a more brutal tone. He twisted Darren's arm behind his back and threatened to break it in half if he didn't hold still. Darren cried like a baby, sucking big gulps of air between hysterical sobs. Empowered by her own anger, Kelly pulled herself from the muck and delivered a swift kick to David's groin. She expected him to double over in pain, but his reaction was much more brutal. He dug his fingernails into Darren's shoulders and held on for dear life. "Fucking bitch!" he screamed.

"Pussy!" she retorted. "Only sissy cunt boys go around picking on kids half their size."

Her hope was that David would turn his attention back to her, but he directed every once of his anger toward Darren. Cursing nonstop, he threw Darren to the ground and tore the leather belt from his waist. Her eyes flooded with tears as she watched him deliver three solid whacks to Darren's bare legs. She could almost feel the blisters rising on her own flesh.

Frantically, she searched the shoreline for stray rocks, but none were large enough to deliver an adequate blow to David's head. With no further options, she took a running start and jumped onto his back. He stumbled backward and came crashing down on top of her. Her spine hit the earth with the force of their combined weight. For one terrifying moment in time, she found herself completely paralyzed.

She could only watch in horror as David tore Darren's shirt wide open and exposed his bare chest to the quickening wind. With a grand, sweeping gesture, he swiped a leech bucket from Darren's critter collection and held it up to the afternoon sun. "I know what queers like," he muttered between clenched teeth. "They like to be sucked raw."

David sprinkled half the bucket over Darren's frail body and dumped the remaining leeches behind the waistband of his shorts. A blood-curdling scream escaped Darren's lips as the slimy creatures attached themselves to his pores.

Laughing hysterically, David walked over to Kelly and kicked her in the ribs. The pain sent violent shudders up her spine and restored sensation to her lifeless limbs. When he bent to open her shirt, she flung two handfuls of dirt into his eyes. "Bitch!" he screamed. "I'm going to kill you!"

When David stumbled over to the pond to rinse his face, Kelly used the opportunity to help Darren to his feet. They ran as fast as they could, linking arms to break through a crowd of children who'd gathered to watch the fight. Adrenaline propelled her legs forward and elevated her mind to a new state of awareness. The woods suddenly smelled of cheap cologne and stagnant water. The trees were sick and wilted. The path leading to the playground swarmed with ugly and obvious humanity.

Up to that moment, she'd always believed Darren led a privileged life on his magnificent wooded estate. In her mind, the suburbs were a safe haven— a luxurious home away from home. People didn't need horse dogs for protection, and little girls like her friend Clarissa didn't end up with broken bottles in their vaginas. As the woods flashed before her eyes in a frightening rush of color, she was struck by the revelation that there were no safe corners in the universe.

They washed up in the guest house to avoid confronting the maid with the horrific evidence of their encounter. Following Darren's instructions, she used basic kitchen matches to burn scores of leeches from places she would never dare to touch under normal circumstances. Like a paramedic running against the clock, she was too wired to be embarrassed about handling his naked body. Her heart bled for him. It was as simple as that.

Sharing a bath with Darren didn't seem so awkward at the time, but the nature of their relationship changed after that. They were created differently, and there was no sense in tromping around the woods like two rambunctious little boys. As spring gave way to summer, Darren made an effort to put the luxuries of his estate to good use. If Kelly wanted to take a dip in the pool, he didn't insist upon going to the pond instead. If she felt like playing wife in his exquisite little playhouse, he let her rearrange the lifelike furniture and fill empty pop bottles with fresh dandelions. They no longer engaged in gross out contests. If she accidentally hocked up a goober while clearing her throat, she refrained from showing it to him. Deep within her heart, she wanted him to start looking upon her as a lady.

By the end of the summer, they missed the woods so much that they were willing to brave the dangers. For his tenth birthday, Darren asked for a pair of camouflage outfits and an expensive set of walkie talkies. He reasoned that they could keep out of harm's way if they avoided the trail leading to the playground and stayed away from the pond. If they found any trouble, they could contact the maid by radio. Kelly's heart fluttered wildly the first time she stepped back into the woods. The fresh scent of pine greeted her on the trail, and the trees appeared strong and healthy again. Their brilliant leaves captured all shades between yellow and red. She finally understood why the pool and playhouse were not among Darren's most valued possessions.

Even when dressed as super commandos, they didn't play as they used to. Darren pestered her to climb trees and pretend to be a princess stuck in a tower. She suspected he liked to rescue her because he'd never had the chance to do it in real life. She put up with his stupid games because she couldn't imagine spending Saturday afternoons with anyone else.

Almost overnight, he grew a little taller and a little stronger. By October, he could outrun her on the trail. He got off on reminding her that he was a few months older and a full inch taller. Sometimes, out of the clear blue, he lifted her off the ground and carried her around like a baby. It was annoying as hell, but she understood that he needed to do it almost as much as she needed to keep gross secrets to herself.

One day, they were flipping through channels on the big television when the remote control died. As Darren roamed the house in search of a new battery, Kelly was forced to watch two horny soap stars making out. He returned to find her sitting on the sofa with her hands closed over her eyes.

"Why are you covering your face? Aren't you allowed to watch this kind of stuff?"

"I always hide my face when people kiss."

"Why? Do you think it's gross?"

"Not gross. Just embarrassing. I mean, why does he have to stuff his tongue down her throat like that? It's a silly place to look for a snack."

"A snack is the last thing on that guy's mind, and you know it."

"Maybe."

"I think you should uncover your eyes."

"Why?"

"Because I'm going to kiss you like that one day, and you should know what to expect."

Kelly's heart skipped a beat. "You are not!"

"Fine. I won't then."

She uncovered one eye. "Never?"

"Never, ever."

"Well, it doesn't have to be never. You can do it one day, as long as you brush your teeth first."

"Are you trying to say my breath stinks?"

"Not at all. I just wouldn't want there to be any food stuck in that space between your cheek and gums."

"Good point. Will you brush your teeth, too?"

"Sure. Why not?"

"We should brush our tongues while we're at it. My dentist says most of the bacteria in a person's mouth lives there."

Kelly ran her fingernail across her tongue and showed Darren the yucky yellowish film trapped under her nail. "Are you sure you want to do this?"

"Yes. When can we start?"

"I don't know. Soon."

"How soon?"

"Darren! I can't predict the day and time. We have to wait for a moment."

"A moment?"

"Yeah. I can't explain it, but you'll know when it comes. There'll be an awkward pause in the conversation, and we'll just start staring into each other's eyes."

"Good idea. We'll wait for a moment."

The truth was, Kelly wanted to kiss Darren more than just about anything, but the very thought of it made her cheeks feel hot and moist. What if they bumped noses and had to start over again? What if she didn't know what to do with her tongue when she got it into his mouth? Even worse, what if she did? What if she liked it a little too much?

For the next few weeks, Kelly paid special attention to her mouth. One afternoon, she brushed her tongue so thoroughly that she could barely taste anything for the rest of the day. Despite all her efforts, Darren didn't seem to notice her ultra fresh breath. He only wanted to play in the woods, and he wouldn't even hold hands when they walked across the pond knee deep in sledge. He was slowly but surely driving her crazy, and she decided to tell him so one day when he had the nerve to drag a whole box of army figurines to the backyard.

"What are those for?" she asked. "You know I don't like war games."

"We could take some battle ships to the pond, if you want."

"Stop it, Darren. Why are you treating me like a boy?"

Instead of answering her question, he plopped down on the ground and began to dig trenches for his little green men. When he finally looked up, tears were streaming down her face. "Geez," he said. "You don't have to cry about it. We could go build a tent or something, if that's what you want."

For some reason she couldn't fully understand, Kelly felt like kicking him in the head. To avoid doing that, she booted his toy box clear across the lawn, sending dozens of plastic figurines into the air. When all was said and done, he looked up at her as if she'd suddenly sprouted horns. "Do you feel better now?" he asked.

"No, I don't feel better! I've brushed my tongue every single day, and you haven't even noticed."

Darren jumped to his feet and took Kelly into his arms. Her pounding heart grew still as he stroked her long, dark hair. "It's not that I don't want to kiss you. It's just that I can't."

"How come?"

"I can't say."

"Come on! You can tell me."

"But it's a secret."

"That's a bunch of crap! I know all of your secrets."

"This secret is different. It's worse than liking the smell of my own farts or eating paste in kindergarten."

"I never told anybody about either one of those things. You can trust me."

"All right. If you tell me your very biggest secret, I'll tell you mine."

Kelly looked down at her feet. "I can't do that," she said firmly.

"See! It's not so easy, is it?"

"Okay, okay. If you must know, my parents are drug addicts, and they steal things from people."

Darren's mouth dropped wide open. "Wow. That's a pretty big secret."

"You don't know the half of it. I was supposed to take things from your house, but I wound up liking you too much to do it, and my dad wound up liking you, too."

Darren couldn't conceal the mile-wide grin on his face. "That's pretty cool!"

"It's *not* cool. It sucks!"

"Well, it sucks that you were going to steal from me, but it's cool that you liked me too much to go through with it. People don't just go around liking me, and the truth is, I can't blame them."

Kelly pulled away from him. "That's the dumbest thing I've ever heard. What's not to like about you?"

"Believe me, there's plenty."

"What are you talking about?"

"I'm talking about my big secret, Kelly. The kids at school are right about me and my dad."

"Don't be stupid. Your dad isn't gay."

"That's what you think. I saw him hugging some man outside the guest house a few weeks ago."

"That doesn't mean anything! Roland hugs everyone, even the maid when he feels like it."

"This was different. It was late at night, and I was upstairs getting the tent ready for your next visit. I looked down into the yard, and I saw him cuddling this dude. They went into the guest house and stayed five whole hours."

"I think you're jumping to conclusions. It could've been an old friend or a long lost cousin."

"Maybe so, but I can't take any chances. Before I kiss you, I have to make sure I don't have anything you could catch."

Kelly stuck her nose in Darren's face. "I'm not afraid. Kiss me!"

"But Kelly…"

"Just do it!"

Darren grasped Kelly's waist and looked deeply into her eyes. He was so close she could smell his raspberry breath and see droplets of sweat forming on his upper lip. She wondered if he was waiting for the precise "moment" she'd described a few weeks ago, but there was much more to it than that. He was frozen in place. It was up to her to make things happen.

At the precise moment when her mouth grazed the surface of his lips, he turned and ran for a patch of trees in the distance. Her heart chased after him, but her feet remained firmly planted on the ground. She watched him grow smaller and smaller until he was finally swallowed by a twist in landscape.

The following day, they struck a bargain. She wouldn't ask to be kissed as long as he stopped treating her like a boy. They could hold hands when walking through the sledge because it was too easy to slip, and it would only be fair to go down together. They could hug when they felt like it, which wasn't very often. On special days, when the sun shone down upon the water at just the right angle, she could lay her head in his lap and look for random patterns in the clouds above.

*****

The Present

Mr. Rivard slammed the phone down in disgust. He'd been trying to reach Darren all day, but the kid was nowhere to be found. It didn't make sense. Just a week ago, he'd seemed so excited about the exhibition. He sent daily e-mails to contribute new ideas and discuss last-minute details. He'd been a little upset about the need to rent mailing lists from a horror magazine, but Mr. Rivard had helped him over that hurdle. He explained that there was no way to reach a target audience without the services of a good list broker, and list brokers didn't come cheap. In the business world, things always turned out to be a little more expensive than planned.

Darren caved on the mailing issue but held firm to other requirements. First and foremost, he wouldn't let Mr. Rivard finance the exhibit with funds from existing accounts. He wanted him to visit the bank and take out a loan like any other would-be entrepreneur. It had taken exactly five minutes and thirty seconds to accomplish that goal. The bank manager took one look at his balance and agreed to loan him the shirt off his back.

Now, after enforcing all of his silly requirements, Darren had dropped out of the project on the very night Mr. Rivard needed him most. He briefly wondered if Darren would be available to paint the winner's portrait. If not, it would take some looking to find a local artist with one third the talent Darren possessed.

Mr. Rivard crossed to his bedroom window and looked down upon the huge, grassy plain that was his backyard. His ex-wife had planned an elaborate landscaping project for the space, but the marriage hadn't lasted long enough to see it through. Mr. Rivard always dreamed of putting horse stables on the property, but he'd lost touch with those plans when caught in the grip of yet another depression.

Tonight, the wide open space seemed more of a blessing than an eyesore. A winding trail cut through the center of the property, directing visitors to a grand display tent decorated to look like a haunted house. The tent was originally purchased to provide a little shade for more than 300 wedding guests. God how he'd enjoyed painting it black and covering it with fake spider webs!

About fifty feet to the left of the display tent, an animated group of youngsters stood before a makeshift stage. A long-haired heavy metal band belted out a scorching medley of cover tunes, compliments of Roger North and his humble staff at Guitar World Incorporated. Roger had been more than happy to provide the entertainment free of charge. It was great publicity for his chain of stores.

The metal band was another one of Darren's little requirements. Mr. Rivard had begged him to consider using a traditional rock-n-roll band that would appeal to all ages, but Darren wouldn't hear of it. He reasoned that horror movie sound tracks were punctuated with a variety of disturbing sounds produced by electric guitars. In fact, horror fans were almost universally attracted to heavy metal music.

The ear-blistering guitars were part of the reason why Mr. Rivard had chosen to watch the evening unfold from his bedroom window. He thought about going down to help his maid supervise the display tent, but it all seemed so pointless. The presence of a metal band had attracted scores of party goers between the ages of 18 and 25. It didn't take an expert in demographics to figure out that genuine oil paintings were out of their price range.

His worst fears were confirmed when he went outside to offer his maid a break from supervising the event. All 57 of Darren's cherished paintings remained firmly in place on their easels. After three hours of whooping, hollering and prancing about the property in full costume, not one person had made a serious inquiry. On the bright side, tee shirts depicting circus accidents were selling like hot cakes.

"They keep trying to talk us down," the maid said. She was a stout, middle-aged woman who understood young people even less than he did. "They seem to think that forty or fifty bucks is an adequate price to pay for a genuine oil painting."

Mr. Rivard wanted to be sick. Each painting in Darren's collection had taken at least a month to complete. If Darren earned minium wage as an artist, it would take about $1,000 worth of his time to produce one portrait. How would those inconsiderate brats like it if they were handed a fifty dollar bill for a full month's work at McDonalds? No wonder oil painters were often referred to as "starving artists." For the first time that night, Mr. Rivard felt grateful that Darren had dropped out of the project. He had no desire to enter the kid's memory as the man who raised his hopes and shot them down in cold blood.

He couldn't help but think of all the aspiring businessmen who'd sent applications to the Have-A-Dream Foundation. Would he lead them all down a path of disillusionment? Would he spend countless hours on their projects only to discover that his ideas were as stale as a month-old loaf of bread? Was it finally time to face the fact that he was past his prime, like the ancient Mustang rotting away in his garage?

Gripped by a profound sense of failure and loss, Mr. Rivard took a long walk around the barren property he called home. A mile past the display tent, where echos stuttered and fell flat, the air was as still as a corpse. The windows of his sparking glass home shone like tiny diamonds in the pale moonlight. He briefly wondered how many rocks it would take to send the whole structure crashing to the ground.

He walked and walked until his thighs rubbed raw against his starchy tweed slacks. He was beginning to wonder how he'd find the strength to wander back home when a pair of headlights sliced through the darkness. "Hey!" Roger shouted through the open window of his pickup. "I've been looking all over creation for you! Some guy is interested in that crazy animal series."

"Really? Which painting does he like?"

"All of them! He wants to buy the whole damned collection!"

Chapter Fourteen: The Past

Kelly tried to hide her budding romance from Carlos, but Darren had to go and ruin it. He insisted upon signing his pictures with sappy adult phrases like, "With love always and forever." For Kelly, it was embarrassing beyond belief, but Carlos couldn't have been happier. He teased her about falling for a rich boy and began to address her as "Miss Kelly." Would Miss Kelly prefer her juice on the rocks or in a wine glass? Did Miss Kelly wish to stay up and watch television, or did she prefer to retire early?

For a time, Kelly believed Carlos had simply lost interest in robbing the Price estate. She didn't think anything about it when he showed up at the playground one day and offered to take her and Darren out for ice cream. What harm could he do in broad daylight?

The questions Carlos asked inside the car made Kelly nervous. Among other things, he wanted to know if Darren could tell the difference between a credit card and an ATM card. Darren explained the difference with the enthusiasm of a teacher's pet who enjoyed blurting answers in class. "An ATM card is used to get paper money from a machine. A credit card is used at the store, and you have to pay a bill that comes in the mail later."

"Very good," Carlos said. "Do you know what a pin number is?"

"Not really."

"It's an access code that you punch into the ATM machine. Understand?"

"I think so. Without the code, you're screwed."

Kelly tried to turn up the volume on the radio, but Carlos squeezed her hand so tightly that her eyes began to water. Keeping his fingers closed firmly around her wrist, he turned down a desolate gravel road and pulled behind a thick patch of oak trees. "How good are you at sneaking?" he asked.

Darren was still playing know-it-all. "I'm the best! Last year, I snuck into the classroom during lunch hour and corrected some of my test answers."

Carlos smiled at Kelly. "I see that your friend is very smart."

"He's not smart at all!" Kelly protested. "He likes the smell of his own farts."

Darren shot her a look of pure horror. "That was supposed to be a secret!"

Carlos was still laughing at their childish banter when he stepped out of the car and opened the trunk. He returned with an adorable young rabbit in his arms. "This is my friend, Peanut. Would you like to hold him?"

Darren stretched his arms out the back window to receive the rabbit. It was a sweet, docile thing with big brown eyes and a light tan coat. He brushed his cheek against its twitching nose.

"Do you know what it takes to kill a person?" Carlos asked.

Finally, Darren was starting to look a little nervous. "A gun or a knife?"

"What if I told you it takes much less than that?"

"I guess I'd have to believe you."

Carlos opened the door and slipped into the back seat beside Darren. "Would you believe I can kill almost anything with my bare hands?"

Kelly pressed the alarm button on Carlos' key chain. "Run, Darren! Run as fast as you can!"

Carlos swung his arm into the front seat and slapped Kelly across the face. Darren dropped the rabbit down the neckline of his shirt and reached for the door. His concern for the defenseless creature gave Carlos just enough time to overcome him. With a flick of the wrist, he tore Darren's shirt wide open, exposing the rabbit's trembling face. "Please!" Kelly screamed. "Don't do this!"

"Kill that God damned alarm or I'll cut you and your fucking dog, too!" Kelly deactivated the alarm and watched helplessly as Carlos grasped the rabbit with both hands and squeezed with ever-increasing force. Blood oozed from the creature's eyes in two thin trails that flowed past either side of its still-twitching nose. A thick, yellowish foam flowed from its tiny mouth. Darren grasped his stomach and leaned forward. Vomit poured from his lips. Kelly was too frightened for him to feel sorry about the rabbit. She regretted the day she crossed to his side of the playground and offered a bite of her peanut butter sandwich. Would all of her friendships end so badly? Was she destined to ruin everything she touched?

In a final display of cruelty, Carlos snapped the rabbit's neck in half and laid the dead creature to rest on Darren's lap.

They buried the rabbit under a sprawling oak tree. Darren dug the hole himself while Carlos leaned back against the tree and enjoyed a taste of his pipe. Kelly sat on the ground with her knees pulled to her chest. Rocking silently back and forth, she cried an ocean of silent tears.

"Do you understand the finality of what has happened?" Carlos asked.

Darren would no longer look at him. "Yes, I do."

"Do you see that the rabbit can never roam these woods again? It will never savor a mouth full of wild flowers or taste cool water from the pond like the rabbits in your picture. It will know no joy and no pain. It will simply cease to exist."

"I understand."

"Are you aware that the same thing happens to people when they die?"

"Yes, sir."

"There is no going back. Death is final. You fade to nothing."

A fire burned deep within Kelly's chest. "Don't listen to him, Darren! Good people go to heaven when they die. You have nothing to fear."

Carlos spun around and kicked her in the head. Searing pain exploded behind her eyes. "Run, Darren!" she screamed. "Please, run away!"

Darren remained firmly planted under the oak tree. "What do you want from me?" he asked.

"I want you to pay attention the next time your father uses the ATM machine. I want the pin number. Do you understand?"

"Yes."

"When you have the number, I want you to carve your initials into this tree as a sign. Can you do that?"

"Yes."

"When I know you have the number, I'll find you at the playground. We'll arrange another meeting for you to bring me the card. Can you handle that?"

"Yes."

"Do you understand what will happen if you say one word to anyone about the things you've seen here today?"

"You'll kill me."

"Wrong. I'll kill everyone you love. Your father, Kelly... everyone."

That night, Kelly locked herself in the bedroom with her rottweiler and remained hidden there for five days. If Carlos had succeeded in draining Roland's bank account, she didn't want to know about it. She had two gallons of water, a loaf of bread, a jar of peanut butter and a big bucket to pee in. It was all she wanted in the world and all she needed to get by. Pizza and movies had a price she was no longer willing to pay. Even the sight of her beautiful doll collection failed to provide comfort. Their twisted smiles haunted her at night. On the third morning, she tossed every one of them out of the window. If Mom and Carlos were going to terrorize people, she would no longer let them blame it on some sick need to provide their little girl with the best of everything.

At least twice a day and sometimes more, her mom stood outside the door and wept. No amount of begging would bring Kelly out of hiding. There was a time when the sound of her mother crying ripped her heart to shreds, but now it was no more moving than listening to a soap star whine over the diagnosis of some rare blood disorder. When Carlos came to the door, she threatened to sic the rottweiler on him. She wouldn't even sleep in the beautiful four poster bed he'd purchased when she first came to live with him. She constructed a fine tent of blankets and filled it with old picture books her mom had found before meeting Carlos. If a tent in the middle of the floor was good enough for Darren, it was good enough for her.

On the fourth night, she came out of hiding to replenish her water supply and dump her smelly bucket in the yard. She had only planned to roam the house long enough to grab some toilet paper and a loaf of bread, but curiosity got the best of her. Crouching beside her parent's bedroom door, she learned that the ATM scam hadn't worked as planned. Roland kept only a few thousand dollars in the account he used for daily spending. They couldn't even get the full amount because there was some kind of limit on cash withdrawals. The credit cards had worked out a little better. They had already been on a wicked shopping spree, and they almost got caught. One of the jewelry stores checked identification, and Carlos ran out of the mall just in time to shake the security guard on his tail.

By the sixth day, Kelly could no longer stand the smell of her rottweiler's urine. Clumps of poop could be picked up with tissue and tossed out the window, but pee stayed inside the area rugs that Carlos had tossed over the old carpet. She was attempting to push the rugs out the window when Carlos appeared before her eyes. Standing on a ladder with tears streaming down his face, he begged for her mercy.

"You've broken my heart," he said.

"You broke mine first."

"I'll regret that for the rest of my life. I should never have laid my hands on you."

"Is that all you regret?"

"Please, Kelly. You can't go on like this."

"I asked you a question. Is hitting me the only thing you regret?"

"I cannot give the answer you want to hear."

"Is it so easy to scare people and take their money? Do you ever feel guilty at all?"

Carlos was silent for a moment. She'd never seen his eyes so full of pain. "Let me explain something to you. A long time ago, when I still lived in Mexico, I worked in a steel mill for fifteen years. Do you remember that day when it was so hot that your mother blistered her hand on the steering wheel?"

"I remember."

"Imagine a place even hotter than it was on that day, and you'll still have only a vague idea of how warm it could get inside the mill. Grown men passed out from exhaustion every single day. In the blink of an eye, they were carried outside and doused with cold water from a hose. If they could be revived, they were sent back to work. One day, my father died in that steel mill, and the owners didn't even have the decency to send a bottle of wine to the funeral."

A tear came to Kelly's eye. "That's so awful. I don't know what to say."

"I'm just a simple man, Kelly. When I was your age, I followed my father around at work and swept the floors in back of him. It was the only way to keep a roof over my head and feed my younger sisters. Your school is not the safest place to spend the day, but at least you have the opportunity to rise far beyond my level. I cannot read the simple pocket books you bring home from the library, and I can't write well enough to fill out a job application. Let me ask you this: If I had to go out looking for work, who in the world would hire a man like me?"

Kelly hung her head in shame. "No one. Not even the steel mill down the street."

"Is the picture any clearer for you? Can you understand my burden?"

"Yes."

"I won't ask for your help again. I would rather die than bring you into another mess that I've created. But don't ask me to apologize for what I do. I have no guilt left in my soul."

Kelly emerged from her room that night and watched an old movie with her parents. The taste of pizza was not as sweet, but she suspected it was just the way of things when you got older. She was finally beginning to see that it was possible to love and hate her parents all at once. The world was neither black nor white. There were good people who did bad things and bad people who did good things. It was pointless to try and make sense of it.

For the next few months, Kelly monitored her parent's nightly discussions like a hawk. She wasn't surprised to learn that they were finding more and more ways to drain Roland's bank account. Her mom visited the Price Estate posing as an irate homeowner in the area. She claimed to have caught Darren spray painting curse words across the side of her luxury home and asked for $7,000 to cover the damage. When questioned by his father, Darren owned up to the senseless act of vandalism. A few weeks later, one of Carlos' white brothers told Roland that Darren had smashed his car windshield with a baseball bat. God only knew what he was doing to assure Darren's cooperation. Perhaps he was killing dogs and horses now.

Kelly understood why Roland was all too willing to believe the worst of his son. Darren was a troubled kid who got into countless fights at school. Roland had no idea his son was tormented by bullies every day of his life, but Kelly knew the boy's secrets. Deep down, he feared that his father truly was gay. He'd heard a lot of folks say homosexuals were born different from other people. If Roland had been born with the tendency, did that mean Darren had inherited it, too? The subject was much too embarrassing to bring up at the dinner table, so Darren allowed his father to believe that he was just a bully who went around picking fights.

Eventually, Darren was forbidden to leave the house without his art tutor. There was no longer a way to trick Roland into believing that his son enjoyed wreaking havoc on the neighborhood. Darren left a note explaining the situation on the tree where Carlos had first encouraged him to carve his initials. Thus ended the most lucrative scam Carlos had ever concocted. When the chips were cashed in, Kelly's parents concluded that they'd earned more than $50,000 from their dealings with the Price family. The jewelry alone was worth $20,000, and that didn't include the money they'd scammed from the ATM machine. It was a sad day when they realized that the well had finally run dry. They couldn't go to work on other children without Kelly's cooperation. She was the key component in their scam. It was her charismatic charm that put other children at ease and whittled away at their defenses.

✵✵✵✵✵

The Present

Dr. Rushing had it all figured out. A fat bouquet of pink roses sat upon the passenger seat beside him. A small cooler in the back seat held a bottle of the very best wine he could afford. Tickets to the symphony were folded into the breast pocket of his rented tuxedo.

Heart racing, grinning ear to ear, he knocked on Claire's door. He wasn't surprised to see the look of shock on her face. "Dr. Rushing! Why are you… what is this all about?"

"You know what it's all about. I've come to see if you'd do me the honor of accompanying me to a real symphony this time."

Without so much as a smile, Claire took the bundle of flowers and laid them across the arm of her couch. "I see."

"Don't you have a vase?"

"I have three of them."

Dr. Rushing's heart sank. He'd expected a much warmer reception. Perhaps her old fear of public places hadn't really been cured by attending that rock concert. "If this is a little too much for you, we could always stay home and watch a movie. I don't actually care what we do, as long as we do it together."

Claire looked down at her feet. "If it's all the same to you, I'm going to turn in early tonight."

"But why? I thought this was what you wanted."

"I *did* want it. I wanted it for much too long."

Dr. Rushing fought back tears. "What happened to change your mind?"

"Darren happened."

"I see. Perhaps I underestimated the depth of your feelings for him."

"It's not that. I don't love him. To tell the truth, I never really did."

"So why are you so opposed to the idea of spending a little time with me?"

Claire straightened her shoulders and faced him with the quiet grace of a swan. "Because I'm not the same person. Don't you see? I've learned that it's possible for a man to accept me exactly as I am with no hangups or hesitations. I don't expect to take the dating world by storm, but I *will* find love if I get off this damned couch and go looking for it. It'll take some time and a whole lot of courage, but I have faith in myself."

Dr. Rushing bent to kiss Claire's forehead. "I have faith in you, too."

* * * * *

The Past

Not long after the Price family fiasco, Mom and Carlos went back to selling crack to feed their greedy addictions. The nightmares that had diminished when Darren came into Kelly's life suddenly returned in full force. Her punishment for the crimes she'd helped to commit was living through hell on Earth. Each night, she found herself trapped in Satan's lair, blistered from head to toe, screaming and screaming until the end of time.

Around age 10, she became obsessed with the challenge of rewriting what she believed to be her ultimate destiny. She gravitated toward the few kids in school who claimed to like going to church and asked them endless questions about heaven and hell. Over time, she patched together her own quilt of beliefs based upon the playground wisdom of various fifth graders. If you could believe the Catholics, it was necessary to confess your sins to a priest to make sure God knew you were very serious about cleaning up your act. If you could believe the Baptists, confessing was a waste of time because God knew everything about you and only cared that you were genuinely sorry for whatever you'd done. His son, Jesus, had died to pay for your sins, and all he really wanted in return was unconditional love. If you could believe the Jehovah Witnesses, the whole Jesus thing was just a line of bullshit invented by lazy folks who wanted to get into heaven the easy way. In their view, getting into heaven was a privilege earned by doing good things for other people and passing out booklets all over town.

Kelly wasn't sure which method was the ultimate answer, but she decided to leave nothing to chance. She confessed her sins to a Catholic girl and sat down with a Baptist boy to say a special prayer allowing God into her heart. She tried to do good things for people whenever she could, taking cans from her mother's pantry and depositing them at various local food banks.

Despite her efforts, she couldn't find happiness living under Carlos' roof. The one thing that gave her a sense of inner peace was the idea that she was getting older. She dreamed of a day when she could have her own apartment with her own couch and her own food in the refrigerator. She already had a decent bed and television set. How hard could it be to get all the other stuff she needed?

Around age 11, Kelly started a hope chest. Any old blanket or frying pan tossed into the garbage was retrieved and washed with loving care. When Carlos noticed she was setting up her bedroom as a miniature apartment, he took her on a tour of neighborhood garage sales and bought her a fine set of towels and a gently used love seat. If his little girl liked to play house, he was going to make damned sure her bedroom was the finest play apartment that ever existed.

By this time, Kelly was used to Carlos buying her love and respect, and she took full advantage of it. Despite the condition of his decrepit house, he was a man with plenty of cash in his pockets. The well that had run dry a few years back was full again. This time, he maintained relationships with two different suppliers so he wouldn't be left penniless if one of them ever got busted. He continued to make friends in suburban areas and charge them double for the stuff they couldn't find anywhere else. He also maintained lucrative relationships with addicts in his own backyard. He upheld strict house rules to ensure that excess foot traffic didn't draw attention to his humble place of business. Only five brothers were allowed to set foot on the property. If anyone else in the neighborhood needed a fix, they had to go through one of the five men to get it. By this time, Kelly understood that true brothers could be white, black or any shade in between. Bonds of trust were stronger than many biological connections in her universe.

The one thing Kelly admired about Carlos was his ability to inspire fierce loyalty in a group of men who cared only for themselves. When one of his brothers got caught peddling a small quantity at the local bar, he went straight to jail to avoid telling cops where he'd obtained his product. Carlos had a way of making each of his brothers feel like the only person in the world who really mattered to him. Kelly was hip to the con. For a very long time, he had made her feel like the sun that lit up his days and the moon that lulled him to sleep at night. She learned the truth the day he slammed his foot into the side of her head. From that point on, she understood that crack was his sun and money was the energy source that fueled it.

By age 12, Kelly was certain that if she could learn to duplicate Carlos' charisma, she could save enough money to buy her own house on her sixteenth birthday. It was the age when most kids learned to drive and the age when people became adults. Four years seemed like an eternity, but it didn't have to be that way if she spent the time productively. It was a fairly simple operation to acquire all of the tools necessary to start her own business. She wasn't particularly worried about getting caught. Mom and Carlos had a tendency to underestimate the amount they could smoke in a single day. They were always surprised by how fast their personal supply dwindled down to nothing. They usually blamed it on the fact that they shared the pipe with so many friends.

Almost overnight, the whole focus of Kelly's life shifted. She shared the pipe with any kid old enough to have a job, be it delivering newspapers or flipping burgers at a fast food restaurant. She only had to give the stuff away once. That's all it took to keep kids coming back with ever-increasing amounts of money. It seemed like the perfect racket until she realized that her friends weren't the only ones who couldn't get by without a fix.

When she started accepting stereos, bikes and compact disks as payment, it didn't take long for Carlos to figure out that his little girl had become a businesswoman. She thought she was headed for a major beating when he smashed his own televison set with a baseball bat and kicked her old rottweiler in the ribs. Much to her amazement, he went to bed that night without laying a hand on her. The following day, he entered an emergency detox center. A week later, he laid out $50,000 cash to assure his placement in a serious three-month drug rehabilitation program at a wilderness retreat in Canada. He promised to do the same for his wife when he was strong enough to rule the house again, but Kelly's mom had no desire to waste every cent left in the safe. She promised to get a job with medical insurance as soon as he returned home, but that never quite happened.

The next few years were a blur. Carlos used a fake GED to get a job at the steel mill, and Kelly's mom suddenly had to hide her habit from him. She had affairs with neighborhood addicts to get closer to their pipes and turned tricks on the side to maintain a personal supply. Kelly hid her addiction from both her parents. Uncle Mark, one of Carlos' white brothers, became her new wholesale supplier. She sold the stuff at malls, seducing well-dressed boys with a wink and a smile. It took only two dates to get them hooked.

*****

The Present

Monday morning at 9 a.m. sharp, Mr. Rivard got the phone call of a lifetime. Allen Trent, the shy young man who had casually written a check for $30,000 to purchase all ten of Darren's crazed animal portraits, wanted to know if Darren had a lawyer.

"A lawyer?" Mr. Rivard asked.

"Yes. A copyright lawyer."

"A copyright lawyer?"

Allen blew into the phone. "Is the connection okay? I'm calling from New York."

"The connection is fine. Why would Darren need a copyright lawyer?"

Mr. Rivard expected the young man to ask for the right to produce framed posters of Darren's work, but his agenda was much more exciting. In a soft, genteel voice that teemed of compassion and humanity, Mr. Trent explained that he was the president and CEO of WildHeart, a non-profit organization dedicated to promoting the ethical treatment of animals. His purpose in calling was to purchase the rights to use Darren's art on posters, flyers, brochures and tee shirts. As fate would have it, Mr. Trent's younger brother was one of 5,000 horror magazine subscribers to receive a flyer announcing the exhibit. A sample portrait from Darren's animal series had appeared on the flyer, which the young man quickly scanned and e-mailed to his brother in New York. Mr. Trent was immediately taken with the image of a young fawn feasting upon the abdomen of a terrified hunter. He envisioned the following caption beneath the photo: "Would you call this a sport?" His hope was that the shocking picture would drive home the point that there was no excuse to kill living creatures for recreational purposes.

Mr. Rivard was quick to jump on the opportunity. "Darren doesn't have a lawyer, but I just so happen to have five of them. If you'd be kind enough to fax your proposal to my office, I'll go over it with Darren as soon as possible."

Just when Mr. Rivard thought the day couldn't get any better, he received a call from a local woman who wished to purchase a painting from the circus series for her husband's birthday. The only problem was that she couldn't come up with $3,000 cash all at once. Would the artist consider letting her make payments over a three month period? Mr. Rivard didn't have to think about his answer. "I don't see why not!"

As the day wore on, a few more calls filtered in. Was the trapeze portrait still available? How about that painting of the dead fish? Could Darren paint a live shark instead? Could he depict the shark attacking another shark? Just how much would that cost, anyway?

Chapter Fifteen: The Past

By age 16, Kelly was a full-fledged businesswoman who ruled the neighborhood from her proud position on the front porch. The little girl who sat on the steps dreaming about her first apartment was gone forever. Moving away was the very least of her concerns. Her mind was set on sneaking to the backyard for a little fix when that stupid motorcycle came barreling down the street and turned into her driveway.

"Watch it," Kelly said as the driver removed his helmet and fixed her with a penetrating gaze. "There's a rottweiler behind this door, and she's not very friendly."

The guy didn't appear to be afraid. He looked a little cracked out himself with his long dark hair and ridiculous eyebrow spikes. "Your rottweiler is no match for my gun," he said.

A shiver crawled up Kelly's spine. She knew robberies occurred every day in her neighborhood, but she somehow felt that her house was impenetrable. "You're wasting your time. This family is broke."

The guy sat there on his bike and laughed his ass off. "Your father should've invested the money he took. He could've done so much with it."

"What are you talking about?"

"I'm talking about the $50,000 your dad stole from my family."

Kelly's heart exploded in her chest. In her wildest fantasies, she never dreamed she'd come face to face with Darren again. Squinting against the afternoon sun, she looked past his long dark hair in search of the sweet expressive eyes that once filled her heart with a joy more tangible than any crack pipe could deliver. As hard as she looked, she could not see the little boy who sketched rabbits in the woods and ate Fruit Loops for dinner. He'd grown into something different—something profoundly sinister and strangely irresistible.

"What do you want from me?" she asked.

Darren left his bike on the driveway and walked over to the porch. "I'm here to settle an old debt."

"I told you, this family is broke."

"I'm not talking about Carlos' debt. I'm talking about mine. I believe I owe you a kiss."

Without further warning, Darren bent to brush his lips across her forehead. The punk who threatened to shoot her rottweiler just moments ago was suddenly gallant and polite. He needed her approval before moving on to her lips, and it was up to her to grant it.

Her stomach churned beneath her flesh as she grabbed two handfuls of his tee shirt and pulled herself up to his level. Their lips met with a loud smack that was considerably more passionate than romantic. She opened her mouth to receive his tongue and savored the very taste of his flesh. She had kissed plenty of boys before, but this was so much different. She felt that she could drink him into her body, swallow him whole, smoke him up like a shiny little rock.

She would've stayed on that porch for an eternity, but he pulled away and hopped onto his bike. Her heart sank in that fleeting moment when he cut across the lawn and made his way back to the street. Was he leaving so soon? Would he ever be back? Was this his way of punishing her for all the horrible crimes she'd helped to commit against his family?

A sudden calm washed over her chest when he tilted his head west toward the setting sun. "Are you coming?" he asked.

With nothing more than a pipe and three rocks in her pocket, Kelly hopped onto his motorcycle and headed straight into the horizon, like the sailboats in that picture she'd loved so dearly as a child. She had no idea where she was going or if she'd ever return, and that was just fine. The little girl who dreamed of a better place was suddenly alive and well, awakened to a state of total awareness after a long winter's nap.

They drove to a place called Donovan's Pub and drank virgin margaritas in a dark corner booth lit by candlelight. Darren offered to escort her to the back room for a real drink, but alcohol was the last thing on her mind. "How did you find me?" she asked.

Darren couldn't look at her. "It's kind of stupid," he said.

"I'll bet it isn't stupid at all. Tell me."

"When I was 10 years old, I had this crazy idea I would show up at your house one day and save you from the man who made my life a living hell. I knew you lived in a little green house on a street by a junkyard and a police station, so I got my hands on a few phone books and called every cop shop in the state. I asked only one question: 'Is there a junkyard around the corner from you?' Only one place fit the description."

Kelly's eyes filled with tears. "That's the sweetest thing I've ever heard. It must've taken you days."

"More like weeks. I was a persistent little fuck."

"I don't know what to say. I'm so sorry about the way everything went down. I didn't know that Carlos was planning to…"

Darren grabbed her hand from across the table. "I know you didn't. Let's not talk about it, okay? Tell me about your life. What have you been doing with yourself all these years?"

"I'd rather not go into that. Let's talk about you. Your life was always so much more interesting than mine."

"It's still interesting, but I can't talk about it."

"That's just great. How are we going to get to know each other if we can't talk about anything?"

Darren thought for a moment. "Tell me how long you can run without stopping."

"Fifteen, maybe twenty minutes."

"How long can you stay under water without coming up for a breath?"

"I don't know. I haven't tried that in ages."

"How much can you eat without puking?"

"A whole medium pizza with salad and bread sticks."

"Sounds pretty good. Would you like to order something? I eat free here."

"Why? Does your dad own the place or something?"

"My dad is not a businessman. You know that as well as I do."

Kelly looked away. "Did you ever find out if he… if he…"

"Queer as a three dollar bill. Makes me sick. We still don't talk about it."

"He's not a bad guy, Darren. The kids at your school were nothing but a bunch of rich, evil brats. I'm sure you see that now. What ever happened to Shelly Whipple, anyway?"

"She slimmed down, but her head grew fatter with each passing year. Maybe it was all that long blond hair. I cornered her in the woods one day and shaved her bald. I threatened to kill her little sister with my bare hands if she ever told anyone about what I'd done."

"Darren! That's awful."

"Not really. Her little sister was a bitch, too. Plus, Shelly didn't exactly suffer any long-term consequences. She got her nose pierced and went for a punk rock look. She was popular, even without the hair."

"It figures. The biggest bitches always seem to have a following. What about her older brother?"

"David made fun of my nose ring one day, so I sealed his nostrils shut with a stapler."

"Darren!"

"He deserved it. He sent kids home from school with black eyes on a daily basis, and he never got expelled because his father contributed thousands to the athletic fund each year. One day, he raped a little girl in the woods, and I saw the tail end of it. When I drove the staples through his flesh, I made him promise not to hurt anyone ever again. The fucker deserved much more than he got that day. He's still on my list."

"Your list?"

"Never mind. Are you hungry?"

"Tell me about this list. Is Carlos on it?"

"He used to be, until I realized how much I'd benefitted from my association with your family."

"What are you talking about?"

Darren looked deep into Kelly's eyes. "I was nothing before I met you. Remember when you told me that the non fighters at your school were barely human at all? They were no better than worms rolling around in the mud or ants crawling along the sidewalk?"

"I remember."

"That's what I was, Kelly. A pathetic little worm waiting for yet another foot to come down and crush me. You and Carlos changed all of that forever. You taught me how to fight, and he taught me that it was possible to scare the living hell out of someone without the aid of a gun or a knife. With a big enough attitude, you can rule the world. Shelly is a prime example of that concept. Fat or thin, blonde or bald, she's the most popular chick in school. She's untouchable."

Kelly studied Darren's face in the warm candlelight. The pointed elf-like features of his youth were more striking and masculine now. He'd grown right into his chiseled face like a caterpillar grows into a butterfly. The old Darren was sweet and adorable, but this new guy was positively provocative. He didn't take shit from anyone, and he sought justice for kids who couldn't obtain it themselves.

They cuddled by the fire in the guest house that night, studying current yearbook photos of the teenagers they knew as children. Darren had turned the place into his own private lair, filling it with gothic style furniture from flea markets and plastering the walls with his own grotesque paintings. He seemed to have lost interest in depicting beauty altogether. Where his young eyes saw a world filled with rabbits and wild flowers, his wiser eyes fixated on a more brutal reality. Kelly was particularly horrified by a portrait of an old woman with raw boils on her neck. She was dressed in an ill-fitting blouse that clung to her ribs and outlined the contours of her sagging cone-shaped breasts. "What's that all about?" Kelly asked. "You like painting old tits?"

"Not exactly. She's a homeless woman who fills her shopping cart at the food bank around the corner from Donovan's. I slipped her a hundred bucks, and she agreed to come back here and pose for a portrait."

Kelly chuckled a bit. "I can just see her hopping onto the back of your motorcycle."

"Yeah, it was pretty funny. The guys at Donovan's whooped and hollered as we drove off into the sunset."

"Why her and not some little girl with ribbons or some stripper with firm tits? You could've paid just about anyone to pose for a portrait."

"Young people are admired and adored by the entire world. Their pictures are recorded in yearbooks and plastered on the walls in every home I've ever seen. This woman's image doesn't appear anywhere else on Earth but here."

"So, you're trying to be original?"

"No, I'm trying to record a life that no one else has bothered to recognize. If anyone deserves to be immortalized, this woman does."

Kelly couldn't believe her ears. Just when she thought that the boy with the fragile heart was gone forever, he crystalized before her eyes like an alien beaming in from outer space.

Around midnight, Kelly retired to the bathroom for a little fix. She had already enjoyed a taste of the pipe in the bathroom at Donovan's, and she was long overdue for another. She didn't worry about Darren smelling anything out of the ordinary. If he questioned her, she would just say she'd burned a cigarette down to the quick. She was fairly confident that he wouldn't know the difference between the smell of a crack pipe and the sharp chemical odor of a burnt filter. She wasn't exactly dealing with an expert.

She felt a little guilty as she extracted the zip lock bag from her pocket and grasped a little rock between her thumb and forefinger. She'd been hiding terrible secrets from Darren ever since she was a little girl. This should've been a prime opportunity to start over with a fresh slate, but it wasn't going to be that way at all. The sad truth was that she had only one rock left in her pocket, and when that was gone, she would have to leave the wonderful guy who'd spent so many years trying to find her.

As expected, Darren begged her to stay the night. He made it clear that sex wasn't what he was after and offered to build a tent in the middle of the floor for old time's sake. As much as she wanted to camp out with him, she simply couldn't stick around. She decided to blame it on some silly curfew that she didn't mind breaking on a regular basis. "It's very important for me to get home," she told him. "Carlos will be worried sick."

"I didn't know Carlos had the capacity to worry."

"He's a different man now. Honestly, you wouldn't recognize him."

Darren rolled his eyes. "Yeah, right."

"You have every reason to hate his guts, but you have to understand that he was a crack addict when you knew him. He would've done just about anything for money."

"There are plenty of crack addicts in the world. Some of them rob gas stations and little old ladies walking down the street. Very few choose to terrorize children."

"You're absolutely right. I can only tell you that Carlos chose the safest route to riches that he could come up with at the time. Believe it or not, he was worried about going to prison and leaving me alone with my mom. I don't expect you to understand, but he really did love me in the only way he was capable of loving at the time."

"He kicked you in the head, Kelly."

"He also enrolled me in the first grade at a time when my mother didn't care if I ever made it to school. He filled my room with expensive treasures and trained a rottweiler to attack anyone who laid a hand on me. Sometimes, you just have to love someone for no other reason than the fact that they loved you in their own twisted way."

"I'll buy that, but why did he have to steal so much? I don't know the going rate for a rock, but it can't be $50,000."

"An addict doesn't want just one rock. The only thing that will comfort a crack head is the knowledge that there's a lifetime of rocks where the first one came from. I don't expect you to understand, but believe me when I say that I've seen people blow through thousands of dollars in less than a month."

"You're kidding."

"I wish I was. It's the most evil addiction in the world. I never dreamed Carlos would kick the habit, but he eventually wound up in rehab. Now, he works from noon to midnight doing the same job that killed his father. At the end of the night, he stumbles in the door, groans in my general direction and flops over on the couch. If I'm not home, he waits up, and he doesn't get enough sleep for work the next day."

"Why doesn't your mom wait up instead?"

Kelly shrugged her shoulders. "She doesn't care enough, I suppose."

"You say that like it doesn't bother you."

"Does that crack in the ceiling bother you, or have you grown used to it?"

"I ignore it."

"Exactly."

"That's sad."

"I know."

They wound up striking a bargain. She would go home, throw a few essentials into a back pack, and meet him out front after Carlos went to sleep. If something went wrong, she'd use the porch light to signal that he should leave and come back the following day.

She was able to slip into the door ten minutes before Carlos arrived. She retrieved her stash from an old doll case and dropped fifteen rocks into 30 different sandwich bags. The stuff was slated for sale at the mall, but she would need every bit of it now. If she could muster the will power to deplete only one bag each day, she wouldn't have to come back to the city for another month. She hadn't exactly been asked to stay at the guest house for any length of time, but she knew an invitation was as inevitable as death and taxes.

She waited for Carlos to slip into bed beside her mother and taped a little note on their bedroom door:

> Carlos,
>
> Today is the day you've dreaded from the first moment we laid eyes on one another. Your little girl is grown up, and there's nothing in the world you can do about it. I've found a new place to stay and a new reason for living. Be happy for me, and feel the reach of my love from many miles away.
>
> A long time ago, you asked me not to force you to apologize for doing what you felt was your only clear option in life. I ask the same of you now. Please forgive me as I forgave you.
>
> Love, Kelly

That night, Kelly's heart burned with desire as she made out with Darren by the fire. She was not a virgin by any stretch of the imagination, and she knew exactly what it meant when a boy's bulging erection raised his sweat pants like a tent. Sex was hers for the taking, and her only challenge was to decide how soon she wanted it. Just like on the porch, he was waiting for her to make the first move. He caressed her back as he ran his lips over her face, steering clear of all the delicate nooks and crannies that define a young woman's shape. She was just about to place her hand on his thigh when he said the most incredible thing: "We can't forget to build the tent."

Kelly glanced down at his sweat pants. "Looks like you've already started."

Darren looked down at his penis as if it were a disobedient child. "Fuck him. He thinks he knows everything. We have work to do."

For the next half hour, they threw all of their energy into building the finest tent ever constructed. They used four dining room chairs as corner supports and draped a king-sized blanket over top of them to create a canopy. To raise the center of the tent, Darren tied a piece of string to a low-hanging light fixture and threaded the string through a hole in the center of the blanket. Their final task was to line the interior with sleeping bags and assemble a box of essential supplies. In keeping with their childhood desires, they packed two flashlights, three picture books, a box of Fruit Loops and a cooler filled with extra sweet raspberry punch.

When their fortress was complete, sex was the last thing on Kelly's mind. Nestled in Darren's arms beneath a fine canopy of blankets, she was struck by the realization that this was a rare opportunity to relive the innocent years that were tainted by her parent's lifestyle. Perhaps she could go all the way back to age nine and start over again, if only in spirit. Maybe she wouldn't need the condoms stashed in her backpack after all. Maybe she wouldn't even go back to the city to replenish her supply of rocks. Maybe sex wasn't the only thing she had the willpower to resist.

The next morning, all of Kelly's good intentions died with the waning moon. Her mind raced ahead to her next fix and her next whole month of fixes. When Darren stirred and opened his eyes, she laid the groundwork for her next several trips to the bathroom. "I think I should warn you that I'm hard to live with," she said.

"Tell me about it. You don't sleep much, do you?"

"Not at all. I'm a raging insomniac. I take walks at night to clear my head. I also hog the bathroom. I take four baths a day, and sometimes five. It drives my parents nuts."

Darren buried his face into the crook of her neck. "No wonder you smell so sweet."

"I'm going to take a bath now."

"Fine. Be sure and brush your tongue."

"Are you trying to tell me my breath stinks?"

"Not at all. I just wouldn't want there to be any food stuck in that space between your cheek and gums."

✸✸✸✸✸

The Present

The dark, mysterious man caused quite a stir among the children at Claire's nursery school. They were playing catch with snowballs when he came strolling along the fence in his faded black trench coat. His steel grey eyes were as cold as the harsh November wind. His dark, bushy eyebrows formed one continuous line above his crooked nose.

A three-year-old boy named Justin had the audacity to point. "Who bad man?" he asked.

"I don't know, sweetie. Get away from the fence."

Justin looked up at her, all eyes and mouth and impatience. "You come!" he insisted.

Just then, a little girl with ear muffs smashed over her pigtails began to cry. "Miss Claire! I have to pee!"

Suddenly every child on the property had an excuse to go inside, even those who usually chose to wet themselves rather than take a break from recess. Brittany Davidson, a precocious four-year-old who often tried to sneak outside during nap time, was seen creeping into the building.

Claire normally shied away from strangers, but in this case, the children's safety was her top priority. This man couldn't just stand there with his nose pressed to the fence, following their every movement with his wicked eyes. Who did he think he was, anyway?

"Would you mind not standing so close to the fence?" she asked. "You're making the children nervous."

The man's voice was harsh and uncultivated. "But I'm just standing here."

"This is private property. Go stand somewhere else."

The man walked slowly along the fence and stopped beside a jogger who had taken a break to watch the children play. "What about him? You gonna make him move, too?"

Claire suddenly realized she couldn't make up rules that applied only to certain people. The sidewalk running along the fence was public property, and the man had a right to stand there and stare at whatever he wished. It was best to gather the children and bring them inside. It was a little too cold for them to be playing in the snow, anyway.

She later regretted her decision to cut recess short. Outdoor breaks provided a much needed opportunity for her young companions to work off some energy. By noon, they were too wired to take advantage of nap time and too restless to concentrate on their puzzle games. For lack of anything better to do, they colored on the walls.

Claire was particularly tired when she left the building that evening. As she fumbled with her key ring, the harsh November wind shot through her flimsy overcoat. She didn't notice the creepy man until he stepped right in front of her car. Her heart skipped a beat when she saw that he was carrying two steaming cups of coffee from the doughnut shop down the street. Did he really expect her to join him in a drink?

"A peace offering," he said, and the voice that floated on cloudy puffs of air sounded curiously like Dr. Rushing's.

Moist heat rushed to Claire's cheeks. "How could you!"

"It was easy. The Halloween shop at the mall is getting rid of everything at half price."

"That's not what I'm talking about, and you know it. How could you scare the children that way?"

"I didn't try to scare anyone. I was perfectly polite. They were the ones who passed judgement."

A warm tear melted its way down her cheek. "I guess sometimes people are afraid of what they don't understand."

"I think you're right. What do you say we just forgive them?"

Claire parted Dr. Rushing's trench coat and pressed herself against his warm body. "I'd say that's the best idea you've had all year."

Chapter Sixteen: The Past

Kelly's first two weeks as Darren's secret roommate were the happiest of her life. They roamed the woods with digital cameras each morning, stopping frequently to share gulps from a large thermos filled with raspberry punch. She was happy to discover that he was an independent soul who didn't mind splitting up to search for photo opportunities. There were plenty of chances to enjoy the pipe in private. In fact, her personal supply was dwindling much faster than anticipated.

She once believed there was no greater joy than the rapture of a fresh hit on the porch, but that was before she'd experienced a fresh hit by the pond. When the sun showered light upon the water, it transformed the woods into her own private nirvana. At certain times of the day, the whole property shimmered, as if infused with the soft, amber light of a candle.

Darren often ate lunch in the quaint tree house overlooking the pond, awaiting rare glimpses of animals interacting with the environment. She nibbled at his famous bacon sandwiches and tossed them to the squirrels when he wasn't looking. She rarely needed solid food to get by, and she didn't want that to worry him.

The sights they were able to capture were nothing short of breathtaking. Kelly's favorite was a snapshot of a giant racoon marching along the edge of the pond with six darling babies in tow. Darren was more partial to shots of dead fish floating in pond scum. She nearly threw a fit when he transferred one such photo to his computer and used it as a screen saver. "Is there any reason why you're hell bent on enlarging that hideous picture?" she asked.

"Yes. I'm going to paint it."

"Why would you even think of doing such a thing?"

"Of all people, I'm surprised you have to ask."

"What are you talking about?"

"When you look at me, you see something more than the freak everyone else sees. Is it so hard for you to believe that I see something more than a dead fish?"

"You're not a freak."

"Yes, Kelly. I am."

"I'm not saying you should stop painting dead things, but would it kill you to paint something a little less disgusting for a change?"

"Like what?"

"I don't know. How about painting me?"

Darren laughed so hard he nearly fell out of his chair. "You want me to paint you, huh?"

"What's so hilarious about that?"

"Come on. I'll show you."

Darren led Kelly to an isolated corner of the wine cellar, where dozens of paintings were wrapped in brown packaging paper. He tore open a few basic outdoor scenes before getting down to the very portrait he'd come to find. Her heart jumped to her throat as she confronted a perfect likeness of herself. Like the angel and cherub paintings in Roland's dining room, the portrait had a distinct ethereal quality. Her long dark hair glistened under an unseen light source that added a soft twinkle to her eyes and surrounded her entire body with a radiant aura. As she struggled to make sense of it all, the truth suddenly knocked the wind from her chest: She gave off light in his mind.

"When did you paint this?"

"About a year ago."

"You've got to be kidding. You couldn't have just imagined me as a young adult. It's so much more than that. It's a near perfect likeness. Have you been... spying on me?"

Darren pulled her into his arms. "Guilty as charged."

Near the end of their third week together, Darren began to take Kelly for short walks along the cobblestone path running behind his father's house. It was almost as if he *wanted* her to run smack dab into Roland. At first he only hinted at it, but he chose to push the subject one night as they shared a picnic of red wine and bacon sandwiches in the tent. "I don't see how it's such a big deal," he said. "I never told him about Carlos. I'll just say I ran into you at the mall, and we rekindled our old friendship."

"It's not as simple as that. I can't look at him, Darren. Do you really expect me to smile over truffles and caviar after everything I've done to him?"

"First of all, we don't eat truffles or caviar. Second, you didn't commit any crimes against my father. Carlos was the man with the plan."

"Maybe so, but I still feel guilty about everything we put him through."

"Your guilt is groundless. He didn't exactly go broke. Credit card companies have fraud investigators. It didn't take a rocket scientist to conclude that my dad's signature didn't match the one on the receipts signed at the jewelry stores. He contested the bills and didn't pay a dime."

"It's not just the money. Your relationship with your father was destroyed as a direct result of my family's interference in your life."

"That's not completely true. How is it your fault my father chooses to believe the worst of me?"

"He didn't choose it, Darren. It was forced down his throat."

"I don't believe that. I've never believed that! If it were my son who'd been accused of spray painting obscenities on luxury homes, I'd have asked how a nine-year-old could've gotten past so many state-of-the-art security systems."

"You confessed to the crimes. What was your dad supposed to think?"

"I confessed because I was young and scared. My whole sense of reality was screwed up. My father was an adult. He chose to believe in a reality he wanted to see."

"That's ridiculous. No father wants to look into his son's eyes and find a maniac staring back at him."

"Mine does. I stayed indoors for a whole year once, and he still looked at me like a clump of shit clinging to a dog's ass. He discusses his sexuality with this snot-nosed frat boy psychiatrist and expects me to trust the guy with my secrets, too. He never tells me anything personal about himself, yet he trusts a god damned student who's been in practice less than a year. Perhaps he thinks I'll stab him with a fork or bash his skull with a frying pan because he likes to sleep with dudes."

"How do you know what he discusses with his friend?"

"Because I'm an eavesdropper, okay! I'm the worst sneak ever, but only because he drives me nuts. I wish he cared enough to spy on me when I was accused of vandalizing every mansion in town. Perhaps he would've learned a thing or two about my real whereabouts."

Kelly laid a hand on his shoulder. "Come on, Darren. I refuse to believe your father is the monster you make him out to be. If you tell him about what happened with Carlos, I'll come to dinner and back you up."

"No way. If I rat on Carlos, my dad will have ten attorneys barking down his throat. That's no way to treat a man who has worked so hard to turn his life around."

"You could care less about what happens to Carlos. You're just making excuses not to talk to your dad. You think I can't see that?"

"I'm *not* making excuses."

"Fine. We don't have to tell him it was Carlos. We'll say it was some dark, mysterious man who hung out in the woods and ate children for breakfast."

"It's all water under the bridge, Kelly. Just let it rest."

"No! I can't let you keep this buried forever. It's not fair to you, and it's certainly not fair to your father."

Darren grasped her shoulders hard enough to leave fingernail impressions on her flesh. "I'll share secrets with my dad when he decides he can trust me with his own secrets, and not a moment sooner. Do you understand?"

"No! I don't understand. This is your father, Darren. He deserves to..."

Darren squashed his sandwich into a napkin and buried his face under the covers. "Thanks for ruining my dinner. Are you going to let me sleep, or will I have to take you home?"

Kelly was seized by the sudden urge to pound his blanketed body with her fists. "What makes you so sure I have to be *taken* home? For your information, I have plenty of cash for a cab. I'm not quite as destitute as you'd like to believe."

Darren popped his head out from under the blanket. "Just calm down, okay? One minute, you can't face my dad, and the next minute, you want to march up to his front door and make a grand confession. Think about what you're saying here."

"I shouldn't have to think every time I open my mouth. I should be able to speak my mind without you threatening to take me home. Is this how it's going to be every time we disagree about something? If so, that really sucks."

He took her into his arms. "You're absolutely right. It was an awful thing to say. I was just scared of you, Kelly. I pictured you banging on his front door at 3 o'clock in the morning without me. i'm so sorry."

Kelly studied Darren's eyes. He certainly seemed sincere, but that was beside the point. Over the past few weeks, she'd come to see the Price Estate as more than just a temporary escape from the city. In her heart of hearts, she'd dared to dream it was possible to make a permanent home of the guest house. It wasn't just the pretty cobblestone path or the hand carved oak trim that filled her heart with so much joy. It was the idea that she fit into Darren's life like a long lost piece to a jig saw puzzle. She was just foolish enough to think she completed him in some profound and earth-shattering way. Now, it was quite obvious he considered another place to be her home.

Kelly grabbed her backpack and slipped out of the house without fanfare. She was near the water's edge when she heard a stay branch snap under Darren's foot. His expensive tennis shoes pounded the trail like the moccasins of a crazed tribal warrior. Just for kicks, she cut through the sledge surrounding the pond, forcing him to waddle through mud on his mission to catch her. Dusk was swiftly closing in, and it was important to confront him with a few obstacles. He knew the woods like the back of his hand. She had no prayer of escaping while light still poured from the sky.

Her goal was to get off the trail leading to the playground. He would expect her to take the path of least resistance. When a twist in landscape provided a moment of cover, she ducked behind a patch of young pines and waited for him to pass. Sure enough, she heard the telltale sound of his tennis shoes sucking the damp earth. He was headed for the playground.

She remained hidden in the trees until the last traces of light disappeared from the sky. She knew a lot of girls who were afraid to set foot in the woods after dark, but she was not spooked by the sound of a lone owl hooting in the distance. She had confronted far worse horrors on the streets of her own neighborhood and in dark corners of her own home.

She was rifling through her backpack in search of the pipe when Darren closed his arms around her from behind. His body trembled in time with the relentless buzz of crickets and katydids. "Please," he whispered. "Don't do this."

"Give me one good reason why I shouldn't."

His shallow breaths sent puffs of air into her ear. "For starters, I love you, but it's so much more than that. I can't imagine going to sleep at night without my arm tossed over your shoulder or waking up without my face buried in your chest. I need you to get through every hour of the day, just like you need your little baths to replenish your spirit and make you whole again. I'm addicted to you, Kelly. You're my drug of choice."

She gasped in the darkness. The cool, damp air filled her lungs with an unbearable weight. "How did you know about the purpose of my baths?"

"I've spent more time than I care to admit in places you'd never imagine. I know exactly what the stuff smells like."

"Damn it, Darren! Why didn't you say anything? How could you just let me make a fool of myself day after day?"

He grasped her shoulders and spun her around to face him. His wet eyes glowed in the pale moonlight. "I believe that if you can't love someone no matter what, you can't really love them at all."

That night, Kelly marched into the guest house and unfastened the shoe string that anchored the tent to the light fixture. Darren watched in horror as the whole structure collapsed inward upon itself. "Why did you do that?" he asked.

"We're not children anymore. It was fun to pretend for awhile, but the truth is I've changed too much, and so have you."

"Does this mean you're leaving?"

Kelly unfastened the buttons on her blouse and let it drop to the floor. "No. It means I'm staying."

They came together slowly, crossing an ocean of carpet to meet at the center of the room. He kissed her with more tenderness than she'd ever known, starting at her forehead and moving down to each eye lid before pressing his lips to her mouth. She grasped his waist and moved herself against him, teasing him just a bit before unfastening his belt. He inhaled his way down her neckline, stopping briefly to run his tongue along her cleavage. They undressed in spurts—a bra here, a rumpled pant leg there—taking innocent pleasure in the unmasking of each new forbidden zone. She caressed his bare legs for the first time, recording the shape and texture of an ancient scar above his right knee. He ran his hands down her back and over her buttocks, massaging her bare flesh with varying degrees of strength and pressure.

He entered her on the floor near the fireplace, looking down into her eyes and through her very soul. She held his gaze from moment to moment, never daring to blink away the intoxicating spell. As his thrusting grew more insistent, she grasped his hips and guided him in precise circular motions. Together, they found a groove so intense that moving a single inch would've destroyed the rhythm. Darren threw himself into that groove, nailing it harder and harder until Kelly's body exploded into a fit of trembling. She'd always thought that noises were for drama queens with something to prove, but tonight she couldn't control the piercing wail that shot forth from the depths of her lungs. Large drops of his sweat trickled down her cheek and stained the corner of her mouth with his salty-sweet taste. She usually hated the part of sex where a man's body oils mixed with hers, but she found herself savoring Darren's personal scent. "It's disgusting how much I love you," she said.

Before Darren could reply, the front door flung open and banged against the wall in the foyer. Kelly barely had time to scramble under the fallen tent before footsteps came barging into the living room. Peaking through the little hole where the shoelace had been threaded, she saw Roland standing face to face with Darren. A little brown Cocker Spaniel pranced about, stopping briefly to sniff the wet spot on the floor by the fireplace.

"I was taking Paris for a walk, and I heard a woman screaming. What's going on in here?"

Darren made a sweeping gesture with his right arm. "I was just practicing my opera."

"Cut the sarcasm. I know what I heard."

"All right, all right. I was watching a little porn. As you can see, I'm dressed for the occasion."

Darren stepped into his jeans as Roland studied the DVD player. "There is no pornography in this machine. That was a cry of terror if I ever heard one."

"Did it ever occur to you that I could've been watching a horror movie on televison?"

"No. Where is she?"

"She's hiding from you, asshole."

"Is she hurt?"

"I don't know. She may have a few carpet burns."

Kelly popped her head out from under the blanket. "It's okay," she said. "I'll be leaving soon."

Roland's face reddened on the spot. "I... I'm terribly sorry. I wasn't aware that Darren had company. Please, stay right where you are."

With no further words, Roland made a break for the door. He was so distraught that he forgot to let the dog follow him outside. It pounced upon the fallen tent and begged Kelly for attention. She fed it a handful of Fruit Loops from Darren's special stash.

For the next half hour, Darren went on and on about his father's rudeness. He didn't seem to be the least bit embarrassed about being caught with his pants down. He only wanted to talk about the fact that his father had automatically assumed the worst. "See what I mean? The man is incorrigible!"

"He has a suspicious nature, I'll give you that. Most dads would've been angry about the sexual aspect of it all. He was just relieved to see you weren't torturing me with an ice pick."

"His attitudes toward sex are pretty liberal, as you can imagine. Too bad he can't loosen up with some of his attitudes toward me."

"In all fairness, he's been confronted with plenty of evidence that you're capable of extreme violence. His suspicion is a conditioned response."

"Let's not talk about it. I'm getting a headache. Are you hungry? We could fry up some hamburger, if you like."

"Actually, I'm in dire need of a bathroom break."

"Why waste the water? You don't have to hide it anymore."

"I hide because I'm ashamed."

Darren flopped over on the couch. "Have you ever considered going through rehab?"

"A basic two-week program at a public facility is the equivalent of slapping a band-aid on a bullet wound. You have to attend classes after you're released, and you begin to forge relationships with a bunch of other weak people who can't wait to go out looking for drugs after class. I've never met anyone who didn't go back to the pipe within weeks."

"It worked for Carlos, didn't it?"

"Not exactly. He went through an aggressive three-month program at a private retreat in Canada."

"I can take you to the same place, if that's what you need."

"It's not as simple as that. Mom and Carlos aren't legally married. I'm not covered by his insurance."

"How much would it cost to get you into that program?"

"The bill came to $50,000 for Carlos. I'm sure it's more by now. If the price of a good hamburger has gone up sixty cents in the last four years, I shudder to imagine how much the cost of intensive therapy has increased."

"We could always ask my dad for the money."

"How tacky! One minute, he catches me screwing his son's brains out, and the next minute, I'm hitting him up for a loan to get rid of my crack problem. Mom always said I was a charmer."

"I told you, he's pretty liberal for an old dude. I'm sure he'll be more than happy to help when he learns that you're the same little girl who used to sketch rabbits with me at the kitchen table."

"I guess I should've reintroduced myself when I had the chance. It'll be even more difficult to face him now."

"Promise me you'll at least consider it."

"Believe me, I already am."

✷ ✷ ✷ ✷ ✷

The Present

Mr. Rivard wasn't sure how Roland might react to a surprise visit from a virtual stranger, and he didn't particularly care. Darren hadn't bothered to return his calls regarding the success of the Halloween exhibition. His motorcycle was standing right outside the guest house, yet he refused to answer the door. If the kid couldn't understand the importance of honoring business obligations, perhaps his father would help explain it to him.

He was surprised to discover that Roland was a pale man with sagging cheeks and lazy blue eyes. He stood in his exquisite Victorian parlor draped in dirty flannel and faded denim. He didn't appear to be the poised and sophisticated gentleman Darren had made him out to be. He drank brandy straight from the bottle and sported flecks of dried leaves in his silvery white hair.

"I'm sure my son isn't ignoring you intentionally," he said after learning of Mr. Rivard's ongoing quest to inform Darren about the WildHeart opportunity. "It's been a very trying week for both of us. Please don't ask me to explain."

Mr. Rivard felt a sudden wave of regret. In his agitated state, he'd painted a mental picture of Darren as a spoiled brat who moved from project to project without a sense of commitment. He hadn't even considered that there might've been some sort of turmoil in the family. "I'm very sorry to have disturbed you," he said. "I didn't mean to barge in here at half past midnight with a briefcase full of contracts. I simply want what's best for your son. I assure you this is a bonafide opportunity and a chance of a lifetime."

Roland looked a little nervous. "Have you made any promises to Allen Trent?" he asked.

"Of course not. No one can force Darren to sell the copyrights to his hunter series, but I do believe he's obligated to paint the winner's portrait and hand over the merchandise he's agreed to sell. I don't want to bring this all down to business, but I have a reputation to uphold. By displaying his art on my property, I've made a tacit agreement with potential customers. I can't just tell them the paintings they love so dearly are no longer available because the artist has lost interest in the project."

Roland shook his head. "Darren hasn't lost interest in this project. He obviously entrusted you to handle the finer details. He's probably assuming you'll distribute the merchandise and cash the checks yourself."

"I'm afraid it's not that simple. The checks are made out to Darren."

Roland nodded his head, as if the whole situation had finally become clear. "Darren will honor his obligations," he said firmly. "And, of course, I'll see to it that he mails your cut of the profits, whatever that may be."

"I'm not after a cut of the action, but I do believe Darren should repay the loan he insisted I take out."

Roland left the room and returned with a little brown checkbook. "How much do I owe you?" he asked.

"Put your book away. I'll take the money from Darren or no one at all. If he's going to dabble in business ownership, he should learn that expenses go hand in hand with profits. It's my job to provide guidance to young entrepreneurs, and I take that responsibility very seriously."

Roland was quiet for a moment. The stern expression on his face slowly melted into a frown. "I believe I owe you an apology. I misunderstood your intentions. Is helping young businessmen a hobby of yours?"

It was precisely the opening Mr. Rivard was waiting for. He dove into an animated discussion of his new charity like a proud father handing out cigars at the hospital. Roland listened with intense interest, his dull eyes brightening with each passing moment. At long last, Mr. Rivard saw glimpses of the poised aristocrat Darren spoke of so lovingly. Even in faded denim and dirty flannel, he was as polished as a brand new penny.

Chapter Seventeen: The Past

Shortly after the encounter with his father, Darren took Kelly for a special late-night ride. He claimed there was nothing like a night on the open freeway to cleanse the soul, but she suspected he had a hidden agenda. When he took the exit ramp leading to her neighborhood, she realized her suspicions weren't so far off base.

They flew past the row of dilapidated houses on the street where she grew up and came to an abandoned school building with boarded up windows. It was the place where Kelly spent most of her days before wide scale budget cuts forced the school district to hold elementary classes in a separate wing of the high school building. An eerie feeling of nostalgia moved through the pit of her stomach as they cut through the old playground and parked beside the rusty metal slide where she'd won her first fight and broken her first bone.

"It's dangerous here," she said. "We really shouldn't stay long."

"I have a gun," he assured her.

"So do half the kids in this neighborhood."

"I'm not worried about it. Crazy Cain is in concert at the Metro Dome. Every thug in town is sure to be there."

Kelly relaxed a bit. "I guess you have a point."

Lost in thought, she wandered along the back of the building and ran her fingers over the cold brick surface. Dated slogans such as "Where's the beef?" and "Homey don't play that" documented the last three decades in bold flourescent colors. Crouching near the lowest portion of the wall, she pointed to a funny little caricature of a frog wearing a baseball cap. "That one is mine!"

Darren's eyes brightened. "I knew it! I came across that picture a few months ago, and I thought it looked like those crazy little frogs you used to doodle in your notebook."

"You've been coming around here that long?"

"Of course. I used to drive down your street looking for the little green house you described when we were nine. I saw you sitting with Carlos a few times, but I could never seem to catch you alone. "

"You never cease to amaze me. Is there some reason why you brought me here?"

"As a matter of fact, there is."

Darren retrieved a can of spray paint from his saddle bag and drew the symbol of a local gang on the wall in front of him. Kelly gasped in horror when she realized what he was trying to accomplish. "Stop! You're going to get people killed!"

"That's the point. Keep them fighting among themselves, and they won't have time to terrorize innocent children, like your friend Clarissa."

Kelly removed her tennis shoe and pegged Darren on the back of the neck. "You mother fucker! I read about this in the paper!"

"Calm down. These kids chose to defend their territory long before I set foot in this neighborhood. I didn't start the war. I'm just engineering another battle."

"But you can't just..."

Darren whipped the can of paint at Kelly. "Take your life back!"

She caught it like a seasoned umpire. "I can't."

"Yes, you can. You're not a victim anymore. You're an instigator!"

Kelly pointed the nozzle at the wall and drew an incomplete circle. Her trembling arm wouldn't allow her to finish the symbol. "I'm sorry. I can't play God with you. I won't punish a new generation of kids for the things their older brothers did to my friend. I can't be the kind of person you need me to be right now."

Darren leaned against the wall and regarded her with detached amusement. "What if I told you there's a reward in it for you?"

"What kind of reward?"

"A natural high more intense than any crack pipe could deliver."

A blinding light switched on in Kelly's mind. "I think you've found the magic words." A double shot of adrenaline pumped through her veins as she raised the nozzle to the wall and completed the symbol. With no further prompting, she darted about the playground covering every printable surface with the same slashes and symbols she'd taught Darren to draw so many years ago. No piece of equipment was safe from the slide to the merry-go-round to the rusted jungle gym where gang members had draped Clarissa's frail body over a metal bar.

An animal rage burned deep within her heart. This was her special place, and they'd littered it with condoms, syringes and blood-stained bandannas. They'd made Clarissa into an example of what could happen to little girls who dared to go bike riding at dusk. They had also made their way into Kelly's nightmares, forcing her to live through unspeakable horrors right along with Clarissa. They didn't deserve to roam the face of the Earth with their switch blade knives and God-sized attitudes.

The rush lasted about seventeen times longer than a crack high. Even as she walked along the cobblestone path leading to Darren's house, her heart raced ahead of her feet. They made love again by the fireplace that night, releasing some of the pent-up energy that burned deep within. Sleep finally claimed them as the night sky faded into day. For the first time in years, she slept for six solid hours.

Around half past noon, the maid showed up with a picnic basket jammed with fresh baked bread and generous slices of roast turkey and ham. The meat was not purchased from a deli: It had literally been roasting in the oven all morning. The basket also contained a variety of gourmet spreads in miniature mason jars. A small note was taped inside the lid:

> Darren,
> I truly regret barging in on you last night. Please accept this basket as my peace offering and tell Kelly she's welcome to join us for dinner this evening at six.
> Love, Dad

When Darren passed the note to Kelly, she nearly choked on a big bite of turkey. "I can't believe he recognized me! I haven't set foot in his house since I was a child."

"What's so hard to believe? You have the kind of face that could stop a train. The moment I saw it, I knew I'd never forget."

"Stop. You're embarrassing me."

"You never could accept a compliment."

"So stop showering me with them."

"Fine. From now on, I'm going to call you Dog Face."

"Call me anything you like, as long as you keep calling."

Darren ran his bare foot up the side of her ankle. "You know something? I'm glad that I don't have to pick up a phone whenever I want to see you. I've always hated that part of dating. If you call every single day, you come off as a leech. If you wait a few days between calls, it appears as if you've lost interest."

Kelly snatched a slice of ham from his plate. "So, tell me. Who did you call every single day?"

"Do I detect a note of jealousy?"

"Think of it as a note of curiosity."

"I'm not going to tell you. You'll laugh me under the table."

"I won't even crack a smile. I promise."

"Fine. It was Shelly Whipple after she slimmed down."

"What! I thought you hated her guts!"

"I did, but she started following me around after I shaved her head. She was suddenly hot for me."

"You've got to be kidding. Since when is forced head shaving an aphrodisiac?"

"I don't know. I just barely understood it myself."

"So, did you draw her little pictures of bunny rabbits and carve her name into your desk? Did you send her flowers and take her to homecoming?"

Darren rolled his eyes. "Do I look like the kind of guy who goes to dances? It wasn't that kind of relationship."

"What kind of relationship was it?"

"Put it this way: I never begged her to come home for dinner."

Kelly breathed a sigh of relief. She didn't particularly care who Darren had screwed in his seven year absence. Her heart was set on being the love of his life, and it sounded as if she had no competition in that department. That, in itself, was cause for celebration. A bathroom break was in order.

She was relaxing in the tub with her pipe when Darren burst into the room and took a seat on the edge of the bathtub. "You're not getting off that easy," he said.

"What do you mean?"

"I told you about the other someone in my life. I want to hear about your other someone."

Normally, that type of question would've made her nervous, but it was nearly impossible to feel bad after a fresh hit. "If you must know, there were several other someones."

"How many is several?"

"You don't want to know."

"Between five and ten?"

"Darren!"

"Between ten and twenty?"

"Stop."

"Forty?"

"Probably less than forty."

"Probably! You mean you aren't sure?"

Still reeling from the hit, Kelly shot him a sarcastic smile. "If you can't love someone no matter what, you can't really love them at all."

Minutes later, when the synthetic euphoria of her buzz had leveled off, Kelly found herself alone and paranoid. She understood that Darren's anger had little to do with the fact that she'd given herself to so many others. What he needed was some kind of assurance that he was the best thing that had ever walked into her life. She could've told him that the love she felt for him was stronger than any emotion she'd ever experienced. Instead, she'd chosen to hit the pipe one more time and enjoy the sensation with her eyes closed. By the time she opened them, he was gone.

Soaking wet and shivering to the bone, she studied her reflection in the oversized vanity mirror. She had no idea why she was considered to be some kind of beauty queen. Her jet black hair had absolutely no warmth and character. She'd tried to lighten it once, but the auburn dye didn't take. Her pale blue eyes were an oddity. They didn't suit her dark skin whatsoever. Worst of all, her bony silhouette was totally void of shape and definition. There was a time when she had reasonably round breasts and an ass that could stop traffic, but her body had gone to shit in the last year. They called it the crack diet, and it worked a little too well. "You're a scrawny ass whore, just like your mother," she said to her own reflection. "You don't deserve him, and you never will."

She emerged from the bathroom to find that Darren had left the house. Peeking through the thick curtains, she saw that his motorcycle was no longer parked out front. Fresh tracks in the lawn indicated that he'd left in a reckless rush. She desperately wanted to cry, but she was somehow beyond that. Tears seemed to be a hopelessly inadequate outlet for her frustration.

Another taste of the pipe gave her the energy to work out a plan. Darren would have to return sometime, and when he did, she would do something special for him. She considered cleaning the house, but it wasn't that messy. When he required that kind of assistance, a maid was just a phone call away. She thought about taking a cab to the mall to find him a present, but he already had every material comfort a teenager could possibility want.

Thinking back to age nine, she tried to remember what kind of things really pleased him. Even then, he was a simple kid who didn't put the luxuries of his estate to good use. He barely ever swam in the pool, and his upscale playhouse was buried under a thick layer of dust. The one thing that brought him great joy was art. He loved pictures of all kinds, even her childish reproductions of animal life in the woods.

Sitting down at the kitchen table with a package of colored pencils, she went to work on transferring her feelings to paper. Amazingly, her artistic skills had grown leaps and bounds without much practice over the years. She was able to sketch a fairly accurate caricature of herself and the flaws she needed to correct. Her long dark hair hung to her waist in a crazy mass of knots and tangles. Her pupils were fixed at opposite corners, like the eyes of a babbling lunatic. Her naked body was twisted and misshapen. You could count every rib in her breastless chest.

When the caricature was complete, Kelly added dozens of little green men to the picture. Each figure had its own little crack pipe and its own toothy grin. She had only intended to illustrate that Darren meant more to her than any of the dope fiends who'd passed through her life, but as she studied the finished product in the afternoon sun, she realized it sent a much stronger message. Without Darren's love, she was something less than human—a thing to be used and discarded by anyone seeking a temporary fix.

Darren returned that evening around half past six. Before she could apologize for her apathetic behavior in the bathroom, he thrust a brightly colored package into her hands. "Put this on!" he demanded. "We've missed dinner, but there's still time for a little conversation by the fire."

Kelly was slipping into her new black dress when Darren burst into the bathroom with the caricature in his hands. She'd never seen so much anger in his deeply set eyes. "This is the most ridiculous thing I've ever seen!" he shouted. "If this is what crack is doing to your self image, I'm flushing it all down the toilet right now."

"Don't bother. I smoked more than my share today. There are only two rocks left, and I need them to get through tonight. If you don't mind, I'd like to face your father with a smile. Believe me, he doesn't want to spend the evening with some nervous bitch who can't concentrate on the conversation."

"Fine. Let's compromise. You can have one rock now, and we'll flush the other."

"It doesn't work that way! I can't get through something stressful without the knowledge that there's a reward waiting for me on the other side."

Darren banged his head against the bathroom door. "Are you listening to yourself? That mentality will keep you between rocks forever."

"Not forever. It's almost gone, remember?"

Going back on her word, Kelly smoked the second rock five minutes after finishing the first one. When the short-lived buzz leveled off, a rush of anxiety set her heart racing against the clock. She begged Darren not to make her face his father. Much to her surprise, he agreed to let her stay home. In fact, he said he was glad that her supply had been exhausted. Perhaps now the healing could begin.

By 8 o'clock, she was craving another hit. She begged Darren to drive her to the city for just an hour, but he wouldn't hear of it. She threatened to walk through the woods and meet a cab at the playground, but he reminded her that it was impossible to outrun him, especially on his own turf.

When threats proved useless, she resorted to lies. "I'm getting sick," she said, clutching her abdomen like a soap star. "If you let me go on like this, I could literally end up in the hospital. You can't just expect me to go cold turkey. It could kill me. Do you understand?"

Darren chuckled. "That happens with heroin, not crack. You're not going to get sick and keel over on me. You'll only wish you were dead."

"You think you're pretty smart, don't you? You've seen a few drug education films at school, and suddenly you're an expert. You have no idea what I'm going through."

Darren smiled down at her. "I wouldn't be so sure about that. I know a thing or two about the need for a rush."

"Oh yeah? Does the need control every aspect of your personality? Does it start in the pit of your stomach and radiate through every nerve in your body?"

"Yes."

"Do you ever feel that no pleasure on God's green Earth could quiet the yearning, not even sex?"

"Yes."

"Would you kill or die for it?"

Darren's eyes flashed. "Absolutely."

Kelly was skeptical. Darren's need to place himself in dangerous situations could hardly compare to her need for crack. She felt the yearning every waking moment of the day and fought with herself to keep from smoking more than fifteen rocks in a 24-hour period. Darren's power trips to the playground were more like a hobby. He could get by with one rush every once in awhile. As much as he liked to brag, he had no idea what it was like to be dependent upon a synthetic substance for day-to-day and moment-to-moment survival. She refused to believe their addictions were related in some fundamental way.

In spite of her doubts, she agreed to take a ride with Darren to calm her nerves. A playground rush was better than no rush at all, and it had the potential to quiet her yearning for at least one more night.

Around 9 o'clock, she found herself sipping lukewarm coffee at a greasy little diner a few miles from her parent's house. She'd wanted a seat at the counter, but Darren insisted upon taking one of the booths situated along the window facing the street. As she studied the curious mix of people shuffling by, she wished that she could fall into step behind them. Every nerve in her body was on fire. The very act of sitting seemed a colossal waste of energy.

Darren's attention was focused on a flamboyant little man who swaggered down the sidewalk with the confidence of a seven-foot-tall basketball star. His three piece suit was made of top grain purple leather, and his wide brimmed hat practically swallowed his tiny head. When he turned to light a cigarette, Kelly was surprised to discover that his skin was only a few shades brighter than paste. Somewhere along the line, he'd adopted the mannerisms of a black man. He was also stuck in the past. His rhythmic walk bore a striking resemblance to Richard Pryor's famous ghetto strut.

"They call that guy Napoleon," Darren said. "Do you know why?"

"I'm sure it has something to do with his height."

"That's only part of it. He's a legend in his own mind. That swing in his step doesn't come from a bottle. He's positively drunk on his own power."

"Let me guess. He's a pimp, right?"

"Not just any pimp. The fucker eats little girls for breakfast. He puts 12-year-olds to work and keeps them strung out on heroin so they'll always have a reason to check in."

"What's so unusual about that? It's how the game is played."

"You don't understand. This guy is particularly brutal. He specializes in providing girls who are willing to engage in masochistic rituals."

"You mean like whips and chains?"

"That and much more. When the price is right, he allows his girls to be killed. They check into special soundproof rooms in his motel anticipating a little spanking, and they don't come out alive."

"That's horrible! Why would you drive all the way out here just to get a look at that piece of shit?"

Darren opened a packet of sugar for his coffee. "Would you believe someone wants to pay me to kill him?"

"Who? An irate father?"

"No. Some bar owner who doesn't like hookers hanging around his corner and directing foot traffic to the motel down the street."

"Donovan?"

"Yes, Donovan."

"So, this is all about business?"

"For him it is. For me, it's personal. I'd waste that dude for free without thinking twice about it."

"Are you serious? You would actually kill a person?"

"Yes. I'd do it for the rush, and so would you."

Kelly shifted positions in her seat. She was suddenly ashamed to be looked upon. "Why would you assume I'm capable of murder? Do you think so little of me?"

"On the contrary, I think very highly of you. You have the instincts of a protector. I've worked very hard to develop a sense of honor and courage. You came by those qualities naturally. You saved my ass from David in the woods, and you stood up to Carlos at a time when you weren't sure if he'd beat the living hell out of you. You're absolutely fearless. If I lived to be 100, I'd never find a stronger hero."

Kelly was too confused to feel flattered. "Let me get this straight. You brought me all the way out here to help you waste some pimp?"

"No. I brought you here to offer you a choice. I could help you find another five-minute rush from one of your suppliers, or I could provide you with a natural high that lasts indefinitely."

"No high lasts indefinitely."

"This one does. I can promise you that the mere memory of it will have you wired."

Kelly should've been appalled, but she wasn't. A few moments ago, she had no sense of control over her own destiny. Her every thought was guided by the need for a synthetic substance she'd grown to hate. Now, she felt empowered by the knowledge that she had the ability to bring about a real change in the world. The mere thought of killing Napoleon was intoxicating. "Let's do it," she said.

"Not so fast. We're not choosing an item on the menu here. This decision is for life. Once you've killed someone, you can never look in the mirror and see the same person again."

Kelly felt a smile tugging at the corners of her mouth. The thought of becoming someone else wasn't as frightening as it should've been. She wasn't comfortable with her identity to start with. She'd always considered herself to be the worst kind of criminal. As a kid, she brought tragedy into the lives of innocent children by endangering their families. In more recent years, she'd introduced a lethal addiction to teenagers who didn't know what it meant to be dependent upon anything stronger than cigarettes or Cherry Coke. This was a prime opportunity to effect a positive change on the very neighborhood she'd helped to weaken and destroy. Instead of contributing to the world's chaos, she could help put an end to it.

* * * * *

The Present

Samantha had never set foot near Darren's house in broad daylight, but she was on a special mission for Donovan. Darren hadn't been around in weeks, and everyone was starting to worry that he'd finally found more danger than he could handle. Samantha was elected to play detective because she'd shared more intimate moments with him than anyone else.

The Price Estate was even more spectacular when bathed in sunlight. A fresh blanket of snow covered the ground, turning the property into a vast winter wonderland. Artfully arranged clusters of spruce and pine were capped by a fine powder that glistened at every turn. The winding drive leading to the northern end of the estate was completely free of ice and debris. She briefly wondered whose job it was to maintain the immense property.

She arrived at the guest house to find a tall blonde slipping a note under Darren's door. A girlfriend, perhaps? She tried not to let pangs of jealousy cloud her judgement. It was high time Darren found someone who could offer him a little more than an occasional dance between the sheets.

"Is there room under that door for another note?" she asked.

The girl turned abruptly, revealing a weary face with a grotesquely exaggerated jaw line. "There's plenty of room."

They stood there for an awkward moment, exhaling steamy breaths that floated on frigid air. Samantha let her eyes wander around the property to avoid staring at the girl's misshapen face. Finally, she extended her right hand. "My name is Samantha Becker. I'm an old friend of Darren's."

The girl's hand shook under Samantha's grasp. "It's nice to meet you."

"If you see him around, could you please tell him that his friends are worried he's laying in a ditch somewhere? We haven't heard from him in quite awhile."

The girl looked down at her feet. "The chances of me seeing him are relatively slim, but I can assure you he's not laying in a ditch. I saw him just a few days ago. He was looking forward to holding an art exhibition on Halloween night."

"Really? That's wonderful! How did it go?"

"I don't know. I was supposed to be there, but I sort of stood him up. I feel awful about it. That's what the note is for—to apologize."

Samantha was stunned when tears came rolling down the girl's face. Why was she so guilty about failing to be there on Darren's big night? Was this the end of some kind of relationship? If so, Samantha finally had evidence to support her theory that Darren had a heart of gold buried beneath his rough exterior. Plenty of beautiful women at Donovan's Pub had shown interest in dating him, but he seemed to gravitate toward select women based on their inner qualities.

Samantha knew nothing about the timid young woman standing before her, but her sisterly instincts led her to slip one arm around the girl's shoulder. "Don't worry about Darren. I've known him since he was a teenager. I can assure you he's very resilient."

"Please don't tell him you saw me like this."

"I wouldn't do anything of the kind."

The girl used the sleeve of her coat to dry her tear-streaked face. "You must think I'm a basket case."

"Not at all."

"I'm not in the habit of hurting people. It doesn't come easily."

"You have nothing to feel guilty about. It's dangerous to stay with someone for the wrong reasons. Trust me, it's too easy to get stuck."

"You're right. And he's got his career to think about. I could very well be doing him a favor."

"His career?"

"He wants to take this art thing to the next logical level. He doesn't feel he has enough challenges in life, and he thinks that opening a gallery would be the perfect solution."

Samantha's heart skipped a beat. "You're kidding me! This is the best news I've heard all week!"

Later that day, Samantha marched into Donovan's office and told him that Darren was purposely distancing himself from the bar in order to start a new life. Much to her surprise, the old man couldn't have been happier.

Chapter Eighteen: The Past

It was quiet on the street when Kelly brushed past Napoleon. Stopping a few feet away from the diner's main window, she attempted to light a cigarette. Each time she brought a match to the tip, a gush of air from her nostrils extinguished the flame.

"Havin' trouble, baby?" he asked.

"Yeah. Fuckin' wind's drivin' me nuts."

He passed a jeweled lighter under her cigarette. "Allow me."

"Thanks, man."

"No problem. You as fine as you wanna be. What's yo name?"

"Kelly."

He grabbed her right hand and brought it to his lips. "It's a pleasure, Miss Kelly. You hungry? Looks like you could use a good steak, and I'm just the one to buy it."

"I couldn't eat if I tried. You down?"

"I might be. Depends on what you need."

Kelly rolled up the sleeve of her sweatshirt, revealing a nasty bruise created with purple eye shadow. "I could use a new friend."

"You in luck. I'm friendly as they come."

"Oh yeah? How much?"

"Whachoo mean how much? Can't a nigga treat a lady around here?"

Kelly bit her lip to keep from laughing. Had he really called himself a "nigga"? She didn't mind white dudes who talked black, as long as they did it with a measure of style and finesse. This guy's speech rhythms were a little off beat. He wasn't born of the city: He'd adopted it for his own purposes.

"Sorry. I wasn't countin' on findin' a gentleman around here. I stay at the Foxton, room ten. Will I see you soon?"

"Very soon, baby. You can count on it."

Room ten at the Foxton was a tasteless hole with yellowing walls and faded red carpet. Cigarette burns dotted the old satin bedspread, dyed purple to cover old stains. A dense floral pattern was still visible through the fabric's shimmery surface. Dime store posters of Marilyn Monroe covered the walls, their dog-eared corners curling inward upon themselves.

"I take it he likes blondes," Kelly said.

Darren positioned himself behind the door. "He likes any woman who is fragile and easily manipulated."

"Oh yeah? How do you know so much about him?"

"He's the stuff of local legends. I shared a park bench with him once. God help me, but I wanted to get inside his head. We traded stories well into the night."

Kelly toyed with the basic butcher knife Darren had provided. It was a humble instrument with a long wooden handle marred by countless dishwasher cycles. "What if I lunge at him and miss? What if he sinks his nails into my wrist, like in the movies?"

Darren shook his head. "This isn't Hollywood. A knife always finds its way home."

A sudden knock sent Kelly's heart racing. Clutching the knife behind her back, she inched toward the door. Napoleon greeted her with a toothy grin. She answered with a seductive smile.

The moment Napoleon stepped inside the room, Darren pressed a gun to his ear. When Kelly swooped in to check his pockets for weapons, he blew a hot gob of saliva into her eyes. "Go on and try it, bitch! I'll nail yo ass to the wall for entrapment. I aine offered to sell you shit. The little bit I got was 'posed to be a gift."

"You got it all wrong. I'm not a cop."

"What the fuck are you then?"

Kelly pressed the cold steel blade to his neck. "Your worst nightmare."

Under Darren's watchful eye, she used strips of torn bedding to secure Napoleon's wrists to the headboard. Even with a gun pointed at his face, the man couldn't keep his mouth shut. "You goin' through a whole lotta trouble just to steal a nigga's dope. The joke's on you, dog. The shit in my pocket aine worth but a dime. Let me go, and I'll take ya to my stash."

Darren laughed. "Nobody's interested in your dope. How about we shove it up your ass?"

"Just shoot the son of a bitch," Kelly said. "I'm tired of his mouth."

Darren eyed the little man with contempt. "A bullet is too quick for him. He should experience the same torment he's inflicted upon others."

Napoleon was surprisingly docile as Kelly sealed his lips shut with a strip of bedding. She'd initially worried that her hands would shake through the whole process, but an eerie sense of inner calm guided her busy fingers. She felt like she was standing outside herself, watching the action from a quiet corner of the room. "What now?" she asked.

Darren ripped the clothing from Napoleon's frail body and handed her a rhinestone encrusted belt. It felt surprisingly good in her hands. The smooth, shiny jewels caressed her fingertips in the most sensual way possible. The sound of her own heartbeat reverberated through her ears. The rhythmic thumping infused her spirit with a grand sense of momentum, propelling her forward like music from a car stereo.

She brought the belt down on Napoleon's chest with a quick, razor-sharp whack. Tiny red depressions from the rhinestones dotted his light skin. His limp penis inflated to full capacity. "What the fuck!" she shrieked. "The freak likes it!"

Darren didn't appear to be surprised. "Fix it so he doesn't like it."

Kelly raised the belt over her head and cracked it down on Napoleon's erection. His whole body shuddered violently. Vomit gurgled in the back of his throat. Darren shot Kelly a cold smile. Fueled by his approval, she continued striking her way up Napoleon's body until his entire abdomen was riddled with tiny round depressions. Multicolored lumps rose from his flesh like boulders from a hillside.

She was about to bring the belt down on Napoleon's face when she caught sight of herself in a chintzy round mirror nailed to the ceiling above the bed. She could've sworn that her pupils were fixed at opposite corners of her eyes, like in the caricature she'd created at Darren's kitchen table. A sudden migraine rocked her skull. Had she finally transformed into the crazed lunatic of her nightmares? Instead of saving the world from freaks, had she let herself become one?

The revelation knocked the wind from her chest and drained the strength from her limbs. "Please!" she shouted, leaning against the wall for support. "Don't kill him!"

Ignoring her cries, Darren drove the dirty steel blade through Napoleon's heart. Blood spurted toward the ceiling in a sudden volcanic explosion. Kelly covered her face to escape the horror, but red fluid dripped behind her eyes and seeped to the back of her throat. Hot liquid poured from her nostrils. The taste of Napoleon's blood burned the surface of her tongue.

From that moment on, there were no secrets between Darren and Kelly. They returned to a guest house bathed in firelight and stretched out upon the fallen tent that had provided them with so much comfort in weeks past. With Napoleon's blood still fresh on their clothes, they sipped raspberry punch spiked with vodka and gazed up at the amazing collection of portraits that held the secrets to Darren's horrifying past.

"I finally understand your art," Kelly said, pointing to a picture of three mutilated birds with flies crawling across the surface of their flesh. "You killed them, didn't you? You kill things and paint them."

A distinct look of shame came over Darren's face. "As a child, my quest for honor and courage was misguided. I tortured small animals to see if I had the stomach for brutality. Back then, Carlos was the most fearless person I knew. I believed that I could develop raw courage by duplicating the horrifying acts he pulled off without flinching."

Tears stung Kelly's eyes. "You wanted to be like Carlos?"

"I wanted to be like any man who could inspire loyalty through fear. I was a pathetic excuse for a male, tormented by every bully who crossed my path in the woods. Shelly and David weren't the first. Half the kids at Parrington had my blood on their hands."

Kelly buried her face in his chest. "I'm so sorry, Darren. I'm sorry for everything."

"Don't apologize. If it weren't for you and Carlos, I might never have discovered the strength contained within my own hands—a strength powerful enough to crush a bird's bones or close a cat's airway in five seconds flat. I'm not proud of these moments, but I'm grateful for them just the same."

"Grateful?"

"Yes. Through my experiences with animals, I discovered that I was a force to be reckoned with."

"So you moved on to humans?"

"Yes. Tormenting helpless creatures is a pathetic pastime. It's much more satisfying to conquer the strong. From the moment I drove that staple through David Whipple's nostrils, I realized I held the power to intimidate almost anyone. With the right weapon, my frail arms could be more lethal than the muscular limbs of a prize fighter."

Kelly looked deep into the eyes of a boy she no longer recognized. "I understand your need to avenge yourself against the kids who tormented you, but there comes a time to let go of the anger. Why turn this into a lifelong pursuit?"

"Because the bullies in my little corner of the world are only part of the story. Innocent children are brutalized to a much greater extent in the city. As I grew taller and stronger, I couldn't get a decent rush from humiliating the same old guys who made my life miserable in elementary school. Why set your sights on a hill when you can climb a mountain?"

Kelly pulled away from him. "I don't buy that. There are better ways to reach a personal summit. What's wrong with you! Did you wake up one morning and decide it would be fun to start killing off gang members?"

"Not exactly. In my sophomore year of high school, I read an article about an inner city gang called the True Bloods. In order to gain admission to the prestigious group, candidates were required to rape, torture or kill an authority figure. Teachers, cops, employers, and even school security guards could qualify. Younger kids could secure membership in the lower ranks by stabbing hall monitors and student crossing guards. I had to do something! Local cops began to record the deaths of children with the same detached efficiency that they documented burglaries and traffic accidents."

"So you took it upon yourself to wipe out every gang in the city?"

"Not at all. I never would've dreamed that big. In the beginning, I was just looking to make a statement. I cornered a True Blood in a gas station bathroom and carved my initials into his back. Quite by accident, the letters "DP" were interpreted as a message from Dan Porter, the leader of a more established gang in the area. The resulting rumble sent four True Bloods to an early grave and landed nine others in the critical care unit. I was moved to tears when I heard the account on the evening news. With the help of my motorcycle and a can of spray paint, I was able to relieve that victory over and over again."

Kelly couldn't believe what she was hearing. Did he say he was moved to tears? Was his whole life based upon the pursuit of a poignant inner peace that came from killing? Perhaps their addictions weren't so different after all. "If you need a mood stabilizer so badly, I suggest you take up drugs."

Darren laughed. "And who would benefit from that? Since the inception of my silent campaign, four major gangs have vanished from the city. Remaining gang bangers spend so much time fighting among themselves that they have no time to torment the innocent. And it's all because of me, Kelly. *All* because of me."

Darren's eyes shone with an inner light as he told her of his personal vow to protect young people who didn't have the strength to protect themselves. He criticized men like Napoleon for being drunk on their own power but ignored his own intoxication. He was riding the crest of a supernatural high—cracked out on his own sense of authority and control.

She begged him not to disclose any further details about the life he'd created, but the words flowed from his lips like champagne. A flood gate had been opened, and she was powerless against the rising currents that threatened to sweep her out of Darren's life.

She was shocked to hear that Darren had learned of Donovan's business from his son Nicholas, who dated Shelly Whipple in high school. Nicholas had the balls to brag that his dad was some big important hit man. He said he could have Darren killed at the drop of a hat if he didn't stop messing with his girl. Darren's first visit to Donovan's Pub was a poorly executed attempt to discover if Nicholas was telling the truth. If he could prove the guy's story was just a line of bullshit, he would have the perfect weapon to humiliate young Nick in front of the whole school. He tried to pass off a fake ID in hopes of securing a private meeting with Donovan. He obtained the best license money could buy so that he'd be justified in demanding the owner's scrutiny. He never dreamed the bouncer would have the balls to treat him so brutally. Grown men weren't supposed to torment scrawny teenagers. It was the stuff lawsuits were made of.

"I could've handled a good beating, but Ron's tactics were considerably more vicious," he explained. "Painting my face with makeup was the equivalent of driving a knife through my heart. As a child, I'd endured unspeakable tortures for being the son of a gay man. Bullies like David had led me to believe I'd inherited the tendency myself. Ron's sadistic head games sent me back to a time when I feared I had no control over the kind of man I'd become."

"So why did you keep going back?" Kelly asked. "If your first trip to Donovan's was so horrifying, what led you to establish an ongoing relationship with him?"

Darren's eyes flashed again. He could hardly speak of his calling in life without lighting up from the inside. "When I learned that Donovan had his eye on some of the most brutal criminals in the city, I recognized the opportunity to combine business and pleasure. From the start, I made it clear that I had no interest in killing crime witnesses, cheating husbands or disgruntled employees who'd stumbled upon closely guarded corporate secrets. I didn't need fancy gadgets and specialized training; nor did I wish to take the most complicated route from point "A" to point "B." I wanted to kill murderers, and I reserved the right to do so in ways that I considered to be satisfying."

A wave of relief passed over Kelly's heart. "So, you're telling me that you've only killed people who have blood on their own hands?"

"That's exactly what I'm telling you. I want to make a difference in my lifetime. I want to die knowing that I've helped others to live."

Kelly couldn't very well pass judgement on Darren. Long before he became infatuated with killing, she'd played a crucial role in the murders of her friend's parents. Even after Carlos got out of the robbery business, she'd made plenty of people wish they were dead by introducing a wicked addiction into their lives. For these reasons, she decided to accept Darren's bizarre hobby for what it was—a disturbed teenager's misguided attempt to avenge himself against the world that crushed him. She knew a thing or two about unconditional love. If she could forgive her parents for raising her in the most unsuitable environment possible, she could learn to look past Darren's gaping flaws. If her mom could sit home and watch televison while Carlos broke into people's homes, there was no reason why she couldn't hang around the guest house while Darren pursued what he considered to be his calling. As she drifted off to sleep in his arms, she vowed to never lose sight of the child within him—a darkly innocent boy who sincerely believed he was performing a necessary service to society.

There was only one problem with her resolution: Her subconscious mind didn't always agree with her wakeful decisions. Since the onset of adolescence, she'd depended upon crack to keep her awake for days at a time. Without the drug, she was powerless against her nightmares.

It took only one night in hell for Kelly to break her vow. The clarity of her nightmare was unprecedented. For the first time, she became aware of the cave's charred clay walls and the flecks of hot ash beneath her feet. She felt the presence of a thousand souls and smelled their foul breath in the air. Looking down upon her blistered feet, she realized she had something the others didn't: a clear and visible body. She was not on fire. Her glistening brown legs were as smooth and flawless as the day she was born. She felt strangely alive. A deep, inner yearning propelled her to a separate chamber within the cave.

Darren was beautiful in a flowing black robe that brushed the top of his bare feet. A small campfire lit his face from below. His dark eyes held her image in their pupils. At the last possible moment, she became frightened. She feared that bonding with him would be the equivalent of becoming just like him. Instead of burning in hell forever, she would rule it at his side.

She awoke with the taste of blood in her mouth—Napoleon's blood. The dirty clothes that carried his essence clung to her skin. She tore them from her body and tossed them into the fireplace. Even while standing at the hearth, an intense shiver shot through her core. An extra hot shower failed to provide comfort. Images of Napoleon's mutilated body flashed behind her eyelids. The sight of a razor blade on the bathroom counter brought horrifying possibilities to mind. She wondered if Darren had ever used such an instrument to slit someone's throat.

While preparing warm milk to settle her stomach, she came across a drawer filled with basic kitchen knives. She wondered how many of them had been used to torment and kill. A cast iron skillet on the stove looked suspiciously like the perfect weapon to bash someone's skull. Every object in the house was suddenly an instrument of death.

It was painfully clear that she'd never be free of Napoleon as long as she remained with Darren. As much as she loved him, she couldn't become the kind of person he needed her to be. She took the wallet from his coat pocket and stole just enough money to meet a cab at the playground.

As the first traces of sunlight broke through the sky, Kelly flopped into her parent's bed like a mangled rag doll. They cried harder than three starving infants, not bothering to wipe their runny noses or censor their sloppy snorts. Later that morning, her mom prepared breakfast for the first time in years. As they feasted on hot buttered pasta and canned beef stew, Carlos joked that he hadn't been grocery shopping since the day she left. He asked no questions, and she told him no lies.

She was relieved to discover that her mom still kept an emergency stash behind an old collection of mason jars in the basement pantry. After Carlos left for work, she helped herself to five rocks in succession. She didn't worry about getting caught. She wanted nothing more than to smoke herself into the grave because only then would she be able to answer the ugly question that burned deep within her soul: What is it going to take to make me stop?

As far as she could tell, there were only two ways out, and one of them involved slitting her wrists. She wasn't afraid to end her life on Earth, but persistent nightmares of hell had taught her to fear mysterious realms beyond the grave. Besides, she'd seen enough blood in the last 24 hours to make a doctor queasy. She had no desire to butcher her own flesh.

Later that day, she pestered her Uncle Mark to front her enough crack to go back into business. Instead of contacting suburban clients, she took her stash to the local high school, where an endless parade of hoodlums and punks attended mandatory summer classes. She conducted business in the open, ignoring drug-free student mentors who would surely inform the principal. Around 3 p.m., a member of the school security staff caught her hitting the pipe under the bleachers in the gymnasium. If she was going up the river, she figured she might as well enjoy a nice goodbye rush.

She kicked the habit during a six-month stay at a juvenile detention center. The first two weeks were a waking nightmare. She roamed the corridors in a constant state of gloom because no activity in the world could keep her mind occupied. She'd lost the ability to find joy in everyday pleasures.

During the third week, she discovered a love for books. She attacked fat novels with the appetite of a serious scholar, stopping only to roam the corridors every few hours. Intellectual tasks seemed to quiet her urges more effectively than television, so she began to keep a detailed journal. She became so absorbed in chronicling her experiences with Darren that she barely had time to think about anything else.

By the second month, she had the patience to sit and socialize with other girls for hours on end. Soon after that, she found that it wasn't so difficult to relax in the lounge and do nothing at all. At long last, she felt the onset of what she could only call grace—a quiet, effortless state of being alive and beholden to nothing.

Upon her release, Kelly went to live with Clarissa in a cramped apartment near the business school where Clarissa took courses in accounting. Without a car or a high school diploma, she was forced to take the closest telemarketing position available.

Whenever possible, she worked evening jobs for extra cash. Since she was confined to a depressing cubicle all day, she made a point to find fun jobs at night, including a gig as Santa's helper and a stint as a zombie at the local haunted house. She often thought of Darren when frightening innocent children out of their wits. She wondered how his life would've been different if she hadn't thrown herself across his path.

She was surprised by how cheaply she could live without a nagging addiction to feed. She could've made payments on a used car, but she chose to help out with Clarissa's tuition instead. She was endlessly proud that someone from her neighborhood was doing something productive and doing it so damned well.

The years slipped by without fanfare. Unlike most girls caught in the grip of post-adolescent madness, she had little time to party and chase boys at the club. A two-hour break between day and evening jobs provided a small window of opportunity to study for her GED. At age 19, she finished the course and found a position as an office assistant.

Just when things appeared to be taking a turn for the better, Clarissa got engaged to her college sweetheart and followed him to New York. With the bills piling up and no roommate to help pay them, Kelly was forced to move back home with her parents. The nightmares returned immediately. Her beautiful four-poster bed and exquisite doll collection reminded her of a time when she played a pivotal role in the murders of her friend's parents. Little pictures and trinkets left behind from her romance with Darren reeked of Napoleon's blood. As much as she wanted to throw them away, she felt that she didn't deserve a fresh slate. Night after night, she found herself trapped in Darren's freakish hell, screaming and screaming until the end of time.

One night, she smashed a glass on her bedside table and sliced her left wrist wide open. She insisted it was an accident, but Carlos wasn't taking any chances. Upon her release from the emergency room, he demanded her immediate transfer to St. Benedict's mental health wing.

✶ ✶ ✶ ✶ ✶

The Present

Roland sat in silence, never bothering to take advantage of the shiny new vending machine with appetizing pictures of hot beverages fused to the front. The room was so clean and bright he could barely look up without squinting. The ticking clock stepped in to fill the terrible silence, lulling him into a state of prolonged agony.

The last two days had been nothing less than torture. With Kelly in a coma and Darren slipping in and out of consciousness, he hadn't had the opportunity to discuss any of the matters that weighed heavily on his mind. When it all got to be too much, he made short trips home to walk along the frozen pond that Darren and Kelly had loved so dearly as children. He passed the rest of his time roaming hospital corridors, avoiding Carlos in general but occasionally spotting him in one of three quiet lounges.

Finally, at half past noon, he dared to take a seat beside the man he hated most in the world. "I suppose you're a lucky bloke," he mumbled from behind a week-old copy of the local paper.

Carlos sat straight up in his seat, as if he'd been addressed by the president of the United States. "What do you mean?"

"If I turn Kelly's journal over to the police, it'll incriminate my son, and worst of all, your daughter. I don't wish to see her on trial for crimes she never would've committed if left to her own devices. She's suffered long enough."

Carlos didn't bother to blot away the tears that flowed from his eyes. "If I could go back and do it all over again…"

"Please! Don't tell me about all the things you wish you hadn't done. The last thing I want is to feel sorry for you. Be thankful that you have your daughter's forgiveness, but don't ask for mine. The least you can do is allow me the right to hate you, completely and irreversibly, for the rest of my life."

Carlos stood up. "You're right. I *am* a lucky man. Kelly's forgiveness is much more than I deserve."

Later that afternoon, while cleaning a spot of chewing gum from the bottom of his shoe, Roland was struck by a panic attack. The dull, listless agony he'd experienced in the last two days was but a walk in the park compared to the paralyzing fear he now felt. He couldn't understand why his nervous system would choose to go haywire this late in the game, but he knew that it was imperative to seek out the man responsible for ruining his life.

He found Carlos pacing the hallway outside Kelly's room. The stout man's padded frame was hardly strong or menacing. His dark round eyes were filled with fear and shame. Could this be the monster who taught young Darren how to make a rabbit's eyes pop out of their sockets?

Still trembling with fear, Roland pressed his neatly manicured hand against the wall for support. "May… may I ask you a question?"

"Of course."

"How does a man who has clearly been unfair to his child begin to rebuild what is lost? I've been thinking about it, and I've decided that you're somewhat of an expert on the subject."

Carlos helped Roland into the room and sat him down in the chair beside Kelly's bed. "If you want the truth, it all starts with a simple prayer…"

Chapter Nineteen

Kelly had never felt more frustrated in her life. The old nurse with the craggy voice kept sticking things in her arm. Worst of all, the bitch wouldn't shut up. "There you go," she whispered, as if the little pokes and pricks were some kind of gift. "How was that?"

Kelly lacked the strength to protest. Her eyelids were hopelessly glued shut. Her arms and legs were like dead weights mixed up in the sheets. She couldn't speak, no matter how hard she concentrated on the group of muscles that controlled her mouth. She wondered if things would always be this way. She couldn't remember exactly how she'd landed in such a horrible predicament. She saw herself laying beneath David Whipple's body in the woods. Is that what did it? No. It wasn't possible. She was just a child when her arms and legs were momentarily paralyzed by the pond. This was something different. If she was truly paralyzed, she wouldn't be able to feel the little pokes and pricks. Or would she?

Perhaps she had overdosed. Clarissa always said the stuff would kill her one day. But wait. Hadn't she kicked the habit years ago? How old was she, anyway? Was she caught in one of her famous nightmares, or was she really stuck in some hospital with a needle happy nurse?

After many hours of blackness, she found the strength to open her eyes. The light stung her pupils and sent sharp spikes through her forehead. Gradually, shapes and colors materialized into solid objects. A heart monitor beeped and blipped its rhythmic lullaby. Carlos was asleep in the chair beside her bed. A tattered Bible lay on the floor near his feet. Since when did the old man know how to read?

She ripped the tubes from her wrist with a good solid yank. The pain seemed minimal compared to the horror of having them inserted without her consent. Her arms were bruised and bloody. A trail of red liquid followed her out of the room and into the clean, bright hallway. Three women shuffled ahead of her; two dressed in white and one in red pumps. She fell into step behind the pumps. Sure enough, they led her to a slow moving elevator that opened into a lobby. One short walk across the carpet, and she was home free.

The parking lot seemed strangely familiar. Something about the way the cars straddled the yellow lines indicated a total disregard for rules and structure. The cracked asphalt burned her bare feet. Sweat soaked her flimsy institutional gown.

A concentrated beam of sunlight glinted on the windshield of a big red jalopy. Squinting past the glare, she spotted a tiny girl sprawled out on the front seat. Her creamy brown skin was glossy and bloated. Dried vomit plastered her jet black hair to the side of her face.

The crack in the window was just wide enough to admit Kelly's arm. The soft pads of her fingertips sizzled against the searing metal lock.

The cooler of ice sat in its usual place on the back seat. As she fumbled with the latch, a pasty grey hand caught her wrist. "Leave the child alone," an angry voice whispered. "She deserves to die."

Kelly raised her head to confront the enemy and found herself sitting face-to-face with a live version of the caricature she'd drawn so many years ago. She recognized the madwoman's eyes instantly. She finally understood why the pupils were fixed at opposite corners. "She deserves no such thing!" Kelly shrieked.

The madwoman dug her fingernails into Kelly's wrist. "She's a murderer. You know it as well as I do."

"No! She hasn't done anything yet."

"She was given plenty of choices."

"How can you say that? Just look at her!"

Kelly swung her free hand over the cooler and plunged her long fingernails into the madwoman's eyes. When she extracted her hand, bits of flesh and gore clung to her fingertips. The bitch screamed and flung herself against the door. Kelly turned her attention to the latch on the cooler. Her bloody wrist throbbed with pain as she lifted the Styrofoam box over the seat and dumped the contents over the tiny girl's body. Entire cubes of ice melted into her hot flesh on contact. Her eyes fluttered beneath their swollen lids.

Kelly was so relieved to see the girl moving that she didn't notice the madwoman's knife. The shiny steal blade whizzed past her face and plunged into the battered leather seat. "My eyes! You took my fucking eyes!"

"I had to! They couldn't see!"

The madwoman scrambled over the seat and flung her body on top of the girl. She kicked and quivered until one of her tiny legs got caught in the big steering wheel. Pasty grey fingers clawed at her tiny throat. Kelly struggled to pull the knife from the cushion, but there was no strength left in her mutilated wrist. Gashes from the madwoman's fingernails circled the spot where tubes had been yanked. She was forced to grasp the handle in her teeth and wiggle the blade free in slow increments.

Holding the knife straight out in front of her, she dove over the seat. The weight of her body drove the blade into the madwoman's spine. A wicked hissing sound filled the car as the woman expelled her last breath of life. Her body deflated before Kelly's eyes. A tattered heap of clothing marked the spot where she'd vanished into thin air.

The girl sat straight up in her seat, as if waking from a bad dream. Fresh round tears glided down her swollen cheeks. "I'm sorry!" she screamed. "I didn't mean to!"

Kelly took the girl into her arms. "It's okay. You're forgiven."

"I'm 'posed to dip my feet when I get hot!"

"I know, baby. I know."

"I'm not 'posed to take a nap. Not ever."

"You'll know better next time. You've learned your lesson."

A cool breeze swept through the car and filled Kelly's spirit with its rejuvenating power. The girl rose to her knees and pressed her nose against the window. Enormous white clouds appeared separately in the sky, as if painted into the scene by an artist's hand.

They stepped out of the car just in time to catch the first blast of frigid rain. Floating pools of water reflected light from the mighty sun, turning the whole parking lot into an icy clean oasis that sparkled with the cool breath of life.

✶✶✶✶✶

Kelly woke to find Carlos hunched over a book. He was so busy sounding out words that he didn't notice her wandering eyes. The tubes in her wrist were still intact. The madwoman's nail marks were not even visible.

A powerful thirst burned the back of her throat. "What does a girl have to do to get a drink around here?"

Carlos flung his arms around her neck. "Baby!"

"Easy! You're crowding my airway."

He withdrew his trembling body. "I'm sorry. How do you feel? Does your head hurt? Would you like a drink of my juice?"

She reached for a small carton on her bedside table. "Thanks."

"Wait! Should you be drinking after me? Hold on. I'll ask the nurse."

"Sit down! I'm fine. How long have I been here?"

"Fifty-three hours."

"Two days!"

"I'm afraid so. You have a very serious concussion. They found you sprawled out on the ground near the guest house of the Price Estate."

"And Darren?"

"He's fine."

"But I shot him!"

"Yes, you did—in the ass. I assume his flesh will heal much faster than his heart."

"He hates me, doesn't he?"

"Perhaps you should ask him yourself."

"He's here?"

"Yes, but you must hurry. They could come for him anytime."

Kelly breathed a sigh of relief. "Let him go. He'll find his own way. We all do, eventually."

"And what about you, my love? Will you find your way home?"

"I can't sleep in that house. You know that, Carlos."

* * * * *

It wasn't supposed to be a work date, but it quickly ended up that way. When Dr. Rushing complained that spending time in his dark, musty basement was more depressing than a walk through the sewer, Claire volunteered to help tear down the old walnut paneling in his home office. The truth was, he'd begun planning the project the moment he regained his freedom. If he was going to spend a lifetime working there, he didn't want to be reminded of the dark, dismal hours he'd spent in captivity.

"Is this what you needed a girlfriend for?" Claire joked as she hammered a screwdriver into the tiny crevice between the ceiling and the top of the wall. He liked the way his big flannel shirt swallowed her up like a cloak. She couldn't have been cuter if she'd been wearing a pair of fleece pajamas with padded feet.

He'd planned on treating her to a home cooked meal and a romantic movie, but that was before the fax machine went berserk. It churned quietly in the corner until excess pages stared spilling over the edge of the desk and piling up on the basement floor. Who in the world would have cause to send him a document long enough to wallpaper the kitchen?

He did his best to rush the evening along when he discovered that the extra long document was a hand-written journal sent by Roland. He wasn't about to share any information about his dealings with the Price family. Claire didn't need to know that the young man who'd guided her through her first romantic adventures was actually a patient conducting an experiment. Her self-esteem was much too fragile for that. It was best to send her along with a kiss and study the journal in private.

It took nearly four hours to read through the terrifying collection of stories that formed the missing link to Darren's childhood. Dr. Rushing tried to evaluate the facts with detached professionalism, but he couldn't ignore the nervous flutter deep within his chest. He took a hot bath to calm his racing heart and dialed Roland's number.

"I'd get him if I could," the maid said, "but I seem to have lost track of him."

"What do you mean?"

"He comes home from the hospital every so often, parks near the guest house and disappears into the woods. I think he may be camping."

"Camping?"

"Yes, camping."

Dr. Rushing had never made it to the Price estate in less than twenty minutes, but he managed to weave through traffic like an ambulance responding to an emergency call. The first place he checked was Darren's old tree house. He was surprised to find Roland sitting over a lantern with a joint dangling from his lips. He hadn't shaved in days, and he was beginning to look like the kind of guy who could hot wire a car on demand. Slats of moonlight filtered through cracks in the roof, casting marbled patterns over his weary face.

Dr. Rushing wasn't sure why the sight of his mentor smoking weed angered him so badly, but he reacted as if he'd just caught his father stealing candy from the dime store. "Would you put that thing away!" he demanded. "It's not the most adult way to deal with this."

Roland took the deepest drag possible and blew the smoke into his young friend's face. "How would you like me to deal with it? My son is a murderer, and it's quite possibly my fault."

"Don't even say that! You had no way of knowing what Carlos was doing to Darren's head. You didn't introduce the animals and teach him to spill blood with his own hands. You dealt with a confusing set of circumstances in the best way you knew how."

Roland stood up to stretch his legs and bumped his head on the low ceiling. An old sleeping bag sat on the floor near his feet with a bottle of wine and a small basket of fruit and cheese. Tiny chairs from years long past were scattered about the place. He wedged his butt into a chaise lounge meant for a nine-year-old child.

"I should've taken the time to investigate all claims against my son. It wouldn't have been so difficult to drive through the neighborhood and look for signs of vandalism."

"Darren confessed to the crimes. He was manipulated, and so were you. Abused children become abusive adults, but that's hardly your fault."

Roland expelled a lung full of smoke. "It's convenient to blame Carlos, but the abuse didn't start with him. It began on the playground with a group of children who felt the need to punish Darren for my indiscretions. It didn't have to be that way, Tommy. I had a wife, for God's sake. I could've held on to her, but instead I chose to treat her like a kid sister. It's no wonder she fled to England. Perhaps she was tired of sleeping next to a corpse. If I'd tried just a little harder to hold things together, Darren would never have been forced to contend with so much cruelty."

"Quit beating yourself up. You can't stay in a marriage when every fibre of your being is screaming to be set free. That's not what Darren would've wanted for you."

"You're missing the point! A boy needs a female figure in his life. My sexual needs should've come second to his emotional development."

"So you were a neglectful husband. That gave Victoria no right to drop out of her son's life! It's plain to see why she left you, but she had no excuse to leave her son. You've made every effort to visit Darren's sister on holidays and call her on a weekly basis. Victoria did none of those things for Darren. You can't absorb the blame for her sins."

Roland turned his attention to the tiny window overlooking the guest house. "It's such a lovely place, isn't it? I never took the time to notice how brightly it glows in the moonlight. Kelly likened it to a little gingerbread house. Do you suppose he's killed anyone there?"

"I wouldn't want to speculate."

"How can I go on knowing what I know? I can't bring myself to visit Darren when he's awake. How am I going to look my son in the eye?"

Dr. Rushing grabbed his friend by the shoulders. "You're going to look at him the same way you've always looked at him. He didn't go around raping schoolgirls or cutting little boys into bite-sized morsels. He killed the kind of people who cut little boys into bite-sized morsels, and don't you forget it."

Roland passed the joint to his young friend. "I acquired this from one of my more creative students. Care to rediscover the inner calm this stuff can bring?"

"No thanks. It doesn't appear to be working for you."

* * * * *

Kelly had never seen a place so happening as St. Vincent's Women's Shelter at dusk. Gals of all ages huddled in small groups of four or five, sharing secrets, telling jokes and trading tattered paperback novels like little blocks of gold. If you saw a group of girls heading outside for a walk in the brutal November wind, it meant that someone had acquired a joint and was willing to share.

Smack dab in the center of the enormous grey room, five women were wrapping up a friendly game of poker. Meg Winter, a tall redhead with an enormous black eye, had just won a pair of gold earrings and a large duffle bag with secret compartments. As Kelly watched Meg collect the jackpot with the excitement of a child on Christmas morning, she realized it was possible for some people to find joy anywhere on God's green earth. She desperately wanted to be one of those people, no matter what it took.

Her first trip through St. Vincent's was depressing because she'd let it be that way. Instead of using the time to make plans and collect her thoughts, she'd waited for a man to come pull her from the depths of gloom and make her life worth living again. This time, she was determined to create her own happiness.

It wasn't always easy. Sometimes, in the dead of the night, she got to thinking about all of her disadvantages. She'd been robbed of a normal childhood, and it was hard not to feel a little resentful. When pangs of self-pity tugged at her heart, she took a good look around and counted the number of women who had it worse than she did. Then, she made a mental list of all the things she could be grateful for:

1. She didn't have a husband who brutalized her.
2. She didn't have children she couldn't feed or support.
3. She wasn't crazy—just a little lost.
4. She could sleep like a baby without so much as a joint or a shot of Nyquil.
5. She wasn't addicted to anything.
6. She wasn't addicted to anything.
7. She wasn't addicted to anything.

By her third night, she could no longer draw strength from comparing herself to others. She began to see that it was a desperate undertaking to look for joy in someone else's pain.

It wasn't long before she found a job as a waitress at the quaint little tavern down the street. Several other women had applied for the position, but Kelly had been the owner's first choice. Sister Mary Louise couldn't have been more proud. She'd sent many women to work at the tavern, but they never seemed to last long. "Drinkers," she muttered under her breath. "You can't go to work in a tavern if you have… *problems.*"

The way she said the word "problems" troubled Kelly, as if people with "problems" didn't deserve jobs at all. What would she think if she knew Kelly was once a crack head who slept with men to get closer to their money?

Sister Mary Louise was the kind of woman who could be your best friend or your worst enemy. If you made curfew every night, stayed out of fights with other women and helped out with chores around the shelter, you could earn a steady stream of smiles, hand squeezes and comforting pats upon the back. If you slipped up, even just once, her opinion of you was forever tarnished. You would be treated to condescending nods and icy stares for the rest of your days in her presence.

The first time she left for work in full uniform, Kelly was bombarded with a variety of nasty insults from her peers. It was a silly outfit with elasticized peasant top, cinched waist, and flaring skirt standing out over a dozen petticoats. "Look at Little Bo Peep," said Deb Mcfadden, the woman who'd harassed her on her first night away from the mental institution. "She lost her sheep, and the bitch can't find 'em anywhere."

"Hey, pretty baby," said Trix Malone, a hard core biker chick with seven tattoos and three drug addictions. "Who'd you have to blow to get that job?"

Kelly ignored the question and continued along the endless row of beds. She was making good progress toward the door when Trix stepped in front of her. She'd never seen a woman with so much pain in her eyes. Her bleach blonde hair formed tight ringlets around her weather-beaten face. A silly red stocking cap stood on top of her head. A tattoo of a tear drop graced the corner of her eye, signifying that she'd killed at least one person in her lifetime.

"I asked you a question, pretty baby."

"I didn't blow anyone! I've only met the guy once."

Trix removed her stocking cap and turned to her group of loyal followers. "Who wants to bet that Little Bo Peep will be blowin' the boss by the end of the week?"

"I'm in," said Deb, tossing a gold ring into the hat.

In a matter of seconds, women were lining up to deposit their personal treasures. There were unopened candy bars and whole packs of gum, fat marijuana cigarettes and trial sized bottles of scented body wash. Meg Winter contributed her warmest pair of mittens.

By the time Sister Mary Louise swooped in to break up the huddle, it was too late. The jackpot was valuable enough to inspire envy in a group of women who had no worldly possessions. They would never drop the subject now.

After completing a full day's work without blowing anyone, Kelly returned to the shelter to find Meg sitting at the foot of her bed. Her black eye had healed completely, and her porcelain skin glowed with the radiance of a woman who'd just recently discovered a thing called hope. "I just wanted you to know," Meg said, "that I'm betting for you and not against you."

Kelly sat down beside her. "I guess they really take this gambling thing seriously, huh?"

"Don't let it get you. They're just jealous because you got the job."

"This whole thing is ridiculous. I mean, how will they know if I've blown the guy or not?"

"That's easy. If you're fired in less than a week, it means you wouldn't blow him. If you stick around for awhile, it means you already have."

"How can they be so sure he'll come on to me?"

Meg rolled her eyes. "Please, honey. You're not the first pretty girl to wander over to that tavern. Sister Mary sends him applications by the dozen."

That night, Kelly stayed up late making mental lists of all the things she planned to do with her first paycheck. She was wide awake when a dark figure crawled over to her bed and inserted a shadowy hand beneath the mattress.

"Get your hands away from my tips."

Trix pressed her mouth to Kelly's ear. "I got a big ole knife that says those tips are mine."

Kelly reached into her pillow case and retrieved a twenty dollar bill. "I happen to know you lost that knife in a poker game, but you can have a few bucks. Something tells me you need it worse than I do. Don't buy coke or anything else that'll have you wired. You can't afford to lose your bed here. A little weed will help you sleep at night. And no Vicodin. Keep it natural."

The next morning, Trix wandered over to Kelly's bed to watch her apply makeup. "Gettin' pretty for the boss man?" she asked.

Kelly refused to look up. "I would do this if I were going to take a walk in the rain. It's a morning ritual. It's who I am."

Trix sat down at the foot of the bed. "What's it like, Kelly?"

"To put on makeup?"

"No. To *be* pretty and *feel* pretty."

Kelly used her lip pencil to draw a small teardrop beneath her left eye. "It doesn't change a thing."

Chapter Twenty

It was nearly dawn when Darren opened his eyes. Roland tried to play the moment casually, but he was uncomfortable in his own skin. He'd never learned how to act around his son, and today was no exception.

"Don't look at me that way," Darren said. "A thousand questions are burning in your eyes, and I don't have the strength to answer a single one of them."

Roland sat down upon the bed. "Save your energy. Kelly filled in most of the blanks. The pain you're feeling right now was caused by a bullet from her gun."

"That must be why you're looking at me like a spot of bacteria under a microscope."

"You're confusing curiosity with contempt. I've never looked down upon you, Darren. I've only tried to stare past the smoke screen."

Darren's eyes shone with tears. "You have no room to talk about smoke screens! You're a master of disguise."

"Am I? It certainly didn't take long for the whole neighborhood to figure out my secret. You've endured unspeakable horrors as a direct result of my silence. You have every right to be angry with me."

Darren nudged his father with his foot. "I thought I told you to stop looking at me like that. It's not your fault that the world can't stand the thought of two guys mixed up in the sheets. It's a poor excuse for violence. If you ask me, those kids were just waiting for a reason to drive spikes into my eye sockets. Everyone needs a place to channel anger. I was just an easy target."

"That's not true."

"Of course it is! This isn't about your sex life or my battles with rich kids. It's about a whole society of people who think they have the right to crush the first convenient victim that comes along."

"It's not your job to wipe evil from the face of the Earth. As satisfying as it feels at the moment, it won't get you anywhere. You'll wake up the next day with the same hole in your heart."

"What would you know about my heart? I've learned to fill it up quite nicely."

"I somehow doubt that. If you're so satisfied with the life you've created, why didn't you just keep going after thugs? What inner void were you attempting to fill when you wrapped a telephone chord around an innocent man's neck?"

"He's not innocent. He's just arrogant enough to believe his friendship can cure the world's problems."

"That hardly makes him evil. Since when do you have the authority to decide a common man's fate? Your need for control has grown far beyond the desire to protect the innocent. Where will it all end? Will your next target be the snotty waitress who ignores your empty coffee mug or the mail carrier who delivers your art supplies with a broken seal?"

Darren turned to the wall. "Just shut up, okay? You don't have to tell me how screwed up I am. I'm aware that I need a little work."

"A little work? That's the understatement of the century. Are you so insecure that you can't bear the thought of me having a friend?"

"You're allowed to have friends, but I resent it when you go out shopping for another son. Just because things weren't working out between us didn't mean you had the right to go out and replace me."

"I resent that. I never sought to replace you."

"That's a lie! There was a time when I would've killed to be included in one of your fireside chats, but you sent me to bed when your intellectual friends came knocking at the door."

"I'm a creature of habit. My parents sent me to bed at a certain time, so I adopted the same policy with you."

"Stop making excuses. I can accept the fact that I'm not the kind of guy you'd invite to a poetry reading, but you're supposed to love me just the same. You could've told me why you and Mom were destined to break up, but you chose to share your deepest secrets with some scatter-brained frat boy who didn't own a pair of matching socks."

"I'm so sorry, Darren. I underestimated your ability to deal with adult issues. I took you for the kind of jerk who has zero tolerance for people who are different. I misread all the clues and misinterpreted all the signs. I was all too willing to believe the worst of you, but that's hardly Dr. Rushing's fault. Please promise you'll steer clear of him. Don't punish an innocent man for my mistakes."

Darren swiped a tear with the back of his hand. "You don't have to get so worked up. It's not good for a man your age. I don't plan on harming anyone ever again. You're right about one thing. It just makes a bigger hole."

$* * * * *$

Kelly felt strangely at peace for a woman who'd just lost the only job available to her. She didn't even mind when the winners dumped the contents of the stocking cap onto Deb's bed and squabbled over who would get what. Her life was just another bet to them, but it was hardly worth getting upset about. She was wrapped in a warm blanket, her belly was comfortably full, and she had more hidden cash than the resident dope dealer.

Close to $1,800 was sewn into the lining of her fluffy white slippers. Half the money had arrived in the form of a check from Carlos. She'd earned the other half at the tavern down the street. It turned out that she was good at something after all. Customers had liked her friendly smile and chatty disposition. Even female clients, who weren't tipping out of some inner need to impress, had reached deep within their pocketbooks. As she drifted off to sleep, she felt a genuine sense of pride for the first time in her life. If she could earn that kind of money in less than a week, there wasn't anywhere she couldn't go and anything she couldn't do.

She awoke to the sound of a woman screaming. The lights suddenly flicked on, sending pinpoints of pain into her weary eyes. She saw Trix and Deb locked in a violent embrace on the floor, their arms and legs bent and twisted like gnarled tree branches. Before she could intervene, Sister Mary swooped in with three of her companions.

"What did I tell you about fighting!" the old woman screamed. "One strike and you're out!"

"But she took her ring back!" Trix shouted. "She's gotta learn to make good on her bets."

Kelly felt as if the breath had been knocked from her chest. Trix must've changed her bet! If she was the rightful owner of Deb's ring, she must've sided with those who believed that Kelly wasn't desperate enough to hand out blow jobs to employers.

"Please!" Kelly cried. "Let them talk it out. Fights don't last long around here. They'll be trading books and making bets again tomorrow, just wait and see."

Sister Mary grabbed Trix by the hair and pulled her to her feet. "This woman is incorrigible!"

"Forgive her! Shouldn't you have some kind of degree in that?"

Sister Mary looked at Trix as if she were a cockroach crawling across the floor. "This woman is beyond forgiveness!"

Kelly pushed Sister Mary with all her might, knocking her down onto the closest bed. "No one is beyond forgiveness."

In that instant, Kelly knew she would no longer be welcome at St. Vincent's, but it was strangely okay. Nothing could touch her now. She threw a stranger's coat over her pajamas and stumbled out into the cold wet night.

*****

Darren woke to find Dr. Rushing looming over his bed. He looked taller than an oak tree in a crisp hunter green sweater and loose tan slacks. For the first time Darren could remember, he felt dwarfed by the older man's hulking presence. "You're not supposed to be here," he said dryly.

Dr. Rushing shrugged his shoulders. "So strangle me."

"Very funny. I'll have your job for this. I'm supposed to start working with another psychiatrist. Your involvement in my life is too subjective."

Dr. Rushing swiped a can of Coke from Darren's tray and helped himself to a nice, long drink. "Threats won't get you anywhere. Do you really want to alienate the only man who knows *all* of your father's secrets?"

Darren eyed him with curiosity. "Okay. I'll bite. What do you know about my dad that I don't?"

"For starters, I know that he's been on the back of a motorcycle at least a dozen times in his life."

"Get out of here!"

"I'm serious. We tested bikes all week before we decided upon your Harley."

"That's just great. I'm so glad you were able to spend some quality time with him."

"It wasn't a boding ritual, Darren. He wanted to surprise you on your birthday. He needed the opinion of a young person, and I knew a thing or two about bikes."

"Yeah, you're a regular mechanic."

"The point is that he always put your happiness first. He never went out of his way to make sure I had the motorcycle of my dreams. He didn't plaster his kitchen walls with my art or brag about my talents to anyone who would listen."

"That doesn't mean anything. You had the greatest gift of all—his trust."

Dr. Rushing laughed. "You think trust is some kind of gift? Someday, you'll understand that it's both a privilege and a burden. Your dad saddled me with his secrets because he felt that you weren't old enough to handle them. You don't know how many times I wished he'd never told me at all. I was content to think of him as a charming bachelor with the world at his feet. I wasn't prepared to face the fact that the man I idolized was living a lie."

"You obviously got over it."

"Of course I did. I couldn't very well turn my back on my best friend."

Darren came dangerously close to cracking a smile. "Don't call him your best friend. It makes me want to pluck your eyelashes with a pair of rusty tweezers. What other secrets do you have?"

"Let's see… I know that he sneaks carrots into the juicer when he makes your favorite fruit coolers."

"He only did that when I was a kid."

"That's what you think."

"Okay. What else?"

"He still talks about that summer in Paris like it was yesterday. I've heard the story at least a hundred times. I know the name of the tour guide who gave you that package of crayons so you'd have something to do on the long ride across the city. I know the subject of your first recognizable work of art and the time of day it was scribbled onto the back of an old bus schedule."

Darren blinked back a tear. "That's nothing. Give me something juicy."

"Okay. Try this one on for size. Your dad was a major pothead in his '20s. He dropped out of college two different times, and no one ever expected him to graduate."

Darren sat straight up in his bed. "You're kidding! He's the fucking head of the English department, and he barely graduated?"

"That's how the story goes. He began his academic career as a business major. He let his father push him down a road that he had no desire to travel. He eventually left England and pursued the career of his dreams at a small private university his family had never heard of."

"So that's why he supports my decision to stay away from college?"

"He doesn't exactly support it. He tolerates it because he remembers a time when his father maintained total control of his life. From time to time, he sends samples of your work to prestigious art schools around the country. He keeps a secret file of acceptance letters."

"I guess I really screwed things up. I could've gone to college, but now I'm probably headed for prison."

"You think you're getting off that easy? I'm pulling for a year-long sabbatical at the funny farm. I feel at least partly responsible for all of this. I was too close to the family to assume control of your therapy. Your case was mishandled from the start, and that's exactly what I told the police."

"A year-long sabbatical? Couldn't you just shoot me instead?"

"If you prefer, I could mail Kelly's journal to your case worker. That'll buy you a one-way ticket to cell block six."

"That's okay. I'll take the vacation. Have you spoken to Kelly?"

"No. I've only read her journal."

"Any professional opinions on why she was standing outside my window with a gun?"

Dr. Rushing shook his head. "Perhaps some things are better left unanalyzed."

"I guess I have a real talent for alienating anyone who has ever loved me."

"None of that matters now. Your father is waiting for you to reach out to him. He's the only person you should be concerned about."

Darren studied Dr. Rushing's face beneath the flourescent glow of hospital lighting. He didn't look anything like the clueless frat boy who'd accidentally charmed his way into Roland's inner circle more than ten years ago. His dark eyes carried a hint of wisdom. A full day's worth of stubble couldn't disguise the fact that he was a handsome man. "All right, Casanova," Darren said with a wink. "What's the deal with Claire?"

Dr. Rushing's face grew red on the spot. "We've been spending a lot of time together, as you can imagine."

Darren could just barely look at him. "Good for you. Good for both of you."

Dr. Rushing backed out of the room, as if making a transition out of the discussion. A few moments later, Darren was surprised to see him wander past the doorway. "Are you lost or something?" he asked.

Dr. Rushing stepped back into the room. "I told myself I wouldn't do this, but there's a certain question that's been eating away at my heart."

Darren rolled his eyes at the ceiling. "For crying out loud, just ask."

"When you were conducting your experiment, did you find that, I mean, in the course of your research, did you..."

"For God's sake, spit it out."

"Fine. Did you have feelings for Claire?"

Darren wished he had the mobility to step backward out the door. "It's safe to say I cared deeply for all of them."

* * * * *

Roland ran his fingertip along the sharp curve of an ocean wave. "I like the lines in this one," he said.

Darren flipped to the back of his portfolio and found a detailed portrait of a middle-aged man with white flakes stuck to his glasses. "How about that one?"

Roland chuckled a bit. "I'd say that fellow needs a good dandruff shampoo."

"That's my new psychiatrist."

"Well, I'll be damned. You aren't going to show him this portrait, are you?"

"Why not? He gets off on pointing out my flaws. I thought it might be fun to illustrate one of his."

"Give him a chance, Darren. He can't be that bad."

"Who says I'm not giving him a chance? I kind of like his lines. See those deep furrows above his brow? That's the sign of a man who takes thinking very seriously."

"Really? I thought it was a sign of perpetual constipation."

Roland shared a good laugh with his son. He found it wasn't so difficult to get a chuckle out of Darren once he stopped playing the straight man.

The mental institution where Darren would spend the next year of his life wasn't such a bad place. If you could get past the lukewarm meals, the smell of Lysol and the sporadic moaning in the corridor, it was a little slice of heaven. Roland had tried to assure his son's placement in a posh private facility upstate, but Darren had chosen to remain close to home. He said he didn't see how it was possible to rebuild their relationship if they could only visit on Sundays.

Roland supposed it didn't matter where Darren chose to rest his head at night. In either environment, he would pass the time painting, watching television and reading from a list of classic novels. It pleased Roland to see his son making an attempt to learn more about the things he held dear. He planned to return the favor by watching more wrestling and studying the rules of hockey.

"Have you given any thought to Mr. Rivard's proposal?" Roland asked.

"Of course I have, but I'm a little conflicted."

"How so?"

"I don't mind selling the copyrights to my animal series, since it's for a good cause, but I'm afraid it'll lead to more work."

"But isn't that the point?"

"I'm not sure I want to go down in history as a painter of suffering and death. I'd like to try my hand at capturing the magic of human expression. There's life behind every pair of eyes, and I want to record it."

"That sounds reasonable. I know you're used to playing the strong menacing type, but you don't really wear it well anymore."

"That's funny. A friend of mine at Donovan's says the same thing about me. Do you really think I've outgrown my image?"

"I certainly do. It was a cool high school image, but I think of you as more of a free spirit now. I can see you in a New York loft, lounging around in a tie-dyed shirt."

"Yuck. I hate the city. How about a houseboat and a big, sloppy tee shirt with a marijuana leaf printed across the front? That's much more fee, don't you think?"

"Yes, I like that image. But you don't smoke pot. And even if you did, it would be rather difficult to roll a joint with the boat rocking and all."

"Good point. How about a beer logo on the tee shirt?"

"That's so unoriginal. Every kid your age has a beer logo on his tee shirt."

"Okay. How about no shirt at all? Just me and the houseboat."

"Perfect! I like that image. It suits you just fine."

*****

Mr. Rivard wasn't sure why certain smells sent him over the edge, but he was driven to thoughts of suicide by an intoxicating blend of vomit and ammonia. The dingy brick walls didn't help either. Even with the bare ceiling bulb overhead, the shelter was like a deep black hole sucking his spirit into a parallel universe where women scratched their genitals in plain view and men were gripped by the compulsion to put stray objects in their mouths.

He was handling himself fairly well until he spotted a young blonde with blood-stained bandanas wrapped around her tiny hands. A substance that looked like dried mustard plastered a section of hair to the side of her face. "Psst!" he whispered in Dr. Rushing's ear. "What's that all about?"

Dr. Rushing turned to Benny. "You know her?"

Benny shrugged. "That's just Chrissy. She likes to chew on her fingers. Nobody knows why."

Mr. Rivard shook his head. "I think I've seen enough."

Roland grabbed the back of Mr. Rivard's collar to keep him from advancing toward the door. "This is important to Darren. He asked us to spend an hour here, and I worked very hard to arrange this meeting."

The previous night, Roland had informed Mr. Rivard of Darren's bizarre quest to fix Dr. Rushing's patients. He could hardly believe he'd been part of a disturbed youngster's psychological experiment. "Where is Darren, anyway?" he asked.

Roland looked at his feet. "In a far better place than this."

Mr. Rivard closed his eyes to block out the sight of a man attempting to suck the last bit of resin from an empty pipe. If anyone other than Darren had asked him to spend the day at a shelter for the deranged, he might've skipped town for the week. "Is there any particular reason why you brought me here?"

Roland's eyes brightened. "Darren seems to think that if we put our heads together, we could move mountains."

"Let me guess. He wants me to convert the local shopping mall into a beautiful shelter with an indoor tennis court and Olympic-sized swimming pool."

"That's a beautiful thought, but I think he's more interested in your political connections. If you can charge $2,000 a plate to raise money for young entrepreneurs, couldn't you do the same with other causes?"

"It would be easier to build a palace brick by brick. Businessmen attend my luncheons to network with industry leaders, not to help struggling entrepreneurs. The only person who cares about that end of the deal is me. Folks are only interested in issues that touch their lives or further their own causes."

Roland's mouth dropped to a frown. "I'm very disappointed to hear you say that."

Anger rose deep within Mr. Rivard's chest. How did someone like Roland have the right to make him feel guilty? "What about you, Mr. Mansion In The Woods? Are you doing your part?"

Roland slipped his arm around Benny's shoulder. "Of course I am. I'd like to introduce you to my new assistant groundskeeper."

Benny's smile was positively radiant. "I do all the stuff the other guy hates to do, like cleaning the gutters and scooping up dog poop."

Roland hit Mr. Rivard with a burning gaze. "Imagine if everyone in our position could help just one person in this shelter."

"Yes!" Benny shouted. "You could adopt a lunatic. Not all of us are so bad. Larry over there used to work as an apartment manager."

Mr. Rivard followed Benny's glance to a small grouping of hard plastic chairs. An emaciated man in army fatigues sat alone with a tattered newspaper in his lap. His cold, expressionless stare was more disturbing than a frown. Mr. Rivard wondered what path he might've taken if he hadn't decided to build an advertising empire. A lack of goals and challenges could've sent him to an early grave. Even with so many advantages, he was prone to feelings of hopelessness and despair. The truth be told, he wasn't so different from Larry.

Mr. Rivard turned to Benny. "I think we could find something for Larry. But what about folks like your friend Chrissy? I don't mean to sound insensitive, but the harsh reality is that she's unemployable."

Dr. Rushing stepped forward. "I think you might be surprised by what some of Benny's friends are capable of. At the very least, they could stuff envelopes or organize stacks of literature dropped by the shelter. Larry could check their work and act as a supervisor. A small income is better than none at all. Something as simple as a candy bar or a bottle of fresh juice can have a profound effect upon the mood."

Roland nodded. "No one expects us to turn their lives around in a day. The purpose of this visit is to identify small steps toward larger goals. Let's get people talking, shall we?"

Mr. Rivard could smell another project on the horizon. If the charity luncheons could give his life purpose, could small employment opportunities do the same for folks at the shelter? Imagine how he would feel at the end of the day if he could institute a program like that! Haggard as they were, Chrissy and Larry held the power to quench his thirst for a meaningful existence.

All of a sudden, the room seemed a few shades brighter.

* * * * *

Vince took a drag from his cigarette and let the rich tobacco stay in his lungs for a good long moment. The smell of impending rain permeated the air, filling his nostrils with a moist, clean scent. He'd chosen the last possible moment for a cigarette break. The inky black sky threatened to release its moisture upon the courtyard at any moment. He was just about to step inside when he caught sight of a dark figure creeping through the bushes. His heart hammered in his chest as he reached for the cold metal gun that decorated his belt. He was a regular cowboy at target practice, but he'd never used a firearm to defend himself. His hand shook with fear as he stepped closer to the bushes.

"Put that damned thing away," said a familiar female voice. "It's just me."

His heart filled with shame as Kelly stepped out of the shadows. How was he going to be a hard-nosed private investigator if such minor incidents filled him with terror? He hoped she wouldn't notice the sweat on his upper lip. He decided to play it cool, just in case. "Long time no see."

She held his gaze with her clear blue eyes. He'd almost forgotten how incredibly beautiful she was. He felt the sudden urge to pull her into his arms. It wasn't an easy decision to leave her at the shelter. For one glorious month, she was his reason for living.

"You hurt me," she said.

He nodded in agreement. "I was weak. The intensity of what we had was terrifying. It almost seemed unreal, like a movie that could be switched off at any moment."

"Stop speaking in metaphors. I can handle the truth."

"I was worried I'd fall completely in love with a crackpot."

Kelly smiled up at him. "I can relate to that. Would you believe I once had the same problem?"

They roamed the empty corridors for old time's sake, steering clear of the nurse's station. Between sips of hot coffee from the vending machine, she told him of her miraculous recovery and her immediate plans for the future. The details made his head spin. Somewhere between a mystical dream and a confrontation with a crotchety old nun, she'd learned about the healing power of forgiveness.

She said she'd spent the last 24 hours in a cheap motel beside an old diner with a "help wanted" sign in the window. She was certain the job was waiting for her. She was certain about a lot of things, and he didn't have the strength to argue.

Around midnight, they came to rest outside the door of room 321. He bent to kiss her forehead before inserting his key into the lock. "Are you sure you want to do this?" he asked.

"I've never been more sure of anything in my life."

*****

She found Darren curled up in a little ball on his bed. The cool moonlight shone through the metal bars on his window, casting a luminous glow upon the side of his face. She was glad to see they'd given him a room with an excellent view of the same courtyard that filled her mornings with a trace of hope during her stay at the institution. Perhaps over time, he would learn to see beauty in the world and paint it with the innocent hand of a child.

She couldn't resist the urge to sit down beside him. The heat from his body warmed the side of her leg. His short hair conjured up memories of the way he looked as an inquisitive nine-year-old child. She never dreamed it would take so long to find out how far he could run without stopping.

She was amazed by how much she still desired him. Even as he lay sleeping, the pull of his magnetism drew goose bumps from her pores. When he slid across the mattress to grasp a stray pillow, his bare leg delivered a blast of static electricity to her hip.

"Ouch!" he shouted.

"Not so loud. You'll wake the neighbors."

His eyes popped open. "Kelly?"

"Yes. It's me."

"How did you get past…"

"Never mind that. I owe you an apology, and I've come to deliver it."

"Don't bother. I deserved to be shot. Some protector I am. I could've killed a decent man. I guess I've passed judgements for so long that I thought I had the right to decide a common man's fate."

"Stop. I'm not here to apologize for putting a bullet in your ass."

"So what are you so sorry about?"

"I broke the cardinal rule. A good friend once told me that if you can't love someone no matter what, you can't really love them at all."

Darren laughed. "That was a bunch of idealistic crap. People don't really love that way. "

"I don't know about that. You loved me at a time when I couldn't love myself. You accepted all of my faults, but I couldn't look past yours."

Darren closed his fingers over her hand. "I forgive you," he said.

"Do you think you can ever forgive Carlos?"

"I don't know."

"How about Shelly and David and all the other kids who made your life a living hell?"

"You're pushing it."

"Am I? Why is it so easy to pass judgement and so difficult to forgive?"

"I don't know. It just is."

"What if I told you that Carlos' father died when he was only twelve years old?"

"That doesn't excuse what he did."

"I'm not saying it does. But what if I told you he was sent to live with an uncle who got off on breaking his bones once in awhile?"

"Geez, Kelly."

"Violence is infectious. People pass it along like the common cold. Let me ask you this: How much time did you spend with Shelly? Was it all just sex, or did you learn anything about her family life with David?"

"No one ever laid a hand on those kids, if that's what you're hoping to hear."

"Abuse doesn't have to be physical."

"If you must know, their mom was a real bitch. She'd scream for hours if she found footprints on the linoleum or fingerprints on the glass coffee tables. She wouldn't let them bring friends home, and she criticized just about every hobby they ever took up. They walked around on eggshells to avoid messing things up."

"There you go. Hate breeds more hate. You can go on hating forever, or you can make a conscious decision to let it go."

"I'll need your help with that. Please say you'll help me."

Kelly took Darren into her arms and held on for dear life. "What kind of hero would I be if I left you now?"